The Collection

A NOVEL

Gioia Diliberto

Scribner
NEW YORK   LONDON   TORONTO   SYDNEY

SCRIBNER
A Division of Simon & Schuster, Inc.
1230 Avenue of the Americas
New York, NY 10020

First Scribner trade paperback edition September 2008

SCRIBNER and design are trademarks of
The Gale Group, Inc., used under license
by Simon & Schuster, Inc., the publisher of this work.

For information about special discounts for bulk purchases,
please contact Simon & Schuster Special Sales:
1-800-456-6798 or business@simonandschuster.com

DESIGNED BY KYOKO WATANABE
Text set in Adobe Garamond

Manufactured in the United States of America

1   3   5   7   9   10   8   6   4   2

Library of Congress Control Number: 2006100020

ISBN-13: 978-0-7432-8065-5

ISBN-13: 978-0-7432-8066-2 (pbk)

Praise for *The Collection*

Named a Favorite Book of 2007 by the *Chicago Tribune*

"A valentine to Coco Chanel . . . beautifully evocative and vivid."
—*Entertainment Weekly*

"The next best thing to a shopping spree in Paris."
—*Elle*

"Diliberto's enjoyable new novel offers insight into the multiple facets of the Chanel persona as seen through the eyes of a young provincial seamstress. . . . One of this book's most engaging features is its meticulously researched account of life in a Parisian atelier: the complicated pecking order, the nasty internecine rivalries, the technical intricacies of assembling couture garments, the at times overwhelming pressures of creating beauty on a deadline."
—*The Washington Post*

"A delicious novel about the life of a seamstress in the early days at Chanel."
—André Leon Talley, *Vogue*

"A fascinating look behind the public salons of haute couture into the workrooms of the imperious Coco Chanel herself, revealing the hierarchies, jealousies, fierce ambitions, and treacheries of an industry that trades in elegance. Seamstress Isabelle Varlet has our sympathy from the first stunning line to the bittersweet ending, and Gioia Diliberto pulls us along on a thread knotted with surprises. A thoroughly enjoyable read."
—Susan Vreeland, author of *Girl in Hyacinth Blue*

"Even if you've never stitched a hem, Gioia Diliberto's novel is . . . a lesson you won't want to miss. . . . Diliberto [writes] with style and attention to detail worthy of the great couturière."
—*Orlando Sentinel*

"Postwar Paris and the ruthlessly competitive atelier of Coco Chanel come to glamorously gritty life in *The Collection*."

—*Vogue*

"A page-turner of a novel."

—*W*

"Acutely observed . . . Diliberto portrays Isabelle's connection to her work with great sensitivity . . . [the] period details throughout are superb."

—*Chicago Tribune*

"Setting her second novel among the glamorous couture houses of post–WWI Paris, Diliberto delves into a Europe inching its way back to caring about fashion . . . with her married lovers and fiery arrogance, Mademoiselle [Coco Chanel] is the true star of the book; each moment she's on the page is sheer pleasure, much like fine couture."

—*Publishers Weekly*

"Diliberto weaves together the intrigue of illegally copied designer gowns, the sweatshop conditions of couture seamstresses, and the cut-throat competition in high fashion to create a seamless and entertaining tapestry. Readers of historical fiction will want this book, particularly if they enjoy the inimitable flavor of Paris in which it is immersed."

—*Library Journal*

"Plenty of intrigue, pathos, romance, and even some sewing tips, as well as multifaceted characters. Definitely entertaining."

—*Booklist*

"Anyone with even the mildest interest in clothing will enjoy this knowledgeable, readable account of a pivotal year in haute couture."

—*Kirkus Reviews*

"Impressive."

—*Chicago Reader*

In memory of my grandmothers,
Rose DeMarzo and Anna Diliberto,
seamstresses both

The Collection

Prologue

*I*nstead of dying, I learned to sew.

I was nine, ill with my first bout of consumption, and the nuns at Saint Foy, the convent school in Agen, where I'd lived for a year, had sent me home with a high fever and a horrific cough, not expecting me to return. For two months I lay in bed while my grandmother cared for me. Despite her ministrations, I grew steadily thinner and weaker, until one day she placed on my quilt a stack of white silk squares and a pincushion spiked with a threaded needle. "Here, dear, let me show you," she said, lifting my limp body from the pillows. Holding me upright, she supported the needle in my fingers and guided it through the silk. Over the next weeks, as she taught me how to baste and overcast, how to turn hems and cut bias strips for binding, and how to patch holes, my fever and cough subsided, and my strength returned. I sewed my initials, IV, in the bottom right-hand corner of each square, and my grandmother tacked them to the walls—monuments of my survival. Determination was in the stitches and also hope. I still feel the bloom of possibility when I put needle and thread to silk.

Another grandmother would have given a sick girl a new doll or a kitten. But I come from a long line of seamstresses for whom stitching is the same as breathing. My namesake, the first Isabelle Varlet, worked at the court of Louis XVI, and, according to family lore, was imprisoned with Marie Antoinette in the Tuileries. I have a gold locket, dulled with age, that belonged to this Isabelle. Inside is an oil miniature of a lovely young girl whose fine straight hair is the same reddish-gold color as mine.

In those years before the first great war, my grandmother and I lived in a two-story cottage on a hill overlooking the road to Timbaut, a little medieval village a mile outside Agen. Our house had an attic and a wine cellar, shuttered windows, a giant oak in front and a vegetable garden in back. Chickens scratched in the yard, where a little goat tethered to the fence gave us milk each morning. Beyond, lay undulating fields of sunflowers and purple heather starred with marguerites. I lacked only parents.

My father, who made hats at a factory in Agen, suffered a heart attack several months before I was born, the event that cost my mother her life. Neither of my parents had siblings. My grandmother, though, had three sisters with whom she once owned a dressmaking shop. They were old ladies by the time I came along, and I never saw them in anything but heavy black dresses. Every day at four, the aunts came to our house for tea, drenched in black, their faces covered by black veils trailing the floor, and carrying little round hat boxes. When they stepped inside, they removed their veils and pinned black caps to their white hair. I asked them once why they dressed like death, and one of them answered, "So everyone will know we are widows!" It was their proudest accomplishment.

After my recovery, my grandmother, in consultation with the aunts, decided to tutor me at home rather than return me to Saint Foy. Over the course of the next eight years, I suffered repeated relapses and was confined for long periods to bed. My grandmother and the aunts worried and hovered over me; my every cough and sniffle sparked grave concern. Because they feared they could lose me at any time, they indulged my smallest whim, and I grew up convinced that life would give me what I asked of it.

My favorite pastime was drawing fashion sketches, inspired by illustrations in the Parisian magazines my grandmother collected. I occupied hours copying clothes from the glossy pages into my sketchbook and then inventing outfits to wear while playing dress-up. For fabric, I used scraps of serge, wool, bombazine, and cotton twill, remnants from my grandmother's shop that I kept in a large box on top of my wardrobe. Most of the pieces were musty and stained, but the box held a few treasures: a square of lush black velvet, some pink organdy, a triangle of beaded white satin, and a baguette-sized strip of mink. I often spread these gems across my bed to examine them, imagining that some day, when I was older and lived in Paris, I would incorporate them into a grown-up gown.

In the August of my tenth year, my grandmother would not let me outside due to a typhoid epidemic that had swept through our region with a wave of severe heat. I couldn't swim in the lake or go to the village to join the other children for games under the thatched roof of the old stone *marché*. I couldn't even go to church. One morning, I pulled out my fabric remnants and began piecing them together, carefully stitching them into a child-sized dress.

Beyond my window, the fields burned, and the sky was white and empty. Cows herded themselves under trees and dogs hid below porches. The whole world seemed to stop moving, and every day was like every other. All I had for company were my grandmother, the aunts, and Jacques Beloit, whose parents owned the patisserie in Agen and who lived up the road. Jacques was a year younger than me, a small, serious boy who often arrived at teatime with treats from his parents' shop.

On the day I squandered my fabric treasures, my grandmother and the aunts went to a funeral for one of their elderly cousins. At four o'clock I heard the door open and close and voices in the front of the house. One of them was Jacques' squeaky soprano. I thought I heard him say something about lemon tarts, a favorite of mine, so I slipped into my gown.

It had a long skirt of gray cotton that I'd taken from an old dress

3

of my grandmother's. I used the black velvet for a bodice and the pink organdy for puffy sleeves. The triangle of white satin fit nicely into the neckline, and the strip of mink made a perfect collar.

I twirled into the parlor. Jacques was sitting on an armchair near the fireplace, munching a lemon tart and swinging his skinny white legs with the scabby knees that looked like burnt toast. He was still too young for long pants, but his wetted-down black hair, severely parted on the right, and his thick spectacles gave him the air of a little man.

I ignored him and glided over to the sofa where the aunts were perched like three blackbirds. The twins, Aunts Hélène and Marie, wore ordinary mourning, but Aunt Virginie, the eldest and wealthiest sister, sat between them in her flashiest black satin gown with the broad weepers' cuffs. Jet chandeliers hung from her ears to her collarbones; ropes of jet glittered around her neck. "It is 1868, and I am lady-in-waiting to Empress Eugénie," I announced in a grand tone.

The aunts were busy arguing, and they didn't notice me. Aunt Hélène rattled her teacup and glared at Aunt Virginie. "You needn't have piled on the mourning," she said. "Cousin Caterine was a silly little nobody."

"You just want an excuse to wear your jet earrings and necklaces," added Aunt Marie.

Aunt Virginie sat erect and unsmiling and looked down her nose at her sisters. "I can wear my jet jewelry whenever I want," she said. "I am *always* in high mourning for my Henri."

Henri, her husband, had been dead for decades. A prosperous doctor, he built the spacious stone house where she lived now with Aunts Hélène and Marie. Their husbands, mere barbers, also had been dead for years.

"You shouldn't drag them out for Caterine then," hissed Aunt Hélène. "It makes us look bad."

"It's not my fault your husbands couldn't afford to buy good jewelry," said Aunt Virginie.

I pirouetted dramatically. "I'm going to a ball tonight, and this is what I'll wear."

They ignored me still. "My carriage will be here soon. If you want to see my dress, you have to look now!"

Finally, the aunts laid down their teacups and considered me. No one said anything for the longest time. Then Aunt Virginie spoke. "Isabelle, *ma chère,* you must have been having a nightmare when you thought that up. It is not at all becoming."

"Not at all becoming," echoed Jacques. "Why don't you wear your burgundy velvet? You look pretty in that."

"What do you know about dresses?" I said, glaring at him. Then, turning my gaze to the aunts, "I copied this gown from *Les Élégances Parisiennes.* I can show you the picture."

"I don't care where you copied it from," said Aunt Virginie. "It's a mess."

Just then my grandmother entered the parlor carrying a fresh pot of tea. She was a small, fine-boned woman with kind hazel eyes and a pink, finely lined face. Her cottony hair was arranged in a neat chignon, and she wore a blue flowered apron over her unadorned black dress. Her husband had been a carpenter, and he couldn't afford fancy jewelry either. "I think it's lovely, Isabelle," she said. "You have a real flair with your needle."

Aunt Virginie shot her an exasperated look. "Don't lie to the child, Berthe. Do you want her to learn about elegance or not?"

"She has plenty of time to learn about elegance. She's not in Paris yet," said my grandmother.

"I've been to Paris!" cried Jacques.

I whipped around. "I don't care!"

Jacques swallowed the last bite of his lemon tart and pushed his glasses in place with a small sticky hand. "Maybe you can come with us the next time."

"Maybe you can go home," I said coldly.

"Isabelle! That's no way to talk," said my grandmother. "I want you to apologize to Jacques."

He looked at me with a hurt expression and waited. But I couldn't apologize.

I fled to my bedroom on the second floor. It was furnished simply with blue cotton curtains, a desk, a chair, a small bookcase, and a wood bureau painted white. Over the iron bed, a Victorian artist's idea of Jesus, handsome and blue-eyed with flowing brown hair, gazed heavenward, and, above it, a plaster crucifix. I said my prayers here every night, watched by my grandmother.

I took my best doll from the bureau and sat with her on the bed. She was made by Jumeau, the most prestigious doll company in France, so I called her Mademoiselle Jumeau. She had large blue eyes and slightly parted pink lips painted on a porcelain face. Her abundant blond hair was arranged in a towering pouf. Mademoiselle Jumeau had arrived on Christmas morning the previous year dressed like a princess in a décolleté white gown with an échelle of perky bows on the bodice and a billowing satin skirt. Gold high-heeled slippers glittered on her dainty feet, a purple ostrich plume frothed from her wide brimmed hat, and she carried a little beaded purse. But what delighted me most was her full set of undergarments: camisole, corset, chemise, pantaloons, tulle petticoats, stockings, and garters, all trimmed with pink ribbons and white lace.

I'd sat on the floor by the Christmas tree, dazed with happiness, absorbing the beauty of the doll, feeling it seep into my marrow, giving me strength. Whenever I was ill or sad, it made me feel better to hold Mademoiselle Jumeau and conjure up her charmed life of parties, opera performances, grand houses, and carriage rides in the Bois de Boulogne.

Now, I took off my play gown and changed into an old brown cotton dress. Then I sat on my bed with Mademoiselle Jumeau. I was in the middle of fantasizing about riding with her in a gold-and-glass landau on the way to a ball, when there was a soft knock on the door. I opened it, and there stood Jacques.

"Let's play something," he said.

I left Jacques in the doorway and flopped on my bed. "I thought you were going home."

"Your grandmother said I could stay." Jacques stepped into the room. "What do you want to do?"

"I don't know," I said. "Make a new dress for Mademoiselle Jumeau, I guess. Do you want to help?"

"Sewing is for girls." Jacques took a volume of fairy tales from my bookcase and sat on the hooked rug in front of my bed with crossed legs.

"Then you can just sit there and look stupid, you stupid boy."

"*You're* stupid," said Jacques.

I took the unbecoming play dress out of my wardrobe and began undoing the seams with a pair of scissors that had belonged to my father. My grandmother said that each time the scissors clicked my father smiled down at me from heaven, and as I worked, I felt bolstered by this unseen love. When I'd finished, I stripped Mademoiselle Jumeau to her camisole and pantaloons. Then I fitted the piece of beaded white satin around her waist, pinning it into a skirt. Next, I cut a piece of the black velvet to make a bodice, keeping the rest for a cape, which I trimmed in mink.

An hour went by. When I'd completed the gown and had it on Mademoiselle Jumeau, I showed it to Jacques. "Isn't she pretty?"

He studied her for a moment, then looked at me with a wondering expression. "She looks just like you," he said.

Two weeks later, the heat broke. A driving rain pounded the village, and the days turned gray and cool, killing the germs that hid in the trees, or so my grandmother said. It was safe now for me to go outside, and my first excursion was to Sunday mass. "I'm so happy to see you, Isabelle. It's been a while," said the gentle old priest, as he greeted me after the service.

I'd brought Mademoiselle Jumeau and held her up for the priest to admire. "We've been cooped up for weeks, and we're very happy to be out," I said.

I followed my grandmother and the aunts down the stone steps of the church and across the village square to a small shaded park. My relatives settled on benches to gossip with their friends, and I wandered to the old thatched-roof marché where two teams of children, separated by a white chalk line, were about to start a game of prisoners' base.

My eyes were drawn to the handsome boy standing in the square at the marché's far end. All sinewy legs and arms, summer freckles in a riot on his face, he looked to be about twelve and had wavy auburn hair and pale, even features. He stood absolutely still as a whistle pierced the air, followed by shouts and the scrape of leather shoes on stone. It took only a few minutes for one of his teammates to scramble through the crowd to him. Then, with a swiftness that startled me, he ran to his team with fists shot triumphantly in the air.

Suddenly, on the sidelines a beautiful little girl appeared in a white organdy frock with a blue moiré sash tied around her waist. A smaller ribbon the same color was tied in her curly dark hair. The boy called to her, inviting her into the game. She hesitated a moment, then darted in, taking her place beside him. The sun bounced around them as they ran, filling their hair with light and bleaching out the boy's freckles. I felt a stab of jealousy and hung back.

"Why don't you play with them?" said a voice behind me.

I turned around to face a tall, slender man with a black mustache and thick gray hair. "My dress is ugly," I said, pointing my chin toward the beautiful girl. "It is not as pretty as *her* dress."

The man laughed. "That is, indeed, a very pretty dress," he said finally. "But it is a city dress. It is not for the country. She is wicked to show off by wearing it here and making you feel badly."

I thought I wouldn't mind being wicked if I could have such a dress.

The following Sunday, I convinced my grandmother to let me wear my best dress—a burgundy velvet with a crocheted white collar.

After mass, I went to the marché to look for the handsome boy and was pleased to see him. A game of prisoners' base was under way, and I prayed to God that the boy would notice me, just *see* me. A minute later, he ran up to me. "My team is short one," he said. "Do you want to play?"

Carefully, I stood Mademoiselle Jumeau against a stone post and followed the boy into the game. I got only halfway across our court, when a child from the other team tagged me. "Don't worry, you'll do better next time," called the boy from the far end of the marché.

That afternoon at tea, Jacques announced, "Isabelle is in love."

"I am not!" I cried.

"Love is for grown-ups," said my grandmother, as she stirred a cube of sugar into her tea.

"She's in love with the tall boy with freckles," said Jacques. He held his *pain au chocolat* with both hands and took a large bite.

"That's Daniel Blank. Madame Duval's nephew. He lives in Paris and is staying with her for the summer," said Aunt Virginie. Then, turning to me, "I don't blame you, Isabelle. He's a very handsome boy."

At the mention of the boy's name, my face turned scarlet. "I'm not in love with anybody."

But I lived for Sundays. During our games, when I thought Daniel wasn't looking, I stole glances at him, my heart swelling at the sight of his narrow, fine-boned face. I loved the lock of auburn hair that flopped across his forehead and how he pushed it aside with the back of his hand. He was a head taller than the tallest of the village children and their natural leader. He dominated our games with his quick, graceful footwork, but Jacques and the other boys didn't seem to resent him. He never made them feel inferior. In addition to being the handsomest boy in the world, he also was the kindest.

I decided to sew him a shirt. I found two yards of blue calico in a trunk in the attic and made a pattern based on an old shirt of my grandfather's. I fit it on Jacques, though allowing for Daniel's larger proportions. I told Jacques that Daniel, admiring the dress I'd made for Mademoiselle Jumeau, had asked me to make it, but that it was a secret. No one was supposed to know, especially my grandmother and the aunts. "You never made *me* a shirt," said Jacques. His eyes were big and moist behind his glasses.

"You're only nine," I said.

"I'd still like a new shirt."

"When you're older."

I worked on Daniel's shirt for a week, and when I finished, I spent another week worrying about how to give it to him. I decided the only way was for Jacques to wear it to church and afterward take it off and present it to Daniel in the marché.

"What am I supposed to tell him?" asked Jacques.

"You don't have to tell him anything," I said. "I'll write a note and pin it to the sleeve."

I agonized over the note for hours. Finally, I wrote simply, "Please accept this gift from the needle of Isabelle Varlet."

I gave the shirt to Jacques on Saturday. He told his mother that I had made it for him (even though it was several sizes too big) and that he had promised me he'd wear it to church, that it would break my heart if he didn't.

On Sunday I awoke with a foggy head and scratchy throat, but I said nothing. If my grandmother thought I was coming down with something, she never would have let me out of the house.

In church, I was relieved to see the blue calico peeking from Jacques' brown serge jacket, and after the service, he ducked behind a tree to remove Daniel's shirt. Children ran about the marché, shouting and squealing. Fall was in the air, and leaves blew across the ground with pebbles and wads of debris. My eyes darted around for Daniel, but he was nowhere in sight. "He's not here!" I moaned, flopping onto the cold stone.

Jacques dropped down next to me. "What do we do now?" he asked.

"Wait. Maybe he'll show up."

"He's probably gone back to Paris."

I was contemplating this dreadful thought, when I felt a presence behind us. Madame Beloit, Jacques' mother. "Why did you take off your shirt? You'll catch your death," she scolded.

I started to cough, first quietly, then with great convulsive hacks. "Look, Isabelle is sick already," Madame Beloit said. "You foolish, foolish children."

Madame Beloit ran off to fetch my grandmother and the aunts, who put me to bed as soon as we reached home. I slept for a long time, and it was only when I awoke and reached for Mademoiselle Jumeau that I realized I'd left her behind in the marché.

Jacques went back for her the next day, but all he found was Mademoiselle Jumeau's battered wood body. She looked like the victim of a toy guillotine. In addition to her beautiful porcelain head, her dress and shoes were missing, and mud smeared her undergarments. "I looked everywhere for the head," said Jacques. "A dog probably chewed it off."

Immediately, my grandmother sent away to Paris for a new Jumeau doll. I didn't forget about the first one, though, and when I was feeling better, we had a funeral for her. I sewed a simple shroud for the body and used the blue silk-lined box she'd come in as a coffin. Jacques dug a hole under the oak in the front yard, and the aunts arrived for the ceremony huddled in mourning coats against the fall chill. Aunt Virginie had draped fox pieces over her shoulders and also donned her best jewelry. My grandmother read from the Bible, and we all sang "Heart of Jesus, Meek and Mild," as Jacques laid the coffin in the ground and shoveled dirt over it.

The late afternoon had arrived, throwing long gray shadows across the yard. Aunt Hélène had scowled at Aunt Virginie's furs and jet jewelry throughout the service, and as we walked back to the house, she said, "It is one thing to pile on the mourning for cousin Caterine, and quite another to do it for a doll."

After that summer, Jacques started boarding school in Bordeaux. For a while I saw him when he came home on holidays, but as the years passed, he visited me less and less. During the rest of my time in Timbaut, I never saw Daniel again, though I got to know his aunt, a tall, efficient dressmaker named Marie-France Duval. When I was seventeen my grandmother sent me to Agen to become her apprentice, and it is because of her I have a story to tell.

One

Madame Duval's shop sat in the middle of Avenue de la République, where a blue canvas awning above the door announced her name in black paint. In front of the store, a small reception area held glass cases with scarves, handbags, and shoes carefully chosen by Madame Duval from Paris suppliers on her twice-yearly trips to the city. The sewing was done at the back of the shop in a small, windowless room, where our clients stood for their fittings behind a flowered curtain.

We served coffee in the morning and red wine at five in the afternoon. A black spaniel named Marat lounged on the heating grate, a couple of cats perched on the counters. A few of our clients stopped in every day after doing their marketing to see if we had put out anything new, to gossip, to discuss outfits they fantasized about having made but could never afford and had no occasion to wear.

When I went to work for Madame Duval, she showed me how to translate the fashion drawings in my sketchbook into actual garments by draping fabric and cutting a pattern. The results sparked in me cataclysms of pleasure; I loved nothing more than taking a raw bolt of cloth and spinning it into a dress. While I worked, Madame Duval chattered nonstop about her life. I'd only been with her for a few days, when she told me about working in Deauville for Gabrielle "Coco" Chanel, a young milliner whom Madame Duval called "a genius."

After marrying a horse trainer in late middle age, Madame Duval moved to the fashionable racing resort and got a job at the Chanel shop on rue Gontaut Biron. Mademoiselle, as her employees always called her, began designing clothes when her hat customers demanded outfits like she herself wore. But her adolescent workers knew little about fine sewing. Only Madame Duval was experienced in couture techniques—she'd taught herself by dissecting Paris garments she'd found in thrift shops—and under her tutelage, the inexperienced seamstresses turned out slouchy belted jackets, jersey dresses, crisp white blouses, and straight skirts with pleats and pockets.

"It wasn't easy working for Mademoiselle," recalled Madame Duval. "She has the worst temper of anyone I've ever known, and the most scandalous private life. She'd been set up in business by her lover, a rich Englishman whom she hoped to wed, but he had lots of ladies and could be faithful to none."

By Madame Duval's account, the briny air in Deauville made everyone a little randy, including her own husband. One day, while strolling the pier during her lunch break, she caught him kissing a waitress from a local café. Almost immediately, Madame Duval packed her bags and returned to Agen.

Later, after Mademoiselle became a *couturière* in Paris, she invited Madame Duval to run one of her workrooms. By then, though, the older woman had settled into a quiet routine, making dresses for provincial housewives and tending to the roses in the terraced garden behind her house. She'd long ago given up on her youthful dreams, but she encouraged me to go to Paris. "Isabelle, you have a real eye for color and line, and you handle fabric so well. Only Mademoiselle has more supple hands. You're young, and your talent is wasted here."

I wanted to believe her. I began dreaming of making ball gowns for duchesses and living in a grand apartment on one of Haussmann's boulevards. Madame Duval nourished this fantasy, though not the part about the grand apartment—she warned me that Parisian seamstresses were as poorly paid as seamstresses everywhere.

As we worked, Madame Duval and I often discussed Chanel's techniques and style, her high standards and artistic eye. Mademoiselle was Madame Duval's dressmaking God, and over time the couturière became mine, too. I sewed in homage to this distant Parisian deity and dreamed of someday meeting her.

My clothes were not terribly original. They mimicked the city outfits I saw in the magazines, and for the most part, they were too flamboyant for the thick-legged country matrons who patronized our shop. Still, Madame Duval displayed my creations on wood mannequins in the front window. The idea that she had a protégé ignited in her a blaze of pride. "Look at what my talented assistant has done now!" she'd say to anyone who stepped through the door.

Not all, however, were dazzled by my work. My grandmother and aunts didn't understand the new fashions. When they came to the shop every Thursday morning after visiting their bank, they sniffed the clothes on display, held the fabric in their gloved hands, and looked down their noses at the frothy silk and lace garments that had come from my needle. "This dress looks like a nightgown," my grandmother complained of a pretty pink silk I'd copied from *Les modes élégantes*. Though the aunts said nothing, I could tell by their shocked expressions that they thought the dress indecent.

When war broke out, the shop became a refuge for worried wives, sisters, mothers, and sweethearts. Women gathered at the counters and in front of the display cases, ignoring the clothes and accessories, their faces smears of pain. When the bodies of their loved ones began coming home in coffins, they ordered dresses made up in black serge and other dark fabrics.

One of the few young men who hadn't gone to war was Jacques Beloit, my childhood friend. After the deaths of his parents in 1915, he'd left school and returned to Agen to run his family's patisserie. It sat directly across the street from Madame Duval's shop, and on his first day back, I stood by the window during slow periods and watched as he worked behind the counter. He'd grown into a tall, slim young man whose only resemblance to the skinny child I'd known was his shiny black hair and thick spectacles. His wretched eyesight, plus a rugby injury that had left him deaf in one ear, had kept him out of the army, to his great regret.

The next morning, I went into the patisserie to say hello and found him alone sweeping the floor. He looked up at me with a warm, wide smile, and that one tender glance changed everything.

"Hello, Isabelle," he said.

"Hello, Jacques," I answered. "A croissant, please."

"The brioche is better this morning," Jacques suggested.

"All right. I'll take two."

The next day, the half-witted old man who ran errands for the shopkeepers in exchange for a few francs delivered a box of lemon tarts to our door. Three days later, he brought over a tray of cookies, and the following morning, a small almond cake. "I think you have an admirer across the street," said Madame Duval, cocking her head in the direction of the patisserie.

One day, when Madame Duval was out, Jacques delivered the pastry box himself. When he walked into the shop, jangling the front door bell and causing Marat to bark a greeting, I was standing behind the accessories counter. He had shed his long white apron, and I noticed that his hair was neatly combed. Without saying a word, he set the box on the counter. Then he leaned across the glass case and kissed me on the lips.

After that I stopped dreaming about Paris. I began planning a trousseau and mooning over babies who accompanied their mothers to Madame Duval's shop. Soon Jacques and I were spending all of our free time together—lunch breaks on a bench in the town square, evenings in one of the local cafés, Sundays at my house. My grandmother and the aunts loved having Jacques around again (and the sweets he brought them every Sunday, balancing the pastry box on the handlebars of his bicycle). Once, after he'd escorted us to church, my grandmother announced gravely, "Jacques was always such a good boy."

"A wonderful boy," the aunts echoed.

Madame Duval, on the other hand, disapproved. Jacques was not the man she would have chosen for me. "He is just a baker, and he is so quiet," she warned one morning, as she looked askance at a chocolate cake he had sent over. "It never turns out well when the woman is more clever than the man."

Indeed, Jacques had little to say. He'd never been a loquacious child, but as a young man, he was downright untalkative. He was a good listener, though; he loved my stories and opinions. If anything, Jacques' reticence enhanced my interest—it was a refreshing change from the female nattering I heard all day. I do not believe that a taciturn nature is evidence of a sluggish mind, and I did not feel more clever than Jacques. He had his own kind of genius, which Madame Duval, not liking sweets, couldn't see.

Ever since he'd visited the Eiffel Tower as a child, Jacques had dreamed of being an engineer. When his parents died, he gave up those plans for the patisserie. Jacques had no interest in baking, but he couldn't bear to close the shop, which his grandfather had opened in 1860 during Louis-Napoleon's Second Empire. So he applied himself to éclairs and tarts, to galettes and *choux à la crème* with the same energy and diligence that he would have bestowed on the bridges and railroads he never had a chance to build.

The result produced pastries that were themselves feats of engineering: cookies in the shape of birds and animals, tarts topped with fruit topiaries; galettes that looked like Picasso paintings. For the window at Christmas, Jacques baked a yule tree frosted with chocolate buttercream made to look like bark. Meringue mushrooms sprouted at its base; candy birds of paradise sat on branches that were dusted with snowy sugar.

People began flocking from surrounding towns to Beloit's. Jacques hired two assistants to help him fill orders, but he refused to expand the shop, and he often turned down requests for weddings and large parties. He had all the work he wanted. He was not ambitious, except to spend time with me.

One of our great pleasures was dancing. We taught ourselves the fox-trot and the tango by watching Vernon and Irene Castle in a newsreel demonstration at the cinema in Agen. Often after the patisserie closed, we flung closed the curtains on the front windows and played records on the Victrola Jacques kept in back. No one bothered us, and for hours we practiced the steps we'd seen on screen. I loved the feel of Jacques' arm around my waist, his hand in mine. The click and snap of heels on the dark wood floor seemed to swell the music, obliterating the glass display cases, the old cash register, the cake stands, and dusty aprons on hooks. We could have been in Paris dancing at the Ritz.

As I became more preoccupied with Jacques, Madame Duval pushed me harder at work. One morning she arrived with a copy of the American magazine *Harper's Bazaar* under her arm and excitedly pointed out an illustration of a Chanel outfit, the first time one of Mademoiselle's designs had appeared in a magazine. The dress was a loose fitting silk chemise with a deep V neck and long narrow sleeves ending in lace cuffs. There was no bodice or waist; a long scarf glided seductively along the hips. The mannequin also wore a broad-brimmed hat with a flat piece of sable twisted along one side of the close-fitting crown, echoing the sable muff she held in her right hand. The dress's unstructured shape, its low waist and raised hem, its skin-baring neckline and simple accessories were in sharp contrast to the fussy models from the other couturiers. "Look at this! With one outfit Mademoiselle has done away with the entire Belle Époque!" pronounced Madame Duval. "Leave it to the Americans to have the courage to print it."

She rummaged in the back of the shop for some blue silk and white lace and asked me to duplicate the dress. I managed as best I could with the old fabric, though the result didn't much resemble the *Harper's Bazaar* illustration. Still, Madame Duval enthusiastically praised my effort and displayed the dress on a wire form in the window with a sign underneath reading, "A charming Chanel design as interpreted by Isabelle Varlet."

Jacques proposed at Christmas in 1916, and we planned to marry in June. But the following May he finally was drafted; the army by this time was desperate for men, no matter how weak-eyed and deaf. Whenever anyone mentioned the war—as people did all the time—a cold terror gripped my chest, and I tried to focus my attention on something pleasant, like choosing lace for my wedding gown.

On his last night in Timbaut, before he was to report for duty, Jacques brought me a box of lemon tarts. We were too sick at heart to eat them, and we sat opposite each other at the kitchen table, the untouched tarts between us. Jacques reached his arm across the table to take my hand, and we sat there for the longest time, not saying anything and me trying not to cry. Finally, at midnight, Jacques said, "I'll be going now."

He kissed me, and I told him to be careful. Those were the last words I ever said to him. As he rode his bicycle home from my house, he was struck by a car and killed. I didn't learn of it until the next morning, when I found my grandmother and the aunts weeping in the parlor. I ran sobbing from the house, finally collapsing under a tree in a field of heather. Though it began to rain, and I could hear my grandmother calling for me, I shivered on the cold ground until it grew dark.

In the following days, I occupied myself making a burial suit for Jacques. I cut the pattern from an old jacket and pants that one of his cousins had brought me, and I sewed it entirely by hand, staying up all night the evening before the funeral. Sewing his suit made me feel close to him, and it staved off the terrible emptiness that overwhelmed me once I'd delivered the clothes to the undertaker.

I did not have a catalogue of regrets, only one, that we had not yet married. Nevertheless, everyone treated me as Jacques' widow. The next day, when I entered the funeral parlor, dimly lit by candles and heavy with the perfume of carnations, the other mourners stepped aside, forming a wide aisle for me to pass. Jacques looked small and pale against the tufted gray satin lining of his coffin. Before the lid was shut, I kissed him on the forehead (I couldn't bear to touch his dead lips), and placed in his hands the rosary he had given me the previous Christmas.

The gathered mourners wept ferociously, as much for their own dead as for Jacques. Nearly everyone in our village had lost a loved one in the war. No doubt the presence of the mayor of Timbaut sparked some of this inconsolable crying. It was his job to notify the families of fallen soldiers, and the mere sight of this kindly old man was enough to start the wailing.

Perhaps because he'd been spared his grim task for Jacques, the mayor had a special place in his heart for the boy who'd died riding his bicycle, innocent of the horrors of battle. Three years later, after the armistice, no one objected when the mayor announced that Jacques' name would be engraved on the village war memorial and called out each year during the Day of Remembrance with the names of the *Enfants de Timbaut* who'd died for France.

When the war finally ended, there was great rejoicing in the village, but it did not last long. Soon an influenza epidemic swept through our region along with the winter storms. Despite my bad lungs, my poor body that wants to break down, that looks for any excuse to do so, I survived. Luck, perhaps, or some coarse strength has kept me alive all these years.

My grandmother and the aunts were among the first to fall ill. Now it was my turn to care for them, and I hardly left their bedsides. The aunts' house was a mile from ours, and I used Jacques' battered but workable bicycle—a gift from one of his uncles—to ride back and forth between the two households. I cooked for my relatives, wiped their brows, changed their bedding, and sat with them through their fevered nights. I remained hopeful until the end, but they were old women, and they were ready to die.

"At our age it is obscene to stay alive with so many boys in the ground," said my grandmother.

"We will see you in heaven," the aunts told me.

Aunt Hélène had a vision of the afterlife in which God had given her a sacred task: caring for heaven's never-to-be born babies, the children of young men who had died before they could become fathers.

I asked her if she would recognize the child that Jacques and I were going to have. "Of course," Aunt Hélène answered without hesitation. "I would know it anywhere. It would be blond, and it would be the only one not crying."

This mythical child had inherited something from each of us—my fine gold hair and Jacques' quietness.

All four sisters died within a week. They went peacefully. I thought I was prepared for their deaths, so it was a shock how hard they hit me, especially the loss of my grandmother. I cried so uncontrollably the doctor had to give me a sedative. He reminded me that I had my whole life ahead of me, and that my grandmother in heaven wanted me to be happy. "Let her joy in your survival give you strength to endure your loss," he said.

I knew nothing would disappoint my grandmother more than to see me in heaven prematurely, and over the years I've felt my subsequent bouts of illnesses not just as failures of my body, but also of my will.

The death of my family settled my future as far as Madame Duval was concerned. "It's time now for you to go to Paris," she told me.

Getting away seemed like a good idea to me, too. After my relatives' funerals in the little graveyard behind the ancient village church, I returned to the house, climbing the hill in the gray chilly morning, past the fields where I had played as a child. In the tiled-roof cottage, I packed a few clothes, some trinkets Jacques had given me, and my lucky scissors that had belonged to the father I'd never known. Then I left, locking the door and turning my back on provincial life.

In Agen, I boarded a train for Paris. As it sputtered out of the station, I turned over in my hand the letter Madame Duval had written on my behalf to Madame Georges, a friend of hers who was the house manager at Chanel Modes et Coutures. Madame Duval had sealed the envelope lightly with a small spot of wax on the point of the flap, and I contemplated opening it. I felt gripped by a need to know the contents, as if they might give me clues to my future. Ignoring the guilt prickling my conscience, I loosened the wax on the envelope with my fingernail and pulled out the creamy paper. "Dear

Madame Georges," the letter began, in Madame Duval's neat, round handwriting:

This will introduce to you Isabelle Varlet, one of the most talented seamstresses I've ever known. Though Isabelle is young in years, she already has surpassed me in her skill with needle and thread.

She is relocating to Paris, which has been a dream of hers for some time. If she seems a bit sad, it is not because she has a mournful temperament (she is by nature, in fact, a cheerful person), but because she has suffered much. Recently she lost to influenza the few relatives who remained to her. She also still mourns her fiancé, a young man who died in a bicycle accident. Though he was a perfectly decent individual, frankly I thought him beneath Isabelle. He did not have her intelligence, her spirit or her ambition.

Of course, his death was a tragedy, and I would never give a hint of this to her. But I can tell you, the poor boy's demise has saved Isabelle from what I am sure would have been a stifled and unsatisfying marriage. Her future now is in Paris, in couture. I hope you can find a place for her at Chanel, and, if that is impossible, steer her toward one of the better houses.

I folded the letter and returned it to the envelope. Did Madame Duval invent that part about my "spirit" and "ambition," or did she see in me something I had not yet recognized in myself? Was Jacques really "beneath" me in intelligence? Had he lived and we'd married, would I have ended up stifled and unsatisfied?

As the brown fields and little stone villages raced by the window, my heart pounded. I was afraid and anxious, wondering if in Paris I would feel the deaths of my family and Jacques as crushingly as I did at that moment. Madame Duval was certainly right about one thing: living in Paris had once been my great dream. Outside, the country-side gave way to the white luminous city, and I felt an unexpected spike of hope. By the time the train had chugged into Paris under the dirty glass dome of Gare d'Austerlitz, I convinced myself that working for Mademoiselle would offer a kind of salvation.

I grabbed my bags from the metal rack and joined the swarm of provincial French as they trudged through the cavernous station, dodging trees that had been planted in boxes to collect soot and freshen the air, redolent of sweat, river, smoke, and perfume. It was my first whiff of Parisian smells, and I sensed glamour in the fragrant mixture, hints of grand apartments, expensive restaurants, rich cars, and beautiful clothes.

Two

After spending the night in a hotel near the train station, I took a taxi to the place Vendôme. The day was extremely cold, though lovely and clear; a bright sun brushed the world in a golden glow. In Agen, the war shrouded even the sunniest days in sadness. In Paris, you'd never know there had been four years of horrific conflict. Elegantly dressed couples admired the jewelry and antiques in the shop windows, while long black cars pulled up to the Ritz, discharging guests under the heavy blue canopy. Around the corner, at 31, rue Cambon, a tall, gray-haired man in white gloves and a crisp gold-braided uniform opened the front door, and I stepped inside a small reception area. Thick beige carpets and heavy draperies imparted a convent hush, sealing out the honking cars and chattering pedestrians in the street. A receptionist sat at a desk with two telephones. "Can I help you?" she asked.

"I'd like to see Madame Georges."

"Do you have an appointment?"

"No. But you can tell her Madame Duval sent me." I handed her my letter.

"Very well. Sit down, please."

I took a seat on a fawn-colored sofa next to a beautiful young woman, whom I examined out of the corner of my eye. She wore a maroon suit, wool and plain, that flattered the slim contours of her figure. A sable coat draped over her shoulders; a huge diamond glittered on her left hand, and a gold choker circled her long, white neck. I thought she was the most gorgeous creature I'd ever seen. Having hardly spoken to a soul since leaving Agen, and, now, giddy with pleasure to be in an authentic couture house, sitting next to a real *Parisienne,* I couldn't stay quiet.

"Is it always this cold in March?" I blurted.

The beautiful woman glared icily. "Do I know you? Does Monsieur Prévot know you?"

"I don't believe so. I'm Isabelle Varlet."

The receptionist looked up from her desk. The beautiful woman stared into space, saying nothing. I felt a hot rush of shame. Obviously, I'd violated some unspoken rule of Parisian etiquette—a protocol of which I knew nothing.

A moment later a *vendeuse* wearing a black jersey dress and a double strand of pearls appeared. "Madame Prévot, I'm sorry to have kept you waiting. You can go back now."

The beautiful woman rose wordlessly from the settee, threw her sable over her shoulders and glided away. When she'd gone, the vendeuse whispered for a minute with the receptionist, then came over to the sofa to speak to me. "I understand you have an introduction to Madame Georges. If you wait here, I'll see if she's available." She studied me with narrowed eyes, taking my measure.

I tried to look confident. *I'm presentable enough,* I told myself. *Nice looking.* I didn't think I was nervous, but my armpits were wet; I hoped no one could smell me. After a few minutes, the vendeuse reappeared. "Come with me, please." She led me down a corridor past the salon where mannequins modeled clothes for the clients, and up a wide, winding staircase. "What kind of experience do you have?" she asked over her shoulder.

I told her about working for Madame Duval. "Maybe you're in luck. Mademoiselle has been talking about hiring a few more *mains.*

We just got finished in February with the spring collection, but she's already frantic about the fall collection in August."

We reached the top of the stairs and the vendeuse handed me my letter.

"You'll find Madame Georges in there," she said, motioning to a door at the end of the hall.

The house manager's office was nothing more than a windowless workroom. Madame Georges sat perched on a stool rummaging through papers in the well of a school desk. She was a small, middle-aged woman with gray hair and even features, dressed exactly like the vendeuse, except with a scarf around her neck instead of pearls. She slammed the desk shut and glared at me over the tops of her wire-rimmed spectacles. "Yes?"

"I'm here about a job," I said. I gave Madame Georges the letter. My mouth was dry and my throat tickled. I worried I'd have a coughing fit and tried to calm my breathing.

Madame Georges read the letter slowly, then removed her spectacles and held them in her small, blue-veined hands. She looked at me with the grave expression of a doctor delivering bad news. "I'll show your letter to Mademoiselle, but I doubt she'll hire anyone who hasn't had experience in couture."

"Oh, but I have."

"In *Parisian* couture."

Just then the door opened, and a small, dark-haired woman with a broad, strong-featured face walked into the room. At thirty-six, Mademoiselle had the short, wiry build of a twelve-year-old boy, and she was dressed simply in a gray jersey suit with a white blouse. The brown curls bobbing about her ears glistened with health; her dark gypsy eyes blazed under thick black brows. She barely glanced at my face, but she took an immediate interest in my dress—a black, low-waisted wool with a white organdy collar and cuffs—noting the perfect fit, the fine cut of the bodice, the graceful skirt that traced the hips. "Raise your arms, girl!" she commanded. I obeyed. "Ah, sleeves that fit properly." She clapped her hands like a delighted child. "Who made it?"

"I did," I said.

Mademoiselle hired me on the spot.

I couldn't believe it had been that easy—I'd walked in and landed a job. The fates were smiling at me, and, suddenly, I felt lucky. I saw my future laid out before me like a sparkling, flower-filled meadow.

When I started work at Chanel Modes et Coutures, I joined a revolution. For the first time, European women wore short hair and showed their ankles in public. The war had dictated that women simplify their clothing, and since the armistice, the most forward-looking of them had retained this casual, unadorned look. The chicest of the chic went to Mademoiselle for their clothes.

By the time I arrived at Chanel, Mademoiselle already was a Parisian celebrity, famous for her glamorous life and her unique personal style. Her February collection—her first as a licensed Parisian couturière—had been an immediate hit. With her next collection in August 1919, she hoped to dominate Paris fashion. The new *mode* would be the Chanel Mode. It was the look of Mademoiselle herself, and it would embody the very spirit of the new age.

I took a cheap apartment on rue du Cardinal-Lemoine in a working-class neighborhood and started work the day after Mademoiselle hired me. In her constant chatter about Paris, Madame Duval had focused on the glamorous aspects of couture; I wasn't prepared to enter a world that operated on a hierarchy as rigid as the Catholic Church. If Mademoiselle was the pope, the vendeuses were the cardinals; the *premières* and *secondes*, the bishops; the *mains,* the priests; the *arpètes,* the acolytes.

At Chanel, there was no such thing as a paid vacation or sick leave. Twelve-hour days, six days a week, were not uncommon, and though the August collection was five months away, the atmosphere was frenzied. We devoted ourselves to making clothes we could never afford for women whose lives of luxury and ease we would never lead. We were the overworked vehicles for Mademoiselle to fulfill her vision, and though not everyone in the shop believed we were changing fashion history, we all had to work as if we did.

I was assigned as a junior *main* to a workroom on the fourth floor. It was a plain square space with gray paint peeling from the walls and ceiling. But the light pouring in from three large windows was excellent. Thirty of us sat crammed together at long wood tables, ten senior *mains* and twenty juniors, including me. The première, Laurence Delaisse, sat at a squat schoolmarm's desk, piled high with papers, trays holding trimmings, and a big black phone. Simple shelves lined the walls. In spots, the seamstresses, had tacked up postcards. The only other personal touches were some family photographs framing a small mirror under the clock.

Laurence and her seconde, aided by the senior *mains,* made most of the toiles, the muslin blueprints that were used as patterns to cut out the models in fine fabric. Every morning, they draped muslin on dress forms, pinning and snipping, pinning and snipping, as soft strips of fabric fell around their feet. After the toiles were pinned together, they were basted with white thread and sent to the studio for Mademoiselle's inspection.

Laurence also decided how our work was organized. We were like an orchestra, each woman playing her part, each garment contributing to the atelier's symphony of beauty and style. Our workroom specialized in *flou,* that is anything soft and unstructured, which was the essence of Mademoiselle's style. Most models were made by a trio of seamstresses—a senior *main* to cut out the model, another senior *main* to help her stitch it together, and a junior *main* to do the less intricate work like hemming and pressing.

After Mademoiselle had approved a toile, it was *mis à plat*—laid flat on the worktable—and gently ripped apart. The deracinated pieces were stitched to fabric and cut out. Then the sewing began. The seamstresses sat elbow to elbow, heads bent over shimmering mounds of fabric—tulle embroidered with pearls, lace, jerseys, velvets, fringed silks, wools—stitching the seams of skirts, setting sleeves into jackets, rolling the hems of evening gowns, fashioning collars and pockets for capes. Near the stove, two junior *mains* pressed the clothes as they flowed from the seamstress's hands. The women chatted as they worked, the hissing of the irons carrying their voices high into the air, moist with the clean laundry smell of steam and linen.

The bulk of our time was spent filling orders for the steady stream of clients who flooded the salon each day. Mademoiselle, though, was focusing on the fall collection, which would comprise some 100 models—suits, day dresses, outerwear, and evening gowns. Illustrations of the models that would be presented on August 5, with small swatches of the fabrics that would be used, were tacked to a board in her studio. The sketches, which were done by one of the premières, since Mademoiselle couldn't draw, changed constantly as models were discarded and new ones added, according to the couturière's vision.

Most of the models I worked on were loose and easy, even the evening gowns had the relaxed, casual feel of sports clothes. There was something new in the air of Paris, a kind of youthful openness. You could see it on the street, in the way the shop girls and young wives wore their short skirts and belted jackets, their floaty chemise dresses and big-collared coats. Mademoiselle had caught their insouciance and refined it into chic.

I wondered, though, if this new fashion would appeal to the average couture client, if even the most avant-garde among them would pay upwards of 4,000 francs for a dress that looked to the unsophisticated eye like it could be put together by the maid at home. Mademoiselle wondered about this, too. She was shrewd—as talented in business as she was in designing. So as not to scare away the conservative, moneyed crowd, she was careful to offer a variety of styles, including some rather dowdy dresses for older women. She would not dwell, however, on these boring models, and she hoped that no one else would either.

The toiles for the collection were stored on metal *rayons* in the back of our workroom, and there was great competition among the seamstresses to see whose models would make it into the final lineup. We all dreamed of sewing the Star of the Collection, the dress that *Vogue* and *Femina* would put on their covers, that department stores in London and New York would pay a fortune to copy, that every fashionable Parisienne would clamor to own.

I'd only been at Chanel a week, when Laurence, my première, told me I had "good hands," the highest compliment you can pay a seamstress. Fast, supple hands—hands that can run a needle through fabric as rapidly as a mouse scurrying across floorboards, hands that can make stitches so fine they're invisible, hands that can cause ruffles to flutter gracefully, shoulders to fit perfectly and skirts to move effortlessly—are couture's currency, more valuable than silver or gold.

I graduated quickly to senior *main*. I was in this job for two weeks, when Laurence's seconde was transferred to one of the tailoring workrooms, and I was promoted to her place. This swift and dazzling rise was the last thing I expected. It buoyed my confidence immensely and reinforced my conviction that I'd done the right thing by coming to Paris. I belonged here in the world of couture.

One of the first toiles I worked on was for the upcoming peace celebrations in June. It was the muslin embryo of a black silk evening dress with a bodice cut in a low V in front that eventually would be covered in jet beads. I'd stayed late to work on it, and I was eager to have it approved by Mademoiselle. On the day I was to present it to her, I arrived early and took the stairs to the fourth floor. I hung my jacket on a wall hook and switched on the aluminum lights. I loved the start of the day: the immaculately swept floors, the bolts of cloth neatly stacked on the shelves, the row upon row of wood dress forms padded out to the various bulges of Mademoiselle's "darlings," as the couturière called the aristocrats, actresses, ministerial wives, rich men's mistresses, and professional beauties who made up her clientele. These women were anything but darling, of course—mean and demanding, the richest tended to be the rudest and the least fastidious about paying their bills.

The seamstresses began arriving. Though she was the première, Laurence often showed up late. A short, compact woman with curly, hennaed hair, she had the confident chic of a woman who'd spent her life in couture. Her grandmother and mother had worked for Paul Poiret at the height of his fame at the turn of the century. Laurence herself had apprenticed to Poiret until he closed his shop at the start of the war, when she was hired by Mademoiselle. Her knowledge of couture technique was superb, but Laurence was man-crazy and inclined to laziness. In the afternoons, she flipped through magazines while the rest of us worked. Often, she slipped out early to keep a rendezvous with a lover. I began to think she was better suited to working in a nightclub or a theater, or as a vendeuse at one of the department stores, where she could flirt all day with the customers.

From a metal *rayon* at the back of the workroom, I retrieved the toile for the silk dress and sat down at a table. I'd just finished fashioning a sash for it, when Laurence approached me holding the jacket of a jersey suit I'd completed a few days before. "You didn't do the seams right on the armholes. They have to be redone," she said. Gently, she turned the garment inside out. "The raw edges should be overcast together. That way the curve lies flatter."

I felt my face redden. The rule on overcasting armhole seams, like dresses that slipped over the head without fastenings, and so much else about Parisian couture, was new to me.

Straightening her back, her voice heavy with authority, Laurence quoted Mademoiselle: "Elegance means something is as perfect on the wrong side as on the right."

"How will I have time?" I protested, motioning to the muslin on the table. "I have this toile to finish."

"Find the time. Amélie Valporin comes in at five for her fitting," Laurence said, referring to the daughter of the *Ministre de la Marine*. Amélie was one of the new garçonne types, slender to the point of emaciation, with no breasts or hips.

"Oh, please. Do you think that skinny nitwit is going to turn the dress inside out and inspect it?" called out one of the seamstresses, an older woman who was rubbing beeswax along a piece of thread.

"No, but her mother might," Laurence said.

The première turned her attention to the girl sitting beside me, a quiet adolescent who'd recently been promoted from arpète to seamstress. The girl concentrated fiercely as she stitched a piece of rabbit fur to the hem of a gray wool dress. "Nice work, Madame Bertaux will be pleased," Laurence said.

The girl looked up, beaming.

"Let's hope she can still fit into it," Laurence added. "Last week she came in with five more pounds on her stomach and a corset from the *ancien régime.*"

From the other end of the room, a seamstress who stood in a cloud of steam pressing a satin gown, shouted, "Her ass is huge, too!"

Plump matrons were a favorite target in the atelier. Mademoiselle loathed fat. If she'd had her way, only young, slender women would wear her clothes. Her contempt for overweight darlings had seeped into the workrooms and infected the seamstresses. Even the ones who weren't so svelte themselves snickered and gossiped about this one's huge bottom and that one's pigeon bosom. Madame Bertaux was particularly loathsome because she was fat *and* stingy.

"Her vendeuse told me she's always fighting over prices," announced an apple-cheeked blonde, as she secured fabric-covered buttons to a blouse. She aped a snooty dowager's voice: "Five thousand francs is too much. Can't you take some more off?"

"Didn't you hear?" Laurence said. "Mademoiselle told her vendeuse she'd give Bertaux a hundred-franc discount for every pound she lost."

The seamstresses shrieked and giggled like schoolgirls, not caring if it was true or not. Most of them had been with the couturière since the start of her career, and they were like missionaries preaching the Gospel of Mademoiselle. The first commandment: Thou shalt make no references to the past. Any superfluous details harking back to Belle Époque opulence—elaborate ruching, false pockets, buttons that didn't button—were regarded as sins. Once I suggested to one of these women that she sew a row of buttons on the back of an evening gown that was fastened with snaps, and she glared at me, as if I'd asked her to add a bustle to the skirt.

I finished stitching the toile and handed the muslin to a junior *main* to press. Over the next three hours, I helped Laurence put together the pieces of a black crepe dress. I sewed the skirt seams, while she sewed the bodice. Soon, the two pieces were ready to be joined, a task I completed by lunch. At one, my colleagues and I were served a simple meal of chicken and vegetables in the lunchroom.

After the break, we had no sooner stepped through the workroom door, when Mademoiselle called. "She wants to see your toile," said Laurence, who answered the phone. "You better come along."

Every afternoon, a steady cavalcade of seamstresses, mannequins, and whomever else Mademoiselle needed for inspiration would take the staircase to the third floor, open the glass doors, and enter Mademoiselle's studio. It was a large, airy room, brightened by the sun sifting through the tall windows. Bolts of cloth leaned against the walls; boxes strewn about overflowed with buttons, pieces of embroidery, sequins, paillettes, spangles, and beading. Belts, shoes, handbags, and gloves piled up on tables. The floor was a carpet of thread and bits of fabric.

A mannequin named Yvette stood in front of the triple mirrors. She was exceptionally pretty, a taller, younger version of Mademoiselle with the same brown hair and dark eyes. What I noticed first about her, though, was her dress. Every inch of it was perfect, from the slender straps at the shoulders to the frothy sash belted at the hips and the airy skirt floating above her ankles. It looked as if it had been sewn by an angel.

The dress had been made by a première from another workroom, a slight, attractive young woman who at this moment was walking slowly around Yvette, studying the white dress from every angle. The première had a spray of freckles on a pale complexion and short ginger hair. Unlike the other forewomen, she didn't wear a smock, but was dressed in a brown Chanel suit.

She was Baroness Susanna Lawson, an English aristocrat who had been with Mademoiselle for a year. Susanna had grown up in a London town house and a grand country estate, but even before the war her family had lost their houses and their money, and she'd been forced to go to work. She discovered she had a talent for sewing, and she learned couture technique by dissecting the clothes she'd bought when she was rich.

The baroness was Mademoiselle's favorite. Though I didn't know it at the time, she made most of the couturière's evening dresses and was the only employee known to see Mademoiselle socially. Indeed, Susanna had introduced Mademoiselle to a world of wealthy aristocrats, a few of whom had become Chanel clients.

The Englishwoman picked up the hem of Yvette's dress and shook it out. "Do you think it's too long?" she asked Mademoiselle in heavily accented French.

"No. It's fine," answered the couturière. She seemed pleased, but there was no dwelling on the success. She ordered Yvette to take off Susanna's dress and put on my toile.

The mannequin shimmied out of the white silk and slipped on the muslin garment. As soon as she did, my heart sank. The toile hung limply on her bony frame. Her shoulders slumped, and her arms were matchsticks. Yvette was one of those young women who straddled the line between exquisite thinness and emaciation. A rounder girl would have shown my toile to better effect.

Mademoiselle moved close to Yvette, studying her from every angle. "No, no. I don't like it all," she snarled. Then, turning to Susanna Lawson, "What do you think?"

Susanna looked my toile up and down. Laurence had warned me that she had an instinct for weakness and would meddle at the first sign of disapproval from Mademoiselle. "It's got no life."

Laurence looked at me and rolled her eyes. I wanted to defend my work, but I was too intimidated to speak.

Suddenly, Mademoiselle attacked the toile with her hands, pulling out the skirt and repinning it to make it narrower. When she'd finished, she stepped aside to study the effect. "No better!" She tossed her arms in the air and glanced heavenward. "You see how it is? I'm tortured like a serf because I demand excellence."

"Maybe you should change the bodice," said Susanna.

Laurence leaned toward me and whispered, "If Mademoiselle changes the bodice, she might as well discard the toile entirely."

I could see exactly how it would go: If the bodice changed, then the skirt wouldn't work, then the trimming, and before you knew it, Mademoiselle would decide to begin again from scratch.

"The loose waist is very graceful," I said.

Mademoiselle whipped around and stared at me with narrowed eyes. She struggled for a minute to recall whom I was. "You're the new girl, aren't you?" she said finally. "So you like the waist?"

"I do, too," said Yvette in a timid voice.

The mannequin had been on her feet for two hours already, while Mademoiselle inspected toiles and finished models. The color had drained from the poor girl's face. She looked like she might pass out. "Can I sit down a moment?"

"You're already tired?" Mademoiselle taunted. "A Chanel dress is made for a woman who moves. Get going!"

Yvette walked across the room, twirled, then returned to her post in front of the mirrors. She was white next to the burnt-sugar color of the muslin. "I must sit down, just for a minute," she said.

Mademoiselle glowered under the furry ledge of her brows. "If you're tired already, you should find another line of work."

Yvette started to cry. Those sloping shoulders quaked pathetically, and tears poured from her eyes.

"Go on, Yvette, let your tears fall, baptize the dress!" Mademoiselle scoffed. Then, turning to Susanna, "How am I supposed to produce a collection by August? My life is one long battle!"

Yvette remained standing, her shoulders slumped, the tears silently slicking down her cheeks. I moved to Mademoiselle's side to get a closer look at the toile. The couturière smelled of starch and lavender soap. Recently, she'd begun plucking her eyebrows in a hopeless attempt to control the fierce growth. I noticed a few black sprouts above her nose. "Maybe if we changed the neckline," I suggested.

Mademoiselle stared at the toile for a minute. "The dress is telling me to leave the neckline alone," she said.

Mademoiselle had incredible flair, an innate, infallible taste. Like natural musical talent, it was a gift one was either born with or not. But the truth was, she wasn't much of a seamstress. I sewed better than she did, all of us did. That's why she'd hired us, because of our technical expertise, our deep knowledge of how to put clothes together—something she herself had never learned.

The couturière dropped to her knees and attacked the muslin with scissors and pins, her hands moving quickly and vigorously over the fabric as though she were sculpting in clay. Behind her hard, dark eyes, she struggled to strike an idea. A moment later, she looked up. "Have we got any tulle?" she asked.

I pawed through the pile of fabric swatches on a nearby table and handed Mademoiselle a piece of light, sheer fabric. She folded it into a wide strap and pinned it to the dress.

"That's very pretty," I said. "But it might work better if we opened up the back." I knew I was sticking my neck out, but I was eager to impress her with my sense of style.

"Oh, is that what you think?" Mademoiselle's tone mocked. Still, she followed my suggestion, repinning the back so it draped into a low U.

My face flamed, and I felt the redness spreading from my chest to my hairline. I began to think my toile actually had a chance.

Mademoiselle took a cigarette from her jacket pocket and held it between square, large-knuckled fingers. The baroness stepped forward and started pulling on the back of my toile. "This line is all wrong, all wrong," she said with grave authority. "Mademoiselle, it is not consistent with the collection. Nothing else you're doing has this draped, Grecian effect."

With the expression of someone who's just eaten something unpleasant, Susanna Lawson pointed to the back of the skirt. "Oh, God, look at this. It isn't hanging right. There's too much extension at the hips, like something from Patou."

At the mention of the couturier Jean Patou, Mademoiselle flinched. She loathed him almost as much as he detested her, their hatred born of similar aesthetics. Both strove to rid fashion of superfluous frills, to produce clothes that were modern and easy to wear. Both wanted to dominate the *mode.* Like beautiful women who can't stand to have

their identities reflected back to them in the form of a rival, Mademoiselle and Patou refused to be in the same room together. If one of them
came upon the other at a party or a restaurant, they would both leave.

Mademoiselle studied the garment for a minute, taking long drags
on her cigarette and releasing the smoke with heavy sighs. "You're
right, Susanna," she said in an exasperated tone. With her left hand,
she yanked the muslin from Yvette's shoulders, exposing the girl's lace-
trimmed chemise and drawers. "It might be beautiful to you," she
said, glaring at me. "Or that phony Patou. But not to Chanel!"

That evening, when I was gathering my things in preparation to leave,
Laurence asked if I wanted to go dancing with her and Yvette. "We all
need some cheering up after that dreadful *pose.*"

"I can't wear this," I said, looking down at my stained and wrinkled smock.

"Of course not. Come with me."

As we made our way to the end of the hall and down the stairs,
Laurence told me that Mademoiselle let the baroness get away with
murder. "She comes in late, and sometimes she doesn't come in at all.
The seamstresses complain to Madame Georges, who complains to
Mademoiselle, but Mademoiselle does nothing."

"Why does she put up with it?" I asked.

"For one thing, Lawson has a lot of rich friends, and she brings
them in as clients. You can't judge anything by today. Today was your
day to get picked on, Isabelle. Mademoiselle treats Lawson as badly
as she treats anyone, actually treats her a little worse. You should hear
her making fun of Lawson's accent. Mademoiselle loves to belittle her.
It gives her a thrill treating a baroness like a maid. Lawson stands
there fuming, then goes back to the workroom and takes it out on
the seamstresses."

"Still, Lawson is the favorite," I pointed out. "She has a special
position."

Laurence snorted. "In this place, being the favorite is the kiss of death. Mademoiselle builds people up just so she can have the pleasure of destroying them."

At the end of the hall on the third floor Laurence opened a door onto a small, windowless room. Metal *rayons* reaching to the ceiling held dozens of dresses, suits, coats, capes, and evening gowns—most of them rejected models and duplicates from previous collections, though a few were garments that had been ordered by darlings and never picked up. Laurence explained that Mademoiselle let her employees borrow from this stash whenever they wanted. "'Why should the clothes sleep here? They like to go out and have fun, too,'" said Laurence, quoting Mademoiselle. "It's one of the perks of the job."

"The *only* perk," said Yvette. She searched greedily through a rack of evening gowns, inspecting and rejecting each dress with quick jerks of her hand. "Black, black, black! I'm so tired of it. It reminds me of convent school."

"What do you expect? All Mademoiselle saw when she was growing up were nuns' habits and peasant frocks," said Laurence. "She acts grand now, but her parents were poor as dirt. And when her mother died, her father dumped her and her sisters in a convent in Aubazine."

"How do you know?" I asked.

"Poiret told my mother." Laurence pulled out a black velvet chemise, exquisitely cut and absolutely plain except for a white lace collar. "This is exactly what he meant when he called Mademoiselle's style *le pauvreté du luxe.*"

I mostly wore black, too, though I wasn't striving for a look of luxurious poverty. I'd adopted the habit of wearing black after Jacques died, and it had become my uniform. Throughout the war, I dressed in the somber tones of my grandmother and aunts. Now, even though peace had come, I still wore black. So did most women. What had started out as a symbol of grief was evolving into the postwar standard of elegance.

Tonight, however, I wanted a bit of color. "What about up there," I said to Laurence, pointing near the ceiling to a *rayon* full of bright silks glittering with embroidery, beads, sequins, and paillettes.

"That's more like it! Which one do you want?" Laurence grabbed a long pole, and after we'd made our choices, unhooked three dresses: a white gown, cut low in front for herself, a gray chemise covered with five rows of fringe for Yvette, and for me, a sleeveless red dress with a tulle-filled slit in the skirt for dancing.

I held the dress against my body, and the tang of perfume in the soft fabric quickened my pulse. With my back to the other women, I shimmied out of my smock and dropped the dress over my head. I'd never before worn anything, even a nightgown, without buttons or some other fastening, and I was amazed at how easily it slipped on.

"You look beautiful," said Laurence. She handed me a wool cape trimmed in turkey feathers dyed the same color as my dress.

"You're sure we're allowed to do this?" I asked, as I draped the cape around my shoulders.

"Just make sure you bring everything back tomorrow."

Outside the air was cool, and we pulled up the collars of our capes. The tall granite buildings looked lavender in the silver moonlight, and the air had a freshness to it, a hint of spring that, in my new Parisian dress, made me happy and excited. We took the metro to Porte-de-Clignancourt, and after walking a few blocks, we were standing in front of the brightly lit portico of Madro, one of those popular dance halls that seemed to open every week in postwar Paris. Gleaming cars slid to the curb, and bright women in bright dresses stepped out, followed by men with their hats pushed back on their heads, slamming doors and dropping keys into the palms of valets. Ragtime music splashed in loud bursts through the swinging doors, and my hips began to sway.

Inside, the club was warm and noisy. The band played a tango, and cigarette smoke hung in the air in thin blue layers. We were seated at a table near the kitchen and ordered drinks. A minute later, the waiter returned with a single glass of champagne, which he placed in front of Yvette. "I didn't order that," she said.

The waiter nodded his head toward a fat middle-aged man sitting in a corner by himself. "Compliments of the gentleman over there."

Yvette craned her neck to see her admirer, lifting slightly out of her seat. When she spotted him, she plopped down and pushed the champagne away. "Take it back," she said to the waiter. "I don't want it."

The waiter left for a minute, then came back with our drinks, which we consumed quickly and ordered more. Three American soldiers at the next table had been watching us since we'd come in, and now they stood, pushing their chairs away with loud scraping noises. The tallest, best-looking one asked Yvette to dance. His beak-nosed, chinless friend chose Laurence, and I was left with the youngest soldier, a smooth-faced boy who couldn't have been more than eighteen and who startled me by speaking fluent French.

"My mother is French," he told me, when we were on the dance floor. He spun me under his arm, pushed me toward the door, and reeled me in. The back of my dress was cut low, and I felt his warm hand on my skin. There was something in his touch—firm, yet gentle—that reminded me of Jacques. "You're not a bad dancer," he said. "I can always tell when a girl is a good dancer. You're not trying to lead. Not like these American girls. They always want to lead."

Laurence and her partner tangoed past us, looking as if they'd been dancing together their entire lives. A rhinestone bracelet with a "1919" charm glittered on Laurence's right ankle, and when she spun around, the green heels on her dancing shoes looked like electric butterflies in flight.

In the arms of her handsome soldier, Yvette stared at the floor, following her awkward feet with solemn resolve not to make a mistake.

After the tango, the Americans dragged their chairs to our table and ordered drinks. "What is it you girls do?" asked the beak-nosed soldier in halting French.

"We work in couture," Laurence told him.

"Is that clothes?"

"In couture, clothes are much more than clothes. It's a kind of art. Everything is sewn by hand and fitted to each client's exact measurements."

The Americans stared at Yvette. They couldn't imagine her doing any work at all. "I don't sew. I'm a mannequin," she said.

"Her job is to be beautiful," added Laurence.

"A woman's chief responsibility in life," said the beak-nosed soldier.

Everyone laughed and raised their glasses. The band played a variety of music, and the Americans knew all the dances: the two-step, the fox-trot, the maxixe, the crab, the bear-step. The boy soldier and I danced nearly every one. He led expertly, but I felt clumsy and out of practice in his arms. It had been more than two years since I'd last danced with Jacques at the village festival in Timbaut. I remembered the little band under the stone roof of the ancient market square, the thick candles on the wood tables where my grandmother and the aunts sat watching, the summer smell of roses and hydrangeas.

After tangoing to "Under the Argentine Sky," the boy soldier and I returned to the table to find Laurence, Yvette and the Americans standing with their coats on. "We're leaving. Going back to their hotel," Laurence whispered to me. "We'll keep the party going there."

On the street, one of the soldiers hailed a taxi. Everyone piled in, but I hung back. "Are you coming?" the boy soldier asked.

A few minutes ago, I'd wanted to stay out all night, but the thought of going off with the boy soldier made me suddenly exhausted. I was not like Yvette and Laurence, these sophisticated Parisiennes, who borrowed men as easily as they borrowed dresses from Mademoiselle's storage room. "I have to go home," I said. "I have to get up early tomorrow."

I told the boy soldier good night and headed for the metro.

The next morning, in the corridor on my way to the storage room to return the red dress and cape, I ran into a puny man with a white goatee, his short-limbed body encased in an expensive blue suit. I recognized him as the Duc de Jacquet, the husband of Adelaide Jacquet, one of our best clients. "Well, hello, there," he said, tipping his hat with a leer.

"Good morning," I mumbled and hurried past him.

No one but the workers ever ventured beyond the first floor. I was wondering what he was doing upstairs, when I opened the door to the storage room and saw Susanna Lawson sitting on a crate in her panties and brassiere, pulling a silk stocking over a curvy white leg. She regarded my shopping bag, then my face. "What are you doing?" she demanded.

"What are *you* doing?" I asked.

Susanna ignored me and resumed tugging on her stockings. But when I pulled the red dress from my shopping bag, she leaped to her feet. "My dress!" she cried.

"What?" I asked, pulling out the cape.

"You borrowed my cape, too!"

"*Your* cape?"

"Everything on the top rack is mine."

"Laurence told me I could choose whatever I wanted."

"That bitch!" snarled the baroness, snatching her skirt and blouse from the floor. "She knows those are my clothes." In two swift movements, Susanna was dressed. She jammed her feet into her pumps and, before running out, regarded me with a sneer. "You should never wear red. It washes you out."

Later, when Laurence arrived, I told her about seeing the duke and finding Susanna. The première snorted.

"He's an old toad," I said.

"He's also one of the richest men in France."

"She said we'd taken *her* dresses last night."

Laurence looked up from the taffeta skirt she was sewing. "Tell that to Mademoiselle."

"I don't understand," I said, lowering myself to the bench beside Laurence, and whispering so as not to be overheard by the seamstresses. "There's so much in the storage room. Is it worth getting Lawson angry?"

With a harsh jerk of her hand, Laurence dropped her needle and angrily squeezed the taffeta in her fists. It sounded like pebbles crunching. "I've got enough to worry about. I don't care if Susanna Lawson is angry. She can die of anger for all I care!"

The next morning, I was going through the models that we'd readied for their final fittings, when I saw that all had *griffes* sewn into the linings. The white rectangles emblazoned with *Gabrielle Chanel* in black cursive were not to be sewn into the clothes until after their final fittings—by tradition, the griffe was the maison de couture's last kiss before the model left home forever. To sew in a griffe before its time was to condemn a workroom to bad luck as surely as if a witch had cast a spell on it. Just the previous month, a première at Worth had been struck and killed by a bus the day after one of her junior *mains,* a new hire from Switzerland, had sewed a griffe into an unfinished suit.

"Did you know there were griffes in those models?" I asked Laurence, pointing to a *rayon* near the door.

"Lawson snuck in here and sewed them in last night," said Laurence. "Look at this."

She handed me a note on beige stationary emblazoned with the baroness's elaborate monogram. "Keep away from my clothes!" Susanna screamed in burgundy ink.

A group of seamstresses had gathered around Laurence's desk to get a look at the note, and now Elise, a junior *main,* asked, "Should we rip out the griffes?"

"Why bother?" said Laurence.

Elise and the other seamstresses exchanged worried glances. "Something terrible could happen," said Anaïs, an older woman who'd been with Mademoiselle since the beginning of the couturière's career.

"You don't believe that crazy superstition, do you?" asked Laurence.

When we were alone, I told Laurence, "If it makes the women feel better, I think we should remove the griffes."

"Fine. If you want to, go ahead."

After lunch, I sat at one of the worktables with Elise, Anaïs and several other seamstresses. We snipped and snipped until griffes covered the table, and the tension drained from the women's faces.

Three

One day, after I'd been in Paris for about a month, I got a *petit bleu* from Madame Duval's nephew, Daniel Blank, inviting me to Sunday lunch at his apartment. Madame Duval had told me that her nephew had become a writer and that he'd lost a leg at the Battle of the Marne. Though I remembered the intensity of my girlish passion for him, I could hardly recall Daniel Blank himself. Only a vague image of a tall child running around the marché had stayed in my mind. I was curious about him and wondered if he remembered me.

The morning of the lunch, I awoke feeling cheerful. Light poured through the windows facing rue du Cardinal-Lemoine. Outside, the clatter of vegetable carts mingled with the harsh cries of an old beggar woman. I made use of the chamber pot I kept hidden under the bed. There was a toilet on the stair landing that I shared with twelve people, but it was unspeakably foul. That wasn't the only drawback of the apartment. It was tiny—only one rectangular room—and sparsely furnished, with an iron bed, an old dresser, a wood chair, and a battered wardrobe. During cold spells, it froze—the only heat came from a small fireplace in which I burned coal boulets. Still, Paris apartments were scarce and expensive, and I felt lucky to have this one.

I poured water from a pitcher into a bowl and splashed the cool liquid on my face. From my reflection in the mirror, I saw the large yellow scars, just below my collarbone, the result of years of blistering and iodine treatments for consumption. I ran my hand over them; they were bumpy and hard. Except for a week of mild coughing soon after starting at Chanel, I hadn't been ill for months, and I hadn't had a treatment in a year. But even on days when I felt well, the yellow scars reminded me of my bad lungs.

I pinned my hair into a chignon and arranged a scarf around the nape of my neck. I was one of the few women at Chanel who had not bobbed her hair. My reddish-gold mane was my only claim to beauty, and I was determined to keep it, though the long hair was a great source of irritation to Mademoiselle, who thought hairpins were as criminal as corsets. Once, she actually chased me around her studio with a scissors, shouting, "Let me cut it." I fled downstairs to the salon, where I hid in one of the fitting rooms. I knew I was safe there, as Mademoiselle never showed her face in the salon, lest she run into a darling. She made a point of never meeting the women who wore her clothes—"A darling seen is a darling lost," she often said.

After gulping a cup of tea brewed on the tiny two-burner stove I'd bought with my first paycheck, I left the apartment and descended the stairs, holding my nose against the elephant stench of the hallway. As I walked up rue du Cardinal-Lemoine, past the flower sellers and the boulangerie blowing warm bread smells into the street, I warmed my face in the sunlight that filtered down through the trees.

Usually at this time on Sundays, I was at mass lighting candles for my relatives and Jacques at Saint-Sulpice. Today, though, I was due at Daniel Blank's at two, so I promised myself I'd go to church that evening.

The bus I boarded at Saint-Germain lurched along the wide avenues. People paraded on the sidewalks, and every flaw in their clothing could have been marked in white chalk. I kept thinking—what if I lengthened the cuffs on that young woman's jacket to give it a better line, or redid the pleats on that dowager's skirt so it hung better? And look at the uneven hem on that child's dress. How sweet she'd look if I could only redo it! Then, a lithe young woman walked by in a perfect tan wool suit. The fresh white collar of a linen blouse flirted from her fitted jacket and her short skirt flared out prettily as she disappeared around the corner.

Daniel lived in a well-kept stone building that had been built in the nineteenth century during Baron Haussmann's modernization of the city. I took the elevator to the third floor and rang the bell. A commotion erupted inside, and then a young man opened the door. He had wavy auburn hair and light blue eyes and walked with a limp. I tried to conjure the boy I'd known as a child, but nothing about this young man seemed familiar.

"Hello. I'm Daniel Blank, and you must be Isabelle all grown up," he said.

Daniel led me down a long wainscotted corridor, through a library and into a small high-ceilinged parlor. The rooms smelled of loss. Framed pictures of a boy and his father and the boy alone. Draperies chosen with indifference and never cleaned. A piano covered in dust. Madame Duval told me Daniel had moved here with his American father after the death of his mother, a French pianist. Now he lived alone, Madame Duval said, endlessly playing his mother's recordings— warped and scratched echoes of famous sonatas—as he pounded out words on a typewriter.

In the parlor, a woman sat on a worn brocaded settee with her legs draped over a man's knees. When I entered, the man pushed her legs aside and stood up. He was portly and middle-aged, dressed in an impeccable gray suit. White spats stretched over his shiny black shoes, and trails of sparse brown hair slicked across his head. Daniel introduced him as Fabrice. He was a well-known couturier, one of those Parisian celebrities who needed only one name.

Fabrice bowed slightly and took my hand. "The room just got brighter and prettier," he said.

I am as susceptible as anyone to flattery, and I might have enjoyed this compliment if its insincerity had not been made obvious by the gorgeous creature at Fabrice's side. He introduced her as Victorine

Dusser. She was a tall bloom of a girl with creamy white skin, straight black hair cut in a severe bob, and slanted green eyes. "So nice to meet you," she said, extending a long white arm. Her rough, slurry voice contradicted her loveliness, as did her fussy dress—a blue silk with voluminous gathers at the hips and an insipid floppy bow tied at the neck.

Daniel explained that I was an old friend of his aunt's from Agen and that I had just moved to Paris to work for Chanel. The mere mention of Mademoiselle's name darkened Fabrice's face. As I settled into a chair opposite him, he launched into a long tirade against her, his chief complaint being that she had taken credit for the revolution he'd begun in 1900. "I was the first person to get rid of corsets, the first to do away with those immense catering hats that weighed as much as babies, the first to splash vivid color on the pale fashion palette of pastels."

I kept quiet, though every provincial seamstress knew it was Paul Poiret who'd rid women of corsets. Daniel carried in a tray of cocktails and set them on the coffee table. Sunday was the maid's day off. "Fabrice isn't a big fan of Chanel's," he said.

"Maybe if he'd slept with her he'd appreciate her more," said Victorine, taking a large gulp of her drink. Fabrice glowered at her.

She glared back. "Why not? You've slept with everyone else."

Were they always this vulgar? A flush spread across Daniel's face, and he whispered, "Isabelle, could you help me in the dining room, please?"

He led me to a dark rectangle off the kitchen. Ancient blue-and-white wallpaper peeled from the walls; newspapers piled up in a basket in the corner. Daniel handed me china, crystal, and silver, and I set the table. "I want to apologize for those two," he said, inspecting a badly chipped plate and laying it aside. "They've been drinking since they got here, an hour before you."

Daniel explained that Fabrice was married to his third wife, and that Victorine was one of his house mannequins. "He's been through just about every woman who works for him, including the seamstresses and vendeuses. The affairs never last long. I think we're seeing the waning days of this one."

"How do you know him?"

"He hired me to write the copy for his catalogue. It's quite a production, a real 'book,' illustrated with paintings by artists from L'École des Beaux-Arts. Seems like a lot of trouble for a few silly dresses."

"Couture dresses aren't silly," I said. "An incredible amount of thought and skill goes into them. Couture is an art."

"They're still just dresses. You don't hang them on the walls or put them in museums."

"Don't you like to look at pretty girls in pretty clothes?" I teased.

"I like to look at pretty girls."

Daniel turned his eyes to the napkins he'd been folding. So he didn't find *me* pretty. I didn't let myself be insulted. He was cool and bookish—not my type.

"If you feel that way about couture, why did Fabrice hire you?" I asked.

Daniel looked up from the napkins and smiled. "He went to my publisher, and the editor recommended me. He knew I needed the money. Fabrice is paying me very well, better than I deserve."

"What else are you working on?" I asked.

"Right now, poems. Gallimard is putting out my first collection in the fall. I've also published a couple of stories—one in *The Dial* and the other in *Revue de France*."

"You're about the only young man I know who survived the war."

"At least three-fourths of me did," he said, nodding toward his wooden leg.

The day before, Daniel's housekeeper had prepared a delicious *suprême de volaille*. Fabrice chose a Burgundy wine from Daniel's father's collection. For dessert there was an apple tart. Fabrice took the largest piece and ate it greedily. Throughout dinner, he'd been on his best behavior, restraining himself from mentioning Mademoiselle. But as the tart disappeared, and with a bottle of wine joining the cocktails under his belt, he couldn't hold back. "You should visit my atelier," he told me. "Anytime. Have Daniel bring you over. I make dresses, not dishcloths and sacks like your employer."

"I think her clothes are beautiful," I said quietly.

He leaned across the table; sweat beaded his reddened face. "I'd like to know what good ideas Chanel has had that she hasn't stolen from me? That little chiffon number in . . ."

"Of course you've influenced her," I interrupted. "What designer hasn't been affected by your work?"

Fabrice's face softened and he leaned back into his chair. "She doesn't like my work very much, does she?" he said.

"That's not true. She's a great admirer of the coats you did last season," I lied again.

"I put art into my dresses. *Figaro* once wrote that my sense of color and form was equal to Matisse's," Fabrice announced.

"And so are your prices," sniffed Victorine. Alcohol had dulled her eyes and put a loopy grin on her face.

Daniel began to clear the dishes. "Why don't you do that later," said Victorine. "You've got a Victrola; let's dance."

Daniel gave her a sidelong glance. "The last time I looked, I didn't have a right leg," he said. "And unless it grows back, my dancing days are over."

Victorine's grin disappeared. "I'm sorry, I forgot."

"I'm sure Daniel wishes he could forget," said Fabrice with elaborate gravity.

"You two go ahead," I offered. "I'll help clear up."

In the kitchen, Daniel filled the old porcelain sink. He rolled up his sleeves revealing sprays of dark apricot freckles, the color of his hair, and plunged his hands into the soapy water. He lifted a plate, rinsed it, and handed it to me.

"I'm glad people forget about my leg. I wish I could," he said. "The strange thing is, I can feel it as if it's still there—even my toes, all bunched up as if I'm wearing a shoe that's too tight."

A squeaky tango floated through the apartment, followed by muffled laughter.

"Does it hurt?" I asked.

"It hurts like hell. Especially at the end of the day. When I take the false leg off and touch the stump, it's sore. But when I take my hand away, I feel the soreness in my lost leg. That's enough to make you think you're going insane. Sometimes, I wake in the night, and it's all cramped up." He looked up from the dishes and smiled ominously. "Phantom cramps in a phantom leg. No wonder I don't sleep well."

He told me he did most of his writing when he couldn't sleep in the middle of the night. "I probably wouldn't have a book coming out, if I still had my leg."

Studying Daniel's pale, narrow face, I went back and forth on whether or not he was handsome, then decided that he was—in a haughty, intellectual kind of way. I preferred less regular, but warmer, faces—faces like Jacques'.

After washing the plates and silverware, Daniel steeped the glasses in the sink, holding back his and mine, into which he poured more wine. He asked me about working for Mademoiselle. I told him I had learned a great deal, but that she was a difficult boss, demanding long hours and impossible standards of perfection. "But the clothes are wonderful," I said. "So fresh and simple. They make the other couturiers look hopelessly *démodé*."

"Poor Fabrice." Daniel sighed. "He doesn't have a chance."

"Not if that costumey dress Victorine is wearing is any indication of his *oeuvre*."

"It's a good thing I'm writing his catalogue, not you."

"Do you know anything about clothes?" I asked.

"Not a thing." Daniel smiled. "You'll have to help me."

We carried the dishes, silverware, and glasses into the dining room on large trays and put everything away in the cupboard. As the last forks and knives were stored in the felt-lined drawers, Daniel said he wanted to show me the illustrations for *Les Robes de Fabrice*, the couturier's catalogue. "Fabrice would kill me if he knew, so please don't tell him."

In the parlor, Victorine and Fabrice tangoed across the worn Turkish carpet. Daniel maneuvered me around them into his study. From a portfolio he removed a series of prints and laid them out on his desk. Each vividly colored illustration depicted an elaborately dressed blonde with an elongated figure, posed in a series of opulent settings. The drawings suggested stories—the stories Daniel had been hired to tell. "I look at these pictures, and I have no clue what to write," he confided.

"How badly do you need the money?" I asked.

"Badly."

"Then you better come up with something."

A shout rang out from the parlor, and we hurried in, just as Fabrice staggered onto the sofa. A low groan escaped from the couturier's throat.

"Are you all right?" asked Daniel.

Victorine stood with her hands lightly on her hips. "He'll be all right. It's Chanel. Anytime he talks about her he almost has a heart attack."

"I'm not having a heart attack. I'm just getting too old for that kind of dancing. Thérèse keeps telling me to slow down," Fabrice wheezed. At the mention of his wife's name, Victorine scowled and, silk dress rustling, marched out of the room.

Fabrice's eyes followed her, weary and sad. "She's turning jealous. I better straighten this out." He took a few deep breaths, then planting his large, square hands on his knees, he lifted his bulk from the sofa and lumbered after her.

"His obsession with Chanel only gets worse," Daniel told me. "It's bordering on the insane. He keeps track of her coverage in the magazines and complains when he hasn't gotten as much space as she has."

Victorine and Fabrice were gone for a half hour. When they returned, they had their coats on. The white afternoon light had faded, and dashes of a red-orange sunset filtered through the window. It was time to go. Daniel walked us to the door, and I followed Fabrice and Victorine into the birdcage elevator. The ironwork door clanked shut, and the cramped machine began its sputtering descent.

Fabrice seemed to have recovered. He had one hand in his pocket and the other on Victorine's bottom. "Daniel is one of the best people I know," he said in a grand tone, puffing a stale wine breeze across my face. "A fine man *and* a talented writer."

Victorine wriggled, dislodging his hand. "What are you, some sort of matchmaker?" she snapped.

"He does seem very nice," I said, trying not to sound too interested.

The elevator landed with a great shaking thud. Fabrice held the door open and Victorine stumbled past him into the lobby. "Sweetie, take my advice," she said. "Find a guy who's got *two* legs."

Four

On Monday morning, I told Laurence about meeting Daniel Blank. She often bragged about her flirtations in the Montmartre nightclubs where she passed most of her free evenings, and though having Sunday lunch with a high-minded poet was not exactly a romantic adventure, I was pleased for once to have my own rendezvous to report.

"Is he handsome?" asked Laurence, as we stood near the stove waxing thread and waiting for the irons to heat.

"He's not bad-looking. He lost a leg in the war."

"Not much good for dancing, then."

"He's not the dancing type."

"What type is he?" asked Laurence.

"Not my type. Too intellectual and very reserved."

The irons began to hiss. We lifted them off the stove and carried them to a worktable holding small ironing boards. "He doesn't sound like much fun," said Laurence.

"He's a writer."

"Writers are all conceited."

I placed the thread between two damp cloths and pressed the iron on top. A rush of steam moistened my face, the heat filling my nostrils. "He thinks clothes are silly, even though he's accepted a lot of money from Fabrice to write his catalogue copy."

"You can't blame him for that."

"I guess not," I said. "Anyway, I doubt I'll see him again. He fulfilled his duty to his aunt by asking me to lunch, and I fulfilled my duty by going."

But on Friday I received a petit bleu from Daniel inviting me to a party the next night at Fabrice's mansion. I was annoyed that he'd asked me on such short notice, and I planned to decline until Laurence urged me to accept. "I hear Fabrice has a gorgeous house. You should go just to see it," she said.

The following evening, though, as I was headed out the door at seven, Laurence stopped me. "Where are you going?" she called from her desk.

"Fabrice's party, remember?"

"You can't leave yet," she insisted. "I can't face Amanda Nichols by myself."

Amanda Nichols was an American art agent who'd recently been all over the Paris papers for a spectacular sale. A Chicago collector paid her a small fortune for a gold ring that Amanda had found in a pawn shop in Greece and that archeologists believed dated to the ancient world. Reporters called it "The Helen of Troy Ring."

"I've already worked for nine hours without rest and hardly anything to eat," I protested.

"I'm not going to her apartment by myself," said Laurence.

"Is she that bad?"

"She's insane when it comes to her clothes. Always ordering things at the last minute and insisting on the most ridiculous adjustments."

That morning at eleven, Amanda had appeared in the salon to order a dress for a party eight hours later. Her vendeuse showed her a few samples, and Amanda picked a model that had been assigned to our workroom. Five seamstresses labored all day to complete it, finishing just as the shop was closing, as the floor was swept and the bolts of cloth returned to the shelves.

We left the shop at dusk with Laurence carrying a box containing the dress, and me holding a leather sewing case. The back door of the Ritz was locked, so we rounded the corner onto the place Vendôme, making our way toward the hotel's blue-and-white canopy. It was a cool night, the sunset softening to lavender gray. From an apartment overlooking the plaza, a piano sonata wafted down. "Ah, Chopin, my favorite," purred a young blond woman, who strolled by clinging to the arm of a portly older man. Laurence eyed them and sneered. "I wonder how much *she's* making tonight—more than we are!"

The Ritz lobby teemed with hotel functionaries, men in blue uniforms with gold braid. But despite the Ritz's luxury, it was a melancholy place. So many displaced people lived there, people without real homes. Lonely women who'd passed the war in hotel suites waiting for husbands and lovers who would never return.

I spotted Tanguy de Navacelle, the dark, curly-haired Ritz concierge, standing near the reception desk. His aristocratic name belied his earthiness. He was humorous and charming, with a large, bumpy nose and a soft, blocky body. Tanguy leaned casually against the polished mahogany counter, his eyes darting about. When he saw Laurence and me, he waved and, smiling broadly, slid through the crowd.

"What's up tonight?" he asked, after crushing our cheeks with his lips.

"Amanda Nichols. Last-minute fitting for a dress," I said.

"I'd like to fit something on her myself."

Laurence screeched, and Tanguy lowered his voice. "I don't believe that ring she sold came from ancient Greece. 'The Helen of Troy Ring.' What nonsense. It probably isn't even that old. She's a good saleswoman, and she knows a sucker when she sees one!"

Laurence and I took the service elevator to the third floor. Amanda's suite was at the end of a long, thickly carpeted corridor. A maid answered the door, and taking the dress box, led us into a large, square salon filled with gilt chairs, huge mirrors, Chinese screens, and marble topped tables. The French doors were open, and the scent of flowers drifted up from a garden below.

Amanda kept us waiting thirty minutes. When she appeared, posing in the archway leading from the salon to her boudoir, she was wearing our dress. It was exquisitely simple, really nothing more than a white silk slip with a swag of fringe falling from the hips. The beauty of this gown, a garment I'd helped create, soothed my annoyance. Every inch was perfect, from the softly falling skirt and the loose bodice draped over the waist, to the sensuous fringe around the hips.

Amanda twirled before us. At forty, she had a pointy chin and a tight little mouth, but her fine clothes and the lustrous curls tumbling around her ears in a fashionable bob bolstered an illusion that she was young and beautiful. "It's gorgeous, just what I feel like at the moment," she said, parading across the carpet. I envied her confidence.

Amanda hopped onto the coffee table to inspect herself in an oval mirror over the sofa. "I think it's a little long," she said.

"It looks perfect to my eye," said Laurence.

Amanda cocked her head to the side and studied the hem's reflection. "No. It's too long. It needs to go up five millimeters. And while you're at it, can you take it in a bit *here*?" She pinched the cloth at her ribs. "I need to walk out of here in two hours."

Laurence and I exchanged glances. Two more hours of work before we'd be free. "Not a problem. We'll get it done," Laurence said.

Amanda hopped off the table, and I sank to my knees. Securing a few pins between my lips, I lifted the silk hem and shook it slightly. I knew this dress so well; I understood how it perfectly expressed Mademoiselle's style. I'd been with the couturière when she "gave birth" to it, as Mademoiselle called the design process. I had helped her pull the model apart and put it together again, working in muslin first. I watched Mademoiselle wrestle with the design, her hands flying over the fabric.

"There," I said, when I'd pinned up the hem. "We'll take it to the shop to finish and have it back by nine."

"See that you do," ordered Amanda. "I'm being picked up at nine thirty." Then, as an afterthought, as if to offer us the gift of a glimpse into her exotic life, she added, "I'm going to a big *fête* at Fabrice's."

I hesitated only a moment. "Oh," I said. "So am I. Perhaps I'll see you there."

Amanda recoiled, then stared at me as if from across a great divide. Without saying anything, she turned and floated through the archway at the end of the salon, disappearing in a cloud of white silk.

"Bravo!" squealed Laurence. "You really stuck her. That was great!"

People still talked about the extravagant parties Fabrice had thrown before the war—the Arabian Nights Ball in 1908, A Night in Versailles in 1910, and The Venetian Summer in 1912. He must have spent a fortune, too, on tonight's Evening in Japan.

His mansion had been transformed into an emperor's palace. The paintings and antiques had been removed from the public rooms, replaced by Japanese screens and floor mats. The vast dining room had been turned into a rock garden with an arched bridge over a little stream. Japanese trees in ceramic tubs lined the terraces, and nightingales perched in cages suspended from the ceilings, their sweet voices almost drowned by human chatter.

When Daniel and I arrived, a line of cars clogged the street—Fords, Rolls-Royces, Packards, Hispano-Suizas, and Stutz convertibles—a string of black pearls. Daniel and I made our way through the stone gates and up a gravel path to the mansion. Lanterns strung through the trees shone like gumdrops, and mannequins in elaborate kimonos, their faces painted geisha white, greeted us at the door.

Inside, the crush was suffocating. Revelers overflowed the halls and salons, the women—even the middle-aged and heavy ones—in sleek sleeveless dresses, the men in uniforms or dark tuxedos and black ties. In the ballroom, waiters bustled behind the long buffet laid out with oysters, turkeys, hams, asparagus aspic, and puffed pastries. The orchestra played a waltz, while couples herded onto the dance floor tried to move. As the music switched to a ragtime tune, the crowd opened slightly for a beautiful brunette in black satin shimmying around a man wearing war medals on his lapels. I noticed the black tulle shoulder straps on the brunette's dress, a signature of Mademoiselle's, and I wondered if the dress had come from our atelier. A rumor shot through the crowd that she was the star of Ballet Russes. Then a guest recognized her as the hatcheck girl from the Bal Mabile. "How did *she* get in?" he asked his companion, a tall redhead in a green dress covered with iridescent spangles.

"She's with the deputy defense minister, *that's* how," the redhead answered.

Fabrice stood in a corner dressed like the emperor of Japan in a yellow silk tunic with enormous bat wings. In his right hand he carried a wood paddle—the emperor's symbol of power—which he drummed nervously in his left palm. Nearby, a large gilded cage sat on a raised platform in front of the windows. Victorine Dusser, dressed entirely in feathers, slumped inside against the bars. She was the star of the evening, the centerpiece of the show, but she was on her way to getting drunk and ruining it. Her assignment had been easy, to look gorgeous for a few hours while everyone admired her ensemble, a camisole and skirt made of bright green-and-blue bird feathers, topped by a little cap with a single ostrich feather secured with a jeweled brooch at the front. Fabrice called the outfit Nightingale. He planned to unlock the cage at midnight and let her fly across the ballroom and pose for the photographers. If all went well, Nightingale would be splashed across the papers, and a new look would be launched—one that would have every woman in Paris clamoring to be dressed by Maison Fabrice.

"I should have fired that girl a long time ago," lamented Fabrice, when Daniel and I were at his side.

"As a mannequin or a mistress?" asked Daniel.

"Both. And I've got Thérèse on my back. She wanted to model the feathers herself. She kept saying, 'I wear clothes as well as that girl of yours.'"

I had never met Thérèse, his wife, but I couldn't imagine that her looks equaled Victorine's. The girl was breathtaking, her black-haired, sloe-eyed beauty perfectly suited to Fabrice's oriental theme.

A tiny old woman dressed in navy satin appeared at Fabrice's side. "Monsieur, I must talk to you," she said in a voice hoarse with age. Her face wrinkled in all directions, and her dyed black hair was piled on her head over a horsehair pad. In her left hand she held an open notebook, and in her right, a gold pen encrusted with four fat diamonds.

"Etincelle, you know journalists aren't allowed in the ballroom until midnight," said Fabrice, stooping to kiss her on each dry cheek. He glared hard over her head at his assistant, Pierre, whose job it was to keep the press outside. Pierre shrugged helplessly.

"I'd like an exclusive," the old woman inisisted. Her column, "Carnet d'un Mondain," had run on the front page of *Le Figaro* every Thursday for the past forty years.

Fabrice seemed to sag in his ludicrous costume. "I can't do that without starting a mutiny in the press corps. Pierre will take you back to the others." He turned her gently in the direction of his assistant, who bowed slightly to Etincelle and took her arm.

In the gilded cage Victorine extended a long white arm through the painted iron grille to accept a glass of champagne from a young man. With her face pressed against the bars, she brought the glass to her lips and gulped.

"I'm putting a stop to this," said Fabrice.

When Victorine reached to grab yet more champagne, Fabrice intercepted the glass and shoved the waiter away.

The mannequin shook the gilded bars, green eyes blazing.

"Are you too drunk to say hello to Daniel and Isabelle?" Fabrice said, trying to distract her.

"You bastard," she snapped.

"No more for now." Fabrice smiled wanly. "I'll let you out in a half hour. You can do your little dance for the photographers, and then you're free as a bird."

Victorine snorted. "You old fart. I'd like to stick these feathers up your ass."

*   *   *

Daniel and I strolled out to the terrace. Even the gravel garden paths were clogged with people. Fabrice had quarantined the reporters behind a beige rope at a remote section of the garden, and several reclined under the chestnut trees, their jackets rolled up as pillows. Photographers stood in small groups smoking. Alone under a trellis foaming with blue hydrangeas, Etincelle dozed on an upholstered chair that a footman had fetched from the house.

"I should sit down," Daniel said. "Let's go upstairs."

We took the servants' staircase to the second floor, almost stepping on a couple necking in a corner of the pantry. Halfway down the hall, Daniel stopped in front of a large door with a concealed peephole. He checked to make sure no one was looking, then lifted the latch and put his eye to the glass. A smile spread across his face before he stepped aside so I could take a look: inside, the actress Gabrielle Dorziat and her male companion sat fully clothed in the porcelain tub, drinking from silver flasks.

The next door led to a small passageway and Fabrice's study. It was an old-fashioned, masculine retreat, cluttered with animal skins, ivory tusks—a present from a client whose husband had shot an elephant on safari—ship models and leather-bound volumes in floor-to-ceiling bookcases. A sheepskin contraceptive hung like a tongue out of the mouth of the bear's head above the mantel.

Daniel lowered himself onto the sofa and lifted his false leg onto the coffee table. "God, that feels so much better."

"Did you do that?" I said, pointing to the sheepskin condom in the bear's mouth.

"Yes. My leg turns into a stepladder when I press a button." He pushed his thumb into his navel.

Leafing through one of the catalogues on the coffee table, I told him, "I'm not a big fan of these harem pants Fabrice did in 1908."

"Who is? Not one of his better ideas." Daniel's face darkened. "This leg is killing me. I might have to take it off." He rubbed the prosthetic through his trousers. "Would you mind?"

"Of course, not. You shouldn't be in pain."

Just then a ripple of feminine laughter pierced the air, and three attractive women in short silk dresses glided by the door. A moment later one of them returned. It was Amanda Nichols. She stood provocatively in the doorway with one hand on a cocked hip, the other raised high against the door frame. She'd spotted Daniel and had scurried back to be introduced to the attractive young man.

Then she noticed me. Her lovely blue eyes opened wide, then nervously darted around the room. I didn't prolong the awkwardness. "Daniel Blank, I'd like you to meet Amanda Nichols," I said. "Mademoiselle Nichols is an art agent and one of our clients."

Daniel struggled to his feet, wincing when his false foot hit the floor.

"That dress looks familiar," Amanda said, glaring at my gray dress, a Chanel I'd borrowed from the storage room.

"Mademoiselle let me borrow it. She likes her dresses to get out."

That was all the small talk Amanda had for me. Turning to Daniel, she said, "I don't know why you're wasting your time in here. The band is fantastic!"

Before Daniel could respond, a short, fine-boned woman rushed into the room, her kimono sleeves flying. It was Thérèse, Fabrice's wife. "Have you seen my husband?" she gasped, looking wildly about. Her round face, dotted on one cheek by a large brown mole, was framed by dark, shellacked hair, set in tight, ridged waves. "There's a crisis with the Nightingale!" she cried.

Back in the ballroom, the orchestra had taken a break, and one of the guests played the piano. The dance floor remained a blur of people, and the mix of voices muffled the music. We pushed through the crowd to the gilded cage. Victorine lay crumpled on the floor with Fabrice leaning over her. Grabbing the limp girl under her arms, he maneuvered her through the swirls of revelers and dragged her into the hallway behind the front stairs, laying her down on the polished parquet. "She's out cold," he moaned. "What will happen to my pictures?"

"Let's put her in one of the bedrooms and try to get some coffee in her," suggested Daniel.

Thérèse leaned over the girl, studying her lunar face. I'd overheard her tell one of the guests that she'd volunteered in a military hospital during the war. Apparently, she'd retained a weakness for creatures in distress, even young women who were sleeping with her husband.

Victorine lay eerily still. Thérèse put her ear to the mannequin's lips and touched her fingertips to the base of the girl's neck. "She's still breathing, thank God."

A group of guests who'd followed the drama into the hallway stared at Victorine and murmured among themselves. One of the women was the hatcheck girl from the Bal Mabile. Fabrice had noticed her, too. His eyes traveled over her body for a moment, then he walked up to her. "Excuse me, Mademoiselle, are you wearing Chanel?" he asked.

The hatcheck girl nodded yes.

Fabrice cocked his head toward the unconscious mannequin on the floor. "Would you mind changing outfits with her?"

"You want me to put on those feathers?" the hatcheck girl asked.

"It would look beautiful on you." He didn't need to mention that her picture would be in all the papers.

"Now, look here," said the deputy defense minister. He tried to block the young woman, but she pushed in front of him. "Please, Arnaud, I want to do it," she said.

Without saying another word, Fabrice pulled the skirt over Victorine's hips and down her long, limp legs and raised the camisole over her head, exposing her small round breasts. He held the clothes out to his new mannequin.

The hatcheck girl had already slipped out of her dress and stood there in her underclothes. She tossed the garment to Fabrice. While the deputy defense minister shielded her from onlookers, the young woman removed her slip and brassiere—one of the new ones that ended above the ribs and had no boning—and tossed them aside. Then she donned the feathered ensemble. Fabrice settled Victorine's cap on the girl's brown bob and secured it under her chin with the jeweled strap.

Lifting Victorine to a sitting position, I held her upright while

Thérèse dropped the black dress over the unconscious girl's head and shoulders, then smoothed the garment down her body. With help from Daniel and Fabrice, we got her to her feet and managed to carry her into the next room, where we laid her out on a settee.

A moment later, Fabrice headed toward the ballroom, leading the hatcheck girl by the hand. Daniel and I followed, watching as the couturier released her into the circle of photographers. Cameras began clicking, as shouts rang out. "Over here, Mademoiselle!" "Look this way!"

Flashbulbs popped, lighting up the girl's feathered slimness. She seduced the cameras with her eyes, spinning toward them, then turning her back and sneering elegantly over her shoulder.

A stir erupted near the entrance. Heads turned, and waiters carrying trays of sloshing champagne stopped in their tracks. Victorine staggered through the arched doorway in the hatcheck girl's Chanel. One side of it had wrinkled up to her hips; the other was falling off her shoulder. "Fabrice!" she screamed, her voice rising above the music, as her drunken eyes scanned the room. "Where is that bastard?"

Five

I had to wait until Thursday, when the papers published their society sections, to see pictures of the Bal Mabile hatcheck girl in Fabrice's ridiculous outfit. On my way to work, I stopped at a kiosk to buy *Le Figaro, Le Matin, La Dépêche,* and *Le Petit Parisien.* None of the photos was flattering and all were buried deep inside the fashion pages in small, nondescript layouts. As if to torment Fabrice, most of the society pages that week prominently featured Mademoiselle. *Le Figaro* ran four pictures of women in Chanel gowns at various Victory Balls. *Le Matin* highlighted a large photo of a well-known actress having dinner at Maxim's in a Chanel chemise dress. *Le Petit Parisien* showcased Mademoiselle herself in a huge above-the-fold picture of the couturière, stepping into a black Packard wearing one of her simple jersey suits. The caption called her outfit the epitome of *"nonchalance de luxe."*

I felt sorry for Fabrice, when I thought of him opening the papers to see his poor feathers so outdazzled. Certainly, Mademoiselle had seen the pictures, too—she read the society pages religiously. At least *she* ought to be in good humor, I thought as I mounted the stairs to her studio on Thursday afternoon. I looked forward to a pleasant, productive *pose.* When I opened the door to the large sun-filled room, however, I was dismayed to hear Mademoiselle raging into the telephone at one of the vendeuses. In her free hand she clutched a copy of *Le Matin* with a large picture of the popular actress Vera Sergine in a pink moiré dress by Jean Patou. "Get Sergine in here this afternoon," commanded Mademoiselle. "I don't care if you have to give her the dresses, but I want her smothered in Chanel. I never want to see a picture of her in Patou again!"

The couturière slammed the phone down and walked toward the triple mirrors, where a tall middle-aged woman stood with a swathe of red satin wrapped around her torso. She was Misia Godebska, Mademoiselle's best friend. "I'm going to see Vera tonight at a dinner at Princess Poix's," said Misia, her voice deep and condescending. "I'll tell her how much you want to dress her. Or would it be better if I just murdered Patou?"

Mademoiselle, who was inspecting a bolt of blue silk, ignored her, and Misia continued to play with the wide ribbon of fabric, unwrapping and rewrapping it around her body, nattering on about how she brought out the genius in her friends and how Mademoiselle should design something for her to wear to a costume ball the following week.

Misia was Mademoiselle's ticket into the haut monde. Everyone in the atelier knew it was Misia who'd introduced her to Picasso, Cocteau, Stravinsky, Diaghilev, and Misia's lover, the Spanish painter José Maria Sert. In her grandly beautiful youth, Misia had been a muse to the stars of late-nineteenth-century art from Bonnard to Vuillard. I went to her house once for a fitting and saw their portraits of her on the walls. Now she was bulky and faded.

"This is a wonderful red—very modern," proclaimed Misia, spinning herself out of the swatch of satin. Modern was her favorite word; she loathed anything that hinted of the past. "I think you should do something with it for the next collection." She dropped the fabric on the floor, and one of the arpètes rushed to put it away.

"Maybe," Mademoiselle responded coolly. She turned to the metal clothes rack and shouted, "Three-fifty-six!" An arpète retrieved the garment—a beige wool suit my workroom had completed the previous week—and Régine, a small, curvy girl with black hair and a round face, stepped forward from the mannequin lineup. Régine shed her robe, and a fitter helped her into the loose jacket and short pleated skirt. Misia stood to the side with Mademoiselle and observed Régine vamping in front of the mirrors.

"It's wonderful!" Misia exulted. "You are the Picasso of dressmaking."

Mademoiselle took a long drag on her cigarette. "No," she said evenly. "Picasso is the Chanel of painting."

The couturière narrowed her eyes, studying the jacket. "Are the pockets deep enough?" she asked. Régine pushed her fists inside them and walked across the room and back. When she paused, Misia stepped behind her, encircling the girl's waist with her arms and lifted Régine's hands from the pockets to insert her own.

"No," Misia said. "I couldn't even get my keys and a lipstick in one." Her large bosom rested against Régine's back. The girl's body went rigid, and she grimaced. Misia pulled her hands from Régine's pockets, gold bracelets jangling on thick wrists.

I turned away in annoyance. I'd redone the pockets myself the previous week after Mademoiselle complained they were too shallow.

"If the pockets are fine for Régine, they're fine," pronounced Mademoiselle. "No one has hands like yours, Misia. You've got Chopin hands. They're huge."

Suddenly, Mademoiselle let out a little shriek. "My God, the back of the skirt! I just noticed it. Varlet, you've curved the edges of the pleats. They look like mountain roads!"

She crushed her cigarette in an ashtray and strode toward Régine. Grabbing two fistfuls of skirt, she glared at me and screamed. "What kind of work do you call this?"

There was nothing wrong with the pleats. They only needed to be pressed. I knew better, though, than to contradict Mademoiselle when she was in the middle of a fit.

"Pleats are difficult," I protested weakly. "I'll redo it."

"At your age, I would have got this skirt right with my eyes closed!"

Mademoiselle dropped the skirt with an angry jerk of her hands and lit a new cigarette. She couldn't sew pleats correctly if her life depended on it. She knew it, and she knew I knew it. She needed my skill even more than she resented it.

"Don't be so hard on her," Misia said, coming to my defense. "When you were her age you were mending trousers in the back of a tailor's shop in Moulins."

"What are you talking about?" snapped Mademoiselle, as if Misia had mentioned a distant planet.

"Don't pretend you don't remember Moulins."

Mademoiselle cleared her throat. She rushed through examining the remaining toiles, rejecting all of them. Then she stormed out of the studio, complaining that all of us—premières, secondes, arpètes, and mannequins—were incompetent fools.

We stood fidgeting awkwardly for a minute, "No one who was born poor ever escapes their past," Misia pronounced finally.

Mademoiselle guarded the secrets of her girlhood closely. Over the first weeks of working for her, I'd gleaned a few details, bits pieced together from gossip picked up in the salon and from my colleagues. The nuns at the convent where she lived after her mother's death taught her how to sew, and in late adolescence, they sent her as a charity case to a finishing school in the garrison town of Moulins, where she had relatives. A job as a tailor's assistant, making cavalry uniforms for young men, was followed by a stint as a singer in a dance hall, where she adopted the nickname Coco.

One of Mademoiselle's admirers set her up in a millinery shop in his Paris apartment and introduced her to Arthur "Boy" Capel, a wealthy Englishman. Mademoiselle fell in love. Capel gave her money to move her operation to rue Cambon, in the center of the couture trade, and the farther she got from her roots, the less she wanted to be reminded of them.

Still, she was not without concern for her family. After the death of her sister Julia during the war, she'd taken responsibility for Julia's son, André, and she stayed close to her remaining sister, Antoinette.

The announcement at the end of March that Antoinette Chanel

had become engaged to a Canadian airman sparked a frenzy of speculation in the workrooms over her wedding gown.

Seamstresses are obsessed with marriage: we even have a holiday devoted to it. Every November 25, on the Feast of Saint Catherine, the patron saint of old maids, couture houses across Paris are closed, and there is food, champagne, and dancing in the workrooms. Those *midinettes* who have reached the age of twenty-five during the year without being married don white caps and are fêted with presents and a prayer:

> *Saint Catherine O lend me your aid*
> *And grant that I won't die an old maid*
> *A husband, Saint Catherine*
> *A good one, Saint Catherine*
> *Handsome, Saint Catherine*
> *Rich, Saint Catherine*
> *Soon, Saint Catherine*

Apparently, Saint Catherine had not been listening in the workrooms at Chanel Modes et Coutures. Except for several widows, few of the women I worked with had ever married, and most probably never would. Romance for them existed in the clothes they sewed. The love lives of Mademoiselle's darlings were a source of passionate concern among the seamstresses, and nothing excited them more than a wedding.

At thirty-one, Antoinette was the youngest of the Chanel girls. She had helped Mademoiselle since the start of her career and now ran our Biarritz maison de couture. We all dreamed of sewing her dress, but no one was surprised when the honor went to Susanna Lawson. One evening, when the gown was near completion, I passed Susanna's workroom and saw it hanging alone on a metal *rayon*. The room was empty except for two junior *mains* sewing at a table near the back wall. I stepped in and approached the dress. It was a short white satin confection with a drapery of chantilly lace floating across the shoulders into a gently cascading train. I held the fabric. In a few months, when Antoinette Chanel would don this dress, when her suits and beaded evening dresses, her nightgowns and robes, her silk underwear embroidered with her new initials, were packed in trunks for her new life across the ocean in Canada, Jacques would have been dead for more than two years.

I twirled a fine gold tress that had escaped from my chignon and recalled when Madame Duval and I tucked strands of our hair into the hems of our clients' wedding gowns—a time-honored couture tradition that brings good luck to seamstresses and brides. I wished I'd married Jacques when I'd had the chance. I didn't think I'd ever want to marry someone else. What I did want, though, was to absorb the beauty of this dress, to harness some of its hope.

I waited until the junior *mains* had finished their sewing and left the workroom. Then, with one swift yank, I plucked a hair from my head and began to work it into the hem of Antoinette's dress. "You cheeky girl!"

I turned to see Susanna Lawson with her hands on her hips and fury sparking in her green eyes. "How dare you touch my dress!" she screeched.

"It's not your dress. It's Antoinette's."

"Why are you snooping in my workroom?"

"I wasn't snooping."

Just then, Madame Georges appeared in the doorway. Her tired eyes took in the scene. "I just wanted to look at the dress," I told her.

"I never want to see you in my workroom again!" cried Susanna before stomping away.

Madame Georges rolled her eyes. "Susanna is difficult, Isabelle, but you must learn to get along with her."

"Why? She's a witch!"

"She brings in important clients, rich clients. What do you think couture is about?"

*   *   *

That evening, I arrived home in a gloomy mood and found a letter from Madame Duval slipped under the door. "Daniel tells me that he had you to lunch and took you to a party," she began. "I'm so glad the two of you have gotten together. It is not healthy to be only with women, to have no life outside of work, and my nephew is exactly the kind of person you should know."

Madame Duval told me she'd closed her shop—something she'd been considering for a while due to the rising cost of materials and the dwindling number of customers. She was looking forward to spring, she wrote, and spending more time in her garden. She ended the letter, "I'm so pleased, Isabelle, that your world is opening up. I'm sure in no time, you will feel like a true Parisienne."

I tore off a sheet from the notebook in which I recorded my expenses and pulled the chair up to my bureau. "Dear Madame Duval," I began. I couldn't continue. I put down my pen and stared out the window. I knew Madame Duval wanted assurance that I was happy, that I'd gotten over Jacques. The truth was, I hadn't, and I didn't know if I ever would.

Outside the sky had darkened, and my room grew cold. An old man in the street stopped to pet a dog, and now the two shadowy forms ambled up rue du Cardinal-Lemoine. I watched them from the window. In the hallway, a door opened, and voices spilled out. Then the door slammed shut. From another apartment, an odor of frying meat wafted in atop a baby's cries. I tried to concentrate on something to tell Madame Duval, but the words didn't come. The sky turned black, obliterating the old man and the dog, and I crumpled the paper in my fist.

Six

![decorative border]

A collection's spirit—its colors, mood, and silhouette—can come from many sources: a radiant fabric discovered on a trip, a painting in a museum, a character in a book, a song, a symphony, a beautiful girl glimpsed on the street. An abstract idea like love or freedom also can give a collection a unifying theme. But Mademoiselle's chief inspiration was herself. She chose and draped fabric according to what would look good on her. If a garment wasn't something she herself would wear, it wouldn't make it to the final lineup.

The toiles and finished models were like living things to me. At the end of the day, when I looked at a dress that I'd brought to life with my needle and thread, when I saw the perfect cut and evenly stitched seams, the graceful drape of the skirt and neckline, I felt I was stepping into my own sunny future. At home, I kept a box of souvenirs of all the models I worked on, and it always soothed me to hold the bits of fabric I'd clipped from inconspicuous seams and hems.

Of course, some dresses, like some women, are more beguiling than others. I fell in love with model 412. When I looked at it, my heart tightened and there was a little catch in my throat—for a moment I forgot my sorrows and deceived myself that the world is a better place than it is.

Unlike many couturiers, Mademoiselle did not name her creations. She thought it idiotic, not to mention hopelessly unmodern, to call a collection, say, "Gowns of Emotion," as the designer Lucille once did, naming her dresses such things as "When Passion's Thrall Is O'er," "Give me your Heart," and "Do You Love me?" Mademoiselle identified her models only by number. To me, though, 412 was Angeline, my mother's name. The crepe de chine planned for it was the same deep burgundy as my mother's silk dress, the only one of her garments my grandmother had saved. She had buried my mother in a plain black cotton work dress, my grandmother told me, because she couldn't bear to part with the silk dress—it smelled like my mother. To me, the dress only smelled like mothballs, like the heavy black serge garments in my grandmother's wardrobe. Still, I loved the feel of the silk, loved its contrasting tones, and when I was a child, I often went into the wardrobe to hold it. The dress was all I had of my mother, and I worshiped it.

Angeline was born on a Friday afternoon in April. Laurence had gone home to be with her mother, who was ill, and I was alone in the studio with Mademoiselle and Yvette. The mannequin stood in front of the triple mirrors in her drawers and brassiere, bathed in a square of dusty light. Beside her, Mademoiselle unfurled a shimmering banner of dark red crepe de chine from a bolt resting on the floor.

The couturière's arms swung in arcs like a dancer's as she draped the fabric across Yvette's hips and chest. Gradually, the outline of a simple sleeveless gown began to take shape, molded with a hundred pins. Mademoiselle stepped aside to study her work. The room was silent except for the trumpet screech of car horns wafting up from the street. "No, that's not right," Mademoiselle said finally.

We pulled the pins out, and she started again, kneading and pulling the fabric, falling to her knees, then standing on tiptoe, then bending deeply at the waist. She worked with her entire body, talking to herself as if she were in a trance. "Oh, yes, this is beautiful. . . . This is something for me. . . . Ah, that's the way it should look. . . . No, no, we don't need any fullness here."

The fading sun cast long gray slants across the wood floor. Shadows flickered around the room, and the rolls of satin, silk, wool, and jersey stacked on shelves against the walls seemed to move, like a chorus backing up the *pas de deux* of Mademoiselle and Yvette.

Suddenly, a shape emerged from the gleam of crepe de chine: a narrow, softly falling skirt, the bodice straight in front and low under the armholes and forming a deep V in back. On each side, beginning at the hips, the hint of a gentle ruffle cascaded to the floor. Mademoiselle looked at me, her eyes bright and intent. "You get the idea, Varlet?"

"Yes," I said. In the lovely red cloud enveloping Yvette, I saw the finished dress, as clearly as if Mademoiselle had drawn me a picture. It had sprung from an idea deep in her mind, a vision I understood completely.

First thing Monday, I began the toile. I draped muslin rectangles on a dress form padded out to Yvette's shape and pinned the pieces together in an approximate silhouette, using a lighter-weight muslin for the bodice lining. Then I removed the garment from the form and sewed it together by hand, using loose running stitches. The skirt was two big rectangles, seamed on the sides, while the cascades were formed from long narrow triangles sewn into the side seams so they would flutter out. The bottom section of the cascades were separate circular-cut ruffles stitched into the sides of the dress.

I was tense as I worked. My toile had to express everything that Mademoiselle intended. The full power of my skills were needed to match the level of her ideas. Had I misinterpreted her instructions? There was no way of knowing until she inspected my work.

I had trouble making the side cascades flutter gracefully, while preserving the line of the dress, and I had to redo them several times. While I worked, one of the *mains* sewed the lining and the shoulder straps, and I fastened them to the toile. I slipped it on the dress form and studied it from every angle. I was pleased. It had an irresistible symmetry, the cascades perfectly proportioned to the skirt and bodice. But something was missing. *A bow,* I thought to myself. I cut a strip of muslin, turned, hemmed, and steamed it, and tied it into a simple, girlish bow that I stitched to the top of the right hip. The toile was done, and the seamstresses gathered around to admire it.

Laurence had been following my progress, and as she moved forward to consider the finished product, the other women stepped aside. She walked around the form, looking the dress up and down, tilting her head, trying out angles, never letting on what was going through her head. At last, she looked at me. "It will be the gem of the collection," she announced.

"Really? You think so?" I asked.

"I know a gem when I see one." Laurence smiled ominously. "You're in trouble now, Isabelle."

Seven

The following Sunday, leaving mass at Saint-Sulpice, I ran into Daniel Blank. The afternoon was bright and cool; the first green blossoms of a new spring flooded the chestnut trees. "How are things at work?" Daniel asked, as we descended the stone steps.

"I finished a toile that everyone thinks will be the gem of the collection."

"That's nice."

"It's not. Mademoiselle can't bear to be dependent on anyone, so she gets rid of the ones she relies on the most. She builds up people, just so she can have the pleasure of knocking them down."

"Who's been filling your head with this?"

"No one. I've seen it. Also, one of the other premières, an English-woman who's close to Mademoiselle, has it in for me. Once she discovers that I've got a promising toile, she'll do everything she can to sabotage me."

"You're worrying too much."

"I don't think so. No one in the atelier ever knows where they stand. Before I arrived, Mademoiselle fired one of the premières—a very talented fitter who'd been with her since the beginning—just because the poor woman asked for a raise."

"If she fires you, you can always work for Fabrice."

"I could, except I hate his clothes."

"You won't hate his Sunday lunch; the food is superb. I'm on my way there now. Why don't you join me?"

"I don't know."

"Fabrice would be delighted to see you."

"You're sure it's all right?"

"I'll call the house and let them know."

At Le Roland, we climbed the marble steps to the mansion and rang the bell. A tall, bald-headed butler opened the door and led us through the house. The antiques, paintings, gilt mirrors, and rugs were back in place, and the enormous high-ceilinged rooms looked completely different from the night of the party. Daniel and I followed the butler across the echoing foyer, past the airy salons where mannequins modeled clothes for Fabrice's clients, down a long, wide corridor lined with statuary.

Fabrice's studio, on the ground floor in a remote corner of the house, was a large beautiful room with tall French doors on three sides opening to a wraparound terrace. The couturier sat in his nightshirt at his desk, tall stacks of magazines covering the surface. More magazines—copies of *Femina, Art, Goût, Beauté, Vogue, La Mode, La Vie Élégante,* and *Desmoiselles,* stretching back to 1916—surrounded him on the floor. Two empty bottles of wine, a tin of opium, and a pipe rested on a table nearby. A large red stain bloomed on Fabrice's nightshirt where he'd spilled some wine, and a few black grains of opium dotted his chest.

The butler left us at the door. When Fabrice saw Daniel and me, he checked the clock on the mantel. "My God, I had no idea what time it was." Gold light streamed into the room, and Fabrice switched off the lamp on his desk. "You must forgive me; I've been up all night."

The couturier explained that the evening before he'd hauled the magazines out and gone through every one. Hoping to reassure himself that the fashion press paid more attention to him than it did to Chanel, he'd counted the number of illustrations of his models versus hers and kept score on a pad of paper.

"I should have stayed in bed and gotten a good night's sleep. I'm not even dressed." He held his arms out from his sides and looked down at his nightshirt with dismay. For all his monumental self-centeredness, I felt sorry for him. He was a child, his disappointments and jealousies spilling out in an unfiltered torrent. "Since the party, I've been in no shape for anything. Thérèse threatened to leave if I didn't get rid of Victorine, and the girl's run off. I don't know where she is. I haven't gotten a thing done. I know I have to snap out of it, but I just can't." He looked at the mess on his desk and on the floor. "I better put these away before my wife gets back and catches me going through them."

At that moment Thérèse appeared in the doorway dressed in a brown linen suit.

"Look at this," she said in a voice shrill with annoyance. "You've got company, and you're still in your nightshirt." Turning to Daniel and me, she added, "I'm so sorry. I must apologize for my husband."

"No need to apologize," I said.

"It's all right. We understand," said Daniel.

Thérèse strode into the room, heels clicking on the parquet. When she saw the magazines strewn across the desk and the floor, she stopped, planting her feet with her hands on her hips. She glared at her husband. "You've been going through the fashion pages again, haven't you?"

"Only a few." Fabrice hung his head like a naughty child.

"Have you lost your mind? If you'd spend as much time working as you do worrying about that little monkey of a woman . . ."

"I will. This afternoon, after lunch. I promise. I'm going to take some of that gold taffeta we bought in Italy and make a ball gown fit for an empress."

Thérèse removed her gloves, yanking them off finger by finger, as she turned to Daniel. "How is work coming on the catalogue?"

"I'm making progress," he said. "Though I'm still waiting for a few illustrations."

Thérèse opened her purse and dropped her gloves inside it. "I've found a new artist I'm crazy about. I've got some samples of his work in the salon. Come with me. Fabrice and Mademoiselle Varlet can catch up with us at lunch."

After his wife and Daniel left, Fabrice led me to a long gallery off the atelier, where an elaborate array of clothes—models from Fabrice's previous collections going back to the start of his career—were displayed on headless wood mannequins. The closed shutters blocked the daylight, protecting the fabrics, and crystal sconces lit the room. A few tables were scattered about, holding large green leather scrapbooks, into which Fabrice had meticulously pasted his press clippings from before the war. "Here you have the history of Fabrice," he said, as he stood next to a voluminous red velvet coat lined in black silk. "This was my very first model. I sold six hundred copies in every color in 1900, and I was launched!"

Next, he pointed out a black satin gown painted with immense pink camellias. His face took on a grave expression, and he lowered his voice. "I did this for Sarah," he said. When I looked at him blankly, he added with annoyance, "Bernhardt! What other Sarah is there? She asked me to design a dress for her to wear in the final act of Camille. I struggled to come up with an idea. Then one night I dreamed this. When the audience saw it, they gasped. . . ." His voice trailed off, and he looked toward the ceiling.

The room was a museum, and like clothes in a museum, Fabrice's designs were interesting mostly for their historical references. None of them looked like outfits a real woman would actually wear.

As if reading my mind, he asked, "Have you been to the Louvre recently?"

"No. I don't have much time off."

"You must go to the Louvre. You must look at sculpture. You must study Ingres, Velasquez, Delacroix."

As far as I knew, Mademoiselle never went to the museums. She took her cues from the street, from contemporary art, from what was fresh and new in the air of Paris.

"If you come to work for me, I'll give you time to go to the museums. And I'll give you time to be with your lover. Is Daniel . . ."

Fabrice stopped in mid-sentence, when he saw my face turn red. "My fiancé was killed in the war," I said.

"I'm very sorry." Fabrice seemed genuinely sad. "If you want to work in couture, though, you must have a lover! You must know how to please a man, how to disrobe for a man. What is a dress, if not an advertisement for yourself? We must find you a lover to take you to the museums!"

Back in his studio, Fabrice asked me how much I was paid. When I refused to tell him, he waved his hands in the air dismissively and shook his head. "Whatever it is, if you come to work for me, I will give you a twenty percent raise."

"You'd hire me without seeing my work?" I asked.

"You're experienced in couture technique. And I like you, Isabelle. I can tell you're smart. You have character. That's a rare thing in a woman. Most women are petty and devious."

"I'm happy at the moment with Mademoiselle," I said weakly. I wondered about Fabrice's motives. Was he auditioning me as a replacement for Victorine? Did he want to have me around so he could question me about Mademoiselle's collection?

"At least go look at my workrooms in Montmartre. You can stop by anytime. By the way, is Chanel doing much with crepe de chine this season?"

Before I could answer, the butler appeared. "Sir, lunch will be served in a half hour. Shall I have the maid draw your bath?"

Fabrice sighed deeply. "I suppose so. I guess I don't have time for a nap."

After lunch, Fabrice sent me off with a gift—a ticket to the opening of *My Lady's Dress,* a play imported from London, and one of several dramas about the couture world that recently had arrived in Paris. He'd designed the costumes for the production, and wanted me to see them. "I've managed to put the spirit of the characters into the clothes. When you see what I've done, I'm sure you'll want to join my house."

I couldn't promise anything, as we often worked late, but Mademoiselle herself left early that evening, so I was able to escape. On the way out, I borrowed a dress from the stockroom—a sheath in beige silk with lace trim at the hem and a matching lace sash around the dropped waist. But when I'd gotten it home and put it on, I discovered it was too low-cut—my yellow scars rose above the neckline like lighted signs announcing my history of consumption—so I went to the theater in my own simple black dress.

Fabrice had bought out two rows in the orchestra section for his friends, and when I arrived, everyone in his party was seated. I recognized the chief of Galeries Lafayette sitting next to the director of Maison Fabrice. Behind them were Jacques Worth, son of the great Belle Époque couturier, and Jeanne Paquin, the brilliant dressmaker and president of the Chambre Syndicale de la Couture Parisienne.

I looked out onto a landscape of flashing jewels, furs, and brightly colored gowns. The French government had lifted its wartime ban on evening dress and Paris was smothering its sadness under a spectacle of opulence.

As I pushed my way to my seat, I noticed Daniel on Fabrice's right, and next to Daniel, Amanda Nichols, looking wonderful in a silk dress the color of a frozen lake. She and Daniel were lost in conversation, and as I passed them, they barely said hello. My dress felt as dull and unattractive as a potato sack, and I wished I had worn the silk sheath in spite of my yellow scars: I could have covered them with a shawl.

As I took my seat, Fabrice whispered to me. "I was worried you weren't going to show."

"The traffic was terrible," I said.

Behind Fabrice sat twelve of his house mannequins in frilly chiffon gowns. The girls giggled and fidgeted. At sixteen and seventeen some of them were still children, and Fabrice turned several times to shush them. Finally, the immense chandelier hanging from the theater's vaulted ceiling dimmed and expired, and the velvet curtain rose on a sentimental set: a woman's boudoir decorated with white furniture, bright carpets, and paintings of nymphs romping through lush gardens.

On stage a young woman argued with her husband over an expensive dress she had bought to wear to a dinner given by his boss. The dialogue made my teeth hurt.

Ten minutes into the action, a maid appeared on stage with the controversial garment, and a chorus of "oohs" and "aahs" erupted from Fabrice's friends. It was an extravaganza of a dress, the kind of theatrical concoction that had made Fabrice famous and that I had seen the week before on display in his atelier: a flowing rose satin gown covered with an overlay of gold lace dotted with jeweled flowers. Sable trimmed the hem and edges of the cap sleeves; a shawl of antique Venetian lace frothed around the shoulders.

The dress was ridiculous, the play even sillier. After the first scene, establishing the gown's significance for the young couple's future, the rest of the first act concerned the making of the dress fabric and was set on a silk farm in northern Italy. The costumes seemed utterly unremarkable—mostly colorful and quaint peasant garb.

I couldn't concentrate on the story. My eyes kept wandering to Amanda and Daniel. She was whispering to him, her head bent close to his, her bare shoulder brushing against his jacket. He couldn't possibly be interested in her, I told myself, but why was she flirting so strenuously with *him*—an impecunious writer with one leg? My feelings were jumbled. I didn't think I wanted Daniel for myself, but I hated his interest in Amanda or anyone else. My mouth was dry, my hands cold. I feared they'd catch me staring at them, and I forced myself to turn away.

At the interval, admirers flocked around Fabrice. "I've never seen such exquisite costumes," said the Duc de Marquesson, patting Fabrice on the back. The couturier shook hands with the mayor of Paris and his companion, the opera singer Marthe Davelli, the hem of what I suspected was a Chanel gown peeking from her Poiret coat.

As Daniel and Amanda left their seats, his hand rested on the small of her back; she held her stole around her waist so everyone could admire her shoulders, round and smooth like white marble balls. A moment before, I wanted to stretch my legs. Now, I sat sullenly in my seat waiting for the next act to begin.

When it did, half the seats were empty. The second act continued the insipid story of the gown's provenance. A lacemaker's daughter complained to her nurse about the man her debt-ridden father insisted she marry: *The whole man's wrong, nurse. He is indeed quite wrong! Quite wrong from head to toe!*

"And so is this play!" shouted someone from the gallery. Laughter echoed around the house, and a few boos rang out.

Daniel nodded off during a scene in a London sweatshop, while Amanda fidgeted with her stole. The end came as a great relief. Men and women in the two rows surrounding Fabrice rose to their feet, shouting "Bravo!" From the rest of the house, hoots and hisses punctuated the tepid applause.

In the lobby, I ran into Daniel and Amanda. The art agent ignored me, but Daniel's face opened into a wide grin. "That was the worst play I've ever seen," he said.

"Me, too." I felt uneasy standing so close to him and strangely tongue-tied. He seemed more handsome than I remembered, his eyes deep and expressive, his chiseled face freshly shaved. I reminded myself that when I met him, I didn't think him particularly attractive.

"I've seen worse," said Amanda. She had her head turned to the side, and she spoke into the air, her eyes scanning the crowd. She looked young and lovely, I had to admit. Her skin glowed, taut and rosy as a girl's. Childless and never married, her aging parents healthy and safe across the ocean, she was unmarked by the war and had no one to mourn.

Amanda said something to Daniel in English, and a moment later she was gone.

"What happened to her?" I asked.

"She has a party to go to."

"Didn't you come with her?"

"No." His face brightened, as if pleased that this mattered to me. "Shouldn't we congratulate Fabrice?"

We found the couturier standing at the bar on the mezzanine surrounded by friends. Fabrice shook hands with Daniel and crushed each of my cheeks with his dry lips. "I don't think people liked the play," he said glumly.

"That doesn't matter," said Daniel. "They liked your costumes."

Fabrice looked from the writer to me. I thought about the chic dresses Mademoiselle had designed recently for Vera Sergine to wear in *Le Secret,* a contemporary drama by Henri Bernstein. After the play opened, we were besieged with orders to duplicate the dresses for our clients.

"The costumes were wonderfully innovative," I lied.

"The whole thing was a flop," said Fabrice. "I shouldn't have wasted my time."

"That's no way to talk. This is *your* night," said Daniel. "Try to enjoy yourself."

When we were outside, Daniel asked me, "Are you tired?"

"I'm wide awake, now that I don't have to watch another minute of that trash."

"Could you come to my place to help me with Fabrice's catalogue? I promised him I'd show him something tomorrow, and I haven't written a word. I've no clue about clothes."

We got into a cab, and it sped through the darkened streets. Daniel sat with his arm across the back of the seat, his fingers brushing my shoulder. I'd never gone alone with a man to his apartment, and I felt nervous, yet also excited. I wondered if Daniel would try to kiss me, and I decided that if he did, I wouldn't resist.

At his apartment, though, Daniel was all business. He led me directly to the dining room and flipped on the lights. "Here they are," he said, pointing to a series of gouache drawings laid out across the table. "The theme of Fabrice's collection is *The Greatest Moments in a Woman's Life,*" said Daniel, rolling up his sleeves. "These are the lead pictures for the sections, which will each include twenty illustrations."

From the clothes and decor it was possible to discern a story: the first high point of a woman's life, and the first illustration, depicted her entering a ballroom in evening dress. The next showed her at a dressing table examining an enormous diamond ring on her left hand, then walking down the aisle of a church in a frothy white gown and veil. Afterward, she's seen reading a book on the deck of an ocean liner, admiring lavish place settings for two in a candlelit dining room, and, finally, kissing a baby held by a nurse.

The illustrations were beautiful, with clean, highly stylized lines and clear, subdued colors. It was best not to explain them, I thought, to let the pictures sell the clothes. "Off the top of my head, I can't think of anything to say that won't sound silly," I said. "The catalogue would probably be better without captions."

"You might be right. But then I'd be out of an assignment and my handsome fee." Daniel retrieved a bottle of wine and two glasses from the sideboard. "Do you have any ideas about the clothes?"

I pointed to the dress in the first picture—a blue evening gown with a tiered and pleated skirt that ballooned from the hips and narrowed to a tube around the ankles. "No one wants to look like that anymore," I said.

Daniel poured two glasses of wine and handed one to me. "I can't write that."

I studied the picture, as I sipped my wine.

"You could say that the greatest moments of a woman's life are over in a year."

"Come on, Isabelle. Help me."

I put down my glass and pointed to the dress in the first illustration. "Did you actually see this model?"

Daniel shook his head from side to side. "No. As far as I know, Fabrice has yet to make any of these clothes."

"Did he give you any information about them?"

"Just the pictures."

I studied the first illustration. "Champagne flowed, and diamonds sparkled, as she entered the ballroom in tiers of silk crepe de chine designed for falling in love," I improvised.

"That's a little purple," said Daniel.

"Do you want my help or not?"

"Okay. Go on."

"A small army of violins played . . ."

Daniel interrupted me. "Why don't you just tell me about the clothes."

"It would help if I knew what the fabrics were."

"I'll try to get a list from Fabrice."

"What about the stories?"

"I'll worry about the stories."

By now it was after three. I promised to do my best for him when he found out more about the fabrics. Daniel took me down to the street, now empty and quiet, the black sky beginning to lighten with a new day. We waited a long time for a taxi. Finally, one rolled by, and Daniel gestured for it to stop. "Good night, Isabelle," he said, kissing me chastely on each cheek.

"Good night."

After that, we began spending Sundays together. In the morning, we went to church, then ate lunch at a café and, afterward, retreated to Daniel's apartment to work on Fabrice's catalogue. We could have been brother and sister, so easily were we in each other's company. My initial impression of Daniel had softened. What I'd construed as coolness was really stoicism. I'd met other amputees—most of them dazed, quiet men who were embarrassed and defeated by their afflictions. Daniel clearly was different. I admired his refusal to dwell on the war, and his brave acceptance of his infirmity.

Often, he looked bored when I talked about my work. But he let me know how grateful he was for my help on Fabrice's catalogue. One day, Daniel brought home swatches of some of the fabrics Fabrice was using in his collection—many of them extraordinarily expensive brocades and silks, and I gave him details and descriptions about the clothes Fabrice planned to make from these sumptuous materials. Daniel particularly liked my description of a blue silk crepe de chine evening dress, which I recited off the top of my head: "It's draped very lightly, the tiers gently pleated, ending in a narrow opening like a tulip turned upside down."

Daniel scribbled in his notebook and nodded toward a picture of a decolleté gown. "What about this one?"

"Mousseline de soie is now judged too heavy and dull for a young woman debuting in society," I said. "The most youthful look for evening is tulle."

"I like that, Isabelle. You have a real flair."

The truth was, Daniel was the one with flair. I didn't think it could be done, but he'd imagined an interior life for the blonde in the pictures and written passages of subtlety and grace about her emotions.

Occasionally, I let myself imagine that I was the inspiration for his blond heroine, an orphan who'd lost her fiancé in the war, but had found a new love. It was a foolish fantasy. Daniel treated me politely, even affectionately, but with no hint of romantic interest. I felt twinges of disloyalty to Jacques for even caring if Daniel was fond of me. But I also wondered why he didn't have a *petite amie,* if something had happened to him during the war that had ruined him for love.

One Sunday while we were working in his apartment, the doorbell rang. Daniel seemed startled by the bell and excused himself to answer it. A moment later, I heard a low, feminine voice. Curious, I wandered into the hall, where I had a good view of the salon. Daniel stood near the mantel talking to a slim young woman with heavy makeup and hair dyed a harsh black. She was pretty, but hard-looking, like the courtesans I'd met who occasionally came to rue Cambon for fittings.

Daniel and the woman began to cross the salon toward the hall leading to the bedrooms. I couldn't concentrate. In the kitchen I found an apple tart and ate a slice of it, though I wasn't hungry. I stared at Fabrice's prints, trying to strike an idea. Nothing came. I walked into the hall and listened for sounds from Daniel's bedroom. But it was very still.

When Daniel finally reappeared after twenty minutes, his hair was disheveled and his eyes sleepy. He stood over my chair, and I thought I smelled sex. "Who was that?" I asked.

"I've hired her to go through my father's papers."

"On Sunday?"

"She was supposed to come yesterday." His voice was tight. He didn't want to discuss it. "Have you made any progress here?"

"I've no inspiration today."

"Then, let's call it an afternoon."

Eight

The notion that Daniel had been with a prostitute saddened and disappointed me, and I tried to push it from my mind. Still, I spent the rest of the night and all the next day pulled around by thoughts of him with the black-haired woman. After work, I stopped for a meal at a café under the arcades on rue de Rivoli. I'd never smoked before, and I can't explain why I accepted a cigarette when an open pack of Gitanes, held by a man at the next table, floated past me in the blue dimness.

I sucked up the smoke, feeling its acrid fire, and almost immediately, my chest rumbled. A pain between my shoulder blades blossomed and I began to cough with loud, angry bursts. I gathered my jacket and purse and fled the café.

Outside, the air was cool, and the clouds looked like shredded muslin in a gray sky. As I walked to the bus stop, a hard rain began to fall, and a bleak wetness penetrated my bones. By the time I got home, I had a fever. I lay on the bed and, mercifully, fell asleep. Coughing woke me at five in the morning. I felt feverish and as chilly as ice. I tried to stand, but in weakness dropped immediately back onto the bed. I wasn't going to make it to work. I lay there for a couple of hours, then managed to haul myself downstairs to the concierge, who agreed to send a petit bleu to Chanel, informing Madame Georges of my illness. "I'd be very grateful if you'd find a doctor for me, too," I said.

A handsome man in his early forties, the doctor arrived at midday carrying a large black satchel. Sitting on the edge of the mattress, he put his hand to my forehead. I still wore my black work smock—I'd fallen asleep in it the night before—and now the doctor lifted me gently from the pillows so he could unfasten it and pull it down over my shoulders. He studied the scars on my chest, moving his right hand over their rough surface. "We don't do that anymore," he said. I remembered the horrible pain, as the *officier de santé* from Agen cut little slits into my chest, then held heated glass cups over the wounds to form bubbly red blisters. The idea was to bleed out the infection, but the treatments only made me feel worse.

The doctor opened his satchel and removed a stethoscope. As he listened to my chest, he pursed his lips and gazed over my head to the plaster crucifix on the wall.

"The congestion is severe. Both of your lungs are affected," he said finally.

"How could one cigarette do this to me?"

"One cigarette didn't cause this relapse. You were overdue for one."

"I always get better," I said.

The doctor's expression was grave. "I think you should go to a sanitarium," he said.

"My grandmother had a friend who had consumption for forty years. She never went to a sanitarium," I protested.

The doctor unplugged the stethoscope from his ears and dropped it into his satchel. "Some people survive ten years. Longer than that is rare."

"Well, then, I'm three years overdue for death."

The doctor smiled coldly and changed the subject, as he palpitated the glands around my neck and armpits. "You have beautiful hair," he said. "Good for you for keeping it long. My wife cut hers last year, against my wishes, of course. A husband has no control over a wife these days."

He stood and picked up his satchel. "You need to go to a sanitarium, Mademoiselle Varlet. There's nothing available at the moment. But I'll put you on a waiting list. In the meantime, rest and nourishment are the best treatments."

Before he left, he advised me that four times a day I should lie on the bed with my head tilted over the side. In this position, his theory went, bacteria would seep away from the apex of my lungs where they were clustered, much the way blood drains down during a headstand. "This will help," he said.

But I had no energy, even for this simple exercise.

The following weeks passed like a long, tormented sleep—periods of unconsciousness broken by horrible coughing and fevered chills. When I coughed or drew long breaths, I felt pain in my lungs all the way through to my shoulder blades. I couldn't remember ever being this ill, and I began to think I *might* die. At some moments I almost longed for it. Dying would mean release from this terrible pain and a new life in heaven with Jacques, my grandmother, and the aunts. Several times a day I prayed to God, asking him either to make me well or to take me to heaven, but to decide quickly which it would be.

Three weeks into my illness, the sanitariums remained full. There were so many new cases of consumption, the doctor told me, that he feared a space would not become available for months. He suggested I go to the hospital to have a rib removed to collapse a lung.

"Your right lung is the most congested. If we can relieve the pressure there, I think we'll see a marked improvement," he told me one afternoon.

The thought of an operation terrified me, though, and I refused the advice, despite the doctor's nagging.

The concierge, who lived in a dark flat on the ground floor of the building, spent a fair amount of time at my bedside, bringing me food, wiping my brow, monitoring my temperature, and making me tea. An overweight woman with dyed red hair, she smelled of patchouli and had the dull, lewd air of an old whore. Before my illness, I'd avoided her. Now, though, whenever she set out a simple meal on a table by my bed, I squeezed her hand in gratefulness. She had a kind heart, and she was lonely.

Laurence came by every evening after work, and on the third day of my illness Daniel showed up. I was flattered by his concern, but horrified that he was seeing me looking so ill and disheveled. He seemed less interested, though, in my appearance than my reading material. I had just finished the last chapter of a serialized novel in *Le Petit Parisien.* Daniel asked me what it was about, and I gave him a quick summary: a young woman finds the fiancé she'd thought killed in battle, alive and recuperating in a hospital in Rennes. After an ecstatic reunion, they are married by the hospital chaplain and live happily ever after.

"It never happens like that in real life," said Daniel in a supercilious tone.

"Finding lost fiancés or happy endings?" I asked.

"Both. Romance was killed in the war."

Daniel's cynicism made me feel sicker. I wanted him to believe in romance, though I wasn't sure I believed in it myself. I started to cough, at first demurely, then with loud hacks. Daniel put his arm around me. "There, there, my poor girl."

He poured a glass of water from the pitcher on the dresser and handed it to me.

I looked into his face, trying to discern in its long, narrow contours evidence of his heart. Daniel's blue eyes were bright and kind, but his mouth had a tightness and severity I'd never noticed before.

Daniel's eyes traveled over me, over my dirty nightgown and filthy, uncombed hair. I felt his eyes seeing everything—my ugly iodine scars, my small, unworthy breasts, the pale inconsequence of my limbs. Suddenly, I resented him, and I wanted him to leave.

"You shouldn't read this trash," he said, picking up *Le Petit Parisien* and flipping through it. He stayed for another hour, and eventually, I fell asleep.

When I awoke, Madame Lebel had arrived with some bread and a bowl of soup, which I forced myself to eat. The next day, when Daniel stopped by, Madame Lebel followed him upstairs and lingered in my room throughout his visit. Daniel brought me a novel by Victor Hugo, a few newspapers, and treats from the neighborhood patisserie, which made me teary with memories of Jacques. "Don't cry, dear, these are delicious," said Madame Lebel, as she helped herself to the almond cookies. While Daniel read to me from the newspaper, she stood in the corner with her arms across her chest, snorting occasionally over something that struck her as stupid.

I knew I was feeling better when her presence began to annoy me. "You've been so helpful, and I've taken so much of your time. You needn't come as much anymore," I told her one day, as I stood by my dresser brushing my hair. My fever finally had broken. I had enough energy to get up and walk around and to make myself a cup of tea. I'd also begun to worry about money, something I'd been too sick to focus on before. At the start of my illness, Daniel had written to Madame Duval about my plight, and she'd sent me a hundred francs disguised as a birthday present. Now that money had nearly run out. I'd considered pawning my gold locket, the one that had belonged to my namesake, though long ago I promised Madame Duval I wouldn't. The gold oval offered evidence, however cloudy, that I was descended from a seamstress who'd worked for Marie Antoinette, and therefore, it connected me in Madame Duval's mind to France's glorious past.

If I didn't go back to work soon, I might have to sell my hair—I'd heard that silky blond tresses fetched the highest prices from the city's wigmakers. I found this prospect so distressing, however, that to act on it, I feared, would cause me to relapse. Of course, I could always go back to Timbaut, to my grandmother's little house on the hill. I would have to borrow the train fare to get there, though, and if I did that, I might as well stay here to look for work.

Along with these worries, and a happier sign of my improving health, I felt an overwhelming urge to sew. One evening Laurence arrived with something to satisfy the craving—a pattern for a blouse and a few yards of white silk. The pattern called for deep cuffs and pin tucks across the front, which I made with small running stitches, occupying me for hours.

Another evening, when the blouse was nearly completed, Laurence brought over some faux pearl buttons, carrying them in a chamois bag. "I thought these would be perfect for your blouse," she explained.

I overturned the bag onto my bed, and a few coins rolled across the blanket with the buttons. "You don't have to do this," I said.

"You have to eat," answered Laurence.

She picked up the buttons and juggled them in her palms. Her face was etched with anxiety. Laurence had been waiting until I felt stronger to tell me the bad news about Angeline, and now her words rushed out.

"Mademoiselle didn't like your last toile. As soon as Yvette had it on, Lawson laid into it, complaining that it wasn't hanging right and that the bodice didn't fit."

"Oh, no." My chest felt tight.

"Don't worry. I'll redo it," said Laurence, as she ran a cube of beeswax across a piece of white thread. She returned the beeswax to her needle bag and sighed. "Lawson is making everyone miserable. Four of her senior *mains* transferred to another workroom."

"Why did Mademoiselle allow it?" I asked. For a seamstress to change workrooms in the middle of preparing a collection was like a soldier switching regiments in the heat of battle.

"Mademoiselle doesn't know. Madame Georges arranged it."

"I'm never going to get my job back," I said.

"That's not true," Laurence said in an emphatic tone. "Mademoiselle promised me you could come back when you were ready."

"Has she asked about me?"

"Once or twice. She asked how you were getting on."

"What did you tell her?"

"That you were feeling better and were eager to come back to work."

Laurence finished attaching the sleeves to the armholes of my blouse and examined them for puckers. Satisfied that they were smooth, she held up the blouse for me to admire. "You rest. I'll take this to the shop to press."

* * *

"Mademoiselle told Laurence I could have my job back when I was ready, but I don't trust her," I told Daniel later that evening when he stopped by.

"I don't blame you," he said with a sly smile. "I don't trust *anyone* who wasn't in the war."

"Mademoiselle is a woman!"

"Not according to Fabrice. Anyway, if you find yourself out of a job, you can always work for *him*."

"I might have no choice."

"It wouldn't be so bad. I bet he'd pay you more than you're getting from the evil witch of rue Cambon."

"Why does everyone say that about her?"

"I've heard *you* say that about her. Why are you defending her?"

"She's a genius. I don't expect a genius to be nice."

"*A genius*? Come on, Isabelle. She's a dressmaker."

Daniel sat on the edge of my bed in his officer's uniform: navy slacks and a horizon blue jacket with brass buttons. Over the jacket he wore a brown leather belt with shoulder straps and two ammunition pouches. I'd never seen him in uniform before. He wasn't one of those flashy veterans, those champions of suffering, who wore their medals everywhere and boasted constantly of their bravery. Daniel didn't consider himself special for having survived the war. "Everyone's a survivor of *something*," he told me once. "Even if it's just their own foolishness."

I had been looking forward to his visit with more eagerness than I cared to allow. At the start of my illness I was too weak to fix myself up, but now I tried to make myself attractive for him. I washed, arranged my hair, and put on clean clothes. He never remarked on my appearance though, and sometimes when he was with me, he acted distracted, as though he were eager to leave. I began to think the reason he'd been so attentive was out of obligation to Madame Duval. He'd promised her he'd look after me, and now that I was better, the visits would peter out.

Daniel removed a box of chocolates from one of his ammunition pouches and handed it to me. He explained that he was on his way to a Victory Ball at the home of Count and Countess Lobrichon. "I never liked dancing much when I had two legs," he said with a shrug.

"You're actually going to dance?" I asked, as I selected a chocolate from the box.

"That's the whole point of the ball—to show the world that us *grands mutilés* are still 'whole' men. We might not have arms or legs, or eyesight, but we still dance! Some guys actually have been taking lessons."

Daniel took a chocolate and popped it in his mouth. "The letter accompanying the invitation said all amputees were required to wear prosthetics," he continued. "No one would be allowed in with a pinned-up pant leg or sleeve. I know one horribly maimed boy, just nineteen years old, who's in a wheelchair at home with his parents. He wasn't invited at all."

I had a vision of Daniel stumbling over his dance partner's feet, and I tried to erase the image from my mind. I was the one who was supposedly dying, yet I felt an urgent desire to protect *him*.

"Take me with you to the party."

"What?"

"Just for a couple of hours. I think I can manage that." I swung my legs over the side of the bed and stood. Walking across the room, I felt strong and balanced. My temperature had been normal for a week now, and my coughing had subsided. I opened the door of the wardrobe and took out my best dress, a black silk I'd sewn from some fabric Madame Duval had sent me.

"I'm not taking you anywhere until the doctor says you're ready to go out," said Daniel. He took the dress from my hands and returned it to the wardrobe.

"If we wait for Dr. Death's approval, I'll be an old lady. You can't imagine how much I want to get out of here."

"Really, Isabelle. I don't think you're well enough. I promise I'll take you to a party soon."

"Can we start going to church again on Sundays?"

"Of course."

"I haven't been to mass in weeks."

"When you're better."

Daniel guided me back to bed. Then he grabbed his gloves and black-brimmed kepi from the dresser by the door. "Good night, now," he said.

For a moment I lay there. My life had begun to feel like a tightly laced corset, growing narrower each day. The thought of the party, of being out in the world, of talking to new people and dancing the tango and the fox-trot to an orchestra, filled me with an irresistible longing. With a burst of energy that surprised me, I got up and put on the silk dress. Checking myself in the mirror, I smoothed my hair and threw a white fringed shawl across my shoulders. Then I scrambled down the stairs. The frantic activity sparked a mild pain in my chest, but did not start a coughing fit. In the lobby, I pushed open the door and stepped outside.

The evening was sweet and still, the sky stippled with stars. As I made my way up the street, a man and a woman stepped from the shadows of a café doorway. The woman was small and slender, the man wore a uniform and limped slightly. I couldn't be sure if it was Daniel. He put his arm around the woman and led her away, around the corner. If it *was* Daniel, I didn't want to humiliate myself by chasing after him. Standing alone in the evening chill, I began to cough. I drew my shawl around my chest, putting off as long as possible going back to my forlorn little room.

Nine

week later, a place became available at a sanitarium in Lausanne, and the doctor wanted to admit me. "If you can get to the train station in an hour, you can be there tonight," he said.

He had just listened to my chest with his stethoscope, and now, sitting on my bed, he wrote a note to himself to put in my file.

"I've no money for the train fare," I said.

The doctor sighed with exasperation. "If that's the case, I'll pay for it."

"No need to. I've decided to go back to work."

"You're in no shape to go back to work."

"I'm going crazy lying here. I think the best thing for me is to get out of bed."

"The best thing for you is to listen to your doctor and go to the sanitarium." He shook his head, grimacing. "I can't be responsible if your condition worsens."

"What did you hear when you listened to my chest?"

"Your lungs are still congested." He removed his spectacles and pinched the bridge of his nose.

"How then do you explain the fact that I've stopped coughing?"

The doctor looked powerless without his spectacles. "I'm not going to argue with you about this, Mademoiselle Varlet." He returned the spectacles to his face and stood. Retrieving his satchel from the floor, he walked to the door. Before opening it and stepping out, he said to me over his shoulder, "I'm warning you, you're endangering your life."

I had to go back to work; I needed the money. I got dressed and took the stairs to the ground floor, where I knocked on the door of Madame Lebel's apartment. The door opened, and the concierge stood under the transom in an old purple bathrobe.

"Can I make a phone call?" I asked.

"You know where the phone is," she said, drawing the bathrobe around her large stomach.

I made my way to a small table near the kitchen. The apartment was tiny and dark, crammed with overlarge furniture. As I crossed the room, my eyes were drawn to a framed photograph on top of the piano of a glamorous beauty. If the picture was of Madame Lebel as a young woman she bore no resemblance to the nosy creature hovering behind me as I dialed Madame Georges's number.

"I'm afraid there's nothing for you right now," Madame Georges said.

"But Mademoiselle promised Laurence I could come back."

"I'm sorry, Isabelle. We promoted Anne to seconde, and the other workrooms are filled. I just don't have a place for you at the moment."

Madame Lebel stood so close to me I could smell her unwashed skin, mixed with the sour apartment odors of bad drains and old cooking. I wondered how the glamorous beauty on the piano had turned into this foul old woman.

"Mademoiselle relies on my work. She needs me for the collection," I pleaded, lowering my voice.

"We have a lot of seamstresses, Isabelle."

"She needs me."

"Call back in a couple of weeks. Maybe things will change."

Madame Lebel was plucking dead leaves from a house plant. After I hung up, I asked her if I could make a couple more calls, and she nodded. To her, this was entertainment.

I dialed Laurence. "Madame Georges says there's no place for me," I moaned. "What happened?"

Laurence burst into tears. "I'm sorry, Isabelle. I just wanted you to feel better."

"You *knew* there was nothing for me?"

"I didn't want you to worry while you were sick."

Then I called Daniel. I'd seen less of him lately, and I suspected it had to do with the woman with whom he'd gone to the Lobrichons' ball, though Daniel said it was because he was busy with Fabrice's catalogue. Without my help, it was taking him twice as long to write the captions, and his deadline on the project loomed.

The phone rang four times before Daniel picked up. "Mademoiselle won't take me back," I blurted. I felt my throat catch and tears welled in my eyes.

"I'm sorry, Isabelle."

"I need a job."

"Fabrice would hire you."

"Do you think so?"

"He'd be thrilled. You know how much he likes you."

Daniel gave me an address: 32, rue Sainte-Cecile. "Let me know what happens," he said.

I hung up the phone and thanked Madame Lebel. "Are you in some kind of trouble?" she asked me when I was halfway out the door.

"Not yet," I assured her.

The next day I boarded a bus for Montmartre. Summer would soon be here, and the days were warm and yellow. Everywhere, flowers bloomed, and the trees fluttered with green coronas. Except for a few dizzying trips to the market and the park, this was my first real excursion since falling ill. I had never before ignored a doctor's advice, and I couldn't shake the thought that I might be making a terrible mistake. Still, the air outside felt like a tonic. I looked forward to going back to work, to being part of the world again, even if that meant sewing for Fabrice. I got off the bus in front of 32, rue Sainte-Cecile, which turned out to be a rundown, six-story building. Taking the fresh air deep into my lungs, I willed my chest to remain calm. I took the elevator to the top floor of the building, stepping into a dark, narrow hallway. A blast of hot air greeted me. Then I noticed the steady whirring of sewing machines and wondered if I'd stumbled onto the wrong floor—perhaps the premises of a factory. Old paint peeled from the walls; naked light-bulbs hung by strings from the ceilings. Piles of debris, filthy fabric, and old boxes made the hall virtually unnavigable.

In the first room, twenty-five women sat crammed together behind rows of sewing machines. Papers bulged from filing cabinets jammed against the walls; fabric bolts were stacked everywhere. A few of the seamstresses looked up at me with dull expressions. A middle-aged woman sat on a stool near the windows flipping through a magazine—the première of this shabby operation.

"Can I help you?" she asked.

"Are these Fabrice's workrooms?"

She dropped the magazine in her lap and studied me from head to toe. "Yes."

"He uses sewing machines?"

"Since he reopened his house. Before the war, everything was done by hand." She snorted in derision. "We had ten workrooms then. Now we have three."

At Chanel the workrooms were by no means palatial, and Made-moiselle did little for her employees' comfort—we sat on hard benches, there was no comfortable dining room or cloak room, the ventilation was bad. But the spirit of artistry compensated for the lack of ameni-ties. The work was organized around time-honored traditions, and most of it was done by hand. How else could you control the fabric and shape a garment? Sewing machines were used sometimes for seams and to assemble the heavier garments. But the machines could never replace human hands.

"Is there no hand sewing anymore?" I asked.

"A little," answered the première. "Special things. For special clients. We have a room for that at the end of the hall."

It was a small space with a narrow oak table at which sat two white-haired women. One of them had a dress turned inside out and was joining the bodice to the skirt with an impeccable seam of tiny, straight stitches. The other woman held a hissing iron, pressing it along a sleeve on a small ironing board.

This is what remained of couture at the House of Fabrice—two old women working silently in a closet in Montmartre. I'd just as soon work in a lampshade factory, I thought to myself as I took the elevator to the ground floor.

"I wouldn't work for Fabrice if he was the last couturier in the world!" I told Daniel later on the phone.

"You need a job," Daniel said.

"I didn't come to Paris to do that kind of sewing."

"You're being silly. It's only clothes."

"It's my craft."

The next day, I used a few of the coins Laurence had lent me to buy stationery and sent letters to several of Paris's leading couture houses inquiring about work. Few jobs were available. Most of the couturiers who'd reopened their houses since the armistice already had hired their staffs. But Madeleine Vionnet, the incomparable design innovator, invited me for an interview.

Her atelier occupied two cramped rooms on rue de Rivoli, separated by several blocks from the palatial couture houses on rue de la Paix. Vionnet had been closed since the war began, and, though her clients were some of the world's richest women, including members of the Spanish court, she'd yet to find a financial backer. She wouldn't have a collection that fall.

Vionnet had a reputation for treating her staff like family. She'd gone out of her way to find jobs for her seamstresses when she'd closed her house, and since the reopening, she'd rehired many of them. Though it would be several years before she would have the money to build her state-of-the-art atelier on Avenue Montaigne with a gymnasium, a medical clinic, and a couture school, she already offered her workers sick leave and paid vacations.

If I worked for Vionnet I'd have earned money throughout my illness, I thought as I sat in her reception area one morning, separated from the rest of the studio by a thin curtain. I could hear the seamstresses' voices and the clatter of a sewing machine. "Madame Vionnet will see you now." I looked up to see a blue serge skirt and a striped white blouse, topped by the severe face of a young dark-haired woman, Vionnet's secretary.

"Thank you."

She flung open the curtain, revealing a large square room, where women sewed at long wood tables. Dress forms held a series of long, pale evening gowns, so soft and flowing they looked like they'd been made from liquid silk.

The secretary pushed aside another curtain at the end of the room—a corner had been partitioned to create an office for Vionnet. She sat on a chair near the window draping muslin on a two-foot-tall doll perched on a revolving piano stool. Plain and white haired, her soft round body clothed in a simple gray dress, Vionnet greeted me warmly.

"Come in. Come in. Isabelle Varlet, is it?"

"Yes, Madame."

"Come closer, Mademoiselle Varlet. See how I'm draping the fabric? A dress must follow the lines of the body. It must accompany its wearer, and when a woman smiles, the dress must smile with her."

As Vionnet worked, the wood mannequin rotated slowly on the piano stool. The doll was amazingly lifelike, with jointed arms and legs and a painted face that looked exactly like the Hollywood movie star Irene Castle. "You see what I'm doing here? I'm putting the grain of the fabric on the bias, and it's spiraling the figure naturally. That's how I get those fluid effects you saw on the dress forms in the workroom."

"Is it cut on the bias?" I asked.

"No, no. In this case, it's cut on the grain, and it *falls* on the bias."

"How do you do that?"

"It's my little secret. If you come to work for me, you'll find out."

Vionnet looked hard at me over the doll's head. "You have a nice body, dear. That's in your favor. I only hire good-looking women. Never anyone who looks like me."

She chuckled softly, shaking her large bosom.

She spun the seat of the piano bench, and the doll twirled. "Look at this!" she cried. In the few minutes I'd been in her office, she had transformed the swatch of muslin into a flowing, sensuous gown.

"It's beautiful, isn't it?" she said. "Wait until it's made up in white silk on a real, live woman. A dress for the ages!" She paused to smile sweetly at me. "You see, I don't make fashion. That's an empty word, completely meaningless to a real dressmaker. I make clothes I believe in."

Vionnet folded her arms in her lap. It looked comfortable enough to crawl into, *too* comfortable. I'd grown accustomed to Mademoiselle's cold disdain, even begun to think it somehow a necessary component of couture. I wasn't sure I could get used to working for this kind, grandmotherly woman.

Vionnet's smile disappeared, and she leveled her gaze at me. "How long have you worked for Chanel, dear?"

"Since March."

"And why do you want to change positions?"

I hadn't mentioned that I'd been sick and lost my job. "It's always been my dream to work for you."

Until a few days ago, I'd never thought of working for her. Vionnet, though, accepted the compliment as her due. "Chanel!" she cried, tossing her hands into the air. "That milliner who calls herself a couturier! Tell me, what have you learned from her?"

She didn't give me a chance to answer. "Chanel does not know how to construct a dress. I've seen her work. It hangs on the body. That's all wrong. All wrong. I don't know where she got her training, do you? Oh, she probably didn't have any. I got mine as a première in the atelier of Madame Gerber, the eldest of the Callot sisters.

"Chanel is a good-looking woman, I'll give her that," Vionnet continued. "She knows how to put herself together. But she makes

Fords! I make Rolls-Royces! And if you work for me, you'll make Rolls-Royces, too. Now, let's see what you can do."

Vionnet reached into a pile of garments on a shelf behind her and pulled out a sleeveless silk bodice with a long center dart. She handed it to me with a pair of scissors and a pincushion holding pins and a threaded needle. "Let's see you make some gathers across the chest."

I'd done this many times before, and it involved a classic couture technique—suppressing the fullness in one area of the garment in order to create it in another, in this case, taking it out of the shoulder to give to the chest. The silk was cut on the bias, which molds to the body, giving it an unmistakable softness and suppleness. But bias-cut fabric can be tricky to manipulate, and my fingers felt dry and stiff, like an old woman's. I picked up the scissors and opened the garment along the dart. Working with the center edges, I made double rows of very fine running stitches on each side to create the gathers. Then I attached the seam in place with tiny backstitches. When I was done, I handed the bodice to Vionnet.

She studied my work, looking through her glasses down her nose. She said nothing. Several minutes passed. Finally, she put the bodice down and stood, smoothing the front of her department store dress with her white square hands. "Good-bye, dear. We'll be in touch."

I went home thinking the interview had gone well. Vionnet seemed to like me, though I was a bit unsettled that she'd said nothing about my sewing sample. I was brooding about that still, when several days later, a note arrived from her secretary. Vionnet had hired a woman who'd worked for her before the war, the secretary wrote, adding that she'd contact me if anything else turned up.

My disappointment was lessened by receiving in the same post, slipped under the door by Madame Lebel, a letter from the house of Jean Patou, to whom I'd guiltily written. On stationery engraved with Patou's motto, "*La Mode c'est la reine,*" his couture manager wrote that Patou was adding two workrooms to his atelier and hiring several new seamstresses. He invited me for an interview.

It serves Mademoiselle right, I thought, as I reread the letter. This is what she gets for not giving me back my job. I'll go to work for her chief rival.

Patou worked out of a grand eighteenth-century mansion that had once been the home of the Comtesse de Flahaut, Talleyrand's mistress. On the day of my appointment, I entered the atelier through the massive carved door with the filigreed iron balcony above, and was shown by a butler into a large reception area with blue satin sofas and Turkish rugs. After I waited for twenty minutes, an assistant appeared dressed in one of Patou's narrow, beautifully cut dresses, as streamlined as the Farman sports cars the couturier loved. She led me through the grand salons with their towering ceilings and ornate carved moldings to an office on the second floor. It was decorated entirely in white: white carpet, white drapes, and white upholstery on the chairs. A white borzoi lounged on the floor, and, as I entered, he leaped to his feet barking.

The couturier, impeccably dressed in a brown wool suit and blue silk tie, sat behind a long desk, the surface empty except for a pearl-handled revolver. He was a slim, handsome man, almost as pretty as a woman, with fine, delicate features and thick dark hair slicked back across his head. I couldn't imagine Mademoiselle or any woman hating him. He was too beautiful.

Patou beckoned me to take a seat. "You want to work for the House of Patou?" he asked.

"That's what I would like to talk to you about."

"Why are you leaving Chanel?"

In my letter, I'd written that I had worked for Chanel Modes et Coutures for nearly three months, but that I wanted to change positions. I mentioned nothing of my illness.

"I'm not happy with the workroom organization," I said, improvising.

"Does Chanel do *all* the designing?"

"Yes."

"She doesn't draw, does she?"

"No. One of the premières draws. Mademoiselle starts by draping, and once she has the idea for a dress, she explains it to the staff."

"So, Chanel makes it up as she goes along?" A smug expression appeared on Patou's face. "It's as I suspected. She doesn't think things through. She throws fabric over a mannequin and hopes for the best."

I wondered if Mademoiselle was as misguided about Patou's methods as he was about hers. "That's not really . . ." I began, but Patou interrupted me.

"I hear that Chanel rules with an iron hand, that she's very controlling."

"She has definite ideas about how she likes things done."

"I do, as well. But I also demand a great deal of independence. Are you used to making your own decisions?"

"I am. Of course, Mademoiselle has the final say."

Patou got up from his chair and walked around to the front of his desk, leaning against it and crossing his ankles. He picked up the revolver and held it in his hand, rubbing the pearl handle with his thumb, like a child stroking the ear of a stuffed animal.

"The war taught me that a certain amount of independence given to one's assistants is essential. Most couturiers hold contrary views, but it's my conviction that a modern business should be modeled on the lines of an army organization. The chief must give his orders, but he must not be expected to bother about the execution of details."

He put the revolver down and folded his arms against his chest, burying his thumbs in his armpits. "Chanel is a woman," he said, as if there was some doubt about it. "This is the first strike against her as a couturier. Whom does she design for?"

He paused, then answered his own question. "Herself. And that's what's wrong with her work. There is more than one type of woman in the world, after all. What looks good on Chanel is not necessarily what looks good on you or Suzette." Patou cocked his head toward the back of the room, where his assistant had been standing silently against the wall throughout the interview.

He walked around his desk and sat down, leaning back in his chair. "Suzette will show you around."

I followed her through the large airy salons, lit by huge crystal chandeliers, up the wide winding staircase to the workrooms. "Go on in. Look around," Suzette said at the entrance to the first door. It opened into a large sun-filled room, freshly painted white. The seamstresses worked at long polished wood tables. A cloakroom and kitchen sat to the right. The pleasant circumstances looked entirely more welcoming than the harsh rooms at Chanel.

I walked among the tables and inspected the finished garments hanging on the racks. Many of the models were loose and sporty and reminded me of Mademoiselle's, though Patou's clothes were less sinuous and more architectural than hers.

Suzette was chatting at the back of the room with the première, an older woman whose expensive dress could not compensate for her thick, lumpy figure. They had their backs to me, and as I approached them, I overheard the older woman say, "She doesn't have much of a figure, does she?"

"That won't matter to him," Suzette answered. "She's pretty enough. And she's young."

Were they discussing me? It was impossible to know, though I felt a spike of anger at the idea that this homely middle-aged première was passing judgment on my looks.

They heard me approach and quickly turned. "What do you think?" said Suzette. She looked at me with cold eyes.

"It seems like a very smooth operation. Of course, I have some questions."

I was trying not to seem overeager. The truth was, I liked everything about the House of Patou: the beautiful mansion, the clean, commodious workrooms, the intelligent professionalism of the employees, the clothes—which were as chic and even more artfully constructed than Mademoiselle's—the couturier himself, so youthful and handsome.

We descended the staircase to the floor with the executive offices. Patou stood alone in the doorway, smoking a cigarette. His dark eyes devoured me. "What do you think, Mademoiselle . . ." He struggled to recall my name.

"Varlet."

"Yes, Mademoiselle Varlet."

"I'm very impressed."

Patou smiled, showing his white, well-shaped teeth. "Now you see how a real couture operation works."

Ten

*T*he next day, I got a petit bleu from Suzette, and I started at Patou the following morning. Over the next weeks, I had to get used to a new way of designing clothes. Unlike Mademoiselle, who worked intuitively, Patou's method was intellectual. He began by thinking out every detail, then explaining his ideas to sketch artists, whose drawings were given to the premières to translate into toiles.

Mademoiselle created a look based on how she wanted to dress herself, but Patou's style encompassed his entire life. He fashioned an aesthetic of cool elegance based on pale colors and clean, geometric lines that defined not only his couture collections, but also—as I learned from pictures in magazines and newspapers—his wardrobe, his cars, his homes, and his offices. It was an aesthetic very similar to Mademoiselle's and, probably more than anything else, that explained his hatred of her. Mademoiselle threatened Patou's originality, and so he strove to distance himself from her as much as possible.

I was assigned as a junior *main* to Madame Lucille, the première I'd met during my interview. Our workroom sat on the third floor, a white airy space. Patou visited the workrooms at least once a day, and his presence always sparked girlish titters among the seamstresses. All chatting stopped. Backs were straightened and stomachs pulled in;

hair was smoothed and smiles composed. Patou would stroll among the long wood tables, hands clasped behind his back, sometimes bestowing a mild compliment. "I like your seams," he'd say to one woman, or, to another, "Those pleats are lying nicely."

Patou didn't flirt; he didn't have to. He knew a seamstress could live for a month on one intense glance from him. Everyone was in love with him—the seamstresses, Madame Lucille, Suzette, the mannequins, the clients. He was handsome, successful, and rich, a war hero who now devoted himself to dressing and pleasing women.

His reputation for glamorous excess enhanced his allure. Patou gambled profligately, drove sports cars at astounding speeds, and changed sexual partners as frequently as he changed his shirt. His romantic liaisons and his exploits at the gaming tables in Monte Carlo and Biarritz regularly showed up in the scandal sheets, and I often wondered if his flamboyant private life was as coolly calculated as his career, a stunt designed to attract attention and build sales. Once, after he'd been to Monte Carlo, I overheard him telling the house director, a man named Georges Bernard, who'd served with Patou during the war, "Don't worry, Georges, each million I lose at the gaming tables sells two million francs in dresses."

Several weeks after I arrived, workmen closed off four of the five first-floor salons at 7, rue Saint-Florentin and opened their interconnecting French doors to create an immense studio. Work on Patou's collection was about to begin. Bolts of cloth—tweeds, velvets, crepe de chines and silk mousselines—were carried down from the storage room and piled on trestle tables. Seamstresses from my workroom and two others moved downstairs to one of the salons where the couches and gilt chairs had been replaced by tables and benches. We would make the toiles for the collection, which, when approved by Patou, would be sent upstairs to be sewn in fine fabric.

Patou moved his office downstairs to the salon next to us to be closer to the action. Here, the mannequins paraded in front of him, as he inspected toiles and finished models. He read his mail at a long polished desk and received guests in an armchair by the fireplace. Unlike

Mademoiselle, who did all the house's designing herself, Patou delegated some of his work to his premières. Months before he had given them antique textiles and bits of embroidery and fabric from which to derive inspiration, with instructions as to the styles he wanted to develop and the colors he wanted to use. The premières had come up with ideas, which they presented to the couturier. Once refined, the designs were passed on to one of three artists, who sat on folding chairs at the back of the room, making sketches throughout the day.

When a toile was completed, it was tried on by several mannequins, until one was found who looked especially chic in it. The toile was assigned a number and then recorded in chalk on a blackboard under the mannequin's name—white chalk if it was a day dress or suit, red chalk if it was an evening gown.

It wasn't long before Madame Lucille recognized my talent, and soon I was given more responsibility, graduating after two weeks from the less skilled tasks such as overcasting and hemming, to making toiles. The first time I presented a muslin mock-up to Patou, I was so nervous that my armpits and forehead dripped sweat. The model was extremely complicated—a suit with godets sewn into the skirt and jacket. I was used to Mademoiselle's simple cuts, and I struggled with this new complexity.

Patou sat in an armchair smoking and considered the mannequin as she paraded in my toile. "Not bad," he said. "Who taught you how to cut? Not Chanel. She doesn't know anything about construction."

"I learned—" Patou didn't let me finish.

"Those shapeless sacks of hers!" he ranted. "They look all right on skinny poles like Chanel, but not on real women."

Patou stood and walked slowly around the mannequin. "All right. It's done," he pronounced.

The mannequin stepped away to change toiles, and Patou and I stood face-to-face. "How old are you, Mademoiselle Varlet?" he asked.

"Twenty-two."

"I don't believe it. You look barely sixteen."

"I'm twenty-two, sir."

A couple of times that afternoon I caught him looking at me out of the corner of his eye. During the *pose* the next morning, he asked me why I hadn't cut my hair.

"I'm fond of it," I answered.

"Don't you ever get tired of hairpins?"

"I'm used to them."

"If you decide to cut it, I know a wigmaker who will buy it from you."

"I'll keep that in mind."

"It's very nice hair. The texture and color are lovely."

That made me blush. I knew I wasn't beautiful or glamorous like the women he was photographed with in the press. But was it out of the question that he would be charmed by me? I stood silently for a minute, red-faced and tongue-tied.

"You can go back to work now," Patou said finally.

When I sat down at my table, my hands were trembling. I had to go to the washroom to compose myself.

After that, whenever Patou spoke to me, my heart beat faster. I didn't want to think I had a crush on him, like every other silly seamstress. Still, I found myself thinking about him throughout the day, and sometimes at night, I dreamed about him. At work, I tried hard to demonstrate my talent and creativity, so he'd notice me. Once, I suggested that a piece of twisted silk braid would look nice around the neckline of an evening gown, and Patou incorporated my idea into the final design of the dress. Another time, I convinced him to use smaller buttons on a fitted jacket with delicate lines.

Not all my ideas were well received. Since many of his suppliers had not yet resumed business after the war, Patou had a great deal of trouble getting quality silks and wools, and once I suggested he use jersey for evening dresses. "You have been here how long?" he asked me, raising one elegant eyebrow.

"Three weeks."

"And you are still thinking like Chanel?" His brow collapsed in furrows. "Jersey is not for evening!"

"I only thought, sir, it was a way to save money."

"That's not the way I dress women!"

I never mentioned jersey again.

Truth be told, I preferred Mademoiselle's work. A lot of the clothes I made for Patou were clumsy: heavy, ankle-length skirts worked in panels, coats with military frogging, jackets with huge collars and cuffs. Nothing he did that season, though, was as unflattering as his shepherdess models—froufrou dresses with low waists and bell-like skirts that fanned out at the hips. I made toiles for several of these dresses, including one that was to be made up in stiffened white organdy, called Dolly, after Dolly Varden, the flirtatious character in Charles Dickens's *Barnaby Rudge,* who was fond of flashy clothes. I was not happy that Patou had assigned it to Jane, an American mannequin, whose tall, angular figure ill suited the model's round, feminine lines.

Recently, Jane had been given all the best models. The chalk marks on the blackboard accumulated under her name, and soon she had twice as many as the other mannequins. Madame Lucille told me it was because she was Patou's *petite amie,* though there was nothing petite about Jane. She stood close to six feet and had a large head and wide, bony shoulders. "He's had a taste for the tall ones lately," Madame Lucille explained.

"Dolly doesn't suit her," I protested.

The stout première peered over her spectacles, lowering her triple chin into the folds of her neck. "If you want to tell him that, go ahead. But I don't think it's a good idea."

By then, Jane and Patou were inseparable. They arrived together in the morning, lunched together at midday, and left together in the evening. When she wasn't working, Jane sat in her smock in a chair by Patou's desk, smoking and reading the paper.

We all thought Patou would soon tire of her, perhaps more quickly than he typically wearied of an infatuation, precisely because this one was so intense. One morning, however, Jane came in wearing a new diamond necklace. A few days later, she arrived with an emerald bracelet on her wrist.

"I think this is getting serious," said Madame Lucille.

"Don't be ridiculous," scoffed a middle-aged senior *main*. "Patou will never settle down."

The two women sat opposite me at the worktable inspecting the seams of several skirts I'd recently finished. "Jane can barely speak French," I pointed out.

Madame Lucille snorted. "Talking isn't what he's interested in. He's never before given anyone such expensive gifts. In a month, you're going to see a ring on that girl's finger."

The première and her senior *main* took the skirts away to be pressed. I felt my face turning hot.

For the rest of the day, I tried not to think about Jane. It was hard to ignore her, though, with those emeralds on her wrist. They caught the light, sending sparks of glitter through the air. Not that she moved much. Maybe, in the whole day, she stood for four fittings. Most of the time she just sat around, smoking and flipping through magazines.

Why did *I* have to work so hard? It seemed I had less stamina these days. Maybe it had been a mistake to come to Paris. I thought of home, of my grandmother's house and the ancient marché in Timbaut with its thatched roof and stone floor. I thought of Jacques and recalled the first time I'd seen Daniel and how my heart had opened in a new way.

We'd not seen each other much since I'd started at Patou. I'd been busy, and then Daniel had gone to London to talk to a publisher about an English translation of his book. Now he was back, and I was glad that I'd made plans that evening to meet him in Montmartre.

When I arrived at the club at nine, I found Daniel at a table near the bar. The band was in the middle of a blues tune, mournful and low, and Daniel's shoulders swayed with the music. "You missed a great trumpet solo," he said, as I took a seat beside him.

A waiter brought me a glass of wine, and as I sipped it, I studied Daniel's face—his eyes sparkling with life, his mouth forming a pleasant half smile. Suddenly I felt very foolish for mooning over Patou.

Quickly, I finished my wine and ordered another glass, then

another. Daniel looked at me with a concerned expression. "You're drinking an awful lot. Is something wrong?"

"No."

"Something's wrong. I can tell."

"Nothing's wrong."

"Things are going well, then?"

"I guess."

"You don't miss Mademoiselle?"

"I don't miss her tantrums. Sometimes I miss Laurence. Usually I'm too busy to think about anything but work."

"What's Patou like?"

"He's a perfectionist, like Mademoiselle. Like they all are."

The band jumped into a fast, jazzy tune, with a thundering drum solo at the end.

"Be careful," Daniel said.

"What do you mean?"

"I've heard things about Patou. He has a terrible reputation with women."

"You don't know him."

"I know men."

The raucous tune ended, and the music slid into a low, dark wail.

"Anyway, he's very involved now with one of the mannequins."

"Still, be careful."

We stayed through the band's second set, and, afterward, we walked out together into the night. "I've missed seeing you, Isabelle," said Daniel, when we'd reached the taxi stand.

"I've missed you, too," I said.

He touched my face, and I closed my eyes waiting for a kiss. Instead, Daniel said, "Where to?"

"Home, I guess."

As I settled into the back seat of the taxi, I watched Daniel duck into the metro and scurry down the stairs. Maybe he didn't want to kiss me. I was so sure, though, that he did. I felt too unsettled to sleep, so instead of going home, I directed the driver to 7, rue Saint-

Florentin. The great old mansion was in darkness, except for a yellow cube of light in one of the first-floor windows. The night watchman let me in, and I groped my way across the marble foyer. I pushed open the double doors leading to the studio and saw Patou at his desk, writing in his ledger. Jane was nowhere in sight. Patou looked up, and when our eyes locked, my heart nearly stopped.

"Mademoiselle Varlet, why are you here?"

"I . . . have a toile to finish," I stammered.

"Why didn't you do that earlier, during regular hours?"

"I had a rendezvous with a friend." My face was on fire; I could feel it turning scarlet.

Patou laid down his pen and smiled. "Where did you go?"

"To Montmartre. To hear American jazz."

"Were you with a man?" He raised an eyebrow and looked at me with a knowing expression.

"Yes. But we're just friends."

Patou clasped his hands behind his neck and leaned his head back. "Go home, Mademoiselle Varlet. It's late. The toile can wait until tomorrow."

Later that week, I finished Dolly. Patou was so pleased with the dress, he decided not to save it for the collection, but to offer it immediately to his clients who needed something new and exciting for the upcoming peace celebrations. To advertise the model, he dressed Jane in it and took her with him to the opening of Mossant, a new restaurant on the Champs-Élysées, where he knew Dolly would be talked about and photographed by the press. He had not, however, counted on the model being pictured next to a dress by Mademoiselle, which is exactly what appeared in *Desmoiselles*. The morning the magazine landed in the news kiosks, Patou burst through the door waving a copy. He marched up to me and threw it down on the table. "Look at this!" he shouted, as if it were my fault. "Your former employer in the same spread with me!"

In the magazine, under the headline, "Chic Parisiennes Attend Opening of Mossant," Jane in Dolly stood next to Régine, who was wearing one of Mademoiselle's simple black silk gowns. "It must have happened at the end of the evening, when I'd stopped in the men's room on our way out," said Patou.

"I'm sorry, sir," I said, though I didn't know why I was apologizing.

Patou's eyes scanned the studio. "Suzette!" he bellowed.

The couturier's assistant rushed over. "Sir?"

"Get Madeleine Savarine on the phone. Invite her to tea this afternoon. Tell her I have something important to discuss with her."

"Yes, sir."

The *Desmoiselles* editor arrived at four, and Patou seated her at the table near the fireplace, where he took tea every afternoon. Then he walked across the salon and drew the French doors partially closed. From my worktable next to the door, I could still see and hear the two of them.

Madeleine Savarine was in her early fifties, a plump little pink-and-white woman with pale powdered skin and bobbed hair dyed an unnatural strawberry-gold. Dressed in a beige wool suit with four ropes of pearls in graduated lengths around her neck, she listened intently as Patou talked, his dark, well-shaped head close to her smooth face. They talked about the problems facing fabric manufacturers and the merits of various handbag suppliers. Finally, Patou said, "I've been disappointed in the coverage you've given the house."

"Really?" Madeleine Savarine arched her penciled eyebrows and looked at him with wide eyes. "It seems to me I've gone out of my way to feature the House of Patou, since you've reopened."

He shook his head and leveled his gaze at the plump editor. "In the past few months, you've been giving Chanel more space. I've counted the pages. She's gotten twelve to my eight."

"You've counted the pages?" The editor's eyebrows climbed higher.

"Yes. Chanel has gotten much more space than me."

"Have you counted the pages I've given to the other couturiers as well?"

"No." Patou paused to light a cigarette. He blew a jet of smoke into the air, then resumed talking. "There is also the matter of your current issue." He looked deeply into Madame Savarine's eyes. "I must ask you never again to feature me with Chanel in the same photograph, and as far as illustrations go, never on the same page or on facing pages."

"I can't promise that!" Madame Savarine's voice rose higher. "I don't make editorial judgments based on such idiotic whims!"

Patou was in a fever, and it had to run its course. "You must never again feature me with Chanel!" he ranted, waving a finger under the editor's nose.

Madame Savarine had heard enough. "Don't shake your finger at me," she snapped, her face growing pinker. She looked like a furious peach. "My job is to cover all the couturiers, not just one or two. If you are this upset about your treatment in *Desmoiselles,* I have the solution. From now on, I will leave you out of my magazine entirely. Au revoir." She stood, and, walking as fast as her chubby legs could carry her, hurried through the French doors leading to the exit.

Curiously, the first casualty of Patou's blowup with Madeleine Savarine was his affair with Jane. The lovers stopped going to lunch and leaving together in the evening. During the *pose,* Patou barely looked at the girl, and when he spoke to her, his tone was icy. One afternoon, a week after the scene with the editor, I saw Patou and Jane arguing in the hall outside the storage room. An hour later, the American fled the atelier in tears. She never returned.

"If Jane hadn't been talking to Chanel's mannequin, the photographer never would have taken their picture," Madame Lucille explained later in an officious tone. "She should have known to stay as far away as possible from anyone who works for Chanel. The girl is so stupid, and he finally realized it, thank God."

Thank God, I thought to myself.

As if he had read my thoughts, the first thing Monday morning, Patou called me over to his desk. "I'm promoting you to senior *main,*" he said.

"Thank you, sir."

"Don't thank me. You deserve it. I thought about it over the weekend, and I decided you're a valuable asset to the house."

During the next week, he asked me to sew two of the most important evening gowns for the collection, and when they were completed, he praised my work extravagantly.

One evening soon after that, I was putting away my needles, when Madame Lucille said I had a phone call. I picked up the extension on the wall near my worktable and heard Laurence's cheerful soprano. "I have good news!" she said. "Anne, my new seconde just quit. You might be able to get your job back. You have no idea how backed up we are. All the premières have been complaining to Mademoiselle, and Madame Georges has been urging her to hire more *mains*."

"Mademoiselle will never take me back since I've worked for Patou," I whispered into the phone.

"She will if she thinks hiring you away would anger him."

"I'm not sure I want to go back."

Laurence was quiet for a moment. "Is Patou paying you more?" Her voice was flat.

"A little. Not enough to make much difference."

"What's so special about him?"

Behind me at the worktable, I could hear the soft rustling of fabric, the click of scissors.

"I like it here," I told Laurence.

A few nights later, as I gathered my things in preparation to leave, Patou stopped at my worktable. He had his coat on and was on his way out the door. "Why don't you have dinner with me tonight?" he asked. "Bignon's at ten. Here's the address."

He handed me one of his embossed cards. On the back, he'd scrawled, "48, rue de Courcelles."

"Thank you," I said awkwardly, my heart knocking about in my chest, as Patou walked away.

Moments later, Madame Lucille marched up to me. "What was that about?" she asked. She considered me carefully through her spectacles. "He's not giving you extra work, is he? You have two toiles to finish for the collection."

"It was about the toile for the green suit," I lied.

I left work early to get ready. At home, sitting on my bed, I thought hard about what to wear. The only things in my wardrobe were my work clothes, my black silk dress and the white blouse I'd recently sewn. Then I remembered the four yards of rose silk that Madame Duval had sent me—every time she cleaned out a closet, I got a bolt of fabric. I pulled it from under the bed and, after removing the brown wrapping paper I'd kept it in, I unspooled it across the quilt. I got out my scissors and chalk and began to cut a pattern for a simple sheath from the wrapping paper. I took a lot of shortcuts, telling myself I would rip out the dress later and put it together properly when I had more time. What was important tonight was not that the dress be perfectly made, but that it dazzled for a few hours.

In the taxi on my way to Bignon's, I imagined a quiet, romantic restaurant with candlelit tables and sparkling crystal. Perhaps Patou had reserved a private dining room. I'd never been in one, though I'd heard all the best restaurants had them.

The taxi turned onto rue de Courcelles and creaked to a halt in front of number 48. Far from the romantic establishment I'd envisioned, Bignon's turned out to be a loud and crowded nightclub. Bursts of tinny music escaped from the revolving doors, as people streamed through. Inside, the air was close and smoky.

The maître d' showed me to a horseshoe booth, and my heart sank to see that Patou was not alone. I settled on one end of the plush banquette. On the other end sat Patou, surrounded by several expensively dressed men and women. The couturier nodded in my direction, not bothering to introduce to me to his companions. The luminous redhead on my right offered me a cigarette, which I declined, and then her long white hand. "I'm Manon," she said.

"Isabelle Varlet. Pleased to meet you."

The pale narrow-faced man sitting to Manon's right leaned across her. "She's a real *beauté*, don't you think?" he said.

Manon rewarded him with a glorious smile. She was an other-worldly creature with flawless skin and perfect features. I tried to figure out how the half-dozen men and women at our booth matched up, but they were all leaning over each other and touching. It was impossible to know who was with whom. It occurred to me that Manon might be Patou's new mistress, but then why was I there? I was reassured that he wasn't paying any more attention to her than he was to me.

The food looked delicious when it arrived steaming on white gold-rimmed plates, and I was famished. I'd ordered *truite aux amandes,* which the waiter now laid at my place. Patou's friends continued to puff on their cigarettes, ignoring their plates. I didn't want to be the first to start, and so I waited until Manon cut a small piece of her steak and slowly placed it in her mouth.

My *truite* was superb. I wanted to clean my plate, but Manon put her fork down after a couple of bites, so I put mine down, too. Five minutes went by before Manon took another bite. She chewed, swallowed, and laid down her fork. Then she pushed the plate away with the pads of her fingertips. How did she survive? On air and admiration? Or maybe she went home at night and swallowed cotton soaked in honey to fill her stomach, as some of Mademoiselle's mannequins did. I looked around the table. No one was eating. Bright talk bounced above the ignored food. Afraid of looking even less sophisticated than I felt, I didn't try to join the conversation. Not talking and not eating, there was nothing to do but drink. The waiter kept filling my glass, and I kept emptying it. Soon, I felt woozy and lightheaded.

Eventually, the party ended—everyone got up from the table. There was a rustle of silk and clinking bracelets and Patou, who hadn't said a word to me during the meal, led me by the elbow toward the door.

The couturier's Hispano-Suiza waited at the curb, the driver holding the door open. Patou guided me into the backseat, sliding to my side. No sooner had the car pulled into the street than he yanked my skirt to my waist and plunged his head into my lap. I tried to push him away, shoving my knee against his chest, as he clawed at my drawers with his teeth. I finally forced him to sit up, but then he started pawing at my breasts, plunging his hand into the front of my dress. "No! Stop!" I cried, but Patou ignored me. The driver kept his attention on the street. I felt Patou's hardness against my thigh, and his mouth was all over my neck, as his hands tried to manipulate my hips underneath him. We were wrestling awkwardly on the backseat when the car stopped on rue Saint-Florentin in front of Maison Patou. The driver hopped out and opened the door. Patou slid out pulling on my arm. "I'm not going with you," I gasped.

Patou looked at me with stony eyes. He dropped my hand and uttered practically the first words he'd said to me all evening. "Very well." He straightened his tie and barked to his driver, "Take her home."

My humiliation was so sharp, I could hardly breathe.

The next morning, I called Suzette from the concierge's flat. I told her I wasn't feeling well and that I'd be in when I was better. I knew, though, that I'd never again set foot inside 7, rue Saint-Florentin.

While Madame Lebel puttered in her tiny kitchen, I called Laurence. "Isabelle, I was wondering when I would hear from you," she said in a bright tone.

"I've been busy," I said, trying to make my voice sound cheerful.

"You don't know what busy is. We're swamped."

"I'm ready to come back."

"What happened?"

"Nothing. I'd just like my old job. Could you talk to Madame Georges?"

"Sure. But don't get your hopes up. She just hired four new *mains*."

Next, I called Daniel, who agreed to meet me at a café near my apartment. At first, I was afraid to tell him what had happened the night before, but once I started talking, the story poured out. It made me feel better to unburden myself, to let Daniel absorb some of the pain. He listened closely, shaking his head. But then he blamed the couturier's behavior on the war. "Don't think I'm making excuses for Patou," he said. "Who knows what he was like before 1914? But unspeakable things happened on the front, things that ruined men."

At first, Daniel's reaction appalled me, but then, I realized that I knew nothing about Daniel's own war. Though he talked openly about his leg, even sometimes joking, he never mentioned the events that led to losing it. His sanity, perhaps, depended on burying the memory.

Daniel must have seen the disappointment in my face, because now he said, "If it wasn't illegal, I'd challenge Patou to a duel."

I thought of him wobbling on his wooden leg. "You'd probably lose," I said.

"Probably."

He leaned across the table and took my hands in his. "What will you do now?"

"I don't know. I'm waiting to hear from Madame Georges."

"Don't worry, Isabelle. Something will turn up."

When I got home, there was a note from the concierge telling me to call the house manager at Chanel. I dashed downstairs. Madame Lebel had heard my footsteps, and the door was opened when I reached her apartment. I stepped into the salon, and she cocked her head toward the phone.

Madame Georges sounded happy to hear from me, and she asked when I wanted to come back to work. My heart began to race. "Would tomorrow be all right?"

"Tomorrow would be great." She explained that the house was backed up with orders, and though she'd brought in a few new seamstresses, the collection still was far behind schedule. Mademoiselle had just given her permission that morning to offer me my old job.

"She doesn't care that I've been with Patou?"

"I told her you hated working for him because you couldn't stand his clothes, they were so inferior to hers."

"She believed that?"

"She wanted to, so she did."

Eleven

The next morning, a bright beautiful June day, I returned to my workroom at rue Cambon. It was a relief to be there, standing under the aluminum lights, seeing the fierce concentration of the seamstresses crowded at the scarred wood tables behind soft mounds of gleaming fabric. The click and slice of scissors seemed to swirl the women's chatter around the tables and dress forms on which half-sewn garments were held together with thousands of basting threads. Through an open window, a whiff of clean air mingled with the citrusy tang of new silk.

Laurence was the first to see me. "Isabelle!" she cried, jumping up from her desk to embrace me.

Heads turned, smiles erupted.

"You're looking well, Isabelle," called one of the women.

"Thank God, you're back," said another.

"We missed you," said Elise, a junior *main*.

"Everything looks the same," I said.

"*Some* things are different," said Elise, nodding towards an arpète, a thin adolescent who was collecting needles from the floor. "That's my cousin, Sophie. Mademoiselle took her on while you were out."

"Hello, Sophie," I said, and the girl looked at me, smiling sweetly.

"She left school for *this*," said Anaïs, a senior *main*, as she took in the piles of old patterns on the floor, the fabric swatches stuffed into bags, the dingy walls and peeling paint.

"Sophie is talented. She'll be a première before you know it," said Elise. "You'll see. Some day, she'll have her own maison de couture."

"Isabelle, while you were out my sister had a baby!" cried François, a junior *main*. "There's a picture on the wall." She pointed to the mirror surrounded by photographs.

I wandered over to the metal *rayon* holding the collection toiles. I looked through them eagerly, noting the neat youthful silhouettes, feeling relieved to be free of Patou's shepherdess dresses and intricate godets. I loved the collection's buoyant feeling. Every model was different, and every model had its charm—from the casual dresses and lighthearted tunics, to the suits with cardigan jackets and pleated skirts and the capes that would be trimmed in fur. The evening gowns were a marvel. Floating above the ankles, they were held up with delicate straps and cut low in back and loose around the waist and hips.

At the end of the rack, I found what I was looking for—the latest toile for Angeline. It had been sewn by Lawrence in my absence, but now that I'd returned, she'd promised it was mine to reclaim—the finished dress would be sewn by me. I ran my hands over the muslin and took it off the rack to study. Something was off—instead of falling gracefully, the side cascades stuck out stiffly from the seams. The toile looked clunky.

It was on the schedule for the *pose* later in the day, and I feared if Mademoiselle saw this version of Angeline, she'd scrap the model entirely.

Carrying the toile, I hurried to the worktable where Laurence was bent over a swathe of jersey, cutting out a dress. "We can't show this to Mademoiselle," I said.

Laurence looked up from her work. "What's wrong with it?"

"The side cascades for one thing." I pulled out the bulky fabric from the right side of the dress.

"I was so backed up," said Laurence.

"Can you take it off the schedule to give me time to redo it?"

Laurence put down her scissors and with her hands pressed against her kidneys arched her back, stretching out the kinks. "If it means that much to you."

Later, in the corridor on the way to the *pose,* I caught Mademoiselle's unmistakable scent—a fresh, elegant aroma, intense, yet not heavy like the perfumes of other women, musks poured on as if to disguise unfortunate secrets. The door to her office was open—she liked to watch the traffic going up and down the staircase—and when I walked by on my way upstairs, she called out to me. "Varlet!"

The couturière sat at her desk in a dark skirt and white blouse, a long strand of pearls dangling around her neck. Squares of fabric samples fanned out in front of her.

I walked halfway into the office, and she motioned me closer. "You're looking fine, Varlet."

"Thank you, Mademoiselle. So are you."

"I see you haven't cut your hair. Never mind. I hear you had a hard time when you were sick."

"It's no fun to be ill."

"A person grows only with pain and suffering. No one ever learned a damn thing from pleasure. Pleasure is overrated. It's a trap. Why do you think I work so hard?" She looked at me, her eyes large and bright. "Work is my medicine," she continued. "I could get depressed, if I let myself. But I don't let myself. As long as I have my dresses, I'm all right."

She leaned back in her chair and studied me for a moment. "I hear you couldn't stand it at Patou," she said finally.

"I prefer to work here." I felt my face reddening and wished I knew exactly what lies Madame Georges had told Mademoiselle about my time on rue Saint-Florentin.

"He's a big phony. Just like all of them." Mademoiselle scowled and shook her head. "What do men know about dressing women?" She glanced away, then returned her gaze to meet mine. "Did he pay you well?"

"The standard, according to the Chambre Syndicale scale." I wondered if Mademoiselle knew that as a senior *main* for Patou, I earned ten percent more than she paid me as a *seconde*.

"So you made out all right?" Her eyes sparkled with mischief.

"No. I was out of work for a month. I still owe my landlady, and I have yet to pay the doctor."

Mademoiselle opened the top drawer of her desk and pulled out a checkbook. After scrawling something in it, she tore off a check and handed it to me. "Here. Take this," she said.

It was made out for 400 francs—a month's salary. At first, I thought it was a joke. Mademoiselle had never been known to give anyone a paid sick leave.

"I don't know what to say," I stammered.

Mademoiselle smiled broadly, dimpling her cheeks. "Don't say anything. And I mean that. If the other girls hear about this, I'm cooked. Yvette's been out even longer than you, and I haven't given her anything. Not a sou. I'm not made of money, you know, and these mannequins are beautiful girls, they can always find a man to pay their rent."

I was too happy to feel insulted that Mademoiselle didn't think a man would want to pay my rent.

"Not a word, Varlet." She put a tan finger to her lips.

"I promise. Not a word."

I worked long hours, and Mademoiselle rewarded me with a renewed confidence in my talent. During the next month, she approved six of my toiles. I was particularly proud of the model for a black tulle evening gown. Mademoiselle had taken my suggestion to put white fur trim on the neckline, armholes, and hem—witty elements that gave the dress character. Angeline, however, remained a work in progress. When Yvette stood in front of the triple mirrors in my latest version of the toile, Mademoiselle shook her head from side to side. "No, no, no! That is not at all what I want!" she cried.

"If you could be a little more specific about exactly the effect you're after," I suggested quietly.

Then a voice from the back of the room. "Mademoiselle is looking for a dress that fits better than something off the rack at Printemps."

I whipped around. Susanna Lawson stood with her arms folded across her chest. "*I'll* redo it," she said with a smirk.

"No!" I felt the blood drain from my face.

Mademoiselle glared at me. "I make the decisions around here."

"It's from my workroom," I said. "I never heard of giving a model from one workroom to another. It's just not done."

"I decide what's done and what isn't done," barked Mademoiselle. She dropped onto the cushion next to the fireplace and took a long drag on her cigarette. As she puffed, she studied Angeline. She didn't say anything for the longest time. Then, she crushed her cigarette in an ashtray and stood. "All right, Varlet," she said with a sigh. "You get one more chance."

"Thank you, Mademoiselle," I said, trying not to sound too relieved. "I know I can make it work."

"*That* will never happen," muttered Susanna, as she strode past me and out the door.

"Mademoiselle almost gave Angeline to Lawson," I told Laurence when I got back to the workroom.

Laurence laid down the jacket she'd been sewing and stretched out her arms. "The baroness is a menace," she said. "I don't know why Mademoiselle puts up with her. She doesn't bring in *that* many clients, and she's cheating Mademoiselle right and left."

"What do you mean?"

"The wife of the owner of Potels told me Susanna gives her free dresses in exchange for meals at his restaurant. I also hear she sells Chanels out of her apartment at greatly reduced prices."

"Mademoiselle doesn't know this?"

Laurence picked up her needle and resumed stitching. "I'm sure she's heard the rumors. Susanna supposedly is a third cousin or some-thing of Boy Capel's. Maybe that's why Mademoiselle tolerates her. If it was you or me, she'd have us beheaded."

It was hard to avoid Susanna during the *pose,* but otherwise, I tried to stay out of her way. Occasionally, I ran into her sitting on the stair-case, surrounded by male acquaintances as they smoked and ogled the mannequins. She never said a word to me, though, and I avoided her gaze.

One afternoon, after I almost tripped over him on the staircase, a friend of Susanna's asked me out to dinner. The young man had no discernible occupation and had not been in the war. Though he was attractive enough, he didn't interest me. I went out with him I'm ashamed to admit for the free meal and the chance to make Daniel jealous. This I tried to accomplish the next day after church, when I went to Daniel's apartment to work on Fabrice's catalogue.

A new group of illustrations were spread out across the dining table. They depicted the catalogue's heroine in a series of *robes d'intérieurs*—flowing, loose gowns that courtesans of the Belle Époque typically wore to receive their lovers. Daniel explained that Fabrice wanted to offer a few models to appeal to the city's seductresses. When Daniel asked how these sexy garments fit into the greatest moments of a woman's life, Fabrice said, "That's why I've hired you. To come up with a story."

Daniel pointed to the first illustration laid out on the dining table—a filmy blue silk gown threaded with gold that clung sugges-tively to the heroine's body. "It looks like a nightgown to me," he said. "Maybe I can write something about the blonde going to bed—with her husband, of course."

"I have no thoughts about it," I said glumly. The dark strains of the Moonlight Sonata, played by Daniel's mother on an old record-ing, floated through the apartment. "Can you change the record?" I asked. "This music makes me want to jump out the window."

Daniel looked at me with a quizzical expression. "You've never complained about Beethoven before."

"I'm tired. I was out late last night."

"Out late? Where?"

"I went out to dinner."

"With whom?"

"Why are you so interested?"

"You don't have to tell me if you don't want to." Daniel poured each of us a glass of wine.

"With a man," I said, accepting the glass.

"I assumed with a man. Where did you meet him?"

"At work."

"You met a *man* in that cabal of women?"

"He's a friend of Susanna Lawson's. Some of her male friends hang around the salon hoping to meet mannequins."

I searched Daniel's face for sparks of jealousy. Instead he wore an impish smile. "And this poor guy got stuck with a seamstress?" he said.

"Is it that hard to believe someone would find me attractive?" The music, melancholy and low, had put a lump in my throat.

Daniel covered my hand with his. "Really, Isabelle. I was just teasing. Where's your sense of humor? You know how lovely I think you are. I'll change the record if you want. What would you like to hear?"

"Debussy."

"Oh. You're in a romantic mood?" Daniel smiled.

"Are you?"

"I'm in the mood to get this damn catalogue done." Daniel gulped the last bit of his wine and, leaning on his forearms, turned his gaze to the illustrations.

"I don't care what you play." My voice came out angry and tense.

Daniel looked at me. "What's wrong with you, Isabelle?"

"Nothing."

"Something's wrong. You're very prickly."

"I'm just tired," I said. "Maybe I should go home." I felt tears erupting, so before Daniel could say anything else, I grabbed my purse and left.

*   *   *

Nothing was wrong. I was changing, that's all.

Growing up, my bouts of consumption had left me feeling vulnerable and weak, as if I might lose my life at any moment. I'd worried constantly about dying, a strange preoccupation for a child. Now, I could feel a quickening of ambition deep in my bones and heart. With the prospect of a long life ahead of me, I began wanting things for myself, first of all to learn everything I could about couture, to perfect my skills as much as possible. Part of my desire to excel was to lose myself in work, to not suffer for what I had lost, for what I couldn't have. Often, when I sewed, I would slip into a meditative state, almost as if I'd become one with the fabric and thread. At these times, I felt a kind of release that was almost like happiness.

Almost.

There remained a yearning, a void left by Jacques' death. I hadn't given up on love exactly. But mostly, I thought about work. With each passing day I felt my fate tied more closely to Mademoiselle's. Then, at the end of June she announced, "I'd like you to make a dress for me, Varlet." I thought she meant another model for the collection until she said, "I need it to wear to a theater opening. I didn't like the last dress Susanna made for me. That girl is losing it."

A grin spread across my face. I didn't try to suppress it.

Mademoiselle had her dress form transferred from Lawson's workroom to mine, and I worked on the couturière's dress for ten days from nine in the evening until two in the morning. It was a simple sleeveless model in cream crepe de chine. Sewing it, though, I felt a sense of solemn responsibility—it could have been a coronation gown for Marie Antoinette.

Mademoiselle ordered the final fitting at her house, a rented villa called La Milanaise in a suburb near the Bois de Saint-Cucufa, fifteen miles outside of Paris. She had taken the afternoon off, and promptly at seven, a shiny dark blue car, bulging with huge headlights and chromium fastenings, its canvas hood folded down, pulled up to the shop to fetch me. The driver laid the dress box in the trunk, and I settled into the black leather seats. Waving a white-gloved hand to the seamstresses who'd gathered in the upstairs windows to watch our leave-taking, the driver started up the engine, and the long lovely car rolled up rue Cambon.

We drove for an hour, beyond the bright city into little suburban villages, then past farms, telephone wires, gated villas, and cemeteries with elaborate monuments like trophies. We arrived at La Milanaise just as the sun went down, and the house and garden were bathed in a soft plum light. The house was much bigger than I'd expected—a tile-roofed, stuccoed affair with turrets, balconies, and extensions branching out on all sides. On the front lawn opposite the circular drive, a marble fountain poured water into a shallow pool ringed with rose bushes. More roses wandered over the lawn and climbed up the house, scenting the air.

At the door, the butler took the dress box and gave it to a maid, who carried it upstairs. I passed into a large salon with French doors opening onto a terrace and the garden beyond. A gleaming black piano stood in one corner. Chinese Coromandel screens flanked the fireplace, where two beefy German shepherds lounged on the hearth.

Mademoiselle reclined on a sofa reading a book. On the sofa opposite her sat a handsome man who resembled her so closely—with the same dark shiny hair, brown eyes, and tawny skin—he could have been her twin. This was Boy Capel. The room was cool and light with white walls and slipcovers, beige carpets, and, on every table, dense bouquets of pale roses. Mademoiselle and her companion were dressed in white—the couturière in a frothy organza dress, the man in a linen suit. Yet there was something between them that brought darkness into the room. Even the Alsatians were edgy. Spotting me, they jumped up barking.

"Soleil! Lune! Hush!" commanded Mademoiselle. Two small terriers nestled at her side, and when Soleil and Lune fell silent, the terriers commenced yapping.

"I've brought your dress," I said.

"How are things in Paris?" asked Mademoiselle. She didn't bother introducing me to Capel.

"Everyone is working hard."

She picked up one of the terriers and scratched his head. "Don't tell me that. I know what happens when I leave early. Everything goes to hell!" She placed the terrier at her side and folded her arms across her chest. "How did you like my car?"

"It's so comfortable, like riding in a cloud."

At the mention of the car, the man looked up from his newspaper and spoke directly to Mademoiselle. "Don't forget to have your driver fix the lock on the luggage box."

Mademoiselle turned to me. "You know how much the car cost? Twenty-eight thousand francs. You'd think for that kind of money, I'd get a car with locks that work."

The man put down his newspaper and stood. He had a stiff, arrogant body with legs too short for his trunk. "I'm going up to make a phone call," he announced.

When he'd gone, Mademoiselle lit a cigarette. "I paid for the car myself you know," she said, a plume of smoke following her words. "Boy saw it at the auto show and told me to buy it. As if I don't know how to choose a car myself! He thinks I'm as ignorant as I was when he found me."

Gossip in the atelier held that Boy Capel still paid most of her bills. Why else would Mademoiselle put up with his marriage to another woman? The year before, he'd wed the daughter of an English lord. Now, he didn't dare appear in public with Mademoiselle, lest they get written up in the scandal sheets.

"Let's see how the dress looks," said Mademoiselle.

I followed her up the stairs into a large dressing room with tall white cupboards and Louis XIV chairs cushioned in silk. A circular table at the center of the room held a garden urn overflowing with yet more roses. Beyond the French doors at the end of the room, an elaborately landscaped garden stretched out.

"All the roses in the house are from my garden," said Mademoiselle, who'd stepped behind a screen to change. "I provide everything for myself—even flowers."

She was silent for a moment, then continued. "A long time ago, before the war, I asked Boy why he never sent me flowers. Isn't a man supposed to send the woman he loves flowers? A half hour later, I received a bouquet. I was overwhelmed with joy. A half hour later, a second bouquet appeared. That was nice. Then, a half hour after that, another one. This was becoming monotonous. Every half hour for the next two days, the bouquets arrived, until I thought I would go out of my mind. It was an important lesson. You can have too much of anything, even happiness."

I thought I heard her sigh. "Varlet, would you close the door? As soon as darkness falls, the mosquitoes take over."

I drew the doors shut, as Mademoiselle appeared from behind the screen in her new dress. She removed several strands of pearls from a drawer, examined them closely, and chose one that exactly matched her dress. She looped the necklace over her head, filled her right arm with gold bracelets, and stepped into a pair of pale kid shoes with graceful heels. She examined herself in front of the mirror.

Working on the dress, I'd thought it pretty, but nothing special, no different from hundreds of other sleeveless evening frocks produced by Mademoiselle or a dozen other couturiers. Now, as I watched her preening, I began to understand the key to her chic. She willed the dress to beauty. It was as if the garments absorbed her personality and reflected it back, enriched, fascinating.

"You know, it was chance that I ended up making dresses," she said, studying her reflection over her shoulder. "I could have done something else with my life. It's not dresses that obsess me; it's work." She put her hands on her hips and looked directly at me. "Varlet, there is time for only two things. Work and love. That leaves no other time. Love is very important. Don't think it isn't. A woman who isn't loved is lost."

Boy Capel appeared in the doorway, looking compact and imperious, his jacket folded neatly over his arm and the dogs yapping around him. "I have to go back to London," he said. I wondered about his wife and imagined a tall, pale blonde with a baby bundled in her arms. Diana Wyndham Capel had given birth to a little girl in April. The announcement had been in all the Paris papers. "I'm leaving now," he said.

"You're not staying for dinner?" Mademoiselle asked.

"Not tonight."

"I don't know why you come for just one day." Mademoiselle ran her hands through the creamy silk skirt of her dress, caressing it gently.

"Would you rather I didn't come at all?"

Mademoiselle worried her pearls. They caught the light from the crystal chandelier and threw off glints that danced around the room. "Well, I think you could arrange to stay a little longer."

I stared at the ground.

"I have to go," he said.

"For just one day, you shouldn't bother." Mademoiselle's voice sounded weary.

"I'll call you."

Boy Capel turned and walked down the hall, the dogs loping after him. Still fingering her pearls, Mademoiselle watched, as he disappeared around the corner.

Twelve

At three A.M. a horse-drawn cart clattered to a halt outside my window and began pumping out the cesspools into which the toilets on our stair landings emptied. The stench was horrid, and the pumping caused a loud racket, which almost extinguished the singing and quarreling of the drunken workmen stumbling home. The next day I was miserably tired, so when the seamstresses broke for lunch, I took the staircase to the salon, where one of the vendeuses directed me to an empty room.

"If I fall asleep, wake me in a half hour," I told her before closing the door and kicking off my shoes. As soon as I lay down on the settee, I heard moaning from the fitting room next door, then a man's voice: "That's it, my girl, that's it!" Fabric rustled and furniture knocked against the wall. I covered my ears to no avail.

Finally, there was silence, then the sound of whispers and shuffling. I peeked out the door. Amanda Nichols stepped from the neighboring fitting room, her blond curls in a frenzy, her face flushed pink. The Duc de Jacquet followed her, pulling white kid gloves over his gnarled hands. They kissed quickly, as the duke slipped on his coat. Then he scurried away, and Amanda darted back to the fitting room. My nap ruined, I headed to the workroom. On my way, I ran into the vendeuse

Monique Thabard. "I just saw the Duc de Jacquet with Amanda Nichols," I said. "I thought Susanna Lawson was his mistress."

"They both are!" cried Monique. "Nichols meets him in the fitting rooms every Tuesday morning. On Thursdays, he meets Susanna. He's a big art collector, you know. Nichols has been after him for years to become one of her clients. Susanna's just after his money. I can't stand it when he's here. I'm always worried his wife will show up."

"Why don't you tell him he's not allowed beyond the salon?"

Monique looked at me as though I'd suggested she murder him. "He's a duke!"

Two weeks later, I saw Amanda Nichols sitting on a gilt chair in the salon—a table holding an unfurled fan of ostrich plumes was all that separated her from the Duchess de Jacquet.

It was one in the afternoon, and the house was mobbed with darlings having clothes fitted for the races and the upcoming seasons in Deauville and Biarritz. I had been summoned for the duchess's fitting, and now, as I padded across the beige carpet, the unhappy receptionist kept her head down and shuffled papers on her desk. One of her duties was to keep wives and mistresses apart.

Mademoiselle had designed this dress for the peace celebrations, and it was one of our most popular models—a satin gown with a low-cut corsage and a skirt consisting of a series of tiny tulle ruffles held out at the hem with a hoop.

It was a youthful, playful dress, extremely flattering to the young society stars who'd already ordered it. But the duchess was old and jowly with three chins and tiny blue eyes shot with red threads. Still, she adored modern fashion.

Monique Thabard took the dress from my arms and followed the duchess. A few minutes later, she called me in. The duchess stood in the middle of the room in the dress, which barely fit her, though it had seemed enormous on the hanger. The fabric pulled taut across her body, and the armholes were so tight she had to hold her arms out like parentheses. She scowled at herself in the mirror.

"Very becoming," said Monique, eager to make a sale. "We'll just take it out a bit here and here." The vendeuse tugged at the garment's side seams and smiled at the duchess.

"I'm not sure it suits me," said the older woman. "And what about these armholes?"

"That's not a problem," I said, unhooking my scissors from the ribbon around my neck. I approached the duchess. "Madame, please raise your arms."

The duchess held up her arms, and two gray flaps of wrinkled flesh hung down. I pushed a fold of her skin away with one hand, as I snipped at the armhole of the dress with the tips of my scissors.

"Ahhhhh!" the duchess cried out.

I pulled my hand away and saw that it was covered with blood.

"You imbecile, you've cut me!"

"I'm so sorry," I gasped, as I looked down to see a dark stain blossoming on the side of the dress.

She dropped onto the settee and glowered at Monique. "If you think I'm paying for it now, you're crazy."

Monique removed the silk scarf from her neck and tied it around the old lady's arm as a tourniquet, but blood continued to seep from the wound.

"Of course, we wouldn't think of asking you to pay for it." Monique raised a threatening eyebrow at me. *I* would have to pay for the dress.

The duchess groaned. "Get my husband."

I fled to the reception area, where through the windows, I glimpsed the duke asleep in the backseat of a Rolls-Royce parked at the curb, blocking traffic. The Jacquets' limousine was among the few that had not been requisitioned by the government, and in grand Belle Époque style they took a car and driver everywhere. "The duchess would like to see her husband," I told the receptionist. Amanda Nichols, still sitting in front, never looked up from her magazine.

Back in my workroom a few minutes later, I wondered how I would come up with 6,000 francs to pay for the ruined dress. Perhaps I could work out some arrangement with Monique whereby I'd pay it off gradually. Quickly, I made a few calculations in my head: at a rate of twenty francs a month—the absolute most I could afford without starving—it would take me twenty-five years to wipe out the debt.

My head started to pound, and I felt a hollowness in my stomach, as I picked up my sewing. Though my needle was moving across the satin skirt in my hands, I was hardly aware of it. Then the phone rang. It was Monique. With the tone of an executioner, she demanded my presence downstairs.

I found her conferring with Amanda Nichols. Monique led me away from the fitting room and Amanda's earshot. I felt tears welling up in my eyes and tried to blink them back. "Listen, Isabelle. If you make a suit for Amanda Nichols to wear at Longchamps this weekend, I'll forget you ruined the duchess's dress."

I was so relieved I could barely speak. "When does she need it?" I asked, my voice a whisper.

"In two days."

I was in no position to object.

At six in the evening two days later, I stood over Amanda's completed outfit—an apricot jersey skirt and jacket trimmed in gray squirrel—laid out on the worktable in front of me. Laurence had cut it out, but I'd done most of the sewing. I turned the suit inside out and checked the seams and linings. Like an iceberg, all the power of a couture garment is below the surface invisible to the eye, in the thousands of hand stitches of varying styles and tension, expertly applied—an unshakable carapace of thread.

With my eyes closed, I pressed my fists into my lower back and kneaded the kinks. My head throbbed and my knuckles ached. For the past week the seamstresses and I had virtually lived in our workroom, sewing orders for the races, the first in Paris since the war. There was great pressure on us to produce dazzling clothes, not only for the darlings, but also for the mannequins to show off in the unofficial racetrack fashion parade. Traditionally, this spectacle was of supreme importance, a prelude to the fall collections and carefully scrutinized by the press and the foreign buyers who'd arrived early in town for the August openings.

It was doubtful that Amanda Nichols would ever appreciate the hours of labor that had gone into this suit—the careful cutting, the meticulous needlework, the fine finishings. Amanda would wear the suit once or twice, then it would be banished to a closet, its life drooping away. Maybe some day, long after she'd forgotten it, she'd happen upon it by chance and slip it on, marveling at the perfect stitching, the impeccable fit, the sturdy fabric. For a moment, she might let herself think of the skill and craftsmanship behind this lovely model. After all, she is a connoisseur of art. But probably she'd decide it was an old model, out of season, and give it to the maid.

Just then, I didn't care. I was exhausted, but happy. I loved the workroom's low hum of chatter, the waves of fabric undulating over the tables, and the soft swishing of silk and velvet as it glided through dancing fingers. I felt connected to my colleagues and to the long line of seamstresses who'd gone before us—the sisterhood of the needle.

That Sunday, I got to go to the races myself. Tanguy de Navacelle, the concierge at the Ritz, had taken a fancy to Laurence, and he invited us to go with him to Longchamps. We took the bus from Paris, and by the time we arrived in midmorning, the track was mobbed. At the rail, a sea of bobbing straw boaters bent over yellow racing forms, while aristocrats and politicians chatted in their boxes. On the lawns beyond, bookmakers and pickpockets mingled with shop girls, demi-mondaines, society celebrities, stage stars, and movie queens. People whispered that Gloria Swanson was hiding behind dark glasses on the restaurant terrace.

In the swirl of bodies, I caught sight of Amanda Nichols wearing my suit and felt a surge of pride. It seemed beyond my dreams that I was here at the Paris races, observing this glamorous woman in something I'd made. Her brown felt hat and simple brown leather pumps perfectly complemented the apricot jersey.

Amanda dazzled as much as the mannequins vamping near the winner's circle. Photographers and buyers, mostly men in department store suits and hats, now crowded the racetrack lawn. As the mannequins strutted and preened, flashbulbs popped, while the couturiers hovered nervously nearby, some of them rushing up to the mannequins from time to time to adjust a hat or a sash.

Yvette and Régine drew attention in identical short, sleeveless dresses with skirts covered in two layers of black silk fringe, and I swelled with pleasure. Their slight, simple outfits looked fresh and modern, particularly compared to the silliness offered by fashion's Old Guard. These comprised a confused jumble of styles, many from France's distant past: high-waisted Empress Josephine gowns, dresses with floating panels of drapery; redingote skirts opening over frilly aprons; Directoire hats, ruffled crinolines. A Marie Antoinette frock from Ardente with an échelle of insipid bows on the bodice and a *panier* skirt pulled out at the hips in voluminous folds made me laugh out loud.

Near the fence, I saw Fabrice leading Thérèse by the hand. She was wearing a green taffeta dress embroidered with pink silk flowers. Her skirt ballooned at the hips and narrowed around the ankles; an elastic strap affixed to the hem made walking tortuous, and the couple proceeded at a snail's pace. Daniel would have enjoyed their ridiculousness, and I wished he was here to see it.

"These clothes are hideous," said Laurence, as she surveyed the mannequins through Tanguy's binoculars.

"The prices are worse!" said a voice behind me. "I'm not paying them, and a lot of the other buyers won't either." I turned to see a short, stout man talking around a cigar at the side of his mouth. He wore cream flannels and a navy blue jacket with shiny brass buttons. "Charlie Spinelli, here," he said, pushing a pale fat hand in front of my chest. "I'm a friend of Tanguy's."

"Charlie, my good man," said Tanguy, slapping the American on the back. "This is Isabelle Varlet and Laurence Delaisse. Charlie's the head buyer for women's dresses at Burlingham and Company in New York."

Charlie Spinelli withdrew his hand from mine and shoved it toward Laurence. "Pleased to meet you, too, sweetie." He spoke fluent French in a heavy American accent.

"Mademoiselles Varlet and Delaisse work for Chanel," said Tanguy.

Charlie Spinelli plucked the cigar out of his mouth and grimaced. "I'm not buying anything from Chanel. Her prices are crazy, the worst."

"Charlie's the cheapest person I know," said Tanguy with a laugh. "He eats at this dive in the sixth, where I used to tend bar. Won't go to a decent restaurant."

"I love this town. But I feel like I'm being robbed from the moment I wake up!" cried Charlie Spinelli. "I'm staying at Les Chênes, and I can't even get a lump of sugar for my coffee without bribing the waiter. This morning, the guy dangled a lump in front of my nose until my mouth watered so badly, I was ready to tip him twenty-five francs." He relit his cigar, inhaled deeply and released the smoke, scribbling the air with a pungent cloud. "I'm not buying any couture."

"What will you do?" I asked. "You have to send something back to New York."

Charlie Spinelli leaned toward me and whispered. "Copyists."

"Copyists?" I said.

"You know about the copyists don't you?"

I shook my head.

"She's new," said Laurence.

"I'll tell you about the copyist, doll, but first let's get out of the sun."

We followed Charlie Spinelli to the far end of the lawn near a copse of trees. He leaned against one, removed his hat and smoothed his nearly hairless scalp. "I can get copies of Chanel, Lanvin, Patou—whatever you want—for a fraction of the original price. The copyists do excellent work. All you have to do is put the word out. It's as easy as pie."

"How is that?" I asked.

"A little bribe here, and a little bribe there, and you can get your hands on anything. With all due respect to you ladies, seamstresses are the most bribable people in the world."

"I'm not surprised, we're so badly paid," said Laurence.

"You think most seamstresses are dishonest?" I asked.

"I prefer to call it enterprising," said Charlie Spinelli. "Last year a vendeuse I know at Doeuillet told me about a client who refused at the final fitting to buy an expensive silk gown she'd ordered. One of the senior *mains* had offered to copy it for her for less than half the price."

"*That's* stealing," I said.

"Stealing is what the couturiers are doing." Charlie Spinelli laughed, causing his whole upper body to shake and setting off a spasm of coughing. Holding his cigar, he pulled a white linen handkerchief from his pocket and with a horrible retching sound, expelled something into it. He balled up the handkerchief and shoved it into his hip pocket. Then he plugged his cigar back into the side of his mouth and resumed talking.

"Take this friend of mind. She works for B. Altman in New York. Last February, she visited a certain house that shall remain nameless and found some models she liked, but the total price the couturier was asking was fifty francs over her budget. Now fifty francs might seem like a trifle, when you're spending thousands, but this young lady's got a tough boss, and if she spent over budget, he'd fire her. She explained the situation to the couturier, but he looked down his nose at her, told her no reduction would be made under any circumstances."

"What happened?" asked Tanguy.

"She walked out and came to me. I got her the models and saved her a hell of a lot more than fifty francs! Now, I don't call that stealing." Charlie Spinelli checked his watch and, holding his hat with one large hand, dropped it on his head. "It's been nice meeting you ladies. But now I gotta study the racing form."

Charlie Spinelli lumbered off toward the betting booths. "I don't believe you can get copies of couture that are as well made as the originals," I said to Laurence, as we wandered back to the winner's circle.

"It depends," Laurence said. "I've seen cheap knockoffs, but I've also seen copies that are so good and in such beautiful fabric that the couturiers themselves wouldn't know the difference."

In the winner's circle, a small crowd had gathered around a tiny man with thick round glasses and sparse brown hair, who sat on a folding chair sketching. This was Georges Coursat, better known as Sem, whose caricatures appeared regularly in the press. Mademoiselle was a favorite subject—he'd been sketching her since she opened her first shop in Deauville, and he anointed her the queen of *vrai* chic. Since then, he'd portrayed her many times as a paragon of harmonious, restrained elegance, contrasting her with the caricatures of *faux* chic—fat, smug matrons who looked ridiculous in the new fashions.

Sem wore a wrinkled gray suit. He drew with the stump of a pencil in a large sketch book, and wads of paper dotted the ground at his feet. I walked slowly by and stole a glance at his drawing. He'd sketched the mannequin parade as a procession of insects with stomachs jutting forward and hips undulating.

Suddenly, a stir erupted near the far end of the winner's circle. Jean Patou had arrived with the actress Vera Sergine on his arm. She was dressed in a white silk sheath, heavily embroidered in a geometric design that resembled a cubist painting. A pair of twin mannequins dressed identically to Sergine followed close behind the couple.

The attention of the crowd bent toward them, like a swift wind that suddenly changes direction. The photographers surrounded the couple. "Over here, Mademoiselle Sergine!" shouted one. "Vera, give us one of those dazzling smiles!" called another.

"Mademoiselle will have a fit when she sees this," said Laurence.

Since Mademoiselle had dressed her in *The Secret*, one of the hit plays of the season, Sergine had been a regular in our salon. The actress and Patou were walking toward me now. They stood very close to each other. Sergine whispered something in his ear, and he smiled.

What a fool I'd been to have a crush on him. I did not want him to see me, and clutching Tanguy's binoculars, I scurried away.

On the pavement outside the winner's circle, I scanned the crowd, spotting Mademoiselle on the terrace. She was chatting with three tall women whose aura of confident superiority made their pedigrees so obvious they might as well have had coronets etched on their foreheads. Comtesse Greuffulhe, Comtesse de Chevigne, and Princess de Polignac were regular features of the society pages. All wore Chanel dresses, Chanel hats, white gloves and little fur wraps. As Mademoiselle talked, her face bright with animation, the three nobles nodded at her words.

An imperious voice behind me said, "Excuse me."

I turned around to face Misia. "Have you seen your employer?" she asked. "She told me she was going to be here, but I can't find her."

Large and ungainly in her sleek Chanel dress, Misia looked like a perfect victim of Sem's *faux* chic. I handed her the binoculars and told her to look on the terrace. "Gabrielle is an idiot!" cried Misia, staring through the binoculars. "She's up there nattering, while Patou is stealing the show down here. She doesn't need to waste time toadying up to those women. They're my friends, and they'll buy dresses from her if I tell them to!" Misia shoved the binoculars at me and stomped off.

Soon the horses appeared, led by stable boys. I joined Tanguy and Laurence in the stands. "Time to place your bets," said Tanguy. On the bus trip from Paris, he had studied the racing form, and he told us Wild Fancy had the best chance to win in the first race. Laurence and I each gave him a few francs, and Tanguy went off to place our bets. He returned just as the bell rang, and the horses shot down the track.

I scanned the crowd through Tanguy's binoculars. Hardly anyone was paying any attention to the race. People were talking; many of them still had their eyes on the mannequins in the winner's circle. Looming into focus to my left were Patou and Vera Sergine, then Mademoiselle and the noblewomen. I found Misia on the terrace with the Maharajah of Indore, a small, dark Indian, impeccably turned out, from his black bespoke suit to his spotless white gloves.

Suddenly, Laurence threw her arms around me. "We won!" she cried. I looked at the board posted above the track. In first place was number 345. Laurence and I were each twenty francs richer. We'd packed a basket of food, and after the fourth race, took the gravel path around the track to a green stretch of lawn, where people were picnicking on blankets and sitting on folding chairs reading the papers.

We polished off two bottles of wine with lunch. Afterward, I lay down under a tree and fell asleep. I was awakened by the heavy, persistent buzzing of an airplane engine, and I opened my eyes groggily. Mademoiselle was standing over me. "Get up, Varlet. I need your binoculars."

As I struggled to my feet, a plane swooped overhead. Its gray belly arched up above the track and turned toward the horizon, disappearing behind a cloud. A moment later it reappeared, flying straight along a swelling blue of sky. Then it slowed, seeming to pause in midair. The tiny figure of a woman crawled out of the cockpit and stood on the wing. Wild cheers split the air. The woman was Alix Vaury, a pioneering aviatrix, whose stunts had won her a blaze of publicity and a movie contract from Metro-Goldwyn-Mayer.

"Would you ever get out on an airplane wing?" asked Mademoiselle. She looked into the sky through the binoculars.

"Never."

"Would you do it if someone paid you a million francs?"

"No."

"I would. For a million francs, I would."

I felt a spike of pity. She'd rather be dead than poor and ordinary.

"Here," Mademoiselle said, returning the binoculars to me. "It's too blurry. I can't get a good look at what she's wearing."

I lifted the binoculars to my eyes. Alix Vaury stood firmly on the airplane wing dressed in black knickers and a white shirt, the wind whipping around her, as she gripped a thin pole anchored to the plane. She looked invincible.

"Did I see you talking to Misia a while ago?" Mademoiselle suddenly demanded.

"Misia?" I said, as if she'd mentioned an exotic animal.

Mademoiselle moved her face close to mine. "I saw you with her. What did she want?"

"Nothing . . . we were . . ."

"Misia *always* wants something." Mademoiselle furrowed her brow. I stood dumbly for a moment.

"Come on, Varlet, let's have it," insisted Mademoiselle.

"She was wondering if I'd seen you. She was looking for you, that's all."

"I don't believe it!" Mademoiselle stomped off, muttering to herself, "That cow! She can't mind her own business for a minute!"

Sem had moved his folding chair to a spot near where Laurence and Tanguy were packing up the picnic things. During Vaury's performance, I'd noticed him studying Mademoiselle, and passing close by his chair, I caught a glimpse of his drawing. He'd depicted Mademoiselle as an aviatrix standing on the wing of an airplane with *La Mode* emblazoned on the side. In the cockpit sat Jean Patou. With one arm he reached out across the airplane wing, ready to push Mademoiselle over the side.

Thirteen

The following week, the papers were filled with photos of Vera Sergine and the twin mannequins in Patou's cubist sheaths. Meanwhile, Mademoiselle's fringed models got no press except for a small drawing buried in *Women's Wear*.

The couturière couldn't take revenge directly on Patou, so she lashed out instead at the brodeuse whose handiwork had adorned his dresses, an older woman named Madame Bataille, who also did embroidery for Chanel Couture.

Because of the difficulty in getting luxurious textiles and fancy trimmings, embroidery was widely used that season to accent plain fabrics, and Mademoiselle had planned some lovely embroidered tunics and dresses for the collection. Sections of these models had recently been cut out, ready to be sent to Madame Bataille. After Patou's triumph, however, Mademoiselle fired her.

From now on, the couturière announced, our embroidery would be done by Madame Petrova, a recent Russian immigrant, who'd come highly recommended through a friend of Misia's and who charged half Bataille's rate.

One hot afternoon, as I sat by the window dreaming about going to the coiffeur for a shampoo, Madame Georges came into the work-room carrying a large brown box. "From the brodeuse," she said, laying the box on my worktable.

I opened the lid and pulled out the first item—the front of a beige silk tunic. To my horror, I saw that it was splattered with black dye around the splotchy imprint of an inky design. Quickly, I went through the box. There were sections of tunics, blouses, dresses, coats, and jackets, which were to be assembled into finished garments after the embroidery had been applied. Now they weren't fit to be dishcloths. All were blotched with dark stains.

"You'll have to cut new fabric. Everything is ruined," said Madame Georges.

"What happened?"

"Whoever tried to transfer the stenciled designs was incompetent."

With the help of a few seamstresses, I recut the silk and wool sections, then packed them in a box and carried it on the metro to the fifteenth arrondissement. Madame Petrova worked out of her home in an enclave of hastily constructed new buildings on rue Blomet. The area was popular with Russian immigrants because of its surfeit of available apartments and jobs at the automobile factories. At number 86, an ugly brick building identical to its neighbors, I climbed the stairs to the second floor, where the whirring sound of machines wafted from an apartment at the end of the hall. I knocked on the door, and a female voice rang out, "Come in!"

The door opened onto a small salon, crowded with mahogany tables, overstuffed chairs, and large display cases filled with porcelain figurines. A stove glowed with coal boules, and irons hissed on the tables. A low archway led to a second parlor where two women sat at foot-pedaled contraptions that resembled sewing machines, only with hooks instead of needles.

An elderly woman appeared in the doorway leading to the bedroom and waddled toward me. She had a wide, thin body, as if someone had squished her between two boards, a lumpy waist, and broad hips. Her face was a collection of knobs—nose, cheeks, and chin—and a cardboard-colored braid wound around the crown of her head. "Madame Petrova?" I asked.

"Who are you?" She fixed me with a hard look.

"I'm Isabelle Varlet from Chanel. I've brought your fabric. Madame Georges said she explained to you that everything has to be redone." I handed her the box.

Madame Petrova's face softened. "Thank you," she said quietly, as she placed it on the oval dining table.

Out of the corner of my eye, I studied the young women at the machines. A fine gray dust covered them—even the hair and clothes of a young woman sleeping on the floor—giving the women the appearance of biblical figures in sackcloth and ashes. Still, they had an air of aristocracy. Most were fine-boned and graceful, and I saw sparkles of gold and diamond in their ears and on their fingers.

"I'm sorry about the fabric," said Madame Petrova. "My girls haven't had much experience transferring designs from the stencils. But they're getting better. It won't happen again."

I moved closer to her and in a low voice said, "Maybe you should hire some brodeuses who've been properly trained."

Madame Petrova shook her head wearily. "These girls are my countrymen. They'd starve without the little I pay them. We've had a hard week. They've been working nonstop, sleeping at their machines. They've thought of nothing but work, not only for Mademoiselle Chanel, but also we're making uniforms for the volunteer regiments fighting the Red Army in southern Russia."

From another room, someone shouted to Madame Petrova in Russian, and the old woman, excusing herself, hurried away. When she'd gone, a small brunette about my age with pale skin and hazel eyes, stopped pedaling her machine. "Things *won't* get better," she said in heavily accented French. "We've taken on too much. We can't possibly keep up."

"It's true," said the blonde at the machine next to her. She was stitching by hand the pocket lining of a man's trousers draped over her knees. When she saw me looking at the trousers, she said, "For my brother. He's all the family I have left."

The brunette stood, pushing her chair away, and came to my side. "I heard what you said to Madame Petrova. We could use some French brodeuses, some workers with real skill," she confided.

"We could use more help, period," said the blonde in a bitter tone. "At Saint Catherine's Institute for Noblewomen in Saint Petersburg, they taught us how to bow to royalty, but not how to sew!"

"You've had *no* training?" I asked.

"Madame Petrova sent us to a factory for a short course on how to use the embroidery machines. We've practiced, and it's really not that difficult," said the brunette. "But it takes years to learn how to prepare the designs on the big sheets of paper for stenciling, and, of course, the hardest part is transferring them to fabric. None of us knows how to do that." She shook her head, releasing into the air a spray of gray dust. She coughed and swatted the air. The dust, she explained, was caused by chemicals in the embroidery backing that burned away when ironed.

"You need some trained brodeuses," I told her. "If you ruin this order"—I nodded to the box on the dining table—"there won't be another."

"In Russia, Madame Petrova was a seamstress, but she'll never hire real workers like herself. She's a snob," said the blonde. "The first thing she asked me when she met me was 'What family do you come from?'" The blonde pointed to the girl sleeping on the floor. "Madame Petrova found out Irina was Prince Volonska's niece, so Irina got the job, even though all she does is sleep."

As I considered the inert girl, I noticed in the cluttered corner beyond her, a tower of fabric bolts in shades of beige, gray, and black. I instantly recognized the material as Rodier jersey, a staple at Chanel, one of Mademoiselle's signature fabrics, a humble cloth that most couturiers shunned. Who could blame them? Jersey was rough and wild. The diagonals went in every direction, making it extremely hard to handle. Also, the loosely worked threads unraveled easily. Whenever I worked with jersey, I resigned myself to many sessions of ripping out and starting over.

But Mademoiselle loved it. It was cheap—Rodier had sold her a truckload of it for practically nothing during the war—and its plain nature suited her simple aesthetic. I wondered what the Russians were doing with so much jersey. "It belongs to one of our other clients," Madame Petrova explained when she returned. Her manner was nervous, and she didn't look me in the eye.

I brooded about Madame Petrova and the jersey all evening and on my way to rue Cambon the next morning. I was the first to arrive, and as I stepped into the workroom, I had a sense of lightness, as if a new window had opened in the wall.

The toiles for the new collection were gone. The night before, the clothes rack against the back wall had been crammed with twenty-five muslin mock-ups completed by my seamstresses—about a third of the collection so far, including Angeline and some of my other favorite models.

Alone in the workroom, I pawed through the other racks, under the tables, on the shelves, even in the cartons holding buttons and trimmings. No toiles. I called Madame Georges. "Did Mademoiselle ask for the collection toiles from my workroom?" I asked her.

"No."

"They seem to be missing."

"They have to be someplace," said Madame Georges. "Call me as soon as you find them."

I told myself that probably someone had moved the toiles and that they'd turn up later in another part of the house. Downstairs, I spent twenty minutes going through the racks of clothes in the storage room. Nothing. I tried not to panic. The missing toiles were *masters,* mock-ups that would be used to make the collection dresses and that, after the opening, would serve as patterns for orders from the darlings and the buyers. We still had copies of earlier versions, and it would be possible to recreate the *masters,* but we'd never have time now, with the date of the opening just weeks away.

My colleagues began to arrive, and by the time I returned to the workroom, a small group had gathered in front of the empty rack. The seamstresses were talking excitedly. "Where are the toiles?" asked Laurence.

"I don't know," I said, flopping onto a nearby bench. My temples had begun to throb. "I've looked everywhere."

"Did someone steal them?" asked Elise.

Laurence ran her hand across the metal bar of the *raym.* "What about the other workrooms?" she asked.

I sent an arpète to make the rounds of the other workrooms. "Look around as much as you can," I told her. "If anyone asks you what you're doing, say Mademoiselle sent you to track down a bolt of lace."

Laurence dispatched two junior *mains* to search the mail room and fitting rooms and to interview the driver of the delivery van. Still nothing. By the end of the day we had to face the inescapable fact that the toiles had been stolen.

Laurence and I made the trek to Madame Georges's office. "There's no trace of them," I said, when I was standing in front of the house manager.

Madame Georges removed her spectacles, carefully unhooking them from her ears, and held them in her arthritic hands. In her day, she had been a fabulous mannequin. Now she was stout and her face blotched and heavily etched, the allure burnt out of her violet eyes. "How many people know?" she asked.

"Just the seamstresses in our workroom," I said. "Are you going to tell Mademoiselle?"

"Not unless you two and the others want to be fired."

"She'd fire us over this?" I asked.

"Over *this*? You must be joking," said Madame Georges. "Of course, she'll blame you and Laurence. It's *your* workroom. You're in charge. She'll probably assume you stole them."

"But we'll remake them," I offered, even though I knew there was hardly time.

Madame Georges exhaled heavily. "Yes," she said, "and meanwhile, in some warehouse off a back alley some clumsy seamstress will be copying them and sewing bad imitations of Mademoiselle's gems, and within a week they'll be offered to the buyers, and you'll see them in the street, at parties, in the newspapers. The whole surprise of the collection—Mademoiselle's one chance to grab attention, to seize the moment, will disappear." The old woman waved her hand. "Do you understand?" she asked.

Laurence rolled her eyes.

"I think so," I said.

Madame Georges looked directly at me. She knew I loved couture, that I believed in Mademoiselle's gift perhaps as much as Mademoiselle did herself. "Isabelle," she said. "Everything you've done here will be in vain."

Back in the workroom, the seamstresses looked at me with anxious faces. "What did Madame Georges say?" asked Elise.

"To keep quiet," I said. "Mademoiselle mustn't know."

"Before the war, I worked for Cheruilt," said Rosa, a senior *main*. "When he lost some toiles, he fired the entire workroom. I didn't have another job until Mademoiselle hired me."

"It's always the worker's fault," said Elise.

"Just be calm," said Laurence. "We'll figure it out."

"I never thought it would happen here," said Rosa.

Every time I looked at the empty *rayon*, I felt life seeping from my limbs. I'd poured so much of myself into those toiles; they were mine as much as they were Mademoiselle's, especially Angeline. The thought of hundreds of Angelines turning up in shops across Paris and in London and in New York crushed my heart.

That evening after the workers had dejectedly filed out, Laurence and I were alone in the workroom. "Do you think Charlie Spinelli could help us?" I asked her.

"He might be the thief," said Laurence.

"You think so?"

"Could be. He seems pretty connected to the fashion black market."

"What if someone shows up in Angeline at Maxim's next week and is photographed wearing it in *L'Illustration*?" I asked.

Laurence had been examining her blemishes in a compact, and now she slammed the lid shut and looked at me. "I'll ask Tanguy to talk to Charlie Spinelli. Let's see what he finds out."

I moved to the window, and as I looked out onto rue Cambon, a mauve twilight marbled the sky, glinting on the tall, granite buildings, outlining their elaborately carved cornices. A sightless accordionist, blinded no doubt on the front, stood on the curb, playing and singing in a smooth adolescent tenor a tune I remembered from my childhood:

> *When I die, I want to be buried*
> *In a cellar with good wine*
> *A cellar with good wine*
> *Yes, yes, yes*

I walked downstairs and dropped a coin into his tin cup.

Fourteen

*I*t took Laurence, myself, and fifteen *mains* laboring Sunday and all night every night for a week to replicate the stolen toiles. We worked from earlier versions of the missing muslins and our recollections of Mademoiselle's comments, taking breaks only to eat sandwiches that one of the women had brought from home and to catch a few hours of sleep on the floor on beds improvised from fabric remnants. We told no one outside our workroom about the theft.

Every time the phone rang, I jumped, imagining the worst. Reading the newspapers and magazines was agony, so fearful was I that some society beauty would be photographed in a dress made from the stolen toiles. Most of all, I dreaded the *pose,* dreaded Mademoiselle examining the new toiles and realizing they were duplicates.

Angeline was the first of the replacements to be presented to the couturière. I'd struggled to make it identical to the stolen one, but when Yvette put it on and stood in front of the triple mirrors, I could see the fit was off. Mademoiselle knew immediately that something was wrong. She shook her lustrous brown curls and asked for a glass of water. She never asked for a glass of water when she was pleased.

"It's a little tight in the bodice," complained Yvette.

"Are you putting on weight? I can't have you getting fat for the opening," said Mademoiselle. She took a sip of water.

"No. I've lost weight. I don't know why it's so snug."

Mademoiselle pulled the fabric around Yvette's hips, then caught hold of the end of the skirt with both hands and turned it up. She glared murderously at me. "Look at this!"

My heart hammered, and my mind raced. She'd figured out this was a copy. It turned out, though, that something else had triggered her fury. "Why is this hem so huge?" she demanded. "Anyone old enough to wear this dress isn't getting any taller." She shook the garment violently and released it.

I'd put in a normal hem, but Mademoiselle sensed something was different about the toile. She secured her cigarette between her lips, freeing her hands. Grabbing the ends of the side cascades, she pulled them taut. "It's as I thought. There's too much fabric here. Didn't I tell you to make these inserts smaller?"

"Yes, but . . ."

"Weren't you listening to me?"

"I was, Mademoiselle."

"Then why didn't you do as I asked?"

She tore out the shoulder straps, then pulled away the bodice. Next she attacked the skirt, demolishing it with two swift yanks. A moment later, the muslin lay in pieces on the floor, and Yvette stood in front of the mirrors in her underwear. I felt my face redden.

"What's the matter with you?" Mademoiselle snarled. "You don't like it that I've destroyed your work?" She pulled the cigarette out of her mouth and smashed it in an ashtray. "Well, get used to it, my girl. These toiles exist to be destroyed."

I stared glumly at the discarded mound of cloth, now nothing but a rag. Angeline wasn't going to make it into the collection. Mademoiselle was silent for a moment. Then she said, "What's going on, Varlet?"

"What do you mean?"

"You're up to something."

"I don't know what you're talking about."

Mademoiselle snorted. She was as intuitive as an old fortune-teller. She stepped closer to me, her dark eyes glowering, "Whatever it is, Varlet, I'm going to find out about it. You know I will."

When Laurence and I were alone together, we talked obsessively about the stolen toiles and who could have taken them. There were no signs that anyone had broken into the workroom, so someone among us must have been the thief. At first my suspicions centered on Susanna Lawson. Her history of dishonesty made her a logical choice. But I couldn't discount the possibility that another seamstress had been bribed by someone from outside.

Despite my vow of secrecy, I told Daniel about the thefts. I'd helped him put the finishing touches on Fabrice's catalogue one Saturday evening, and afterward, we'd gone to an expensive restaurant to celebrate. I knew Daniel wouldn't say anything, and I had to know if he thought Fabrice could be involved.

"Absolutely not," Daniel almost shouted. "Fabrice is a lot of things, but he's not a thief."

"It's just that he hates Mademoiselle so much, and he seems so desperate these days."

"You're right about that." Daniel sighed and gazed past me out the window, to a manicured garden that stretched to the Champs-Élysées. He propped his elbows on the table and looked at me. "Fabrice is a mess," said Daniel. "He's drinking heavily, sleeping poorly, and spending wildly. Thérèse has about had it with him. He needs a success to stay in business. Yet just when he should be working the hardest, he spends almost no time in his studio. He stays in his bathrobe until noon everyday, reading the papers. Then he goes out to lunch and spends the afternoon prowling the antique shops for furniture he can no longer afford."

"Has he made any models from the catalogue?" I asked.

"I don't think he's completed a single toile. To motivate himself, he's actually hired a spiritual adviser, a middle-aged woman named

Emmeline who specializes in contacting spirits through the Ouija board. It's bunk, of course, but Fabrice actually thinks she's going to save him. Poor man. During one of his sessions, Emmeline claimed to contact Eugène Delacroix himself. The artist had plenty of things to say about Fabrice's work, starting with a directive to use deep, vivid colors. At least that gave Fabrice a spark of hope. He's pushed back the date of his opening to the end of August. But I doubt he's going to put out a collection at all."

Daniel pulled an envelope from his jacket and handed it to me. "Fabrice asked me to give this to you," he said.

Inside was an invitation to join Fabrice "twenty thousand leagues under the sea" at a fête inspired by the Jules Verne novel. "Another party?" I asked. "With his finances in shambles?"

"Fabrice promised Thérèse this would be the last, a treat to cheer himself up before he buckles down to work," said Daniel. "Do you want to go with me?"

"Of course."

We left the restaurant and rode in a taxi across the Seine. The trees looked like inkblots above the garden walls of the old faubourg mansions. Something about Daniel's relaxed posture and the confident set of his mouth reminded me of the boy I'd mooned over as a child. "You know, I fancied you when we were kids," I confessed.

"You didn't know me very well."

"Don't you remember playing prisoner's base in the marché?"

"Oh, yes."

"I thought you were very handsome."

"And I thought you were very pretty."

"Don't lie. You hardly noticed me."

Daniel shrugged. "I was just a kid."

"I made you a shirt. But it was the end of the summer, and you'd gone back to Paris."

"I didn't know that."

"Well, you wouldn't."

I wondered what had happened to the shirt. *I'll have to make some-*

thing else for Daniel, I thought. Maybe a jacket, or even a winter coat. I went over in my head the fabric remnants I'd seen around Mademoiselle's atelier. There might be some black wool from the last collection, or even some gray English tweed. I was still dreaming about the tweed, when the taxi reached my building and pulled to a halt.

Fabrice had asked that everyone dress in black, the color of the sea at night. So, the following Saturday, I arrived at the party on Daniel's arm, wearing my black silk dress. At the front door, mannequins in mermaid suits handed out blue chiffon scarves embroidered with rhinestone fish. I draped mine around my shoulders and followed Daniel through the mobbed salons. Outside, in the garden, a group of mimes dressed like deep-sea divers sat reading newspapers through the windows of their brass helmets. We walked around them and ducked under the flap of an enormous tent. It had been decorated to look like the inside of a giant aquarium with walls covered in pleated blue tulle, backlighted with electric light. Swimming among the pleats were an array of fabric fish glittering with spangles, sequins, beads, and rhinestones.

A jostling crowd of revelers had surrounded the dance floor, where two girls in extremely short, nearly topless dresses shimmied to a jazz tune, their bobbed hair and fringed skirts in an uproar. "No stockings. And that décolletage is indecent. I can see their little bosoms," sniffed a middle-aged woman with an American accent. "What do their sweethearts think?"

"They're French, my dear," answered her companion, a veteran wearing a jacket smeared with medals. "Their sweethearts, no doubt, are dead."

Thérèse advanced toward us in a loosely draped black gown, the top half of her face covered in a mask made to look like diver's goggles. "Isabelle and Daniel! Thank you for coming." She crushed each of our cheeks with her lips and pointed toward a corner of the garden. "My husband is over there. Go say hello to him and brighten his

mood. He's upset because he thinks everyone is wearing Chanel." Her eyes rolled heavenward, as she shook her head from side to side.

"I'll get some drinks," said Daniel and headed off toward the bar.

I found Fabrice near a hedge strung with colored lanterns talking to Etincelle, *Le Figaro's* ancient society columnist. The couturier was dressed like Verne's fictional Indian prince Dakkar, Captain Nemo's alter ego, in a gold tunic and turban. "Isabelle, this is Madame de Perony, or as we all know her from her fabulous column, Etincelle."

The tiny black-haired woman offered me a dry, bony hand. "I was just telling Monsieur Fabrice that I've heard a lot of complaints from American buyers. They think the French mode is confused. Some of them are planning to do most of their ordering with a new crop of American designers, and I'm wondering if this means the demise of Parisian supremacy."

"Nonsense," said Fabrice, stiffening his back and looking down his nose at her. "It's only because of the war, with the impossibility of travel, and the French luxury tax that the Americans have had to take up designing. There's no real artistic inspiration behind their efforts. The idea of Yankee style is absurd. Style is French, just like painting is French."

Etincelle nodded in agreement, while scribbling fiercely. Then she stopped moving her pen and gave Fabrice a perplexed look. "But, Monsieur, how do you explain all the strange variations we've been seeing? The *panier* skirts, the Second Empire styles, the crinolines? You must admit, this does not encourage the foreign buyer."

"I, for one, won't be doing anything historical," said Fabrice grandly. "But I will be making beautiful evening gowns." He leaned toward the little woman; I thought he was about to kiss her on the top of her head. "Because you are such an old friend, Marie, I'm going to give you some advance information about my collection. I've told no one else about this." Here Fabrice paused dramatically. "I will be using the colors of a bruise—rich, deep colors—yellow, red, green, blue."

"A bruise?" Etincelle scrunched her brow; it looked like a piece of corrugated paper.

"Yes, like what your skin looks like when it's bruised." Fabrice sounded annoyed.

"Is this like the Reign of Terror look Doeuillet is doing?"

"No!" Fabrice's voice rose. "I'm not copying Doeuillet or anyone else. It's not Doeuillet's Reign of Terror look. It's my own Reign of Elegance."

"Reign of Elegance. I like that." Etincelle's eyes opened wide, then narrowed, as she scrunched her brow again. "What about the silhouette? Are you launching a new silhouette, too, or are you staying in the mode?"

Fabrice looked blankly at her for a moment, as he tried to strike an idea. Then he said, "I will not be departing dramatically from the look of the moment, which, as you know, is loose and narrow. But there will be some surprises."

"I can't wait!" Etincelle snapped her notebook shut and tucked her jewel-encrusted gold pen into her purse. "Monsieur Fabrice, you've given me my story. Thank you." She shook Fabrice's hand, then mine, and scurried away to file her fashion scoop.

Fabrice nodded toward the dance floor, and I saw that his expression had changed, taking on the pale, tense cast I'd come to recognize as the start of a rant. "Do you see those fringed dresses on the dance floor? Are they Chanel?"

"I don't think so," I said. In fact, I knew that they were, as they'd come from my workroom.

Fabrice wrung his hands and looked uneasily across the garden. "Over there, near the buffet. Isn't that Elaine de Pougy in Chanel? Oh, God, why is everyone wearing Chanel at *my* party?"

"You were just interviewed by Etincelle. You'll be in her column tomorrow," I said politely.

"I don't care about that old hag and her silly column! It's the French beauties I want to see wearing my clothes in the picture sections—the Baroness de Rothschild, the Countess de Pracontal, the Princess Faucigny-Lucinge. I don't understand why they've left me for *her*."

"There's enough business to go around. Women haven't changed. They tire quickly of their clothes. They need an endless supply."

Fabrice no longer was listening to me. He'd spotted Gloria Swanson near the buffet. "Is that Gloria? My God, I think she's wearing something of mine! Excuse me, Isabelle. I need to say hello to her."

I returned to the house to look for Daniel, but he was nowhere in sight. Near the buffet, Thérèse was talking to an exceptionally tall woman with frizzy copper hair who was dressed, contrary to the party's rules, in a spanking white gown. This amazon turned out to be Emmeline, Fabrice's spiritual adviser. As Emmeline folded at the waist to meet my gaze when we shook hands, two tiny dolls made of multicolored silk threads, the mascots Ninette and Rintintin, popped out from her cleavage. During the war, you could buy these tiny effigies on any street corner; women and children—and some men—wore them dangling from cords around their necks as protection against bombs. Emmeline said that hers had saved her the year before when a bomb exploded in front of her in the Tuileries, pulverizing a statue. "I've never taken them off since," she said.

She bowed dramatically again and looked intently at me. "Did you lose anyone in the war?"

Before I could answer, Emmeline pulled a card from her purse and handed it to me. "Come see me anytime. I'll help you contact your loved ones. But I must warn you. I don't make predictions. So it's not going to do you any good to ask me if you're going to inherit money or live to be ninety."

"I'll keep that in mind," I said and excused myself.

In the dimly lit corridor on my way to the toilet I passed Fabrice's studio. Throughout the evening, I couldn't shake the feeling that I was close to my toiles. Now, that feeling had grown more intense. I hesitated at the door. Probably, it was locked. But when I turned the brass knob, the door swung open easily. I stepped into blackness and felt my way to Fabrice's desk, where I switched on the light.

The room was a mess, though there was no evidence of any dress designing having been done, let alone the launching of a new Reign of

Elegance or a line of evening gowns in the colors of a bruise. There were no toiles to speak of. It looked less like a couturier's atelier than a war bunker. Newspapers and magazines were strewn about. Ashtrays overflowed with tobacco; empty bottles of wine were lined up on the floor.

Plastering an entire wall behind Fabrice's desk were clippings torn from newspapers and magazines. The couturier had arranged them in three groups under handwritten signs—IMPORTANT, NOT-SO-IMPORTANT, and IRRELEVANT. Some of the clippings were articles in which various phrases had been underlined; the others were fashion illustrations. All the items had to do with either Fabrice or Chanel. The couturier had devised this system to keep track of who was getting more publicity. But he had skewered it to deceive himself that he was winning. Chanel had twice as many items on the wall as Fabrice, but hardly any in the IMPORTANT section, which included the conservative journals *Les Élégances Parisiennes* and *Les Modes*. In the NOT-SO-IMPORTANT group were *Femina* and *L'Art et la Mode,* which virtually ignored both Fabrice and Chanel, and under IRRELEVANT, where Chanel had the most clippings, were *Vogue, Harper's Bazaar,* and *Women's Wear,* the American publications.

There were shopping bags scattered about, and I began rummaging through them, looking for my toiles. "Isabelle!" Someone shouted my name, and I turned around to see Fabrice in the middle of the room with Daniel. "What are you doing?" the couturier asked. He looked at me with a tightened jaw and waited for me to say something.

"I was looking for the water closet," I said.

"You're not going to find it in those shopping bags," said Daniel sternly.

"You're on the wrong end of the house," said Fabrice in an indulgent tone. "Can't you remember where it is?"

"I guess not."

Fabrice moved toward me and put his arms around me. "Poor thing. You've been working too hard."

Daniel turned and walked unsteadily away, his whole body drooping, as it always did when he was tired or upset.

Fifteen

s I rode the bus to church on Sunday morning, I kept playing the scene over in my head. I wanted to apologize to Daniel, but he didn't show up at Saint-Sulpice. Throughout mass, guilt and anger at myself filled my thoughts. After the service, I called him, and he agreed to let me come to his apartment. "Why didn't you go to church?" I asked, when I was standing in Daniel's doorway.

"I have a lot of work to do," he said. He stood with his fists jammed into his pockets. His eyes were cold.

"I'm sorry about last night."

"I assumed you'd had too much to drink. You weren't yourself."

"I guess that's true." I waited for him to invite me in, but he said nothing.

"Well, I just wanted to apologize. I never wanted to embarrass you."

"No need to." Daniel cocked his head in the direction of his study. "I better get back."

When I got home, I called Laurence from the concierge's apartment and asked her to meet me at the public bathhouse by the river at the end of my street. I thought a bath and some sympathetic company might cheer me up.

At the women's entrance, we each paid thirty centimes, and the attendant gave us towels and bars of soap as small and crumbly as pieces of nougat. At the top of the stairs, rows of private cells lined a steamy maze of hallways covered in cracked, gray tiles. Women, mostly from the lower classes and many with children in tow, wandered the halls, their voices loud and echoing. Ashes and cigarette butts covered the infrequently swept floor. Steam hissed through leaky pipes, and the air smelled of sweat and cleaning fluid.

In a small windowless cell, the changing area, I removed my clothes, hung them on a hook, and entered the adjoining bath. A long chain used to summon attendants hung from the ceiling next to a naked lightbulb; a glimmer of light filtered through a dusty netting covering the skylight. The attendants were supposed to clean the tubs after every use, but mine was filthy. The previous occupant had shaved her legs in it, and a film of black hairs circled the rim. I ran the water as hot as I could get it and rinsed the hairs down the drain. Afterward, I filled the tub and lowered myself in.

I closed my eyes, and I was a little girl again, floating in the lake in Timbaut on a warm summer evening, my hair swirling around my arms and torso. I hadn't trimmed it in several years now, and it reached to my hips—a fine gold curtain that I draped over my chest when I was naked so I didn't have to see my scars. I would never cut my hair, never. Short, it would be nothing; it would lie flat on my head like a schoolboy's bob. It was a pretty color, but so fine! It had no strength, unlike Mademoiselle's hair, which seemed to grow an inch every night like some wild black weed.

I sat soaking for a long time, oblivious to the bathhouse's twenty-minute time limit. The water cooled and the skin on my fingers turned bluish and began to shrivel. Out of the tub, I wrapped myself in a towel and squeezed the water out of my hair, then combed it carefully, removing every tangle. I loved its silky weight, the feeling of pulling it back and twisting it into a chignon, securing it with six pins and two mother-of-pearl combs—presents from my grandmother on my eighteenth birthday.

When I was dressed, I joined Laurence next door. Though hair dyeing was against bathhouse rules because the dye stained the tubs and tiles, Laurence had smuggled in a sack containing hennaing materials, and she asked me to wait with her while she colored her hair.

She sat on the edge of the tub in her chemise and drawers, the towel wrapped around her head. On the floor, a paintbrush plunged into a bowl holding bright green goo. "I have to sit here for an hour while the henna sets," she said. "I could have done it at my mother's. She's got a tub, but then I would have to haul the water upstairs myself from the pump in the courtyard." She adjusted the towel on her head. "How was your bath?"

"There were hairs in the tub."

"This place is horrible. Some day, I'll have a house with running water."

"Mademoiselle has two baths. One for herself and one for Monsieur Capel."

Laurence narrowed her eyes at me. "How do you know that?"

"I was at her house, remember?"

"Oh, yes. I forgot. You're the new favorite."

"I am not!"

"Sewing clothes for Mademoiselle's personal wardrobe makes you the favorite."

"It was just one dress."

Laurence shifted her position on the tub and looked at me with a sour expression. "Don't think I'm jealous," she said. "I'd be happy for you to have my job when I leave. I'm seriously thinking of taking a position at Lanvin. I know the manager over there, and she says she can get me in whenever I want."

"You'd leave before the opening?"

"Lanvin would pay me more. I'd get the première's salary that's been set by the Chambre Syndicale, which is twenty-five percent more than what Mademoiselle pays me."

"I'm broke, too."

"You think you're poor. I'm supporting myself *and* my mother.

Not to mention that she sends a little every month to her brother in Toulouse, who's out of work and needs an operation."

My bath had distracted me from my worries, but now the talk about money pushed the stolen toiles into my mind.

"I wonder how much someone was paid to steal our toiles?"

"Let's not talk about it," said Laurence, raising her hands to adjust the towel on her head.

"Did Tanguy ever find out anything from Charlie Spinelli?"

"I don't want to talk about it, Isabelle. It's depressing."

"What did Tanguy say?"

"I didn't tell him. I decided it was better not to. The fewer people who know, the better."

"Do you think your friend could get me in at Lanvin?"

"So now the little favorite wants to leave, too?" Laurence said sarcastically.

"Mademoiselle is going to find out about the toiles, and she's going to fire us," I said glumly.

"How do you know she's going to find out?"

"She just will. She knows everything."

"Like God?" Laurence snorted.

"It's uncanny."

"She's a gypsy huckster like all her people, and she's got that gypsy intuition."

A loud banging on the door was followed by the attendant's harsh voice. "Twenty minutes is the time limit. You must leave!"

"Don't pay any attention to her. She's not going to kick me out with my clothes off." Laurence sat with her arms across her stomach, drumming her foot. "All this show about how Mademoiselle is transforming the mode. What bull! A lot of what she claims to have started really was begun by Poiret. Just ask my mother; she was there when it happened before the war."

Laurence was silent for a minute, then she said, "When the fashion history books are written, Mademoiselle will be a footnote. She doesn't even know how to sew."

"The nuns taught her *something*."

"You think some old nuns in the provinces know couture technique? Please! What little she knows, she learned from your Madame Duval and the others she hired when she opened her shop in Deauville. She has style, I'll admit that. But her real talents are for self-promotion and cruelty." Laurence stood to stretch out her back and settled herself again on the enameled rim. "Do you know why I had to stay late last Thursday? During the *pose* Mademoiselle heard me say I had a rendezvous, so afterward, she called me to her office and kept me there until nine, helping her choose fabric." Laurence leaned toward me, and spoke in a tone filled with bitterness. "If it wasn't for the war, Mademoiselle would be nowhere. She got to build her business because the male couturiers had to close shop to fight for France."

"Yes, but she's shrewd. She saw her opportunity, and she knew how to take advantage of it."

"I still say it was mostly luck. And now with the toiles missing and Patou back in business maybe her luck is running out."

The clock on the bell tower of a nearby church clanged three o'clock. "Finally, I can rinse this out!" Laurence removed the towel from her head, and, bending deeply at the waist, leaned over the rim of the tub to stick her head under the faucet. A stream of hennaed water ran down, staining the porcelain. Laurence towel-dried her hair and removed a pocket mirror from her purse to examine her curls. They were the deep purple of ripe eggplant. "Tell me your honest opinion. Is it too artificial?"

"Maybe a little," I said.

"I'm not going through this again. I'll have to look like a *fille publique* for a while."

We were making our way down the hall to the exit when the attendant, an old woman in a gray smock, shouted after us, "Mamzelles, Mamzelles! Can't you read? Hair dyeing is not allowed! You must pay a fine!"

"Oh, God, let's get out of here," said Laurence. We darted to the end of the hall and down the stairs to the street.

*   *   *

Laurence was wrong; Mademoiselle's luck hadn't yet run out. The next day, employees from most of the other couture houses went out on strike, sending a windfall of new clients to Chanel.

On my way to work, I turned the corner onto rue de la Paix to see a small group of women gathering in front of Paquin's lowered iron curtain. By the time I went out to lunch at one, the street was mobbed. Knots of women chanting, "Eight hours! Eight hours!" marched with their fists in the air. Around them, the scene was festive. In front of Doucet, waiters from Café André, who themselves had been on strike a few weeks earlier, passed out champagne from large trays held on upturned palms. Farther down the street, under the awning at Worth, a soprano from the Paris Opéra serenaded the strikers with a Verdi aria. At Paquin, women danced to folk tunes played by an accordionist.

Since the armistice, strikes had been breaking out all over France. Now the troubles had hit the Chambre Syndicale de la Couture Parisienne, a private organization run by representatives from the top couture houses that set wage and work hour guidelines and organized the schedule for the collection openings. Mademoiselle had steadfastly refused to join the Chambre. It was abhorrent to her to follow anyone's rules but her own.

"How long do you think you'll be out?" I asked a young woman who was sitting on the curb in front of Paquin's, eating a croissant.

"Until they reduce the work day from ten to eight hours and give us half of Saturday off!"

"Ten hours would be nice. I work for Chanel, where it's more like twelve and fourteen hours these days."

The young woman swallowed a bite of croissant. "Chanel is the worst!"

The condition of the workers who sewed the dresses seemed to be of little concern to the women who wore them. By the time I returned to our atelier after lunch, the salon was mobbed. New clients crowded the chairs and settees; a few stood around the reception desk waiting to make appointments. As I passed through the salon, I saw women I'd never seen there before, but whose faces I recognized from their pictures—actresses, aristocrats, society beauties, the wives of politicians, and celebrated figures in the arts.

Near the staircase, I overheard two women in a heated debate discussing the merits of Jean Patou versus Mademoiselle. One of the women, a tall brunette, was devastated because the strike was preventing Patou from fulfilling her order for a blue suit. "It was exactly what I wanted to wear to the American ambassador's lunch next week," she said to her companion, a redhead with a curvy figure. "You saw it, remember? That navy serge model with the white godets sewn into the skirt and sleeves."

"You'll find something you'll like better here," said the redhead.

"I doubt that," said the brunette.

"Have an open mind! You've never even tried on a Chanel. Wait until you put on one of her evening dresses. You won't believe how they slide over your body, how wonderful they make you feel."

Upstairs in the studio, Mademoiselle looked happier than I'd seen her in weeks. "Did you see the salon?" she asked me. "There's no place to sit, and the phone's been ringing off the hook."

"Coco's got them all now!" said a small muscular blonde at Mademoiselle's side. Elsie Toule, better known as Caryathis, was an avant-garde dancer who ran a Montmartre school. Mademoiselle had taken lessons there when she'd first arrived in Paris and still imagined she might make a career on stage. The two women had become friends, and now Caryathis sometimes attended the *pose*.

Mademoiselle began fussing with a column of white chiffon covered with row upon row of fringe worn by a gray-eyed mannequin named Solange. When she was satisfied the dress looked right, Mademoiselle told Solange, "All right, let's see you move."

Solange began to walk across the studio, and the column of fringe moved with her, swaying slowly as if blown by a gentle breeze. Caryathis glided toward her, and grabbing Solange by the waist, twirled the mannequin in an impromptu dance, faster and faster, until the myriad silk strands on the girl's dress flew out in magnificent circular sweeps. "Now that's a dress that's alive!" cried Mademoiselle.

"Did it take longer than eight hours to sew it?" asked Caryathis. The dancer released Solange and sat on the floor among piles of fabric bolts, her legs tucked under her like a child.

"Actually about fifty hours," I said.

"You can't get anything done in eight hours," said Mademoiselle. "Ask any artist." She knelt on the floor to adjust Solange's hem. "And people want to know why I never joined the Chambre Syndicale. Because I'm not a moron, that's why! I'd never tolerate mutiny." She was on her feet again, hands on her hips. "Now, let's see how the cape looks over the dress." An assistant helped Solange into a taupe velvet cape trimmed in rabbit, while Mademoiselle chattered.

"Women on strike! Very alluring, isn't it, to see them marching up and down rue de la Paix with their fists in the air. If only they knew how ridiculous they looked! What does striking have to do with elegance?"

Caryathis and I exchanged glances. The dancer raised her eyebrows high, and they disappeared under her curtain of bangs. "This isn't about elegance, Coco. It's about decent hours and wages."

"You don't know what you're talking about. You've been doing too many headstands." As she talked, Mademoiselle's hands moved fast over the cape, molding it with her pins.

"How much are *you* paid?" Caryathis asked me.

"Enough," interrupted Mademoiselle. "The salaries here are good."

Caryathis rolled her eyes. "Is it so terrible for these girls to want a better life?"

"What a bore you've become," said Mademoiselle. "I don't want to hear anything more about strikes and wages. I'm trying to get ready for a collection."

Mademoiselle made a few final adjustments to Solange's cape, and the lovely mannequin disappeared behind the dressing screen. Another mannequin appeared, then another. As the beauties paraded before Mademoiselle in a series of dresses, she continued her monologue. "I believe in this gown. I could build a religion around it. . . .

Yes, that's for me. Finally, a dress, I'd actually wear. . . . That's a lucky one, and the woman who wears it will be lucky. . . . Take away some of the fullness on the hips. . . . No, that's not right yet. . . ."

Then came some coats and capes in brown wool, red satin, and gray jersey trimmed in fur. Régine appeared in a floor-length cape of black velvet drenched with ostrich feathers and tied at the collarbone with two tassled cords. "Now that's what I call a cape!" cried Mademoiselle. "Just the thing to wear to the opera next winter."

Caryathis, who'd been whispering with one of the mannequins at the back of the room, looked up and shouted, "Or to keep a girl warm on the picket lines!"

I couldn't wait for the strike to end. The business that had been diverted to Chanel because of the walkout only meant longer hours for us. But Mademoiselle was thrilled. Of all the new clients she'd picked up since the strike, she was most gleeful about dressing those of Jean Patou. She gloried especially in outfitting Louise de Rochas, an aristocratic young beauty who'd worn nothing but Patou since the war ended, and whose picture regularly appeared in the press. Louise went out almost every night to theaters, restaurants, receptions, and parties, and since she couldn't be seen and photographed in the same thing twice, she needed an endless supply of clothes.

Soon after the *pose*, Monique Thabard called me to the salon to fit Louise for a series of evening gowns. When I arrived, the young woman stood in front of the mirrors in a frothy pearl chiffon dress. She had shiny chocolate hair and large, wide-set blue eyes.

I dropped to my knees to adjust the hem, and when I'd finished, Louise said, "This is gorgeous, as beautiful as anything Patou has done. It feels wonderful, so light, almost like being naked."

"You will have to come here more often," said Monique. The thought of the commissions she would make off Louise had lit up her face.

I began to put away my pins as Louise continued to admire herself in the mirror. "Do you know why I go to Patou?" she asked.

"I don't, Madame," answered Monique.

"It's not that I like his clothes better than the other couturiers. It's because he lends me things."

"He lends you things?" said Monique.

Louise whipped around to face us directly. "You don't actually think I pay for all those clothes I'm photographed in?" She looked expectantly from Monique to me, then said in a grave tone, "Chanel has never offered to lend me a dress."

The brightness disappeared from Monique's face, as Louise added, "Maybe you could speak to her about it."

"I'll see what I can do," said the vendeuse.

"Oh, that would be lovely." Louise's eyes greedily scanned the pile of silk and satin on the settee and the beaded chiffon fantasies hanging from the hooks on the wall.

I went back to work, and two hours later, the phone rang with the urgent jangle it always seemed to make when the caller was Monique Thabard. "I lost three month's commission today!" she screeched at me.

"Mademoiselle let Rochas take those dresses?"

"Everything! The little vixen walked out of here with twenty thousand francs' worth of clothes!" she shouted, before slamming down the phone.

Patou was not one to accept losing even a minor skirmish. This was war, and when he heard that Louise de Rochas had defected to Chanel, he struck back by trying to hire away Mademoiselle's star mannequin, Yvette.

Our mannequins were famously underpaid, receiving only 200 francs a month, which was half of *my* pathetic salary. It was not enough to live on, and most of them depended on relatives for room and board. Periodically, Madame Georges pointed out to Mademoiselle the injustice of paying them so little and urged the couturière to increase their salaries. Mademoiselle refused. "Let their rich boyfriends support them," she scoffed.

Yvette's boyfriend, however, wasn't rich. She'd fallen in love with the American soldier she'd met at the Madro, and until the day when she hoped to marry him, she was living with her mother in a little cottage in Saint-Cloud. One evening, I was standing by the shelves looking for some fabric, when Yvette rushed into the workroom in tears and flung herself into my arms. "Patou has offered to double my salary!" she wailed.

"And you're crying? What's wrong with you?" I could feel the bony wings of her shoulders through her white smock.

"I don't want to leave Mademoiselle."

I didn't want her to leave, either. In the first place, Angeline had been fitted on her, and it would be hard to find another girl who looked as well in it for the opening. My initial impression that Yvette was too thin and angular for the dress had been wrong. Actually, she suited it perfectly. But Yvette would be foolish to turn down a doubled salary; I'd accept it myself in a minute.

The mannequin stopped crying and lifted her head to look at me. "I believe in the collection. I want to stay through the opening."

"Can you afford to turn down a doubled salary?"

"No."

She began sobbing again. I held her shoulders firmly and drew her away from me so I could look into her eyes. "Don't be a ninny. You should take Patou's offer. He isn't exactly a gentleman, but his clothes are wonderful, except for those stupid shepherdess dresses. If you behave coolly and professionally with him, you'll do fine."

"What do you mean, he's not a gentleman?"

I wasn't sure what Yvette had heard of the couturier's reputation, but I didn't want to talk about my own experiences with him. "He has an eye for the ladies, especially mannequins. So you need to be careful around him."

"You really think I should take his offer?"

"You're insane if you don't."

Still, I worried about Yvette. When Daniel called—this time it was *his* turn to apologize for treating me coldly after Fabrice's party—I told him my concern.

"Yvette's a Parisienne, she can take care of herself," Daniel said.

"It's you, the little provincial I'm worried about." His tone was teasing, affectionate.

"I hope I'll see you soon," I said.

"I'm on deadline. I have a story due at *The Dial* on July 2. Why don't we have dinner that night?"

"I'd like that."

"I'll see you then."

It took Yvette two days to get up the courage to tell Mademoiselle. At first, the couturière exploded, screaming at Yvette that she was a traitor. Then she calmed down and raised Patou's offer to Yvette by twenty-five francs. This started a bidding war that ended with Yvette agreeing to stay at rue Cambon for a salary of 500 francs a month, a colossal sum that Mademoiselle forever afterward resented having to pay. She made Yvette's life miserable, forcing the mannequin to stand for hours without a break during the *pose*. One afternoon, as Yvette shivered in her underwear, waiting to don her tenth toile of the day, Mademoiselle said, "Tell me, Yvette, how does it feel to be rich?"

Yvette's body trembled, as the other mannequins looked on enviously.

"Come on," taunted Mademoiselle. "What did you spend your millions on this week?"

Yvette's tears erupted in a single burst and she released a loud sob. Mademoiselle enjoyed that immensely.

As the strike wore on, the crowds in the street outside the couture houses slowly dwindled. Two weeks went by, and finally, seamstresses from houses belonging to the Chambre Syndicale accepted a modest increase in pay and a reduction in their daily hours from ten to nine with Saturday afternoons off. The salon at Chanel Modes et Coutures calmed down, as some of our new clients returned to their regular couturiers. Still, the darlings were as demanding as ever, and our workday continued to stretch to the grave. Twelve-hour days were not uncommon, even on Saturdays, as we struggled to fill orders.

So much new business had been diverted to Mademoiselle because of the strike that we'd run out of jersey for our most popular daytime models, and Mademoiselle had sent the arpètes to the storage room to fetch the bolts she'd been saving for the collection. When the girls got there, though, the jersey was gone. I found out about it during the *pose*. Mademoiselle was so furious she couldn't concentrate on anything else. "Everyone steals from me!" she ranted. "They'd take the sinks if they weren't cemented to the walls!"

After the *pose*, I called Madame Georges. "I think Madame Petrova has our jersey," I said.

"The Russian?"

"I saw a tower of jersey in her apartment. Why would Petrova take our fabric?"

"For the same reason she probably also has our toiles. Someone paid her to do it, to sabotage the collection," said Madame Georges.

"You think Petrova has the toiles?" I asked.

"Maybe. Why don't you go over there, see if you can get everything back."

After work, I took the metro to rue Blomet and knocked on Madame Petrova's door. She opened it a crack and peeked her head out. "The embroidery isn't ready yet," she said.

"I'm not here about the embroidery. It's the jersey."

"What jersey? We don't have any jersey."

"The last time I was here, I saw bolts of jersey stacked in a corner." Madame Petrova stared at me and said nothing.

"The jersey Mademoiselle ordered from the collection is missing."

"I didn't take your jersey," said Madame Petrova.

"Please, if you have Mademoiselle's jersey"—here I paused meaningfully and looked hard at Madame Petrova—"or *anything* else of hers, just return it to me. I promise I won't tell Mademoiselle."

"I don't know what you're talking about," said Madame Petrova.

"Think about it," I said and walked away.

* * *

I heard nothing from Madame Petrova, but one afternoon the following week, I entered the studio to find her deep in conversation with Mademoiselle over a box sitting on the couturière's desk. "You cannot miss your deadlines," said Mademoiselle. "It is *insupportable!*"

"Is Mademoiselle unhappy with the work?" Madame Petrova lifted a black satin rectangle embroidered in white and red silk from the box. "See, how gorgeous this is," she said.

"I don't care how gorgeous it is. If it is two weeks late, it doesn't do me any good."

"Is it not worth waiting a bit for this?" Madame Petrova reached into the box to retrieve the front of a white blouse embroidered in an elaborate, brilliantly colored floral pattern.

"No!" Mademoiselle banged her hand on the desk. Madame Petrova flinched.

"If Mademoiselle would permit me to explain . . ." Madame Petrova began, but Mademoiselle wouldn't permit it.

"Explain what? That your order is late because you've hired workers who don't know their behinds from their noses? Do you understand what's at stake here, how important my collection is? I am creating the look of the twentieth century!" Mademoiselle leaned across her desk and pointed her chin toward the back of the room where I stood, awkwardly observing the scene. "Mademoiselle Varlet has told me about your operation, about the graduates of Saint Catherine's School for Noblewomen whom you're trying to turn into brodeuses."

"My girls need the work. They'll starve without it."

"And I'll starve if I continue to use you!"

This last bit of hyperbole put a spark of life into Madame Petrova's heavy-lidded eyes. "With all due respect, Mademoiselle, I don't think that's true."

Mademoiselle stared hard at her for a moment, then lit a cigarette, blowing a jet of smoke into the old woman's face. "You are hardly the only brodeuse in Paris," the couturière said. "I've got them lining up for the honor of working with me. Good day."

There was nothing left for the vanquished Petrova to do but retreat. She backed away from Mademoiselle's desk and without looking at me, fled the studio.

After exacting a promise from Madame Bataille that she would drop Jean Patou as a client and never stitch so much as the corner of a collar for him again, Mademoiselle sent the rest of the collection's embroidery order to the Frenchwoman.

When I told Madame Georges about it, she moaned, "Now we'll never find our jersey or our toiles."

Sixteen

"Were some toiles stolen from your workroom?" Monique Thabard looked at me expectantly as we stood in a fitting room rehanging clothes that had just been fitted on Elisabeth de Gramont, one of the vendeuse's richest clients.

"Where did you hear that?" I asked, trying to sound nonchalant.

"Everyone's talking about it." Monique plopped onto the settee holding a velvet dress with a fringed hem. It deflated in her lap with a soft sigh.

"Does Mademoiselle know?" My heart nearly stopped.

"I don't think so."

"Thank God."

"So it's true." Monique had wrapped the dress's sash around her left wrist, and she was plucking the pile from the velvet with nervous jerks.

"What do you hear?" I asked.

"That Susanna Lawson is behind it. She's been stealing from Mademoiselle since she got here, selling old models from the storage room at greatly reduced prices."

"I hear she also sells new models out of her apartment and gives free clothes to her friends in exchange for favors."

Monique's plucking had left a bald spot on the velvet sash. "Look what you've done!" I cried.

"I'm such a wreck," moaned Monique. "I have too much to worry about with the spring orders. I don't want to have to worry about some stolen toiles, too."

"Don't worry about it. It's my problem—and Laurence's. The toiles came from our workroom."

"You don't work on commission. Those dresses mean money to me!"

I looked hard at her. "Do you really think Susanna Lawson is responsible?" I asked.

"Yes. And so does everyone else." Monique handed me the velvet sash. "You don't mind making a new one, do you, Isabelle?"

Over the next few days, I looked for an excuse to visit the baroness's workroom. She wouldn't be so stupid as to keep our toiles there, but I thought I might see or hear something that would lead me to the purloined muslins. My opportunity came one morning after Susanna borrowed a box of buttons from us, and Laurence sent me to retrieve it. I found the Englishwoman talking on the phone, and while I waited for her to finish her conversation, I strolled around the tables, listening to the seamstress's chatter, peering into shelves and *myons*. I was casually searching through a pile of muslin at the back of the room when a young arpète dashed in carrying several large shopping bags from Galeries Lafayette. Mademoiselle ignored the education laws, and I was used to seeing underage girls working in the house, but this child looked barely older than ten. She overturned the bags on the table, and dozens of fabric hats of various shapes and sizes tumbled out. The seamstresses picked through them, selecting a few to take back to their tables.

"Excuse me, what are you doing with those hats?" I asked one woman.

"We'll pretty them up a bit with ribbons and feathers and give them to Baroness Lawson," she said. Then, lowering her voice, "She sends them to a shop owned by one of her friends where they're sold for five times the Galeries Lafayette price."

A phone slammed down with a loud crack, and Susanna called to me. "What do you want?" She'd been overusing the curling iron, and her hair looked like burnt wheat, the ends singed as if held to a fire.

"The buttons you borrowed."

"On top of the file cabinet."

I grabbed the box of buttons and went straight to Madame Georges's office. When I told her what Susanna was doing with the Galeries Lafayette hats, the house manager sighed. "I'm not surprised. I suppose I have to tell Mademoiselle."

"I suppose you do," I replied.

At the *pose* that afternoon, Susanna Lawson looked tense. Her hard eyes and the grim set of her mouth told me that Madame Georges had already chastised her about the hats. Régine stepped in front of the triple mirrors in one of the Englishwoman's wool suits. Mademoiselle walked slowly around the mannequin. "Come here, Lawson," she barked. When the baroness stood in front of her, Mademoiselle said, "I'm transferring you to millinery."

"I don't understand . . . I . . ." stammered Susanna.

Mademoiselle took a drag on her cigarette and blew the smoke out in a long, hissing jet. "Since you like hats so much, you can stay with them until you die!"

Susanna's body was rigid; her face white. She seemed frozen in place, like a statue.

"Go on!" shouted Mademoiselle. "That hats are waiting!"

As Susanna dashed from the room, Laurence whispered to me, "It takes one to know one."

"What do you mean?" I asked.

Laurence leaned toward me and lowered her voice further. "When Mademoiselle started as a milliner and was desperate to make a profit, she sometimes bought inexpensive department store hats, which she sold as her own creations for high prices."

"I don't believe it."

"Where do you think Susanna got the idea?"

Later that day, I was cutting out a black wool suit that was to be sent to Madame Bataille, when Mademoiselle called. "I need you to go to Biarritz for Antoinette's fitting," she said.

With Susanna Lawson exiled to millinery, the job of finishing Antoinette Chanel's wedding gown had fallen to me. "Now?" I asked.

"Tonight."

This was the evening of my dinner with Daniel. I didn't want to miss it. "Maybe I could come down tomorrow. I've got a lot of work to finish here."

"Tonight, Varlet."

Antoinette, apparently, couldn't be bothered to come to Paris for another fitting, so the plan was for me to take a train that evening and meet the Chanel sisters at the Biarritz atelier the following morning. "I'll bring the dress with me in the car," Mademoiselle told me. "I'd give you a ride, but I have André with me. He's got a little vacation, and he's spending the weekend with Antoinette."

André was the young nephew of Mademoiselle and Antoinette, the son of their sister Julia who'd died during the war. André's father, an itinerant peddler, couldn't take care of the child, so Mademoiselle had enrolled him in boarding school in England.

Reluctantly, I sent Daniel a petit bleu cancelling dinner and boarded an overnight train for Biarritz. I arrived the next morning, a bright sunny Friday. From the station, I could see the tower of the château that housed Chanel Coutures, and I set off in that direction on a long white road that stretched to the beach. The air was filled with salty ocean smells, and the tile roofs of stucco villas gleamed above forbidding dark cliffs. In the distance, the sea rolled away to the horizon, tranquil and blue. Maybe it was the sea air, or just putting some distance between myself and Paris. Suddenly, I was less anxious about the toiles.

Soon, I stood in front of a small stone castle opposite the town's massive, crenelated casino. A gold plaque announced Chanel Coutures. Here in 1915, when the enemy was at the gates of Paris, when people who had money and still cared about pleasure and elegance fled to Biarritz, Mademoiselle had opened a bona fide maison de couture. Throughout the war, she'd supplied clothes to a steady clientele of prosperous women from across the border in neutral Spain, to the girlfriends of war profiteers, and the wives of military officials on leave who gambled every night at the casino and danced at the Miramar, as if the world was at peace.

A tall man in a gold braided uniform opened the door, and I stepped into a large cool foyer, empty except for a receptionist behind a desk. The decorations in the salon beyond recalled rue Cambon, with the same pale carpets and sofas, embroidered pillows, and an ostrich feather fan unfurled across a polished table. Vitrines held gloves, hats, shoes, purses, scarves, and an assortment of knitted beach costumes.

The receptionist told me to wait while she called Antoinette. A moment later, Mademoiselle's sister appeared wearing a white marquisette dress as thin as handkerchief linen. "Mademoiselle Varlet! So good of you to come." Antoinette took my hand, clasping it in both of hers.

"Is Mademoiselle here?"

"She's with the premières. The dress is in the fitting room."

I followed Antoinette down a long wide corridor flooded with sunlight from tall windows to a large square dressing room. The wedding gown hung from a hanger on a wall hook. As I buttoned Antoinette into it, a child's laughter erupted in the hallway, followed by the sound of running feet. A moment later, Mademoiselle opened the door and entered the fitting room, gasping for breath. "I told André to stay in the courtyard, but he's running up and down the hall. I tried to catch him, but he's fast!"

"It's all right. No one's in the salon," said Antoinette. Then, turning to me, "Everyone in Biarritz sleeps until noon."

Another childish whoop pierced the air.

"What a character that kid is," said Mademoiselle. "I took him to tea at Angelina's. Sitting next to us was a faubourg dowager with ropes of pearls draped on the biggest pigeon bosom I've ever seen. André couldn't take his eyes off it. He stared at it for a half hour. Finally, he announced in a voice loud enough for the entire room to hear, 'Tante Gabby, that lady has some bosom!'"

The sisters laughed. "He says whatever comes into his head. Just like Julia," sighed Antoinette, her expression darkening. Then she caught her reflection in the mirror, and the darkness lifted. "Didn't Mademoiselle Varlet do a beautiful job?"

Mademoiselle scanned the dress. "It looks good, Varlet, but I'd like it a bit snugger in the shoulders," she said, marking with pins where she wanted the adjustment.

The day passed quickly. By the time I'd finished work on Antoinette's gown, the light outside had turned pale silver, and the sweet smell of night-blooming jasmine floated through the windows. I worked a strand of my hair into the gown's hem, then snipped a tiny square of a seam and dropped it into the pocket of my smock to add later to my stash of souvenirs.

That evening, I ate at a café, then strolled the boardwalk, as a black mass of waves slapped against the cliffs. Passing one of the more modest hotels, I rented a room and slept late the next morning. After dressing, I went down to the beach. The sun was hot and shimmered over the long stretch of sand, dotted here and there with black-and-white striped tents. Men and women in street clothes sat on folding chairs reading the paper. Children darted about, some searching for shells in the receding waves. Young women paraded by. Many of them wore morning costumes from Mademoiselle's salon that were as spare as bathing suits—little knee-length shifts, cut deep under the armpits and loosely sashed around their hips. On their feet they wore beige flats with black toe caps.

Passing the pier, I saw Mademoiselle and Boy Capel. They lay on a blanket on the sand, propped up on their elbows. The sun baked my face, and I wished I had a hat. Barefoot, I wandered along the beach.

I walked for a long time, until the boardwalk ended and there was nothing but the unwinding ribbon of sand, the craggy cliffs, and the water. The sea air made me hungry and walking back along the boardwalk, I found a café with tubs of bright red geraniums flanking the door.

I sat down with my newspaper and ordered an omelette and a glass of wine. Afterward, I wandered back to the beach. Boy Capel was gone, but Mademoiselle hadn't moved. She lay on her stomach on the blanket staring out at the sea. Lying there, watching André chase a retreating wave, she seemed less fearsome than she did in Paris. I trudged through the sand to her side. "I want to thank you for giving me this opportunity," I said. "I've enjoyed seeing Biarritz and, of course, it's a treat to have Saturday off."

She squinted at me, shading her eyes from the sun with her hand. "For God's sake, Varlet, don't tell anyone you had the day off. I'll have a mutiny on my hands."

"Tante Gabby! Tante Gabby!" André shouted as he clamored up the sand to Mademoiselle's side. He dropped his little shovel and pointed to a coal barge in the distance. "Our boat."

"That's Boy's," said Mademoiselle, her voice sharp with irritation.

"But he said you were engaged to him."

"When did he say that?"

"After Mama died."

"That was a while ago. He doesn't mean it anymore."

"Why not?"

Mademoiselle flopped over, turning her back on the child and the boats and the pleasant blue sea. "He's married to someone else."

That afternoon, I boarded a train, but instead of riding it all the way to Paris, I stopped in Timbaut to visit Madame Duval and attend the unveiling of the village war memorial. I arrived at the train depot in Agen in early evening. A warm breeze fluttered the leaves on the chestnut trees lining Avenue de la République, but the town looked dismal.

Many of the shops had closed permanently, their fronts boarded up. A few widows strolled the sidewalks arm in arm; old men sat on crates smoking and playing chess. I saw several young women, but almost no young men.

I walked past Jacques' patisserie and Madame Duval's shop, both now empty, the awnings ripped and streaked with dirt for having been neglected all winter. At the taxi stand, a slight, pleasant-faced driver took my bag and carried it to his car. I followed him, and as he opened the door for me, a thin middle-aged woman with graying brown hair ran out of the boulangerie. She grabbed the man by the arm. "Robert! My own son!" she cried.

Gently, he withdrew from her, and holding her elbows, stared into her face.

"Don't you recognize your own mother?" she whispered.

"Madame, I don't . . ."

A young woman darted out of the boulangerie and ran to her side. "Mama, please, let's go."

"I want Robert to come with us."

The young woman held her mother's shoulders and tried to lead her away. But the mother planted her feet in the street and stared at the driver. A deep vertical crevice marred her brow; her eyes were so light they looked almost transparent. "Won't you come to lunch?" She turned to me. "Is this your girl? Bring her, too."

"We have an appointment," the driver said quietly.

"Then you'll come later. This afternoon."

The woman reached up to hold his face in her hands. "Good boy. You were always such a good boy."

The driver let her caress his face for a minute. Then he removed her hands and placed them at her sides. "Good-bye," he said softly.

"Thank you for your kindness," said the daughter. She had a lovely voice. "Let's go, Mama," she said.

"I'm sorry about that," said the driver, as he helped me into the taxi. "She thinks I'm her dead son."

"Did you know him?"

"Yes. A nice boy. Killed in the trenches. He looked nothing like me."

It was difficult to avoid crying when I saw Madame Duval. Her own eyes overflowed as she hugged me tight, and it was only the distraction of her ill-fitting dress—a blue chemise that she wore without a corset, revealing all the lumps and bulges of her fifty-six years—that kept me from sobbing. Later, as we ate dinner in her dining room with the copper pots lining a high shelf above a mural of Versailles, Madame Duval told me the woman in the street was a former client of hers. "Poor thing, she's been out of her mind for a year, since Robert died. She thinks every young man she meets is her son."

Madame Duval had prepared a *pot au feu*, and, in honor of my visit, had set the table with her good china and silver. "Veronique, the daughter, takes good care of her mother," she said. "You used to play with Veronique when you were little."

But I could not remember that, and when I shut my eyes, only Jacques appeared. In Paris, I didn't think about him as much, and I never dreamed about him anymore. Being home reminded me that my memories of him were fading, and now I felt sad and guilty.

After supper, Madame Duval and I sat on the terrace drinking coffee and gossiping about Mademoiselle. I thought of telling her about the stolen toiles, then decided against it—why worry her? I'd brought her small samples of the fabrics we were using in the collection and the little square of satin from Antoinette's gown.

"If I still had a shop, I'd like to do something with this," she said, holding up a thin slice of blue silk.

"You'd have no trouble finding clients if you came back," she told me. "Someone with Parisian experience would do very well here."

"You were the one who pushed me to leave, and now you want me to come back?"

Madame Duval lifted the white linen napkin from her lap, folded it into a small square, and placed it on the table. She had aged. The hollow pits under her cheekbones had deepened, and sharp etchings divided her neck into three distinct cylinders. "I miss you, Isabelle," she said. "It's lonely, especially now that the shop is gone."

"Everything is gone."

"It'll come back. We need more young people here. Remember when you marry, have a family, this wouldn't be a bad place to settle."

"When I was planning to marry Jacques, you thought staying here was the worst idea in the world."

Madame Duval looked at me hopefully. "Tell me about Daniel. How are you two getting on?"

"We're friends, that's all," I told her. "I think he's seeing someone."

"Who?" she looked crushed.

"I don't know who she is. I saw them together in the street."

"He never said anything to me about it."

"He wouldn't."

"You probably imagined it."

"Also, once when I was at his house, a woman came over who I think was a . . . professional."

"A professional?"

"You know . . ."

Madame Duval looked shocked, and I regretted mentioning it. "Daniel with a prostitute? At the apartment? Really, Isabelle, you *are* imagining things."

"Daniel said she was helping him go through his father's papers, but she seemed more like a *fille publique* than a librarian. Very hard looking, with dyed black hair and vulgar clothes. They disappeared for a half hour, and when Daniel joined me again, he looked like he'd been tumbling around in bed."

Madame Duval sighed heavily. "I suppose I have to tell you, though it will ruin the surprise."

"What surprise?"

"That woman is Josephine Martine. Her father was a friend of Blank *père*. They have an antique store in the sixth, and they recently returned from Japan with a stash of ancient kimonos in the most exotic silks. Daniel bought one for you."

"I don't believe it."

"When he got it home, he discovered a small tear in the sleeve.

Mademoiselle Martine was picking it up for repair. Daniel told me about it in his last letter."

I smiled, delight filling my entire body.

"The fabric apparently is extraordinary. Daniel thought it would thrill you to make a dress out of it."

After the last plates were stored in Madame Duval's cupboard, I set out for my grandmother's house, walking past the familiar fields with grazing cows and sheep and the oblong lake where I'd once swum on hot afternoons. As I walked, I held a brown envelope of pictures that Madame Duval had given me for Daniel. When I reached the old stone church, I sat on the steps and studied them. The old prints showed a little girl of about ten whom I assumed was Daniel's mother—her narrow face and light eyes were exactly likely his.

Behind the church, I found the graves of my relatives and Jacques and pulled at the weeds that had grown up around their headstones. Then, leaving the cemetery, I set out on the old road, finally coming upon our cottage at the top of the hill. It was a shock to see it. The paint on the front door was peeling. One of the windows was cracked; the others were streaked with dirt. The garden, once lovely, had become a jumble of weeds and dry earth.

I pushed the door open and stepped inside. Everything was just as I had left it. In the kitchen, a brown circle from a cup of tea I'd spilled still stained the white lace tablecloth. Jacques' bicycle still leaned against the wall, and my grandmother's bonnet still hung on a hook by the sink, its ribbons neatly tied.

In my grandmother's bedroom, I opened the wardrobe and removed my mother's silk dress. As a child, it had seemed to me the most beautiful garment I'd ever seen, a dress fit for the wonderful life I was sure my mother had lived. Looking at it now, I saw that it was shapeless and dowdy. The burgundy color had begun to fade, and the hem was fraying. It was a sad, provincial dress, and so, probably, had been my mother's life.

My bedroom looked smaller and shabbier than I'd remembered, the blue cotton curtains faded and worn, the ceiling low, the table in the corner that served as my desk, scarred and wobbly, the wood chair next to it barely large enough for a child. The linen, lace-trimmed nightgown my grandmother had made for me one Christmas, years before, lay across the old iron bed. One of the pintucks in front had begun to unravel, but the others were pristine, and in the even, meticulous stitches I felt the fierceness of my grandmother's love. I slipped the nightgown on and, laying down on the bed, cried until I fell asleep.

In the morning, I left my grandmother's house and started for the village, taking an old path that wound through the woods past meadows and farmers' fields. A cavalcade of clouds appeared in the sky, and I could smell rain in the humid air. The path opened onto the road leading to Timbaut. Pony traps and handcarts clattered by, and a lone car sped past, scattering a flock of sheep who'd come down from the hills with their owner. I entered the village on the east end of the ancient cobblestone square. The war memorial stood opposite city hall in the dark shade of an immense oak. It had just been completed, and the mayor had decided to dedicate it now, rather than wait for the official day of remembrance in November. I searched for Jacques' name among the fifty-two engraved in the tall stone obelisk and found it near the bottom. I ran my fingers across the etched letters and felt a sharp yearning. Soon, Madame Duval arrived, and we joined the crowd gathered around the memorial.

At nine o'clock, the bell in the church tower clanged, and a line of children, each holding a blue cornflower, trooped out of the schoolhouse at the end of the square. A weak rain began to fall, and two old men, veterans of the Prussian war, carried tricolors up to the memorial. The mayor nodded his head, and the first child, a little boy of seven with carefully combed hair and brightly polished shoes, stepped forward. In a soft, thin voice, he read the first name from the roster of casualties. *"Mort pour la patrie,"* intoned his classmates. The boy stepped back in line, and another child, this time a little girl in a crisply starched dress, came forward to read the second name. *"Mort pour la patrie,"* repeated the children. And so it went until the names of all fifty-two dead men had been read. Then, starting for the schoolhouse, the children tossed their flowers on the monument's base and marched away silently, leaving behind them the weeping adults and the wet, gray morning.

Seventeen

When I boarded the train for Paris that afternoon, a fresh wave of grief washed over me. It was as if everyone I loved had just died. A great sob rose in my chest, but I thought of Angeline and willed it away. As the train rumbled through the countryside, I concentrated on how I would sew the final version of my dress, how I would achieve perfection with my scissors and needles. Every stitch of Angeline would be flawless.

My fifth toile for the model was on the schedule for Monday's *pose*. I did not expect Mademoiselle to approve it; I thought I'd be making toiles for Angeline into eternity. But when Yvette stepped into the studio wearing the muslin dress, Mademoiselle cried in delight, "I told you it could be done, Varlet. If you can capture this gracefulness with the finished model, I'll be very happy."

The hardest part was over. I'd conquered the proportions and lines of the model. Now all I had to do was translate from humble muslin into elegant crepe de chine. Because I was so busy, Laurence wanted to assign the dress to a group of senior and junior *mains*, but I insisted on sewing the finished model myself, starting that afternoon. I pulled the toile apart, and using the deracinated rectangles as my pattern, attached them with small thread tacks to a length of burgundy crepe de chine laid out across the worktable. Being careful to allow enough fabric for generous seam allowances, I cut out the dress. When that was done, I laid out the pieces across the table, snipped the thread tacks and lifted the muslin from the crepe de chine.

I waxed and ironed a long piece of burgundy thread and fastened it with a knot, which I made as small and inconspicuous as possible— half the size of a head of a pin—so it would be virtually invisible. Now, I was ready to begin. As I assembled the dress over the course of the next several days, I made thousands of stitches, most of which were preliminary and ended up being ripped out. I did all the work myself, except for the bodice lining, which I gave to one of the *mains*. Another *main* had the task of reassembling the muslin toile, which would become the master blueprint to be used after the opening for making copies of the dress for our clients and the buyers.

Slowly, the dress began to take shape—the bodice—with its gathered sides and low back, and the skirt, a large rectangle with long narrow triangles sewn into the sides to form the cascades. After the fourth day, the dress was done. Now, all that was left was to overcast the seams and raw edges, with small, close stitches to prevent unraveling. Starting with the seams of the skirt and making my way to the left side, then to the bodice, I made slanted stitches, 1.5 millimeters deep and 1.5 millimeters apart, over all of Angeline's raw edges. Overcasting seals the dress against time and the vagaries of fate. It is the varnish on the oil painting, the glaze on the apple tart.

What is more important than making the center hold? If God had overcast Creation, there would be no earthquakes or erupting volcanoes, no avalanches or floods, no hurricanes and no tornadoes. If thought could be overcast, all demons would be held at bay. We'd be strong and true forever, our love and faith never unraveling.

I sent the dress to the studio, and when I arrived myself a few minutes later, Yvette was wearing it, standing in front of the triple mirrors. As familiar as I was with every millimeter of Angeline, as many toiles as I had sewn and taken apart and sewn again, it was a revelation to see the finished garment on a live mannequin. "If there's no woman, there's no dress," I heard Mademoiselle say many times. Yvette made Angeline come alive. When you saw her in it, you knew that was how you wanted to look. Like all good fashion, Angeline celebrated the moment. It caught the spirit and freshness of the present. It was a modern dress, a dress to wear into a new century.

A group of fitters gathered around Yvette, murmuring admiration. *What a beautiful line. Those cascades are so pretty. I wish it was my dress.* Mademoiselle had been watching Yvette intently. Now she rose from her cushion near the fireplace and walked slowly around the mannequin, inspecting Angeline from every angle. "Good job, Varlet," she said, finally. "Good job."

I felt a spike of elation, but tried to keep my face composed. My grandmother always told me to keep my emotions as even as possible. If you learned not to soar too high during triumphs, she said, you wouldn't sink too low in times of trouble.

Eighteen

The day after I returned from Agen, I called Daniel to tell him about Madame Duval's pictures, but there was no answer. I called again the next day, and the day after that. Still nothing. When he failed to show up at Saint-Sulpice on Sunday, I began to grow concerned. Immediately after mass, I took a taxi to Daniel's apartment. The elevator was out, so I climbed the stairs and pounded on his door. "It's Isabelle," I cried. "Open up!"

I waited a moment, then ran downstairs to ring the concierge's bell. A middle-aged man in a suit answered. In the dining room behind the foyer, his family were enjoying lunch. Clinking glassware. The smell of poultry and potatoes. "I'm a friend of Daniel Blank's. I'm worried about him. He's not answering his phone or the door," I said.

The concierge's expression turned grave. "Monsieur Blank has been ill."

"Ill?" My voice came out in a desperate gasp.

"Some kind of infection. The doctor was here yesterday."

"Did he go to the hospital?"

"I don't think so," said the concierge.

He disappeared into the dining room and said something to his family. When he returned, he held a large ring clattering with keys. "Let's see if he's all right."

At the top of the stairs, the concierge opened the door to Daniel's apartment, and a blast of fetid air wafted across my face. "Daniel!" I called out. I dropped the envelope with Madame Duval's pictures on a table and hurried from room to room, turning on lights. In the hallway outside Daniel's bedroom, his wooden leg lay against the baseboard, cracked in several places, the shoe and sock missing. I found Daniel in bed, delirious but alive. The bedclothes had fallen off him, and he lay in his underclothes, pale and thin, the sad stump of his leg deathly purple. A new wound oozed blood from his scar, and a week's growth of beard darkened his face, erasing his freckles. It was as if he'd already slipped away, and I couldn't bear it. "Call the doctor!" I screamed at the concierge.

I pulled the covers over Daniel and pressed a moistened towel to his brow, as my grandmother did for me when I was feverish. The doctor arrived within the hour, a short, stout man in a gray flannel coat that was too warm for the weather. "It looks like he's taken a turn for the worse," said the doctor in a flat tone, as he sat on Daniel's bed and removed a stethoscope from his bag.

The concierge by this time had returned to his family, and I waited alone in the salon, while the doctor examined Daniel. A half hour went by, and then the doctor appeared in the doorway. "Are you his sister?" he asked.

"No, friend." I flung aside the magazine I'd been nervously flipping through.

"He needs an operation on his leg."

"What happened to him?"

"A few days ago he fell from a chair he was using as a stepladder to reach a box on top of a cupboard. He said he was looking for paper. The prosthetic cracked, and a broken edge pierced the stump. It's become infected, which is why he's so sick. But the stump was in bad shape before that. The first time I examined him, I noticed a piece of exposed bone that was hindering his healing. That's why he was in so much pain."

"He didn't complain much."

"He's a soldier."

I walked the doctor to the door. "I've called an ambulance. It'll be here soon," he said.

During the following days, I pushed through the motions at work, as if under anesthesia myself. I listened to Mademoiselle's instructions. I discussed facings and pleats, sleeves, and pockets. I assembled toiles and ripped them apart and assembled them again. But my mind and heart were at the hospital with Daniel.

The operation was done on Friday morning, and I visited Daniel that evening. A driving rain had begun to fall on my way to the hospital, and by the time I arrived, the huge square building glistened in drizzle. My steps echoed through the bare hallways, harshly lit with naked white bulbs and filled with the sickroom smells of chemicals and disinfectant. The bleak surroundings brightened, though, when I found Daniel sitting up, looking weak but well enough to chat with the nurse who'd brought him a bowl of soup. I returned every evening for the next ten days, and spent all of Sunday at his bedside. I brought Daniel books, treats from the patisserie, some oranges and even smuggled in a bottle of red wine, which we shared one evening.

"This is no life for a young girl, spending your free time visiting a cripple in the hospital," said Daniel, sipping his wine.

"You won't be in the hospital forever," I said.

Daniel laughed bitterly. "But I'll always be a cripple."

I glanced at his bony form under the meager blanket, lingering on the hollow where his leg should have been. An image of his younger self running through the marché in Timbaut flashed in my mind.

When I'd walked in, I'd found Daniel flipping through a catalogue his doctor had given him, Arnaud Baudot's *Guide to Artificial Limbs and Their Uses,* and now he pointed to an illustration of a man walking on a tightrope with an artificial leg. "Look at this," said Daniel. "And the doctor thinks I'm reckless for standing on a chair."

"It's all relative," I said, then, pointing to the catalogue. "Are you shopping for a new leg?"

Daniel threw the catalogue aside. "No. I've had it with that fancy contraption. I'm getting a peg."

"You're going to hobble around like a pirate? Very elegant," I said.

"You sound like Chanel." Daniel folded his arms across his chest and leaned his head against the pillows. "What does it matter? I'm home alone most of the time anyway."

"But when you do go out, a peg just draws more attention. . . ." I couldn't continue.

"To what? The fact that I don't have a leg? If I'm not embarrassed by it, you shouldn't be."

"Monsieur Blank needs his medicine. I'm afraid you'll have to leave." A nurse, an older woman with gray tendrils sprouting from her white cap, appeared by Daniel's bed. I wanted to embrace him, but felt shy in front of the nurse, so I squeezed Daniel's hand.

"Good night," I said.

"Good night."

Later that evening, I called Madame Duval from the concierge's apartment.

"I can't believe you didn't tell me immediately," she said.

"I thought about it, but decided it was best not to worry you."

"You're sure he's all right?"

"He'll be all right," I said. "He goes home in a few days."

"I'm coming to Paris."

"He told me to tell you not to."

"He needs me."

"I know. He needs me, too."

Madame Duval arrived in town on July 13, the morning Daniel

was released from the hospital. The doctor had wanted to keep him a few more days, but Daniel insisted on being home for Bastille Day and the grand victory parade that was planned to celebrate the signing of the peace treaty the previous month.

After getting Daniel settled at his apartment, Madame Duval came to 31, rue Cambon, where I met her in the salon. Her eyes grew wide, as she scanned the large, high-ceilinged rooms, the over-groomed women on the plush settees, the imperious black-clad vendeuses trailing the scent of money.

"I didn't expect such luxury," she said. "I had no idea Mademoiselle had gotten so far."

"Would you like to see anything? Any of the new models?"

Madame Duval shook her head no. "Before you came down, I called Mademoiselle, but I didn't get through."

"She's very busy. The collection is looming, and the holiday has everything backed up."

"I'd like to see her."

"I'm sure she'll call you. Did you leave Daniel's number?"

"Yes."

That evening, I joined Madame Duval and Daniel for dinner in Daniel's apartment. He greeted me at the door looking amazingly strong despite the ungainly leather strap reaching across his shoulders and the side of his body to fasten around a black painted peg. "You look great," I said.

Daniel smiled. "I've astonished everyone."

Madame Duval had prepared a bouillabaisse and for dessert there were pastries from my childhood—lemon tarts, *coeurs à la crème,* éclairs, and almond cookies—that Madame Duval had carried from Agen on the train. After coffee, Daniel hobbled off to his study, and when he returned, he placed in front of me a bundle of papers— proofs of his new book. The first page was a dedication—"To the memory of Horace Nathaniel Blank, my father." On the following page appeared a poem titled "Requiem." It began:

The mind stops
Petals of soul
Drift through the uncaring air

"I wrote it soon after my father died. The first lines came to me in a dream," Daniel said. He looked at Madame Duval. "Did you tell Isabelle what happened to him?"

"He committed suicide," she said flatly.

"Suicide?" I was shocked.

"Because he thought *I* was going to die," Daniel explained. "After I lost my leg, I was in a hospital on the front for a while. I developed a high fever that wouldn't go down, and I was slipping in and out of consciousness. My father hounded the authorities until they agreed to send me back to Paris. I was in the hospital for two months, but I was only getting worse.

"The doctor kept telling my father I was going to die, and, finally, one night he called Papa and a priest to my bedside. Three hours into the death watch, after the priest had administered the last rites, Papa walked out of the hospital. He passed a nurse who heard him muttering, 'I can't live without Daniel, I can't live without Daniel.' He took a taxi to Pont Neuf, filled the pockets of his coat with stones and threw himself into the Seine. Two days later my fever broke, and a week after that I was home hobbling around on crutches." Daniel knuckled a drop of moisture from the corner of his eye, and that one errant tear nearly broke my heart.

The clock over the mantel chimed midnight, and I stood to leave. "You can't go until I give you your present," said Daniel.

He disappeared into the back of the apartment and returned a minute later with a large box. I opened the lid and lifted out a gorgeous white silk kimono. Embroidered in shiny lacquered threads from the hem to the waist were delicate vines holding pink blossoms and fluttering nightingales. The embroidery was so lifelike I thought the birds would start singing.

"It's the most beautiful fabric I've ever seen," I said.

"You deserve it. I couldn't have written Fabrice's catalogue without you."

Daniel carried the box with the kimono to the door, his peg clomping rhythmically like a giant metronome. "What will you do with it?" he asked.

"Save it," I said, taking the box from his arms. "For something special."

The next morning, July 14, I awoke early to church bells ringing, dressed quickly and left my apartment. It was Bastille Day, a national holiday, so Mademoiselle had been forced to grant us the day off. Daniel had given his aunt and me tickets that provided access to an area along the Champs-Élysées. From there we could view the parade, perhaps even spot Daniel, who'd insisted on participating. Dodging puddles, I made my way to boulevard Saint-Germain, where revelers who'd been up all night drinking and dancing to a jazz band now slept on the sidewalk wrapped in blankets. A waiters' strike that had closed many of the city's cafés and restaurants for two weeks had just been settled. I bought a croissant and walked toward the Seine. Every inch of the pavement was mobbed with people and soldiers on horseback. Families with picnic baskets camped out in the grassy areas; young men perched on lampposts and in the trees. A few had brought stepladders and were balanced precariously atop them. I'd arranged to meet Madame Duval on a corner of rue Marbeuf, but there was no chance of finding her.

I elbowed my way through the crowd and showed a policeman my ticket. The officer allowed me to enter a restricted area. Standing on my tiptoes and craning my neck, I could see the Arc de Triomphe. Four gigantic angels sculpted from aircraft scraps guarded its four corners, while an empty casket, inscribed on its plinth with the words "aux morts pour la patrie," stood nearby.

Trumpets pierced the air, followed by booming guns. The crowd roared, and, for the first time since 1871, when the Prussians had marched through it, soldiers passed under Napoleon's triumphal arch. Heading the procession were three broken young men in wheelchairs, followed by a thousand more of France's wounded, halting along on crutches and canes, the blind leaning on the arms of friends. It was impossible to read the faces of the men marching under the rain of flowers tossed from the viewing stands above by schoolgirls in provincial costume. Somewhere among the marching soldiers was Daniel.

For two hours, soldiers from the Allied forces passed through: Frenchmen with flowers on the ends of their bayonets, khakied Americans, turbaned Moroccans, kilted Scots, Africans in flowing caftans, flag bearers, and aviators. When General Mangin appeared in his scarlet kepi and bright blue jacket, a small boy standing next to me with his mother began to cry. As the crowd shouted "Vive Mangin! Vive Verdun!" the child's chest heaved with terrible sobs. His mother pulled him to her, and I noticed that he wore a military ribbon around his neck and war medals pinned to his shirt. "Don't cry," his mother urged. "Think of what a beautiful parade this is for your father."

I did not fight my own tears. After several hours, the last troops, trailed by nine massive armed tanks, passed from the Étoile Circle toward the place de la Concorde. I thought of Jacques cold in his grave, my poor fiancé who at least was spared the sin of having to kill another man. I thought of Daniel who for the rest of his days had to endure his violent memories and the loss of his leg. The wild cheering, the dazzling fireworks now bursting over the Seine, the fluttering flags and pretty girls throwing flowers, seemed almost obscene—a vulgar attempt to bury tragedy under the cold mantle of glory.

I didn't see Daniel or Madame Duval until nine that evening, when we met for dinner at Taudière's, one of the most venerable restaurants in Paris. Though it had opened in 1873 in the aftermath of the Paris Commune, the restaurant's rococo paneling, ornate chandeliers, and "tous les Louis" furnishings harked back to a pre-Revolutionary era of royal glamour. The monarchist aura made it an odd choice for Bastille Day. Taudière's, however, was a favorite of Le Cent, a private club composed of the hundred self-anointed best eaters of France, of which Fabrice was a charter member. He'd recommended the restaurant to Daniel as a special treat for Madame Duval.

The maître d' sat us at a table on the far side of the dining room under an immense Fragonard-style painting of a hoop-skirted girl on a garden swing. Madame Duval soon began lamenting that Mademoiselle was avoiding her. "I've called three times and sent four petit bleus and gotten no response."

"She's swamped. But if you want, I'll mention it to her tomorrow," I said.

"Would you, Isabelle? That would be very helpful."

I knew it probably wouldn't do any good.

A waiter dressed like a footman at Versailles, in a white wig and knee britches, appeared at the table to take our orders. He left and returned a few moments later with a parchment document that listed the ancestors of the game and fowl we were about to eat and the names of the luminaries who'd consumed them.

"Look at this. My duck is descended from one that was eaten in 1875 by Victor Hugo," said Madame Duval, smiling softly.

Perhaps because I'd never dined at such an expensive restaurant—or perhaps because I'd ordered a hen that was descended from one that had been consumed by Leon Gambetta, the gluttonous Republican leader of the Belle Époque—I ate more that night than I ever had before.

The food kept coming, and I consumed it with an appetite I didn't know I possessed. There were three courses before the entrée and two after, all accompanied by side dishes and expensive wines. The gray twilight outside the windows fell to blackness. Neighboring tables emptied and refilled with new parties, and still our meal continued.

I was preparing to tuck into a slice of *crème renversé,* when I heard a commotion near the reservations desk. Two waiters held aloft in an armchair a tiny white-faced woman, barely visible in the folds of a pink satin dress.

"It's Sarah Bernhardt!" gasped Madame Duval.

The actress recently had lost her right leg from an abscessed injury, and there she was, in all her glorious decrepitude. The waiters carried her past our table, and I got a good look at her face, powdered to a chalk whiteness to hide the wrinkles. Two bright blue eyes beamed under her nest of dyed red hair; her mouth was a gash of purple lipstick.

"It is she, the one-legged wonder," said Daniel.

"I thought you were the one-legged wonder," I said.

"He's a wonder, period," said Madame Duval with grave pride.

Bernhardt's chair was placed in the center of the cavernous room, and the diners fell silent. The owner of Taudière's, a large bald man with a ferocious moustache, introduced her, going on too long about her great service to France throughout the war, when she risked death to entertain troops at the front. Then Bernhardt, in her still powerful theatrical voice, spoke about the bravery of the fallen soldiers, and we all wiped tears from our eyes. At the end, she raised herself to her full height, standing erect and steady on her remaining leg. Lifting her arms and eyes to the heavens, she cried, "Weep, Germany! Weep! Your eagle has drowned in the Rhine! *Vive* France!"

The musicians in the balcony struck up the Marseillaise, and the diners jumped to their feet, clapping and cheering, as Bernhardt was carried to a table in the far corner. "My God, isn't that Chanel she's with?" said Daniel.

Madame Duval and I craned our necks and looked in the direction of Daniel's gaze. There sat Mademoiselle with Bernhardt, Misia Godebska, Caryathis, and their four male companions. Mademoiselle was dressed in a frothy white chiffon gown, her bare, well-sculpted arms laden with gold bracelets. She looked astonishingly young and beautiful.

"I don't believe it," said Madame Duval. "A few years ago, she was a little milliner-cocotte. Now she's dining with Bernhardt. No wonder she doesn't have time for me."

"Go on, say hello to her," Daniel urged.

Madame Duval's features crumpled, and she looked like she was about to cry. Daniel put his hand on her arm. "Come on, let's say hello."

"I'll go with you, too," I said.

"No, I just want to leave," said Madame Duval.

Daniel paid the bill, and we walked out of the dining room and the restaurant into the yellow light of the street lamps and a boisterous swarm of singing, dancing revelers.

The celebrating continued the following day in Mademoiselle's studio, where a party atmosphere pervaded the *pose*. Misia and Caryathis, still in their silk gowns from the night before, stumbled in with several bottles of champagne. Corks popped and glasses were passed around. Bright fabric from shelved bolts floated up on the warm breeze pouring through the open windows and rippled into the room like handkerchiefs waved by phantom revelers. Seamstresses chatted in small groups at one end of the room; at the other, mannequins in white robes lounged against the wall.

Mademoiselle stood in front of the triple mirrors examining a toile. Someone handed her a glass of champagne, and she pushed it away with the back of her hand. "Time to get to work!" she snapped.

Misia and Caryathis had settled into a settee at the back of the room, and I overheard them whispering. "Gabrielle's angry because she had to give everyone the day off yesterday," said Misia.

She never called Mademoiselle "Coco." She thought the nickname vulgar—a washerwoman's name.

"She's more upset about not being invited to Princess Poix's," said Caryathis.

"I'm angry about it, too."

"The Poixs are royalty. They'd never invite a dressmaker to their home."

"But Gabrielle's a friend of mine. They should have included her."

"Anyway, the Poixs are bores." Caryathis yawned elaborately. "I wish we hadn't gone dancing afterward. I could have used some sleep."

"Five twelve!" Mademoiselle's voice boomed from the front of the room.

Yvette entered the studio and stepped to the triple mirrors in a narrow skirt and tunic. "Bonjour, Mademoiselle," she said.

"Bonjour, Yvette," said Mademoiselle without looking at the girl's face. She had her eyes on the muslin. I'd prepared myself for the couturière's disdain, but Mademoiselle looked pleased.

"I like it," she said, walking around Yvette and inspecting the ensemble from every angle. "So nice. Look at how it follows the body." She moved her hands over the hem of the tunic, which would be trimmed in nutria in the finished model.

Mademoiselle dismissed Yvette and moved on to a velvet coat with voluminous wrapping scarves. I tried to keep my face from breaking into a grin, as I settled into a chair next to Misia. "May I have a refill?" I said, holding out my glass.

After pouring the champagne, Misia laid the bottle on the floor and pulled a gold cigarette case encrusted with diamonds from her purse. She removed a cigarette and put it between her lips. Mademoiselle lifted her head from the tray of buttons she'd been pawing through and glared at Misia. A moment later, she dashed across the room. When she was standing in front of Misia, she pointed to the gold cigarette case in her friend's hand. "Where did you get that?" she demanded.

Misia looked stunned. "You gave it to me." She tipped her head back, expelling a straight line of smoke into the air.

"I did no such thing."

"You did. Last year. Don't you remember? At that dinner at Maxim's. I admired it, and you said it was mine."

"Why would I give you something that Boy had given to me?"

"Are you saying I stole it?" Misia opened her mouth and started to shout something. Then she remembered who she was. She drew her back straight and looked down her nose at Mademoiselle. "Monsieur le Couturier, you are crazy!"

Once, in the salon, I'd overheard the writer Colette refer to Mademoiselle as "Monsieur le Couturier." I couldn't believe anyone would dare to call her that to her face.

"Shut up," said Mademoiselle.

"You shut up," said Misia. She threw the cigarette case at Mademoiselle and stomped out, slamming the door behind her.

Mademoiselle slipped the case into her pocket. The room fell silent. Everyone stared at Mademoiselle with amazed faces, as the couturière resumed her place in front of the mirrors. "Five twenty-eight!" she cried.

Yvette changed into another of my models—a sleeveless black silk evening gown with tiers of ostrich feathers on the skirt. A delighted sigh escaped from Mademoiselle's throat, the unpleasantness with Misia forgotten in her excitement over the dress. "Just the thing for a girl with a nice figure. Even with a dog's face, she can go anywhere in this, and everyone will say she's pretty!"

"I'm glad you like it," I said.

The couturière took Misia's case from her pocket, removed a cigarette, and held the jeweled box toward me. "Want one?" she said.

I shook my head from side to side. "No, thank you. I never smoke."

Mademoiselle started to walk away, and I followed her. "Could I speak to you a moment?" I asked.

"What is it?"

I told her Madame Duval was in town and that she'd been trying to reach her. To my surprise, Mademoiselle's face brightened. "Marie-France Duval! One of the best people who ever worked for me. A wonderful woman. Tell her to call me."

"She has. Several times. And sent petit bleus."

Mademoiselle furrowed her brow. "Really? I never got them. Tell her to try again. We'll have dinner."

During the week she spent in Paris, Madame Duval went to several art exhibitions and visited Notre-Dame. She shopped at Galeries Lafayette, took walks along the Seine, and had tea at the Ritz with Daniel. I joined them a couple of times for dinner. By Madame Duval's last night in town, she told me that she never reached Mademoiselle. "I called her every day and left messages, but I never heard a thing," she said, her voice full of sadness.

The next morning, Daniel took her to Gare d'Austerlitz, and she boarded a train for Agen. Later that day Mademoiselle stopped me on the staircase. She was with Misia. Their spats, which both of them seemed to find energizing, never lasted long. "Is Marie-France Duval still here?" she asked me.

"No. She left this morning." I didn't tell her that her silence had nearly ruined Madame Duval's visit.

"The next time you see her, give her this." She shoved a shopping bag at me and continued up the stairs.

"I told Gabrielle she shouldn't give this stuff away, but she never listens to me," said Misia.

When she and Mademoiselle were out of sight, I pulled out of the bag a gorgeous wool cape trimmed in sable, a model from the last collection which sold for 18,000 francs.

Nineteen

One evening after Madame Duval's departure, Monique Thabard phoned, asking me to meet her in a fitting room downstairs. I found her sitting on a velvet settee, puffing nervously on a cigarette. She explained that Amanda Nichols had just left, after showing up without an appointment to insist again on a last-minute dress.

"Absolutely not," I said. "I'm not going to do it. It's less than three weeks before the opening, and I'm swamped." Because I'd spent so much time on Angeline, I was far behind on my other work, and Laurence was nagging me to finish several models that were on the schedule for the next *pose.*

"Mademoiselle would want you to do this for an important client," Monique said dryly. "I might point out, Mademoiselle Nichols already this year has spent 35,000 francs here."

Whiffs of the art agent's perfume—heavy and pungent—lingered in the air underneath smoke from Monique's cigarette. I said nothing.

"I'll give you fifteen percent of my commission," offered Monique. Ninety percent of her salary came from commissions.

"You can't tempt me with money."

It was seven, near closing time, and only two darlings—the last appointments of the day—remained in the salon. Through the fitting-room curtain, I could hear their voices, soft and content, oblivious to our argument. Monique took a long drag on her cigarette and stubbed it out in an ashtray. "Look, I'm going to have to tell Mademoiselle that you've refused to make a dress for one of our best clients."

"Be reasonable. You know the pressure we're under. How am I supposed to fit it in?"

"I'm not interested in arguing with you. I'm going up to Mademoiselle now."

At that moment, I became aware of someone outside the fitting room. Muffled footsteps. A cleared throat. Then the curtain tore open. Mademoiselle stood with her feet rooted in the carpet and her nostrils flaring. The creator of modern chic looked hard at Monique, then at me and roared, "What dress have you refused to make?"

"For Amanda Nichols, one of our best clients," said Monique, her voice dripping with righteousness.

"We're always doing rush orders for this woman," I said. "I've no time. I've got two models for the collection on the schedule for Friday and . . ."

Mademoiselle didn't give me a chance to finish. "Make the dress, Varlet."

It took four of us two days to sew Amanda's dress—a lace shell over a black satin slip striped in bright green ribbon. We completed it on a Friday evening at nine, and I brought the dress to Amanda's apartment at the Ritz. An attractive brunette greeted me at the door. She looked familiar, though I couldn't place her. "I'll take that," the brunette said, lifting the dress box from my arms. She disappeared down the hallway, and I settled on the sofa.

Through the walls, I heard a phone ring, followed by feet running across the floor. Then Amanda's voice, rising with anger. She appeared to be talking to a dealer, though I could discern only snippets of the conversation. "In twelve years, I've never been mistaken once . . . No . . . I'm sure it's a fake. . . . What? . . . If I were a man, no one would question my judgment on this for a second."

I picked up a magazine from the coffee table in front of me and began flipping through it absentmindedly, while I struggled to hear Amanda. "They've got quite an operation. . . . Paintings and sculpture . . . all over Europe . . . jewelry, even couture dresses." At the mention of couture dresses, I tossed the magazine aside and cocked my head in the direction of Amanda's voice. It was faint, however, the conversation suddenly inaudible. A moment later, I heard the phone click. Thirty minutes went by, and, finally, Amanda appeared in her new dress, the brunette standing by her side. She looked stunning. I was annoyed, though, that she'd failed to apologize for keeping me waiting, so I didn't compliment her. "How does it fit?" I asked.

"I think the straps need to be taken up." She pulled out the fabric on her shoulders.

"Let's take a look." I stepped behind her and ran my hands over the straps and the back of the bodice, feeling where I should make adjustments.

The brunette poured herself a drink from a carafe on the sideboard, and plopped into an upholstered chair. I studied her out of the corner of my eye and decided she wasn't really pretty. She had a small, almost childlike figure and her face was heavily made up. Her jaw was thick, her nose beaklike, her mouth tiny and thin. In her floaty, blue chiffon dress, with the black aigrette nodding on her sequined headband, she looked like an exotic bird who'd flown in and alighted on the furniture. Still, there was *something* about her.

Then I remembered where I'd seen her—on the cover of last month's *Desmoiselles*. She was Jeanne Gaudel, a former cabaret singer who'd taken up car racing. She'd been in the news recently for beating twenty rivals in an all-female tournament in the Swiss Alps. And last summer she'd survived a fiery crash while racing her Burgati in Italy. The pictures were in all the papers. "What do you think, Jeanne?" asked Amanda.

"I think it's too loose in the waist," answered Jeanne.

"Perhaps," said Amanda, smoothing her hands over her hips.

"It's fine to my eye, but I'll take it in, if you like," I said. I wanted to ask Amanda about stolen couture, but feared she'd think I'd been eavesdropping on her conversation.

"Where are you ladies going tonight?" I asked.

"A gallery opening," said Amanda coolly.

"Which one?"

"Demont's. There's a Bourdin exhibit."

"I love Bourdin," I said.

"You know his work?" asked Amanda in an arrogant tone.

"My grandmother had one of his paintings—of a little girl in a blue dress in a garden." I didn't tell her it was a copy, made probably by some impoverished art student from our region.

"I know that painting. I thought it was in a private collection in America."

I tried to stop my face from flushing and buried my head behind Amanda's dress. "I think that about does it," I said, after I'd marked with pins where the waist and straps needed to be readjusted.

"Let me look." Amanda hopped on top of the coffee table and studied the dress in the mirror over the sofa with grim determination not to overlook any flaw. "I guess it's fine." She jumped off the coffee table, stumbling as she landed and twisting her right ankle. "Yeow!" she cried.

Jeanne sprang out of her seat and helped Amanda to a chair. "You should be more careful."

"I'll be all right," said Amanda. Slowly, she raised herself to standing and shimmied out of the dress, leaving it in a heap on the floor. "You can fix it while I'm taking my bath," she commanded, starting for the door with a slight limp.

I picked up the dress off the floor and sat with it on the sofa. As I snipped out the waist seam with my scissors, Jeanne poured herself another drink. Her presence grew larger, filling the room. While I sewed, I asked her polite questions about car racing, and she gave light, bored answers. At one point she said she'd like to see some of Mademoiselle's clothes. "Amanda says they're the chicest in Paris. She has a great eye for dresses, as well as art. Much more than me."

I told her I'd be happy to set her up with a vendeuse, thinking how impressed Mademoiselle would be if I could deliver Jeanne Gaudel as a client. But Jeanne only nodded distractedly, and I didn't think she was serious.

Finally, Amanda appeared, fresh from her bath, wearing a terry-cloth wrapper. Her limp had vanished, I noticed, as she moved to the secretary to retrieve her cigarettes. She lit one and took a seat next to me on the sofa. "How long is that going to take?" she asked, pointing to the dress with her cigarette.

"Just a few more minutes."

"I don't want to get there too late." Then turning to Jeanne she said, "There's a painting in the Demont exhibit that I'm sure is a fake."

"Which one?" asked Jeanne.

"*Redhead Dreaming*. It's the nude, brushing her hair. At least I'm almost sure it's a fake. I saw it yesterday in a preview, but I need to examine it more closely tonight."

Amanda explained that *Redhead Dreaming* was Bourdin's master-piece, the finest example of the artist's innovative use of color and light. Gallery Demont had borrowed it for the exhibition from a private collector—a wealthy faubourg aristocrat whom Amanda hoped to lure as a client, and that was why she'd been invited to examine it the pre-vious day. "I think it could have been done by a forgery ring in Arles," she said. "Their representatives have been trying to sell me things for years. They deal not only in art, but also in furniture, jewelry, and cou-ture. I got a call tonight from a detective I know who's investigating it."

Jeanne looked directly at me. "Amanda likes nothing more than finding fakes. It's great publicity for her business."

"You're always saying that, but you miss the point," insisted Amanda. "I'm offended by forgeries, really hurt by them. Anyway, they're never as good as the originals. Take *Redhead Dreaming*. I knew something was wrong with it the moment I saw it, because it didn't move me. It seemed cut off from the passion of creation, the drive to capture light which is so characteristic of Bourdin's work."

My heart had been beating faster since I'd first heard Amanda men-tion stolen couture, and now I thought it would burst if I didn't ask her, "Do you think that forgery ring in Arles might have some Chanels?"

"Could be," said Amanda. "They've got a lot of stuff." She looked over her shoulder at me. "Now are you done?"

"It just needs to be pressed."

Amanda sent me to the maid's room at the far end of the apartment, a tiny cell with a window overlooking an air shaft. An ironing board with an iron atop it stood near a rusted sink. I carried the iron to the kitchen next door, turned on the stove, and placed it on a front burner. As I waited for the iron to heat, I thought about Amanda's dress, about the exquisite fabric from the best silk weaver in Lyon, about the expert cut and flawless stitching. The iron began to hiss. I removed it from the stove and returned to the maid's room. Placing a dampened cloth under the iron, I pressed Amanda's dress with painstaking care. No fake Chanel could match the beauty of this garment. No fake would be this alive.

With the dress draped over my forearms, I made my way down the hall through the deep stillness of the apartment, lit only by the soft yellow light of wall sconces. The kitchen was dark, the door to the bedrooms closed. I thought the women might have been called away by some unforeseen emergency. As I approached the salon, though, I recognized Amanda's low monotone. "Come here, you," I heard her say, as I reached the doorway. Then I saw the two bobbed heads—one blond and one brown, rising above the back of the settee. Amanda and Jeanne, their noses locked and lips crushed together.

One evening a few days later, I was at home reading *Le Figaro*, when my eyes wandered to a small headline buried at the bottom of page 33:

RAIDED AS FASHION SPIES
Two American Women Are Arrested

On complaint of the Paris couture firm Ardente, police raided the hotel rooms of two American women today and found them in possession of muslin toiles (dress patterns cut from cheap cloth) and an alleged secret code for transmitting information about them to fashion wholesalers in New York.

The two women, Mrs. Olivia Davis and Miss Ida Jones, denied they were acting as fashion spies and declared that the toiles in their possession were purchased legitimately from agents of Ardente.

"That is a preposterous lie!" said Philipe Ardente, proprietor of the firm on rue de la Paix, adding that those so-called "legitimate agents" were two employees whom he'd fired recently for selling swatches of the fabrics he was using in his collection to his competitors.

Monsieur Ardente said next year he plans to install a dyeing facility in his atelier so he can change colors at the last minute and thus thwart the illegal copiers. "At least that aspect of my collection will be safe. The copyists won't have time to reproduce it," he said.

Also in possession of Mrs. Davis and Miss Jones were toiles and finished outfits made in fine fabric from several of Paris's leading couture houses. The investigation is continuing.

The next morning, I called the police from the phone in the concierge's apartment, and I was put through to an Inspector Morain. I asked him if any Chanels had been found in the raid of the Americans' hotel room. He put me on hold for a few minutes while he checked the report, and when he came back on the line he told me "no."

"Do you know anything about an art theft ring in Arles that deals in stolen toiles?" I asked.

"Art theft is a different department entirely," the inspector said. "But I doubt anyone in Arles is mixed up in this. Whoever took your toiles was American, like those women we arrested. It's the Americans who are desperate for French couture."

Twenty

*A*mericans were everywhere in Paris that summer. As July drew to a close, shiploads of American fashion buyers and journalists arrived in Paris. For most, it was their first trip to the city since war had broken out five years before, and some of them, like the editor from *Harper's Bazaar* who opened an office on rue de la Paix, had come to stay.

In my off-hours, I began prowling the lobbies of hotels and cafés frequented by Americans. When I told Daniel what I was up to, he volunteered to accompany me. "What exactly is it we're looking for?" he asked one evening, as we sat on a settee in the lobby of a hotel on rue de Rivoli, watching fashionable people come and go.

"Dresses that have been made from the stolen toiles," I said.

Daniel shook his head. "This is an insane waste of time."

I knew he was probably right. The chance of one of the stolen models suddenly crossing my path was as unlikely as a daisy sprouting in the desert. Still, this was high season for style theft in Paris, and it made me feel better to be doing *something* besides sitting in my flat worrying.

One night when Daniel and I were strolling boulevard Saint-Germain, I thought I recognized Angeline peeking out from a large shawl worn by a woman walking ahead of us. I left Daniel sitting on a bench near a newspaper kiosk, while I ran to catch up to her, just as she and her companion ducked into a restaurant. I followed them in, but her dress looked nothing like Angeline.

"I can't take another night of this," said Daniel, when I'd found him again. He was sitting on the bench with his peg extended onto the pavement, angrily drumming his foot. "From now on, Isabelle, you're on your own."

A few nights later I went alone to a café near the Madeleine and ran into Tanguy de Navacelle. The Ritz concierge was sitting at a table with two women, one middle-aged and the other young. Tanguy introduced them as buyers from Rosenfeld and Company in New York. He said the women were friends of Charlie Spinelli, and that he'd met them at the racetrack earlier that month.

Both spoke decent French. The older woman, Mae Hagan, had a pale angular face and brown hair arranged in an old-fashioned bun at the nape of her neck. She wore a dress that reached to the ground in "Eveque," an insipid purple shade that was said by the society pages to be Mrs. Wilson's favorite color, and a rope of pearls that hung to her knees. The younger woman, Nora Kimble, was blond, short, and stocky. She'd affected a garçonne look with bobbed hair, a skimpy dress, and bare legs.

"Isabelle works for Chanel," Tanguy told the women, as I took a seat between them. The table was cluttered with empty glasses and an overflowing ashtray.

"Chanel's prices are horrible! I can't believe what she's asking for even the simplest jersey frock," said Mae. Her face was crisscrossed with tiny lines, which she tried to disguise with white powder.

"It's much worse than I expected," added Nora, her stale wine breath flowing into my face. "You French have gotten so accustomed to wartime prices, that now you're not satisfied with normal profits."

"I personally would be satisfied with any profit at all," I said. The waiter laid a glass in front of me and poured wine into it.

"It's time to have Charlie take us to one of the copyists," Mae said to Nora.

"I'm definitely ready for that," said Nora.

An image of Mae and Nora cramming dresses made from my toiles into a steamer trunk flashed in my head. "That's stealing!" I said.

"Buying copies is not a crime," said Nora.

"You mean buying the *right* to copy. Purchasing illegal copies *is* a crime, and the police are starting to crack down on the fashion thieves."

Nora grunted. "After what we did for you during the war."

"After what *you* did?"

"The money America handed out to the French Red Cross, not to mention the several million bandages we sent over."

"You're using the war to justify buying illegal copies?"

Mae shrugged. "Anyway, what's coming from the Paris couturiers isn't so hot. We can buy better clothes at home."

"It's true," agreed Nora. "The only French house we can't do without is Callot Soeurs."

Mae nodded her head vigorously. "The French are no longer the leaders in fashion. The only thing the French are leaders in is starting wars."

"That's the stupidest thing I ever heard!" I said.

"All right ladies, this isn't the Chamber of Deputies."

I looked up to see Charlie Spinelli standing by the table holding a fat cigar. He nodded to Nora and Mae and pumped my hand. "Nice to see you, again," he said.

"Charlie, my good man," said Tanguy. He considered the small, marble-topped table. "Let's move to a bigger one."

"Don't bother," said Mae. "We've got to go. Come on, Nora."

"I'll call you tomorrow," Nora said to Charlie Spinelli, as she stood. "Mae and I need to visit a copyist."

"All right, doll." Charlie Spinelli kissed Nora, then Mae.

Grabbing their purses off the table, the women said good-bye to Tanguy and me.

After they'd left, Charlie Spinelli lowered his bulk into a chair and relit his cigar. "Don't mind them," he said, expelling a foul stream of smoke. "They're nice girls when they haven't had anything to drink."

"Which copyist are you taking Nora and Mae to?" I asked.

"The same one I took them to last February." Charlie Spinelli leaned his body toward me and lowered his voice. "This couture house whose name I won't mention held its opening at which one of the gems of the collection was a black and white satin dress, at fifteen hundred francs a real lollapalooza, as we say in Brooklyn. A few buyers ordered the original model, but Nora and Mae held back on account of the price. I was able to get them the same thing at a little shop I know for a mere three hundred francs." Charlie Spinelli flashed me a smug grin.

"I had some toiles stolen from my workroom a few weeks ago," I blurted, staring hard at Charlie Spinelli. "I don't suppose you'd know anything about that?"

"I *might* know where they are," he said.

"Is that because you *might* have had something to do with taking them?"

"Charlie isn't a thief!" cried Tanguy, patting his friend on the back.

Charlie Spinelli looked at me with wide eyes. "I understand you're upset," he said. "But I didn't take your toiles."

"This shop you mentioned. Do you think they have any Chanels?" I asked.

"They've got everything. I'll take you there tomorrow if you like." He reached under his jacket to adjust the belt on his trousers. "When can you get off work?"

"Probably not until nine."

"I'll pick you up at nine."

I bounced through the following day on a cloud of high spirits, certain that Charlie Spinelli would lead me to the stolen toiles. At nine sharp I was waiting in front of the atelier, when Charlie Spinelli, who loathed being jostled on the crowded metro more than he hated high prices, pulled up in a taxi. He directed the driver to rue Mireille, an old street in Montmartre. "Do Mae and Nora really think they can get by without French fashion?" I asked, as the taxi climbed a steep hill.

"Nah, they're just frustrated with the prices, as everyone is," said Charlie Spinelli. He pointed his three chins downtown. "I was at Rizzi's last night looking at the women's toilettes. It might cost a guy three hundred francs to feed himself and his lady, but she's gotta put out a fortune just to get dressed. I was alone, so I had time to figure it out. A modest restaurant outfit, not counting the jewelry, costs seventeen thousand francs if it costs a sou." Using the index finger of his right hand, he ticked off a series of items on the fingers of his left hand. "First, you got your mantle, and it's gotta be fur-trimmed. That's fifteen thousand francs. A little dress with no trim but a fancy label means another sixteen hundred francs—and that's a low estimate. A hat, even with no feathers, is four hundred francs. You can buy a lot of *canard à l'orange* for that!"

A soft rain began to fall, and when we arrived at number 82, the sidewalks were slick. The old buildings looked indistinct in the darkness, their sagging window shutters and crumbling facades clouded in a haze of pale light from the street lamps. I could almost smell my toiles.

"This is it," said Charlie Spinelli.

He led me up two flights of narrow stairs through fetid air thick with the odor of tobacco and spoiled fruit. At the landing he flipped the light switch, illuminating flocked rose velvet wallpaper, faded with age and grime, and a narrow door covered with layers of green paint.

Charlie Spinelli rummaged around his suit pockets and pulled out a long chrome-colored stick, the size of a pencil. "No one will be here at this hour, so I'm going to have to use this," he said.

With a groan, he lowered his bulk to one knee and applied the pick to the lock. As he twisted it back and forth, I asked, "Are you breaking in?"

"Nah, my friend just forgot to give me the key."

I felt queasy. The only time I'd ever committed a crime was in convent school in Agen when I was eight. Juliette, the little girl who slept in the cot next to me had a collection of hair ribbons that I coveted. She kept them in a box under her bed, and one day when I stayed behind in the dormitory because of a cold, I removed the box and took one of the ribbons—a thick blue velvet delicately embroidered with white marguerites—and slipped it in the pocket of my uniform. I counted on Juliette not missing it, since she had so many ribbons. Then one morning the following week, after the tower bell had rung calling the students to morning chapel, I was hurrying across the courtyard when a child screamed, her anguish wafting from the top floor dormitory where the junior girls slept to the stone pavement below. I looked up to see Juliette at the window holding her box of ribbons. "Someone stole my blue velvet!" she shrieked.

Later that day, the nuns interrogated everyone. When no one confessed to the crime immediately, they assumed the imbecile servant girl who swept the floors in exchange for a few francs was the culprit.

I hid the ribbon in my Bible and brought it home the next weekend, where I displayed it on my dresser with my china statue of the Virgin, my rosary beads, and the pictures of my parents in painted wood frames. "Where did this ribbon come from?" my grandmother asked.

"Juliette, a little girl at school gave it to me," I lied.

"She *gave* it to you?"

"Yes."

Perhaps my grandmother had heard about the theft at the convent, or perhaps she simply understood the greediness of little girls. In any case, she didn't believe me, and she badgered me until I confessed. I brought the ribbon back to school and gave it to Mother Superior, a kindly old woman who allowed me to tell Juliette that I'd found it under a cupboard in the hallway. My remorse, Mother Superior said, was punishment enough, though she still made me say twenty Hail Marys and copy out an entire chapter from *The Lives of the Saints*.

"Got it!" said Charlie Spinelli. He hoisted himself to standing with great difficulty and turned the old brass knob. The door flung wide, not on the shabby criminal enterprise I'd envisioned by the looks of the filthy hallway, but on a charming little shop.

The walls were freshly painted white. Rose taffeta curtains framed the tall French windows. A collection of reproduction Louis XIV chairs and tables were arranged on a plush carpet on one side of the room. On the other side were glass display cases holding an assortment of handbags, hats, scarves, shoes, hosiery, and lingerie. On one stood an open, empty cash register. My eyes darted around frantically. Somewhere in this shop were my toiles.

"Let's see what's here." Charlie Spinelli opened one of two doors at the back of the room. It led to a corridor and a series of fitting rooms. Then he opened the other. I followed him in.

It was a workroom like any other with scarred wood tables, piles of fabric bolts, a sewing machine on a table in the corner, pin cushions, scissors, tape measures strewn about, pictures of dresses torn from magazines tacked to the wall, a carpet of needles, thread, and fabric bits on the floor. A few headless dress forms wore outfits in various stages of completion—a wool jacket pinned together, a coat awaiting its fur trim, a dress yet to be hemmed. I made a beeline for the two *rayons* behind the work tables, which were crammed with toiles and pawed through them quickly. A few models seemed to be Lanvin's; others reminded me of Poiret and Jenny. None were Chanel.

I felt as limp as an empty sleeve. I had no idea where else to look. I could only hope that the toiles wouldn't show up on the street or in a magazine before the opening.

"Well?" Charlie Spinelli stood over me, still red-faced and sweating from his exertions with the lock.

"Nothing."

"None of those toiles in there are yours?"

"No."

He grabbed my shoulder with a large square hand and massaged it tenderly. "Don't worry, doll. I'm sure they'll turn up."

* * *

Outside, I said good night to Charlie Spinelli and ducked into the metro. At home, I pulled down my box of treasures, and reached through the fabric pieces to retrieve the kimono. I held the silk to my face, letting the luxurious scent of the fabric quiet my mind. Maybe I couldn't have my toiles, or a nicer flat, or Daniel. But I could have a new dress.

I took the sheet off of my bed and laid it across the floor with the kimono on top. Carefully, I snipped out the garment's seams and smoothed the fabric flat. Using a pattern I'd made based on one of Mademoiselle's old designs, I cut out the bodice and skirt for a dress and began stitching them together.

I'd modified the pattern's décolletage to cover my iodine scars, and I cut the back low, nearly to the waistline. Now, it would be impossible to wear a brassiere with the dress, and that made me feel bold and daring. I attached the bodice to the skirt, matching the embroidery so that the delicate vines of the kimono appeared in an unbroken line from the hem to the shoulder. By the time a golden sash of sunrise appeared beyond my window, the dress was complete.

I slipped it over my head, experimented with the kimono's obi as a shawl, then decided to save it for another garment, perhaps to line a jacket. Hopping atop the bed, I studied myself in the mirror in a twirling imitation of the mannequins at work. For a moment I let myself imagine a man's warm hand on my back, leading me in a tango. The man had Daniel's face, but he had two legs, and he moved with the unhindered grace of Jacques. As I stepped out of the dress and hung it in my wardrobe, I felt the ball of sorrow that had been with me since my fiancé's death swell in my chest. I got into bed. I was too tired even to cry, and I promptly fell asleep.

I got a chance to wear the dress on Sunday, when Daniel took me to a concert at La Salle Pleyel to hear a young pianist named Aurélie Tranchevent, who had lived for many years with her parents in the apartment next to Daniel's.

A long black piano gleamed on the stage, and as Daniel and I took our seats, a dark-haired woman in a white dress glided out from the wings. She settled herself on the cushioned bench and stared into space to compose herself. A moment later, her hands floated up from her lap, and the first poignant notes of Debussy's Clair de lune vibrated through the air. Aurélie's playing was intense and romantic. She'd started the piece tenderly and built to a feeling of deep yearning. Daniel listened with a soft expression, and by the time the last notes splashed into the air, his eyes brimmed with tears. "That was one of my mother's favorites," he whispered to me.

Next, Aurélie played a Beethoven sonata and two Chopin Nocturnes. After the interval, she switched to ragtime, handling the muscular rhythms and dense chord clusters as skillfully as she'd played Chopin's and Debussy's cascading notes.

Afterward, Daniel and I met her in a dressing room back stage.

"You were amazing," Daniel said, taking hold of Aurélie's thin shoulders and kissing each of her cheeks. Then, turning to me, "This is my friend Isabelle Varlet."

"Enchanted," she said. Her smile lit up her deep intelligent eyes.

I resented her talent, her loveliness, her friendship with Daniel, and tried to hide it with flattery. "I've never heard Chopin played with such perfection."

"Thank you, but I was a little off in the second Nocturne." Her voice was as rich and sensual as her playing.

Why hadn't I ever learned to play the piano? At convent school, I took lessons from a birdlike nun with round spectacles, but the endless droning of the metronome on the old out-of-tune upright, and my inability to catch on quickly discouraged me, and I gave it up after a few months.

"Will you join us? We're going to grab something to eat near Saint-Sulpice," said Daniel.

"Why go all the way over there?" asked Aurélie. "There are a lot of good restaurants in this neighborhood."

"We're going to evening mass. Isabelle missed it this morning, and she feels guilty if a Sunday goes by without church. You know how these provincial girls are." He patted me on the head like I was a pet he needed to walk. Daniel and Aurélie laughed lightly, and I hated them for their Parisian sophistication.

"Another time," said Aurélie. "I have my mother and brother here."

Daniel and I took a taxi to rue Bonaparte and sat at a café across from the beautiful old church. It was late evening, and the square before us glowed with a quiet plum light. We ordered a bottle of red wine and two charcuterie plates and chatted about work. Daniel said he'd started a couple of short stories. I told him about Charlie Spinelli and my continuing anxiety over the stolen toiles. I couldn't stop thinking about the way he'd looked at Aurélie, and finally, I asked him, "Have you ever had a girlfriend?"

"Sure," he said.

"A serious girlfriend."

"What do you mean by 'serious'?"

"Like in love. Were you ever in love with Aurélie?"

"For about a week, when we were sixteen." He smiled mischievously at me. "Are you jealous?"

"I'm not jealous. Why should I be jealous?" I glared at him. "I was just wondering."

When he didn't say anything, I blurted, "I'm never getting married."

"I don't think I will either."

"Because of the war?"

"I don't know. What about you?"

"I don't know. I guess I didn't mean it."

"About getting married?"

I nodded my head, and Daniel reached across the table to take my hand in his. "I'm sure you'll find someone, Isabelle. A lovely girl like you."

We drank the wine, talking casually and watching the activity in the square. Daniel announced that he'd be leaving Paris soon for Timbaut where, away from the distractions of Paris, he hoped to finish his stories. I asked him when he'd be back, and he said he didn't know.

He told me he was thinking of going to America to meet some of his father's relatives, and that he might sail directly from the south.

I wondered if he'd ever come back. Perhaps in America he'd find it easier to forget the war, easier to cope with his infirmity, easier to write. Despite what he'd said about not marrying, he would probably wed an American woman, have American children, and never even speak French. Meanwhile, I'd be stuck with no one to go home to and nothing to think about but buttonholes and collars, sleeves, and hems. These thoughts, and the possibility that I might never see Daniel again, put a cold hollow in my stomach.

Night had come, and the city lights faded out the sky's blackness. A little boy was trying to climb into the fountain in front of Saint-Sulpice, and when his mother restrained him, he started to shriek.

"Do you think I should cut my hair?" I asked suddenly.

"I love your hair," Daniel answered.

"I'm getting tired of all the pins. And the tangles, getting them out every morning. Also, I think it's becoming dull, losing some of its color." I yanked the pins out and let my hair fall around my shoulders. A man at the next table stared at me and shook his head.

"That's crazy," said Daniel. "It's beautiful."

"I'm going to cut it. If the toiles are found." I sipped my wine and looked past Daniel to the brightly lit church. "I promise God. If the toiles turn up, I'm cutting my hair."

Twenty-one

The following Saturday night, Tanguy de Navacelle borrowed a car to take Laurence and me to a nightclub in Neuilly.

"How are things at work?" asked Tanguy, after he'd picked me up in front of my building, and I was settled in the backseat.

"Still no word on the stolen toiles," I said.

"Charlie Spinelli couldn't help you?"

"No. I'm just holding my breath till the opening."

Laurence, who had her head on Tanguy's shoulder, lifted it to say, "Then Mademoiselle will be the fashion dictator of the world. At least that's what she wants."

"And will she succeed?" asked Tanguy.

"She might. She's tougher than everyone else," I said.

"And how tough are you, Mademoiselle Varlet?" asked Tanguy, smiling at me from the rearview mirror.

"I'm alive."

As the car left the city and raced along the dark suburban roads, something Mademoiselle had said began to play in my head: *A woman who isn't loved is lost.* When I sewed, the hollow in my stomach disappeared without my even realizing it. But the emptiness always returned. I felt it less when I was with Daniel, I thought, resenting his absence.

We'd been driving for an hour, when the road turned extremely narrow and began winding up a dark hill. The motion of the turns made me queasy. Reaching forward, I put my hand on Tanguy's shoulder. "Could you slow down a bit, please."

"Sorry!" Tanguy cried.

Just when I thought I couldn't stand another curve, we reached the top of the hill, and the car halted. A group of men stood in front of us with torches. One of them approached the car and pointed toward the darkness ahead. "There's an iron gate a few hundred feet up," he said. "Go through it and follow the road."

It led to a small château with turrets and balconies, surrounded by a forest of oaks. We parked the car and stepped onto a gravel path that meandered up to the house. Tanguy told us it had been built during the Belle Époque for the mistress of a candy manufacturer and had been vacant for years. A former croupier who'd spent most of the war in jail for illegal gambling recently had leased it to start a nightclub. Inside, the house showed its neglect, with peeling plaster and bare, creaking floorboards. The air smelled stale and sour, a mixture of tobacco, liquor, and mold. The staircase sagged; some spindles were missing from the banister. Tattered drapes hung from the windows of the salon. In the ballroom, where a few couples danced to a small orchestra, part of the ceiling had caved in.

While Laurence and Tanguy searched for the bar, I went to the dining room where a blackjack game was underway around a large table. Two middle-aged men with gray, exhausted faces sat opposite a young Spanish-looking man. In front of them, cigarettes burned in ashtrays next to glasses holding thick gold liquid. At the back of the room, two women wearing cheap department store dresses and bored expressions lounged in chairs.

I hung back near the wall. The middle-aged men ignored me, but the Spanish-looking man nodded to me meaningfully. Thick, dark hair rippled from his forehead over deep-set black eyes. Under a thin moustache, he had a girlish mouth with soft, full lips and very white teeth. He slapped a few bills on the table, and the dealer, a skeletally thin man with a hard face above a stiff white collar and black bow tie, pushed a pile of chips in his direction.

The Spanish-looking man won his hand and the next. While he played, he'd stolen a few glances at me, and now he asked, "Would you like to try?"

"I don't know how," I answered, my face reddening.

He grabbed the chair next to him and motioned me forward. "Sit here, and you'll learn."

Shadows from candles in the chandelier flickered over the walls, making them appear wobbly. It was a relief to sit down. I could still feel the motion of the car in my stomach, and my head pounded. The dealer turned the cards over with a violent snap, and I moved closer to the Spanish-looking man, feeling the solid weight of his arm next to mine.

He kept winning. Finally, one of the exhausted men mumbled something about "Miguel's good luck," and the other said, "It has nothing to do with luck. It's skill."

"I got good at this during the war," said the Spanish-looking man in an apologetic tone. "But I know to quit while I'm ahead. I'm done for tonight." Then pushing his chips forward, he said to the dealer, "Hold these for me, okay?"

The dealer nodded, and the Spanish-looking man turned to me. "Would you like to dance?"

"Is your name Miguel?" I asked.

"Yes. And yours?"

"Isabelle."

Miguel led me out to the ballroom, where the orchestra was in the middle of a fox-trot. He knew a lot of fancy steps that I had trouble following. After the fox-trot, we sat at a table and ordered cocktails. Then we danced again. As we navigated the dance floor, I tried to push Daniel from my mind. I thought about how much I loved to dance, about the pleasant feeling of moving my body to the music. I was enjoying Miguel's attention. I liked the warmth of his arms as he held me, the pungent laundry soap smell of his white shirt.

I watched the door for Laurence and Tanguy. At one point they walked by, laughing and holding cocktail glasses. But I didn't see them after that. I began to feel nervous and distracted. In the middle of a tango, I tripped, and Miguel caught me a second before I would have tumbled to the floor. "I think someone's had a bit too much to drink," he said. "Let's go upstairs."

I can't explain why I followed him to the second floor. The cocktails, the strange surroundings, the music—made me lose all balance; I wasn't myself. At the top of the stairs, Miguel pulled me to him, kissing me hard on the mouth. I didn't resist, and he kissed me again, this time pushing his tongue between my teeth. He led me to a room at the end of the hall and opened the door. When we were inside, he drew me to him again. He did not attack me, as Jean Patou had, but his hands moved urgently over my body. He was kissing me now and fumbling under my dress. My excitement was mingled with uneasiness and shame. "I have scars," I protested, but he ignored me. He pushed my dress down over my shoulders and hips, and it fell to the floor. With a groan, he buried his head in my neck and fondled my breasts. When he reached under the swell of my stomach, I grabbed his hand. "No," I said.

He tried again. After I stopped him the third time, he pulled away. He walked toward the window and switched on a lamp, illuminating the room's sparse furnishings: a battered wardrobe, a wood table and chair, a narrow bed, and a rusty sink. Miguel sat on the bed and removed his trousers. I could feel his eyes devouring me. I reached for my clothes on the floor. "No, let me watch you," he said.

He began to pleasure himself. I stood as still as death, my arms pressed to my sides, my head turned away, and my eyes closed. Tears stung the inside of the lids. I forced myself to think not of what was happening, but instead of Angeline, of the moment Yvette had slipped on the finished dress, and everyone in the studio—from Mademoiselle to the arpètes—saw it come alive, saw the perfection of the fit, the elegant flutter of the cascades, saw the skill and determination that had gone into every stitch.

"You can leave now," said Miguel.

I didn't look at him as I slipped on my clothes. Without saying a word, I fled out the door, down the stairs, through the house, to the terrace. It was empty and quiet. I sat on a stone bench and looked at the sky with its high white moon, surrounded by a smattering of stars. They looked like silver sequins, harmless and pretty, but I knew they really were explosive balls of fire. As a child, I'd had a telescope and a book on astronomy. On summer nights, I'd lie on my back in the field behind my grandmother's house to study the stars. I wondered what had happened to the book and the telescope.

The French doors opened, emitting from the house a jumble of nightclub sounds—music, laughter, and clinking glasses—followed by Laurence and Tanguy.

"Where've you been? We've been looking everywhere for you," said Laurence.

"Here. Watching the sky." I didn't want to explain further.

We piled into the car and took off down the winding country road. It was a beautiful drive back to the city. The sky was lightening, and the first warm rays of a new day rose above the treetops. "You scared the hell out of us, Isabelle," said Tanguy. "We thought you'd gone off with that creepy guy you were dancing with."

"He wasn't *that* creepy," I protested.

"You're so naive. We shouldn't have left you for a second."

"You shouldn't have."

"The next time, we won't."

Twenty-two

The next day I got a petit bleu from Daniel saying he was back in town and asking me to meet him at Fabrice's as soon as possible. He wrote that he was fine, but that Fabrice was in trouble. He promised to explain when he saw me.

After work, I took a bus to Le Roland, arriving a little after ten. The mansion was dark. I felt my way to the front steps and hammered the immense brass knocker. A light went on, the door opened, and Fabrice stood on the threshold in a worn bathrobe and slippers. He had a bad cold, and his face was white, except for his eyes and the tip of his nose, which were bright red. "I don't have a butler anymore," he said, his tone as humble as a cotton shirt. As he led me through the hall, he explained. "I'm broke, Isabelle. Everything is gone."

Though Daniel had finished his catalogue weeks before, Fabrice said he'd been unable to make any of the clothes depicted in it. He'd given up the idea of producing a fall collection. All but a few of his clients had left him, and he'd closed his workrooms.

"I'm very sorry," I said.

"Thank you, dear." He sighed heavily. "I've got no one but myself to blame."

In the salon, lit by a single floor lamp, the mirrors and pictures had been taken down, leaving only dusty lines where they'd once hung. Muslin shrouds covered the furniture; large packing crates were stacked in the middle of the floor. Daniel sat on one of several upturned crates near the lamp, and he motioned me to sit next to him. He looked pale and distracted.

"Fabrice has something for you," he said.

The couturier shuffled around the packed trunks and crates, the temples in his forehead throbbing nervously. He stopped at a metal locker and took a ring of keys from a pocket in his robe. He tried a couple of keys before he found one that fit the lock. The lid creaked open loudly. "Here they are." He pulled out several bundles of muslin garments and laid them, like a religious offering, at my feet.

"Are those my toiles?" I asked. I felt dizzy with relief.

"Yes." Fabrice lowered his gaze to the floor.

I looked at Daniel, whose face was tight with embarrassment. "I only learned he had them this morning. It was Fabrice's idea to give them back to you."

Quickly, my heart racing, I went through the piles, looking for Angeline. I found it near the bottom, wrinkled and musty. It thrilled me to have it safe in my arms.

"A special dress?" asked Fabrice.

"Yes."

Fabrice lowered his bulk to a crate next to the light. "I picked apart those toiles, and frankly, I don't get what all the fuss is about," he said, as I examined the rest of the bundle. "They're nothing special, as far as I can see. Shapeless jackets and skirts. Little nothing dresses with no backs and not much in front, held up with lingerie straps. Where's the artistry there?"

"It's all in the cut and the fit," I said sharply.

"Maybe you have to see them on."

"Maybe *you* do."

"Listen, Isabelle, Fabrice wasn't trying to hurt Chanel. He only wanted to see what she was up to," said Daniel.

"It's true," said Fabrice.

"Do you know how long it took us to make replacements? I hardly slept for a week."

"I'm deeply sorry."

"I thought we were friends," I told him.

Fabrice shook his head slowly and stared at his white, veiny feet.

In the front hall, the door opened and shut, and high heels clicked across the floor. Fabrice's back stiffened. "Thérèse," he said. "Poor woman. This has all been very hard on her. She needs to get away, so I'm taking her to America. I've got some lectures lined up that will keep me busy for a few months. I don't know what will happen when we get back. I might open a restaurant or a nightclub. I've an offer to design for Galeries Lafayette. The name Fabrice still means something in Paris. But I don't know." His eyes looked so sad that it nearly crushed my anger.

"Does Thérèse know about the toiles?" I asked.

"Oh, God, no."

The clicking heels faded, then vanished into another part of the house. Fabrice lifted his bulk from the crate where he'd been sitting. "I better put on some clothes. She doesn't like seeing me in my bathrobe."

"You go up. I'll see Isabelle to the door," said Daniel.

Fabrice started to walk away, and I put my hand on his arm. "Who helped you, who actually took the toiles?"

Fabrice sighed deeply and bowed his head. When he raised it to meet my gaze, sadness seeped from his eyes. "It's difficult to tell you, Isabelle."

"I think I know who it was," I said, dropping my hand from his sleeve.

He looked amazed. "You do?"

"Susanna Lawson."

He stared at me, looking bewildered. "I don't know that name."

"An Englishwoman. She works for Mademoiselle."

He shook his head.

"So?" I said.

Fabrice's soft body seemed to deflate as he expelled a puff of breath. "Your friend. Laurence Delaisse."

There was a cold rush through my veins. "I don't believe it," I said. "I'm very sorry, Isabelle."

My head started to pound, and my limbs felt as heavy as sandbags.

"Don't think too badly of her. There was a lot of pressure on her," said Fabrice. "Her mother worked for me briefly after leaving Poiret, and I still see her from time to time. She'd been telling me for months how unhappy Laurence was at Chanel. Her uncle, her mother's brother, is ill and out of work, so Laurence has been supporting his family, too."

"What about the jersey?" I asked.

"The jersey?" Fabrice looked confused for a moment. Then he said, "Oh, that."

"Did Laurence steal the jersey, too?"

Fabrice nodded.

"Why was it at Madame Petrova's apartment?"

"I didn't want Thérèse to find it. The toiles folded up easily, but it's hard to hide twenty-five bolts of fabric. Laurence sneaked it out one bolt at a time and gave the Russian a little money to hold it."

"I thought you weren't trying to hurt Mademoiselle."

"That was a little vengeful, I'll admit."

"Thank you at least for returning the toiles."

"I am truly sorry, Isabelle. I hope you'll forgive me someday."

I gathered up as many toiles as I could carry—Daniel said he'd bring the rest to my apartment in the morning—and walked with him to the front hall. We stood awkwardly for a minute, Daniel with his fists plunged in his pockets, me hugging my toiles. Finally, Daniel opened the door, letting in a warm draft. I took a step over the threshold and paused. "Good night," he said.

"Good night," I answered, though it was the last thing I wanted to say.

* * *

I couldn't wait until tomorrow to confront Laurence. At her apartment, a crumbling eighteenth-century building on a narrow pre-Haussmann street, I climbed the stairs and rang the bell. Laurence's mother answered the door. She looked exactly like her daughter, except she was old with wrinkles and a frizzy gray topknot on her head. "I'm Isabelle Varlet," I said.

"Isabelle Varlet! I'm delighted to meet you at last!" She looked at the toiles in my arms, and her face darkened. "Laurence isn't here. Was she expecting you?"

"No."

"You can come in and wait if you like. She's out with Tanguy and probably won't be back until late." She glanced again at the toiles. "What are you carrying there?"

"That's what I want to talk to her about. Will you ask her to call me?" I scribbled the concierge's number on a piece of paper and handed it to her.

"I will," she said, shoving the paper in her pocket without looking at it.

I slept fitfully that night, and the next morning I awoke to find a petit bleu from Laurence under my door. "Dear Isabelle," it began:

So you know. It's a relief in a way to have it over, the stress of it all nearly killed me. I'm sorry that I hurt you, as I am fond of you and admiring of your work. Someday, I hope, I'll have a chance to tell you about the financial pressures that led me to accept Fabrice's offer. I am ashamed of what I did, of course, but under the circumstances you might have done the same thing. My mother and I are leaving Paris. I suppose it is too much to ask that you not tell Mademoiselle about this. If you could see it in your heart to make up some benign excuse about why I've left, I'd be eternally grateful.

Regretfully yours, Laurence

I sat on my bed for a long while staring at Laurence's letter. Then I stood, splashed some water on my face from the pitcher on the nightstand and got dressed. The room was hot, and the air had a stagnant odor. I felt exhausted and numb.

At eight o'clock, Daniel picked me up in a taxi with the rest of the toiles hidden in shopping bags. We got to 31, rue Cambon early, and he helped me carry the bags up to Madame Georges's office. I left a note on her desk to call me when she got in. Later in the morning, when I finally stood in front of her, I handed her Laurence's letter. "What do you think?" I asked when she'd read it. It was a relief to let the decision be Madame Georges's.

The house manager removed her spectacles and rubbed her eyes with the heels of her hands. "I'll have to tell Mademoiselle that Laurence is gone. But I think we should remain quiet about the toiles," she said. Madame Georges replaced the spectacles on her face and folded her hands in front of her on her desk. "Mademoiselle never has to know."

"There have been a lot of rumors in the atelier. I think the doorman at the Ritz knows, too."

"What?"

"He's been seeing Laurence."

"Anyone else?"

I thought of Charlie Spinelli, but decided not to mention him. "No."

"Put the toiles in the storage room, Isabelle. Somewhere in the back where no one will find them."

I started to walk out the door and remembered my promise to God. Turning to Madame Georges, I asked, "Do you know a good coiffeur?"

"Why?"

"I made a vow that if the toiles were found, I'd cut my hair."

"Silly girl. I don't know. Ask Mademoiselle."

I didn't have to think too hard about what to tell the seamstresses. The lie appeared in my head and rolled easily off my tongue. "Laurence's mother is gravely ill, and she's taken her to the country to care for her," I said. I was standing in the middle of the workroom between the tables where the women sat with their sewing. None of the seamstresses seemed very surprised or disappointed.

"Are you the première now?" asked one of the junior *mains*.

"I don't know."

At the end of the day, Mademoiselle called me to her office. I found her sitting at her desk going over paperwork. The window behind her was open, and the warm August light held something new, a kind of couture glow. Sifting in, it looked faintly like ribbons of lemon chiffon. "I'm promoting you to première," said Mademoiselle.

"Thank you."

"You haven't heard from Laurence?"

"No." I hoped she couldn't read the lie in my expression.

"I never thought she'd skip out on me before the opening, but to tell you the truth, I'd lost confidence in her a long time ago. She was lazy."

"She had her problems."

"We all have problems. Don't make excuses for her." Mademoiselle lit a cigarette and blew a jet of smoke into the air. "Now, what's this I hear about you cutting your hair? Madame Georges says you promised God you'd cut it in time for the opening?"

"Yes."

"You shouldn't go around promising things to God. That's a bad habit to get into."

"Can you recommend a good coiffeur?"

"You don't need a coiffeur. I'll do it myself. Sit down."

I dropped into the chair behind me, as Mademoiselle advanced toward me with a scissors in her hand. Suddenly, I was very afraid. I already missed the lovely long sheet of my hair. I was terrified of what I would look like without it.

"Take the pins out," Mademoiselle commanded, as she smashed her cigarette in an ashtray.

I obeyed, and my hair tumbled down over my shoulders. Mademoiselle grabbed a section and hacked it off below my ear. "Not too short," I pleaded. "I don't want to look like a boy."

Mademoiselle's lips curved up slyly. "You don't think short hair is sexy?"

She grabbed another chunk of hair and snipped again. I sat erect and tense, afraid to move a muscle.

"I want to tell you something, Varlet. A woman's mind is the sexiest thing about her. Even a plain girl who keeps herself neat, who doesn't get fat, who dresses nicely and has interests, is sexier than a beauty with no intelligence and no style."

A big piece of hair fell onto my cheek, and I twitched my nose and mouth to dislodge it.

"What do you think happens to those women with perfect faces and nothing up here?" she continued, jabbing at a temple with her left index finger. "At nineteen they're goddesses, but by thirty they're washed up. No man of any worth stays in love with a woman like that."

As she warmed to her argument, her snipping grew more furious. The scissors clicked loudly in my ear. "I'm telling you, work and independence are what keep women young and attractive. But most women don't understand that," she continued. "Most women want to get married so a man will take care of them, and they can retire from life. What would have happened to me, if I hadn't had ambition, if I'd stayed in the Auvergne? I probably would have ended up married to a farmer, milking cows, and, eventually, blowing my brains out."

This thought made her snip faster and more furiously still. "Long hair doesn't make women feminine. Femininity is a state of mind."

When it was over, a ring of blond hair circled the floor around me. As Mademoiselle studied me, her face took on a pained expression. "Maybe you *should* go to the coiffeur," she said.

"Can I see?" I asked.

I stood and walked to the mirror on the back wall above the settee, and when I saw my reflection, I burst into tears. My hair looked like it had been hacked off with a knife. It stuck out from my head in uneven chunks; one side was two inches longer than the other which barely covered my ear.

I was sobbing now, trying to stifle the sound with my hands.

"Don't be such a baby," scolded Mademoiselle. "Go to the coiffeur tonight. He'll fix it."

Mademoiselle scribbled something on a piece of paper and handed it to me. She'd written: "Émile, The Garden Salon, 23, rue Lantier."

When I arrived there later, I found a small shop decorated like a garden with wrought-iron furniture and silk roses climbing on white trellises. Émile greeted me at the door. He was a portly man with stained false teeth and a black toupee, dressed in a too tight pinstriped suit.

"Mon Dieu!" he cried when I took off my hat. "Who did this to you?"

"Someone who didn't know what she was doing."

Émile drew himself up to his full height, which was only a couple of inches over five feet. "You've come to the right place. I am an artist, the Da Vinci of coiffeur," he said. "Come with me."

He led me to a room in the back with a barber chair in front of a dressing table and mirror. "Now, we get to work."

An hour later, I walked out of the Garden Salon with a chic, very short bob, known as a pineapple, because of the feathery layers starting at the crown of my head and extending to the nape of my neck. Everyone said it was becoming, but I just missed my hair.

Twenty-three

For days, nobody left the house except to catch a few hours sleep. We drank coffee to stay alert and ate food fetched by the arpètes from nearby cafés. Madame Georges had hired a couple dozen temporary workers to help during the final crush before the opening, and the workrooms were overcrowded to suffocation. Coals to stoke the irons burned all day in the stove, and even with the windows open and a fan blowing, the air sizzled, like a desert at high noon. Our fingers turned red and rough and ached with exhaustion. Whenever we had a chance, we rubbed our hands with a mixture of sugar and oil or one of the pumice stones that lay on the worktables with the wax and spools of thread.

Mademoiselle put in as many hours as we did. She moved into a room at the Ritz and arrived at work at nine sharp every morning. Dressed every day in the same blue jersey skirt and slouchy jacket with the sleeves pushed above her elbows, she went straight to her studio and worked late into the night, taking a break only to gulp a cup of coffee and a sandwich delivered at five o'clock by the maid.

The mannequins lived in their underwear on the landing outside the studio, wrapped in white smocks, or sometimes with just a sheet thrown over their shoulders. One by one, Mademoiselle would call them in, usually for final fittings of models she'd already approved, but sometimes to drape fabric for a new model, based on an idea that had just occurred to her and that she was determined to get into the collection, though only days remained until the August 5 opening.

Mademoiselle had noted the official Chambre Syndicale schedule when it had been published in the press the previous spring, and afterward chose August 5 as her opening day. Five, she said, was her lucky number. It also put her first, ahead not only of her archrival Jean Patou, who'd been assigned August 17, but also every other couturier of consequence.

As the opening approached, the collection's mood of radiant simplicity became more sharply defined. All models were pared down to their essentials; everything superfluous was cut away. The silhouette grew sleeker and more narrow. The colors, too, were restrained and neutral—beige, gray, brown, white, an occasional shot of red, and for evening, black, black, and more black.

On the eve of the opening, the entire staff gathered in the salon, where Mademoiselle stood holding a stack of white cards emblazoned with black numbers. This was the ultimate test, the moment when she decided if our models would actually make it into the collection. Mademoiselle was merciless in her sacrifices; at the last minute, pulling garments that had gone through dozens of toiles and been lovingly, meticulously sewn by women who for weeks had sacrificed their dinners and evenings at home. She didn't care that the collection would be small. She cared only that it was perfect. If something wasn't good enough for the couturière herself to wear, it was out.

"Four fifty-three!" she called.

Régine stepped forward wearing a velvet dress with a tiered skirt and a ruffled collar. Mademoiselle glowered. "Too girly. No one wants to look like that anymore."

The dress was out. The vendeuses sitting in chairs against the wall nodded approvingly to each other. Next came a fur-trimmed wool suit. "Very elegant, but the buttons are horrid," said Mademoiselle. "Get me those gold buttons from last season."

A commotion erupted in the back of the room, while several women rummaged through boxes overflowing with jewelry and accessories that crowded the tables like wares at a country bazaar. "Come on, come on," snapped Mademoiselle. "You haven't eaten them, have you?"

At last, the buttons were found, and an arpète hustled the coat up to the workroom so they could be sewn on. And so it went for hours. Mademoiselle seemed to grow more alive as the evening wore on, though the rest of us were on the verge of collapse. When two vendeuses fell asleep on chairs at the back of the room, she shouted at them to wake up. "How can you sleep at a time like this? Don't you understand what we're doing here? We're choosing clothes for a woman to meet her fate in."

Hats, gloves, shoes, and jewelry were selected from overflowing shopping bags and tried out for their effect with the models that Mademoiselle had approved. Accessories were the final notes of her collection, the last chords of her symphony. One unnecessary note could ruin the harmony of a model.

Recently, Mademoiselle had begun working with an accent coach, a friend of Misia's, to squeeze the peasant roughness from her voice. In her focus on the collection, though, her effort to speak like a sophisticated Parisienne was lost. Now orders flew out of her mouth in a low, gruff monotone. She sounded like an old housewife yelling at a country market. "Don't forget to put that brooch on. . . . Are those earrings clean? Why are you heaping on so many necklaces? She's not a display case!"

A tall, splendid blonde named Célestine stepped forward wearing a red jersey dress with a matching coat featuring large, deep pockets. "Where's the hat that matches this?" demanded Mademoiselle.

A milliner appeared with a cloth cloche and fitted it on Célestine. "You call that a hat?" Mademoiselle barked. "Where's Lawson?"

"Here," called out Susanna Lawson from the back of the room where she sat gossiping with the milliners.

"Maybe that hat would fit you," snarled Mademoiselle. "But it's not big enough for a head that actually has some brains in it."

The room rippled with snickers. Susanna sat silently.

"I know what your problem is," Mademoiselle taunted. "You're used to all those English pinheads, those dumb duchesses and dull ladies." She plucked the cloche from Célestine's head and flung it at Susanna. The Englishwoman caught it and clenched it in her fist.

Mademoiselle glared at her. "I don't want to see you again until you've made a new hat. This time for a Frenchwoman who's got something more than you do between her ears."

Susanna stomped out, and Yvette stepped in front of the mirrors in Angeline. The mannequin looked terrible. She'd lost flesh from her already excruciatingly slender frame, and the dress hung limply on her shoulders. Her face was gray; her hair had lost its luster. Mademoiselle frowned. "What's wrong with you?"

"Nothing," said Yvette. Her words were barely audible.

"Don't tell me that. I can see something's wrong with you. Are you sick?"

"My boyfriend broke up with me. After some sleep I'll be fine." It turned out that Yvette's American soldier had a fiancée at home, and he'd just announced that he was returning to her.

"Sadness is bad luck," growled Mademoiselle. "You can take that off now. Régine will wear it. And Célestine will take your other models."

I felt a sharp stab of disappointment. Angeline's beauty and elegance depended on its fit, and it would not fit Régine, who was shorter and curvier than Yvette. "Yvette's just a little sad. She'll be fine tomorrow," I offered.

"A little sad?" mocked Mademoiselle. "She looks like Bernhardt dying in *Camille*."

Yvette turned to the couturière, tears swimming in her eyes. "Please don't take it away from me. It was designed on *me,* my body."

Mademoiselle moved closer to the unhappy girl and stared hard at her. "It's *my* collection. I'm sorry for your problems, but I'm not going to sacrifice a dress to your feelings." Her eyes jumped around the room. "Where's Régine?"

The curvaceous mannequin stepped from the lineup, dropped her white robe and slipped on Angeline. One of the fitters fastened the four hooks and eyes at her lower back and adjusted the shoulder straps. Régine's shiny black hair and olive skin suited the burgundy fabric, but the dress pulled unattractively over her bosom and hips, and the shoulder straps kept slipping.

"This will never do," said Mademoiselle. She turned to Madame Georges, who stood nearby recording the numbers of the approved models in a spiral notebook.

"It's out."

"No!" I protested, more loudly than I intended.

"It looks like hell," said Mademoiselle.

"With a little adjustment . . ."

"I said, it's out."

I felt a gripping in my chest; my hands and feet turned icy. "You're making a mistake. It's one of our best models."

"Whose collection is this?"

"It's just that—"

She cut me off. "If you want it in so badly, make a new one."

"A new dress?"

"No, a new parachute. Of course, a new dress! Fitted on Régine."

"It's one o'clock in the morning."

"I know what time it is."

"The *défilé* is in fourteen hours, and I haven't had any sleep."

"Suit yourself. If there's a new dress that Régine can wear, I'll consider it."

Was she out of her mind? Perhaps in fourteen hours I could cut out the dress, sew the lining, and do the preliminary overcasting. Maybe sixteen hours was enough time to seam and turn the shoulder straps, attach the bodice to the skirt, and hem it. But make the entire dress? It had taken me several days working full time to complete the original. And that was when I'd felt rested and well. Now, I was exhausted, having worked all night with only two breaks and hardly anything to eat.

Mademoiselle must have known that the dress was doomed if I

tried to copy it. No doubt for her, it already was doomed. The choice between Yvette and Régine, between a girl who sapped the life from the dress and one who ruined its lines, was no choice at all. By making it my problem, the failure would be mine.

In the workroom, I switched on the aluminum lights. My stomach rumbled fiercely, and I ordered it to hush. I cut out the dress, using the master toile as my pattern and taking care to allow enough fabric for Régine's larger proportions. Next, I fitted the pieces to a wire form that had been padded out to the mannequin's measurements. In the middle of my work, Elise, the junior *main* who'd helped me sew replacements for the stolen toiles, walked in. "Why are you doing this, Isabelle?"

I dropped my hands to my sides and looked at her. "I can't give up on it."

"I agree it's a mistake to take it out of the collection. But it's *her* collection. Why don't you go home and get some sleep."

"I think it's better if I stay here."

"It's only a dress; it's not your life."

"I feel like it is, though."

"All right, I'll help you." She left and returned five minutes later with two seamstresses.

While Elise sewed the lining from a piece of smooth, tightly woven silk, the other women assisted us, basting and ironing the pieces as we went along. We were working with the finest silk crepe de chine. It was a fabric of beauty, strength, and vitality, with a fierce will of its own. If the crepe de chine was mishandled or mistreated, it would protest—"bounce," in seamstress parlance—by literally standing up to announce that it was not lying correctly on the grain.

Gradually, the dress began to take shape, and I forgot my hunger and exhaustion.

The side cascades were as difficult as ever. Each one demanded careful draping of the fabric so the extensions at the hips would flutter out in graceful folds. The added ruffles at the bottom required painstakingly tiny stitches down the length of the skirt to form fine, almost invisible seams. So the ruffles would ruffle, the stitches had to have just the right size and tension.

By midmorning, I had finished the cascades. Elise now had completed the lining, and I sewed it into the top of the bodice, then secured the bodice to the skirt. While one of the seamstresses finished the long straps, I sewed four fastenings at the back of the dress that crossed over left to right and were invisible to the eye. Then I added the side bow and sewed on the straps. Now, all that remained was to trim down the seam allowances, overcast the seams, steam, roll, and sew the seam and stitch on some decorative detail.

By noon, the dress was done. I slipped it over the dress form and stood back. It was perfect. Carefully, I lifted Angeline's skirt, clipped a slice of seam, then dropped it into the pocket of my smock.

When Régine donned Angeline in the studio, the fabric flowing gracefully over the girl's curves, the waterfalls of crepe de chine at the hips ending in delicate points on the floor. Mademoiselle puffed on a cigarette, as she walked around the mannequin, studying Angeline from every angle. She looked pleased. "Fan!" she cried.

My heart hammered. "Does this mean the dress is in?" I asked.

"We'll see," said Mademoiselle.

An arpète reached into a box and pulled out a huge ostrich feather fan that had been dyed the same wine color as Angeline.

"Stockings and shoes!"

The arpète went into another box for a pair of silk stockings and pumps. They, too, had been dyed burgundy. Régine slipped them on, and they fit perfectly.

"Headband!" Mademoiselle barked. Another arpète retrieved a burgundy headband, an idea Mademoiselle had appropriated from tennis star Suzanne Lenglen, who'd worn a similar one during her championship match at Wimbleton. The arpète helped Régine secure it low over her forehead.

"All right, you better get down to the dressing room with the others," Mademoiselle told Régine. "And if you see Yvette, tell her to go home. I don't want her and her sadness anywhere near the house today."

"Thank you, Mademoiselle!" I could have kissed her.

"What are you thanking me for?" the couturière asked, as she removed the ribbon holding her scissors from around her neck. "I'm not doing this for you."

While Mademoiselle attended a lunch in her honor at Misia's house, I went outside for some fresh air and a quick meal. When I returned at two, a large crowd, mostly men, had gathered in front of the door at 31, rue Cambon. The buyers were under great pressure to place their orders before their competitors, but only representatives from the most important manufacturers and stores had been invited to this first opening. The other buyers, as well as the press and the darlings, had to content themselves with seeing the collection later in the week.

No one got in without an invitation, though that didn't stop many of the buyers from trying. They were shoving and shouting. "I should have gotten an invitation!" cried a small man in a white linen suit. "I bought practically the entire collection last February!"

"Why do Marshall Field and Franklin Simon get in and not Rothstein and Pitofsy?" called a thin bald man with a Swiss accent.

"This is outrageous!" shouted an Italian baritone from the center of the crowd. "I demand a seat!"

The white-gloved doorman stood erect and fierce, his body blocking the door as he tried to stare the crowd into submission.

"Isabelle!" Charlie Spinelli was calling my name and pushing through the crowd. "Can you get me in?" he asked, when he was standing by my side. His straw boater was pushed back on his forehead and sweat beaded his reddened face.

"I couldn't get the Sun King in without an invitation. You know the rules."

He looked at me with an expression of grave concern. "Did your toiles ever turn up?"

"Yes."

"Who had them?"

"Someone sent them back anonymously," I lied.

"Lucky for you."

"Yes, it was lucky."

"If you're not going to get me in, will you at least have dinner with me?"

"Not tonight. I haven't slept in days."

It took several minutes to push my way to the entrance, where the doorman opened the door just wide enough for me to squeeze in. A group of Mademoiselle's friends whom she'd invited for moral support stood in the salon. Fashionably dressed, the men in dark suits, the women in silk dresses, they were chatting and sparkling, holding the gleaming light from the chandeliers and the freshly polished floor.

Boy Capel was with a tall man in a black suit. "I'm surprised to see you here," said the tall man. He had gray hair slicked back on his forehead and a stubby gray moustache.

"Why would that be?" asked Capel. He wore an impeccable brown suit and white spats over his shoes. "I'm as interested in beautiful women in beautiful clothes as the next man."

"I only thought . . . because of Diana . . ."

"Don't think. It'll ruin the afternoon."

"Did that Chanel shop in Biarritz turn out to be a good investment?"

"She's paid me back already."

"How much?"

"Three hundred thousand francs."

The tall man chuckled through his moustache. "She's not a bad businesswoman."

"Better than most men I've known."

I moved away from Capel and his companion and made my way upstairs. Seamstresses crowded the stair landing, and I struggled to find a spot with a good view of the salon, finally settling on the floor, where I could peer through the banister spindles.

Mademoiselle's friends had gathered on the top stairs: Misia Godebska and her fiancé, the painter José Maria Sert; Caryathis; the opera singer Marthe Davelli. Boy Capel was not with them. He was crossing the salon, negotiating his way through the maze of chairs. Near the door, he paused to look at gloves in one of the vitrines. He checked his watch. Then he slipped out.

A moment later, the swarm of buyers burst in. After they'd settled in their seats, Mademoiselle appeared, wearing the cream crepe de chine dress I'd made for her in the spring. Around her neck hung a long string of pearls that swung gently as she crossed the hallway, then stopped to sit on the top step. A mannequin stood in the wings wearing an unlined, simple beige suit, trimmed minimally with picot edging on the long jacket's shawl collar, sash, and cuffs. At exactly three o'clock, she stepped into the salon. The voices damped down, then fell silent. The défilé had begun.

Like portrait subjects who'd stepped from their canvases at the Louvre, the mannequins strolled through the salon with otherworldly grace. Holding white cards announcing in bold black lettering the numbers of their models, they stared straight ahead, pausing occasionally to let a buyer fondle the fabric of their hems. There were frocks in gray, brown, and black jersey, long coats with loose belts and great pockets, suits and capes generously trimmed in fur. Older buyers inspected the clothes through lorgnettes, an expression of bright eagerness on their faces. Everyone was searching for *the* dress: the one that would increase their profits and make them happy; the department stores sought a dress that would look good on a variety of ages and sizes; the wholesale manufacturers wanted a dress that could be copied easily and cheaply for the firms where they had contracts; the luxury-shop owners needed a dress that would charm one or two special clients.

During intermission Madame Georges ran up to me, wringing her hands and looking alarmed. "We've a little crisis with four twelve."

My chest tightened. "What's wrong?"

"Some of the stitching on one of the cascades has come out."

"That's impossible. Those stitches are as strong as steel."

"I think someone stepped on the dress and pulled it out at the hip."

"Oh, no!" Clutching my needle bag, I hurried through the salon, following a line of butlers carrying trays holding canapés, glasses, and champagne. In the mannequins' dressing room, my eyes darted about for Régine. The square, windowless room was hot, the air heavy and close with cigarette smoke and perfumed skin. Clothes hung on double *rayons* from the floor to the ceiling of every wall, giving the room the feeling of a padded jewelry box. With the close quarters, the jars of makeup lying about and everyone smoking, it was amazing that accidents didn't happen more often, that the dresses didn't get smeared and stained or go up in flames.

Régine stood in front of her mirrored dressing table in Angeline. The seam on the right side of the skirt was ripped, and the cascade at the hip had flattened out into an unattractive lump of fabric.

"How did this happen?" I wailed.

The mannequin pointed her head in the direction of a beautiful girl with a black bob as shiny as lacquer. I hadn't seen her since the night of Fabrice's party, but I recognized Victorine Dusser immediately. Since Fabrice had fired her, she couldn't find work as a mannequin. Everyone knew about the scene she'd made at Le Roland, and no couturier would have anything to do with her. I'd heard that during the August openings, she'd taken to prowling the mannequins' dressing rooms, hoping to fill in for some girl who'd gotten sick at the last minute.

Now Victorine lay on the floor in a simple gray dress, her head propped up on a chair cushion, her long white legs stretched out in front of her like the legs of a statue.

"She wasn't watching where she was walking," moaned Régine. "She stepped on the dress and pulled it with her. She's such a big girl!" Régine started to cry. "She doesn't belong here, anyway."

"Never mind about her. I can fix this with my eyes closed." I pulled a needle out of my bag and threaded it—there was no time to wax or press it—and began sewing, making small, even stitches, finishing just as Madame Georges announced that it was time for *les robes du soir*.

I watched the rest of the défilé from the mannequins' entrance.

The silk and satin dresses—all sleeveless, trainless, and above the ankle—spun out a lightness, a feeling of romance and hope. Angeline appeared last. Everything about Régine looked right, from the burgundy headband she wore low over her forehead, to the long chandelier earrings dusting her collarbones, to the simple burgundy pumps with the curved Louis heels and the immense ostrich feather fan waving in her right hand. Gasps of pleasure rippled through the audience. The buyers lifted their eyebrows and nodded in solemn approval.

Régine made her circuit through the aisles flanked by the tightly packed rows of buyers. I watched their faces, the greedy look in their eyes. They did not understand Angeline, the artistry and love that had created it. They would make lifeless, ill-fitting copies for women who wouldn't be worthy of it.

Régine disappeared behind the stairs, and loud applause rang out. The défilé was over. Several people threw bouquets of flowers. Others jumped to their feet shouting, "Bravo!" A woman in the front row, a buyer from Rome, had tears in her eyes.

I felt the triumph as my own. *My* skill, *my* dedication had led to this moment. Mademoiselle couldn't have done it without me.

Now she was standing, smiling halfheartedly with her lips closed and staring beyond the gilded chairs and the people, as if she saw through the walls of the salon to the world outside. She looked up to where the seamstresses were crowded on the landing. The women jumped excitedly about, squealing like schoolgirls. Mademoiselle nodded to them. I watched her face, expecting to see happiness, or, at least, the warmth of satisfaction, but her eyes were the dull black of old nails.

Later, in the studio, we celebrated with champagne left over from the interval. "Everyone loved your dress!" Monique Thabard said, raising a glass to me.

"There's a stampede for it!" added Madame Georges. "All the buyers want it."

When Mademoiselle came through the door, she was scowling. She marched directly to me. "The bodice on four twelve was so loose, I thought it was going to fall off Régine," she snapped.

The bodice fit perfectly. No one in her right mind would say that it didn't. Anyway, Mademoiselle had seen the model before the défilé and had said nothing about a problem with the bodice. If I pointed this out, though, I knew she'd explode. Something had poisoned the evening for her, and she needed to vent. Was it exhaustion, or had Boy Capel ruined it by leaving before the défilé? Perhaps she simply couldn't enjoy success, her mistrust of good fortune having convinced her that to celebrate it was the first step toward losing it. "Pleasure is a trap," she'd once told me.

"What if the top had fallen down?" snarled Mademoiselle. "Very chic that would have been with Régine's titties on display."

"The men would have liked that!" blurted a seamstress from the back of the room.

"You're an imbecile, Varlet. I can't believe I hired someone so stupid."

My chest felt tight, like someone was squeezing my heart. But I had to defend myself. "The dress is beautiful. Everyone loved it," I said.

Mademoiselle's dark eyes bored into me. "Anyway, you approved it," I added.

I waited for one of the women to echo my words, for Madame Georges to tell Mademoiselle again that all the buyers were ordering the dress, for Monique Thabard to repeat her lavish compliment, for the seamstresses to rise up in my defense. The room was silent. Mademoiselle had her face close to mine. Her eyebrows, as black and thick as eels, knitted together threateningly. "Don't contradict me!" she screamed.

"I've been up all night."

"You think you're the only one who hasn't slept?"

The couturière swung around, heading toward the door. Before marching through it, she barked out one last command. "Tomorrow we go back to work!"

* * *

I would not be going back to work. I picked up my purse and walked out the door. As I made my way down the hall, I heard fading voices from the salon below and the scrape of wood on wood—the cleaning crew moving chairs. I entered the mannequins' dressing room. The air was sweet with the scent of bouquets piled several feet high in the sink. Some of the mannequins already had left; others lounged at their mirrored tables, removing makeup and gossiping. The girls' dresser, an old woman with a gray bun and thick-soled shoes, shuffled about, gathering the earrings, necklaces, bracelets, pins, and rings that had been worn in the défilé and restocking them in wooden boxes. I headed straight for the far wall, where metal *rayons* held tonight's collection. I pawed through the rack until I found Angeline. In a minute, I'd shed my smock and slipped the burgundy dress over my head. I was about the same size as Régine, and the dress fit well, though it was a little long and loose in the shoulders.

"Isabelle, what are you doing?" Régine was at my side in her slippers and wrapper, her arms crossed over her chest.

"I'm taking my dress."

"Take these, too!" cried Victorine Dusser, as she hurled a pair of burgundy pumps, followed by the fan Régine had carried in the défilé, across the room. The shoes landed at my feet, but the dresser caught the fan in midair and carted it away. Heading out the door, I grabbed my smock and the shoes and took the stairs to the storage room. I found my toiles and stuffed as many as I could into two large shopping bags.

Outside, the August air had cooled, and a gold twilight raked the narrow street. I walked to rue de Rivoli and descended into the metro. As I waited on the grimy platform, Angeline drew stares from the plainly dressed working people, and I was glad when the train roared in, blasting heat through the tunnel. The steel doors parted, and I took a seat in an empty car.

I closed my eyes, and when I opened them, the euphoria I'd felt a few minutes ago was lost. I was heading into a void as black as the tunnel racing by the window. What would I do when I got back to my room? I did not want to be alone. I had taken a bold step tonight, and more bold steps would be needed if I was to move away from darkness.

At the next stop, I got off the train and hurried through the station to the street. It was crowded and noisy, full of life. I hailed a taxi and directed the driver to 43, rue Sevran. Inside the apartment building, I did not wait for the old iron elevator, but walked up the three flights of stairs. I rang the bell outside number 3B, and Daniel opened the door. "Isabelle! My God, you cut your hair," he said, taking the shopping bags from my hands and kissing me on each of my burning cheeks. His eyes traveled over my hair. Then he stepped back. "Let me see the rest of you."

Daniel put the shopping bags on the floor and studied me with an alert intensity, as though I were a long lost lover he thought he'd never see again.

I held my arms out, turning slowly in a circle.

"Nice dress," he said.

1962

Epilogue

The letter arrived on a sunny day in April, and I knew it was important from the scent and feel of the beige envelope, as luxurious and soft as the finest linen. I pried open the flap and removed the typewritten sheet inside. "Dear Madame Blank," it began:

> *I am writing you because of an exciting upcoming exhibition at our museum called* Les Années Folles *1918–29, scheduled to open September 10 and run through October 28. The exhibition will highlight the achievements of thirty couturiers whose visionary designs have had a lasting impact on the mode.*
>
> *The years 1918 to 1929 represent an historical landmark in couture, and we hope to mount an exhibition that will demonstrate the insistent authority of the high aesthetic quality that characterizes it.*
>
> *Gabrielle Chanel's work, perhaps more than anyone else's at that time, reflects a chicly formulated modernity, one that stormed the barricades of the old mode, transgressing class to revolutionize fashion.*
>
> *We are searching throughout France for the best examples of*

her work from this period. We hope to bring to our selections the same standards of connoisseurship and judgment that are used to address any work of art. We are particularly interested in a dress in your possession, which we understand from Madame Ursula Georges dates back to the 1919 Chanel collection. We are wondering if you would consider giving us the privilege of examining it, with an eye toward including it in the exhibition?

Please call me at your convenience. I look forward to meeting you.

> *Sincerely,*
> *Antoine Perret, assistant curator*
> *Musée de la Couture Parisienne*

I sat near the window fingering my glasses. I lingered over the phrases "insistent authority of aesthetic quality" and "chicly formulated modernity," which I wasn't sure I understood. Then, rising from the chair with stiff legs, I went to the phone in the hall and dialed Antoine Perret's number. A secretary put me through, and I invited Perret to tea the following afternoon.

He arrived at five, carrying a leather briefcase. He looked to be about thirty, an exceptionally tall man with close-cropped hair as black as the rims of his glasses. We made small talk as we drank our tea in the salon. After twenty minutes, Perret set his cup and saucer on the table. "I'm very eager to see the dress," he said.

I led him into the hall, where I opened the door to the linen closet and pointed to a box on the highest shelf. Perret reached up to retrieve it and carried the box to the dining room.

He removed a pair of white gloves from his pocket and pulled them over his long slim hands, as I spread a clean cloth across the table. Carefully, as if he were handling a wounded child, Perret lifted Angeline from the box and laid it on the cloth. I had not looked at the dress in fifteen years, since the day I'd taken it out for my daughter to try on. Julie is a pianist; like all the women in her family, she creates beauty with her hands. At fourteen, when she made her professional debut at Salle Rameau, I suggested that she wear Angeline, mostly for sentimental reasons, since it was what I wore the night her father and I decided to be in love. It looked wonderful on her, but Julie thought it made her hips wide, and she refused to wear it. I made a new dress for her concert instead.

Perret inspected every inch of Angeline, then turned the dress inside out and examined the seams. "All these perfect hand stitches, as fresh as if they'd been sewn yesterday," he exclaimed, then turning to me, "You did all this?"

"I had some help, but, yes, I cut it out and sewed most of it."

I could never make those tiny meticulous stitches now. Last year, because of my worsening eyesight, I had to give up the dressmaking shop I'd owned since returning from America with Daniel in December 1919. We had been married aboard ship and spent several months touring the East Coast. One day, while walking on Broadway in New York, the strap holding Daniel's peg snapped. I was there to break his fall, but the mishap alarmed Daniel, and he decided to try a new prosthetic. We found a wonderful doctor who made him an elm and leather leg—the best on the market—and Daniel has worn it ever since.

Back in Paris, I rented a storefront near the rue Sevran apartment, where we still live. Madame Duval sent me fabric left over from her Agen shop and money to buy a sewing machine. Using Mademoiselle's toiles for inspiration, I made up a collection of dresses and suits. The simplicity of the designs made them easy to copy, and though my machine-made, ready-to-wear versions had none of the precision fit and elegant finishing of couture, they were fresh and chic and appealed to the young working women who were my clients.

From time to time over the years, Daniel had urged me to move the shop to a more fashionable quarter, where my clients would be more fashionable. But I was not ambitious. I liked staying close to home and Julie.

Though my stitching is slower and less even now, I still sew things for myself and Julie, and I make all of Daniel's shirts. I can't imagine a life without stitching, and I pray that my vision will last as long as the rest of me.

"The dress is in perfect condition, and it's a good example of that period. It was all about symmetry in those days," said Perret. "If you had a cascade on one side, you had to put one on the other side, too. But it doesn't say 'Chanel' to me. It could have been done by any number of couturiers."

The pride I felt a moment ago vanished in disappointment. "It's all I have, I'm afraid."

"It's hard to find early Chanel. I don't know what happened to all those beaded flapper dresses. They got danced into the ground, I suppose. A lot of what I've seen is in tatters."

Perret looked hard at me, his eyes small and flat behind the thick lenses of his glasses. "I can't promise it will make it into the exhibition, but I'd like to borrow the dress. We'll take good care of it."

"I don't see why not," I said. "It's just been sitting in the closet."

When Perret opened the box containing Angeline, a ribbon of memories had spiraled out. I asked Perret if he'd tried to contact a woman named Laurence Delaisse. "It doesn't ring a bell," he said.

The last I'd heard from Laurence was after Julie's birth. I don't know how she knew of it, but she'd written to congratulate me. She said her mother had died and that she managed a small hotel in the countryside. She gave no other details of her life and no address, though her letter was postmarked Andalucia, Spain.

As it turned out, Angeline did make it into the exhibition, and I was invited, as were all the donors, to the opening of *Les Années Folles,* which was held on a warm evening in September. Daniel was in London, visiting the offices of *The Truth,* the newspaper he'd been the Paris correspondent for since Julie's birth, so I went alone. The Musée de la Couture Parisienne sits behind towering gilded gates on boulevard Haussmann in a grand eighteenth-century building that had once been a private home.

Tubs of white chrysanthemums flanked the stone steps and a perfumed cavalcade of VIPs streamed up the red carpet, as silver light from the paparazzi's cameras flashed in the air. Inside, the marble lobby was mobbed. The catalogue I'd been given at the door told me thirty couturiers were represented, and as I made my way through the first floor salons, I found exhibits for Vionnet, Patou, Lanvin, and Poiret.

Despite the polished setting, the clothes displayed on wood dress forms behind velvet ropes looked sad and lifeless. I remembered something Mademoiselle had said long ago—"If there's no woman, there's no dress." *They should have hired mannequins to wear the clothes* I thought.

On the second floor, I came upon a lone model by Fabrice, a black velvet and brocade cape embroidered with an immense dragon from his last collection in February 1919. Poor man. Thérèse, after threatening to leave him for years, finally had made good on her word, and two years later, Fabrice had died alone and broke in a little apartment near Saint-Germain.

Just then, a clatter of voices erupted behind me. Students from the École de Chambre Syndicale, the school that trained young people for couture careers, had trooped in. They looked like American beatniks, the boys in black jeans and jackets, the girls in black skirts and sweaters, their hair long and stringy, their eyes lined in kohl and their lips red. They were looking at Fabrice's cape and giggling. "What kind of freak designed that?" said a boy who had his arm around a sullen, skinny girl.

She pulled away from him and slapped him affectionately on the shoulder. "I'd like to see you do better," she said.

I found Mademoiselle's display on the third floor in a salon that was feebly lit by old sconces. Locked glass cases held a collection of her costume jewelry and hats. A huge empty bottle of Chanel No. 5, as big as a stove, stood in front of the fireplace. Once in the twenties, when it had been filled with perfume, it had belonged to the Jazz Age sensation Josephine Baker.

As I looked at the models on display, I saw that many of the highlights of Mademoiselle's early career were here: Angeline, of course;

also: a jersey cardigan jacket and skirt from 1920; the short little black dress that became a fashion icon in 1926 after American *Vogue* pronounced it as innovative as Ford's Model T; a printed silk dress with a coat lined in the same silk print, from 1922. This model, the catalogue noted, had been loaned by Amanda Nichols, who, Antoine Perret told me, now lived in New York and still worked as an art agent at age eighty-three.

Perret, who had been downstairs greeting people, just then rushed into the room. "She's here!" he cried.

"Who?"

"La Grande Mademoiselle!"

I followed Perret to the ground floor. There near the spiralling staircase, surrounded by admirers, stood Mademoiselle. It was the first time I'd seen her in forty-three years, and it was a shock. Dressed in a trench coat and boots, she looked like a parody of her younger self, still slim and wiry, but with withered limbs and a deeply lined face. A black fringe of bangs peeked out from her large hat; it had the flat fake look of a wig. "Why is it so dark in here?" she grumbled.

"So the paintings won't fade," said one of the guards.

"Would it kill the paintings to put a few lamps around? I'm sure they'd like to see what's going on."

"I'll suggest it, Mademoiselle."

"She doesn't look bad for an old lady," Perret whispered to me. "But I'd lose those boots."

Talking nonstop and gesturing with her cigarette holder, Mademoiselle walked along the velvet ropes, examining the garments on display. She had nothing good to say about any of them. When she passed a black satin *robe de soir* by Agnes, Mademoiselle snarled, "Agnes had no taste."

She scoffed at a brocaded coat by Jenny—"That looks like the back of a sofa!"—snickered at a hobble skirt by Poiret—"What a genius he was; corsets were more comfortable"—and laughed at a hoop skirt by Doeuillet—"What is the woman who wears that supposed to do when she sits down?"—apparently forgetting that she had done a similar model in 1919.

When one of the women in her party admired a marine jersey chemise with a matching jacket by Beer, she said, "Of course, it's elegant, he stole it from me." And of another Beer suit, she added, "Now that's chic. It looks like Chanel."

A moment later, she stood in front of a sweater with a geometric pattern and a pleated skirt by Patou. "Oh, God, look at that. Like something you'd wear to play golf. What a phony he was!"

The reporters lurking nearby scribbled down everything Mademoiselle said. Over the years, I'd read her impolitic comments in the press and chuckled over them. The things she'd said privately to us in the studio, things that made us cringe and roll our eyes, she now announced boldly to reporters, and the comments were published in newspapers and magazines. It amazed me that she got away with it.

"Okay, I've seen this garbage," she said, then turning to one of the guards. "Where are the Chanels?"

"Upstairs, Mademoiselle," he answered.

"Why are you hiding them?"

The guard started to say something, but Mademoiselle cut him off. "Never mind; let's go."

Mademoiselle scrutinized each of her models, commenting volubly on them all. "Oh, yes, that was a hit. . . . Everyone wanted that dress. . . . I started a revolution with this one. . . . They're still wearing things like that today!"

She was standing next to me now, our shoulders were only a few inches apart. I could feel my heart beating and told it to slow down. "What do we have here?" she asked, as she scrutinized Angeline. She tried to read the sign posted on the metal stand in front of the dress, and when she couldn't, reached into her purse for her glasses. She put them on and read out loud: "Silk crepe de chine evening dress, 1919. Courtesy of Isabelle Varlet Blank."

If the name meant anything to her, she showed no sign of it. She removed her glasses and turned to me. Her eyes hadn't changed; they were exactly as I remembered them, dark and mischievous, full of fire and determination. "Nineteen nineteen," she said. "That was the year I woke up famous."

She looked approvingly at my simple black wool suit and the single strand of pearls at my neck. She didn't recognize me, though. I've changed a lot over the years, and the world is full of seamstresses. She's seen hundreds of us come and go.

Great success has attended the absolutely simple model of burgundy crepe de chine sketched at the left on page 56. It is closely wrapped around the figure and has cascades of material at each side, which end touching the floor. With it is carried a huge fan of uncurled ostrich, the sort of fan which always decorates the table in Chanel's salon; the slippers and stockings exactly match the gown, so that the effect of gorgeousness which the gown undeniably gives comes solely from the color and is obtained by such simple means that one wonders how it is achieved.

Simplicity, the sort of simplicity that always has been and always will be expensive, is the characteristic of the Chanel frock; but once the winter gaieties of Paris begin again, there will be no models more often seen than hers, for her success is distinctly among the true Parisiennes.

—*Vogue,* NOVEMBER I, 1919

Author's Note

At the dawn of the Jazz Age in the early twentieth century—long before she gave the world quilted handbags, black-toed sling-backs, boxy bouclé suits, and costume jewelry emblazoned with interlocking "C"s—Coco Chanel created a style of casual elegance that still influences how women dress.

The Collection is an imaginative account of how a seamstress might have experienced the birth of this style. The character of Isabelle Varlet, the young woman who narrates the novel, is wholly invented, as are the other main characters, with the exception of Chanel, Jean Patou, and Misia Godebska. Arthur "Boy" Capel, Madeleine Vionnet, and the cartoonist Sem also make brief fictional appearances. Fabrice is an invention, though his extravagant entertaining and pompous pronouncements are inspired in part by the legendary turn-of-the-twentieth-century couturier Paul Poiret.

The plot, too, is a product of my imagination, though in fashioning my story, I've incorporated actual events, including the Bastille Day celebrations of July 14, 1919, the reopening of the Longchamps racetrack after World War I, and a brief strike by Parisian couture workers in the spring of 1919. The rivalry between Chanel and Patou depicted in the novel reflects their real-life hatred of one another.

Though the toile theft in *The Collection* is fictitious, illegal copying was a major issue in the fashion press of the day. French designers were plagued by style theft until laws allowing them to copyright their work were passed in the 1930s.

Chanel was often quoted saying she had no objection to being copied. It was flattering, she claimed, and, anyway, you couldn't stop it. But she never tolerated outright theft of her designs. In 1930, she joined Madeleine Vionnet in suing Suzanne Laneil, a copyist who was caught in a police raid with thirty-six Vionnet copies and twelve Chanels. A French court found Laneil guilty, concluding that "by a combination of fabrics, colors, accessories and the like, the originating couturiers had given to the garments a personal and creative artistic character—they were real works of art and as such entitled to the same protection accorded authors and copyright holders."

Little is known about the early years of Chanel's Paris maison de couture. In 1910, she set up shop as a milliner at 21, rue Cambon. Some of her biographers have reported that she moved to 31, rue Cambon only in October of 1919. But she is listed in the 1919 *Bottin de Commerce,* the city's industrial directory, which was published every January, as "Chanel, Gabrielle, modes et coutures, rue Cambon, 31." So, I have placed my story at this address.

According to Chanel executives, there are no extant photographs or descriptions that show what the interior of 31, rue Cambon looked like in 1919 or how the space was organized. In creating my fictional atelier I've used accounts of Chanel's working methods from subsequent years and my reading about the practices and traditions of French couture.

The clothes in the novel are drawn from descriptions and pictures of Chanel's 1919 models as featured in the newspapers and magazines of the day. Prices are based on the 1919 French franc, which had a purchasing power of about one and a half 2006 U.S. dollars. Thus, a Chanel dress that cost 3,000 francs in 1919 would cost the equivalent of about $4,400 today. It is difficult to compare actual costs, however, since the price of labor and materials has skyrocketed.

In writing *The Collection,* I have relied on the work of many authors for atmospherics, anecdotes, background information, and, in the case of characters who are based on real people, reported quotes. My chief debt is to Chanel's biographers, and in particular to these books: *Chanel Solitaire* by Claude Baillén; *Chanel* by Edmonde Charles-Roux; *Mademoiselle Chanel* by Pierre Galante (translated by Eileen Geist and Jessie Wood); *Chanel: The Couturiere at Work* by Amy de la Haye and Shelley Tobin; *Coco Chanel* by Axel Madsen; and *L'Allure de Chanel* by Paul Morand.

My portraits of Jean Patou, Madeleine Vionnet, and Misia Godebska draw on Meredith Etherington-Smith's *Patou,* Betty Kirke's *Madeleine Vionnet,* and Arthur Gold and Robert Fizdale's *Misia,* respectively. Other indispensable books are listed in the bibliography.

I could not have written *The Collection* without the help of Billy Atwell, formerly an instructor in the fashion department at the School of the Art Institute of Chicago and a designer in his own right. Billy gave me a short course in couture technique and recreated Angeline based on his deep knowledge of design history and dress construction. My diligent researchers Régine Cavallaro, Elizabeth Calleo, and Thomas Faliu came up with a wealth of material and were a delight to work with. I would also like to thank Gillion Cararra, Betty Kirke, Michael Vollbracht, Maria Pinto, Timothy Long, Stéphane Houy Towner, Jamilla Dunn, Debra Mancoff, Elinor Mancoff, Meredith Etherington-Smith, Stacey Jones, Isabelle Taudière, and the librarians in New York at the Fashion Institute of Technology and the Costume Institute of the Metropolitan Museum of Art, and in Paris at the Musée de la Mode et du Costume. Thanks also to Geneviève Madore at the Marie de Paris and Marika Genty at Chanel. To Teresa and Didier Varlet, thank you for translation help and for providing my heroine with a *nom de famille.*

Throughout my writing life, I've been lucky to have the support and guidance of wonderful agents and publishers. Lisa Drew has been a dream of an editor through three books, and though this is our last together due to her retirement, I will never forget her help and kindness to me over the years. I am grateful also to Rhoda Weyr and Jennie Dunham for their intelligence and unfailingly astute advice, and, at Scribner, to Alexis Gargagliano, whose vision and talent with a red pencil have greatly improved *The Collection.*

Thank you to Maureen Dowd, Kathy Henderson, Kerri Weitzberg Herman, Victoria Lautman, Trish Lear, Maud Lavin, Kaarina Salovaara, Rachel Shteir, Dinitia Smith, Sara Stern, and Monica Vachher for being yourselves.

As always, my husband, Richard Babcock, was by my side through every stage of writing the novel, spending long hours discussing it with me and carefully scrutinizing various drafts of the manuscript. I am everlastingly grateful to him for his strength and patience, his brilliance and wit, and, above all, his love and devotion. He and our son, Joe, make books worth writing and life worth living.

G. D.

ear Reader,

Though I can't sew a stitch, I come from a long line of seamstresses and tailors. During the late nineteenth century, my maternal great-grandfather made vestments for priests in a small town outside Naples, Italy. After the family emigrated to New York, his son, my mother's father, became a hatter. Several of my great aunts and both of my grandmothers worked for clothing manufacturers in Manhattan and Newark, New Jersey.

Of all the residents of this ancestral heaven, Rose DeMarzo, my maternal grandmother, looms the largest. She died when I was a baby, and I never knew her. Yet my mother, who revered her, regaled me with stories about her, and in an odd way, I feel close to her. Rose was one of those immigrant superwomen who supported her out-of-work husband and five children throughout the Depression and still managed to cook, clean, and sew everyone's clothes, including her sons' shirts and her daughters' winter coats. My mother saved some of these garments well into her own old age. I remember a beautiful wool suit in blue tartan and a black and white printed silk dress with a red organdy flower on the belt. Those disappeared long ago, but I still have a black crocheted evening bag that Rose made for my mother's trousseau. I've also recently acquired, thanks to my aunt Filomena Farley's closet cleaning, the white satin and lace gown that my grandmother wore to her 1914 wedding. Short and low-waisted with a white satin sash loosely tied over the hips, it is gorgeously hand stitched in luxurious fabric, and it is probably the closest my grandmother ever got to couture sewing. I imagine her stitching it after putting in a long day on Seventh Avenue, after washing the dinner dishes and putting her younger siblings to bed, staying up into the wee hours, pouring all her love for my grandfather into this one dress that she would wear for only a few hours. For her, the gown must have been a symbol of the future, and when I hold it now, it seems to transcend the details of my grandmother's story and evoke an entire generation of immigrant dreams.

When I was growing up, Rose's shiny black Singer sewing machine had pride of place in the bay window of our guest room in suburban Washington, D.C. Decorated with gold metalwork and lacy floral decals, it was set in a walnut art deco cabinet that also held the original manual, its pages mildewed and curled at the edges, and a few ancient spools of thread, their colors faded by time and coatings of dust.

The machine was strictly for show. The only person who actually ever used it was my *other* grandmother, Anna Diliberto, on the one visit she made to us a few years before her death. She preferred that we come to her, which we did twice a year, visiting her in the Orange, New Jersey, two-flat where my father had been raised, a few streets away from the Italian grocery the family owned.

Anna would have fit nicely in a Sicilian village at the turn of the last century. Dressed in black down to her sturdy shoes, her yard-long gray hair in a hastily tied bun at the nape of her neck, she spoke little and regarded the world through rimless glasses perched on the end of her nose. She is the only one of my Italian grandparents I was able to trace through Ellis Island records. On the log of the *Sicilian Prince,* the ship she rode to America in 1903, Anna is described as a literate, healthy thirteen-year-old. Her place of origin is listed as Lecara Friddi, the dusty mining town outside of Palermo that also spawned Lucky Luciano and Anthony Martin Sinatra, Frank Sinatra's father.

My grandmother passed most of her visit finishing my project for junior high home economics, a class I'd signed up for in hopes of learning to sew and thus satisfying my endless craving for new, beautiful clothes. Even as a little girl, I loved fashion; in fact, I can't remember a time when I didn't. One of my first memories is being three years old and wearing a black velvet dress with a white lace collar, a present from my mother's sisters. I never seemed to have enough dresses, skirts, blouses, jumpers, and Capri pants. There was a limited amount I could nag my mother into buying for me, however, and she herself didn't sew.

I decided to start with an orange cotton "skort," a kind of culotte with a panel of fabric over the front that was popular in the sixties. I'd cut it out at school from a pattern and several yards of cotton that my mother and I purchased at a local mall. Grandma took one look at my crooked stitches and ripped them all out. Her own sewing was impeccable, and I was delighted with her work—that is, until the end. The skort was meant to be fun and flirty, but my grandmother insisted on hemming it two inches below the knee, which ruined the look. I wore the skort only a couple of times, on both occasions rolling it up at the waist as soon as I left the house. That was my last attempt at sewing, until writing *The Collection*.

After the publication in 2003 of my last novel, *I Am Madame X*, the story of the woman who was the subject of John Singer Sargent's most famous painting, I thought I'd like to set another novel in Paris. I know it pretty well by now (though my French refuses to improve) from researching two books there (in addition to *I Am Madame X*, *Hadley*, my 1991 biography of Ernest Hemingway's first wife and muse, is set largely in the city). Paris is a wonderful place to be, if only in your head.

I've always been fascinated by Coco Chanel, and I was thinking it would be interesting to write about her. She's one of the most original, dazzling charcters of the modern era, one of those people who emerge in every epoch, who in their personality and accomplishments seem to embody the very spirit of their age. I've never understood why she hasn't shown up in more novels over the years. Perhaps it's because most people who write novels consider fashion an ephemeral and frivolous art and, therefore, an unsuitable subject for fiction. To me, though, clothes are much more than items to hang on the body—they're clues to cultural currents, and they have great symbolic power. We all have clothes we can't bear to part with because of their special meaning: that twenty-year-old dress you'll never give away because you were wearing it the night you met your husband; the old moth-eaten sweater you won't throw out because your mother made it for you; the box of baby clothes you can't part with because they remind you of your children's childhoods.

I wasn't sure, though, how to write a Chanel novel. I didn't want to do another faux memoir like *I Am Madame X*, and anyway, Chanel's life had been well documented in several fine biographies. Around this time, my aunt Filomena found (as a result of more closet cleaning) and sent to me a scrapbook containing Rose DeMarzo's student sewing samples. My grandmother was twelve when she made this little clothbound scrapbook, and as soon as I saw the charming little fabric squares so meticulously sewn into the pages with my grandmother's initials stitched in red thread underneath, it just hit me: I'd write about a seamstress who works for Coco Chanel.

I decided to set my story in 1919 during preparations for Chanel's fall 1919 collection, because Chanel always said that 1919 was the year she woke up famous. It was her first big collection, the one that anointed her the Queen of Chic. And it was a pivotal year in fashion history. The cataclysm of the Great War had just ended. The world was being remade in every way, and the revolution in fashion was tied to the revolution at the core of society, in science, politics, and the arts.

Because sewing is at the heart of my novel, I needed to understand it, and I needed to re-create the dress called Angeline, which is as much a character in the book as the people. Working on Angeline is the way Isabelle Varlet beats back sadness. She feels that her very future is tied up with the dress; as long as it turns out, things will work out for her, too.

I read sewing expert Claire B. Shaeffer's *Couture Sewing Tech-*

niques, trying to imagine what it would be like to actually make a fully lined tailored suit or a puffy ballgown. My friend Billy Atwell let me sit in on his fashion design classes at the School of the Art Institute of Chicago. I watched his students cutting and draping fabric, and Billy showed me how to execute the most basic stitches used in hand sewing—the running stitch, the backstitch and the slip stitch. He threaded a needle, made a pinhead knot at the end of the thread, and taking up a piece of muslin, began executing a perfectly straight line of tiny, even stitches. Then it was my turn. I was terrible at it. No matter how deeply I concentrated, I could not make the stitches even and straight. I was just as incompetent at sewing as I'd been in junior high. I knew I'd never be able to re-create Angeline myself. I'd have to sew it vicariously through Billy.

All he had to go on were two sketchy illustrations—one in *Women's Wear Daily* and one in *Vogue.* Billy spent hours poring over Jazz Age pattern books and studying Chanel's construction techniques. The bodice was easy, but the skirt posed a problem. It was impossible to tell from the illustrations (and the one description of the dress in *Vogue*) if the side cascades—the element that distinguished the dress—were extensions of the skirt or separate pieces that had been sewn into the seams.

Eventually, he decided that the cascades were separate pieces. After trying to get a fluttering effect by opening up a strip of fabric that had been cut in a coil, he concluded that the desired result could only be achieved by rectangular tubes sewn into the sides of the dress. When the toile was completed, Billy draped it on a dress form, which I keep next to my desk. Hanging above it is a black-and-white photograph of Chanel given to me by my husband. In the picture, the couturière reclines on a sofa in her rue Cambon apartment, dressed in one of her signature bouclé suits with braided trim. She cradles her head in her arms as she looks down the length of the sofa, past the enameled boxes and gilded lion on the coffee table, directly at my toile. A faint smile plays around the cigarette dangling from her mouth. I think she approves.

Selected Bibliography

Books about Chanel:

Baillén, Claude. *Chanel Solitaire*. London: Collins, 1973.

Baudot, François. *Chanel*. Translated by Sharon Hughes. New York: Universe Publishing, 1996.

Charles-Roux, Edmonde. *Chanel*. New York: Alfred A. Knopf, 1975.

——*Chanel and Her World: Friends, Fashion, and Fame*. New York: Vendome Press, 2005.

Galante, Pierre. *Mademoiselle Chanel*. Translated by Eileen Geist and Jessie Wood. Chicago: Henry Regnery, 1973.

Haedrich, Marcel. *Coco Chanel: Her Life, Her Secrets*. Translated by Charles Lam Markmann. Boston: Little Brown and Co.,1972.

de la Haye, Amy, and Shelley Tobin. *Chanel: The Couturiere at Work*. New York: Overlook Press, 1996.

Kennett, Frances. *Coco: The Lives and Loves of Gabrielle Chanel*. London: Victor Gollancz, 1989.

Madsen, Axel, *Coco Chanel. A Biography*. London: Bloomsbury, 1990.

Morand, Paul. *L'Allure de Chanel*. Saint Jean-de-Braye: Hermann, Éditeurs des Sciences et des Arts, 1996.

Wallach, Janet. *Chanel: Her Style and Her Life*. New York: Doubleday, 1998.

Other:

Beaton: Cecil. *The Glass of Fashion*. Garden City, New York: Doubleday, 1954.

Beckett, Alice. *Fakes: Forgery and the Art World*. London: Richard Cohen Books, 1995.

Bertin, Célia. *Paris à la Mode*. London: Victor Gollancz, 1956.

Bolton, Andrew, and Harold Koda. *Chanel: The Metropolitan Museum of Art*. New Haven: Yale University Press, 2005.

Chase, Edna Woolman, and Ilka Chase. *Always in* Vogue. Garden City, New York: Doubleday, 1954.

Etherington-Smith, Meredith. *Patou*. London: Hutchinson, 1983.

Fizdale, Robert, and Arthur Gold. *Misia: The Life of Misia Sert*. Morrow Quill Paperbacks, 1981.

——*The Divine Sarah: A Life of Sarah Bernhardt*. New York: Alfred A. Knopf, 1991.

Grumbach, Didier. *Histoires de la mode*. Paris: Éditions du Seuil, 1993.

Kennett, Frances. *Secrets of the Couturiers*. London: Orbis, 1985.

Kirke, Betty. *Madeleine Vionnet*. San Francisco: Chronicle Books, 1998.

Koda, Harold, and Richard Martin. *Haute Couture: The Metropolitan Museum of Art*. New York: Harry N. Abrams, 1995.

Lynam, Ruth, ed. *Couture: An Illustrated History of the Great Paris Designers and Their Creations*. Garden City, New York: Doubleday, 1972.

Mackrell, Alice. *Paul Poiret*. New York: Holmes & Meier, 1990.

Marie, Grand Duchess of Russia. *A Princess in Exile*. New York: Viking Press, 1932.

Milbank, Carolyn Rennolds. *Couture: The Great Designers*. New York: Stewart, Tabori & Chang, 1985.

Poiret, Paul. *King of Fashion: The Autobiography of Paul Poiret*. Translated by Stephen Haden Guest. Philadelphia: J. B. Lippincott Company, 1931.

Radiguet, Raymond. *Count d'Orgel*. Translated by Violet Schiff. New York: Grove Press, 1953.

Shaeffer, Claire B. *Couture Sewing Techniques*. Newton, Connecticut: Taunton Press, 2001.

Steele, Valerie. *Paris Fashion: A Cultural History*. New York: Berg Publishers, 1999.

——*Women of Fashion: Twentieth Century Designers*. New York: Rizzoli, 1991.

Tindall, Gillian. *Célestine: Voices From a French Village*. New York: Henry Holt, 1996.

Troy, Nancy J. *Couture Culture: A Study in Modern Art and Fashion*. Cambridge: MIT Press, 2003.

Vassiliev, Alexandre. *Beauty in Exile: The Artists, Models, and Nobility Who Fled the Russian Revolution and Influenced the World of Fashion*. New York: Harry N. Abrams, 2000.

SELECTED BIBLIOGRAPHY

NEWSPAPERS AND MAGAZINES:

Art, Goût, Beauté
Les Élégances Parisiennes
Femina
Le Figaro Illustré
Harper's Bazaar
L'Illustration
Journal des Dames et des Modes
Vogue, U.K. and American editions
Women's Wear

About the Author

Both of Gioia Diliberto's grandmothers worked as seamstresses in New York in the 1920s. The inspiration for *The Collection* came from the discovery, in a relative's basement, of her maternal grandmother's student sewing samples, which had been carefully preserved in a scrapbook. Ms. Diliberto grew up in Bethesda, Maryland, the daughter of a junior high school English and Latin teacher and a NASA engineer. She has worked as a newspaper reporter and a magazine journalist and is the author of three biographies and a novel. She lives in Chicago with her husband, the writer and editor Richard Babcock, and the couple's son, Joe.

A SCRIBNER
READING GROUP GUIDE

The Collection

If there's no woman, there's no dress.
—Coco Chanel

Set in post–World War I Paris, Gioia Diliberto's novel *The Collection* opens the door to 31, rue Cambon—the atelier of Coco Chanel. Through this door, we witness both the glamour and the dark side of high fashion during the Jazz Age.

Our narrator is Isabelle Varlet, a provincial seamstress who suffered from tuberculosis, the loss of her entire family, and the tragic death of her beloved fiancé. Now, at twenty-two years old, Isabelle has left her small town to work a low-level job for Mademoiselle, the rising star of haute couture.

Working tirelessly for little pay and even less encouragement, Isabelle is determined to thrive in this new and exciting world. When her ill health, Chanel's outrageous perfectionism and demands, and the theft of Angeline, her creation for the upcoming fall collection, threaten to force Isabelle back to her old life, the seamstress relies on her true passion to guide her: "At the end of the day, when I looked at a dress that I'd brought to life with my needle and thread, when I saw the perfect cut and evenly stitched seams, the graceful drape of the skirt and neckline, I felt I was stepping into my own sunny future."

Containing "plenty of intrigue, pathos, romance, and even some sewing tips, as well as multifaceted characters" (*Booklist*), *The Collection* is an inspiring story about the simple women who were behind the sophistication and success of fashion geniuses like Coco Chanel.

DISCUSSION QUESTIONS

1. "I wasn't prepared to enter a world that operated on a hierarchy as rigid as the Catholic Church. If Mademoiselle was the pope, the vendeuses were the cardinals; the *premières* and *secondes,* the bishops; the *mains,* the priests; the *arpètes,* the acolytes" (page 27). Discuss the importance of hierarchy, both to the House of Chanel and to the plot of the novel.

3. Do you think Isabelle belonged in the world of haute couture or do you think she was too provincial for such a cutthroat industry? What similarities did her life have to that of Chanel?

4. "What had started out as a symbol of grief was evolving into the postwar standard of elegance" (page 38). What else does black symbolize in *The Collection*? Where are there great splashes of color in this novel?

5. Why do you think "seamstresses are obsessed with marriage" (page 68)? How did Isabelle reflect or reject this stereotype? Did

the characters of Jacques and Daniel help to influence or limit Isabelle's independence?

6. What single item of her mother's did Isabelle possess? How was it significant to Isabelle's craft and success?

7. "Often, when I sewed, I would slip into a meditative state, almost as if I'd become one with the fabric and thread. At these times, I felt a kind of release that was almost like happiness" (page 131). Is sewing an escape for Isabelle? Or is it a trap that keeps her within a certain class level?

8. "You can have too much of anything, even happiness" (page 134). What does Mademoiselle have too much of in this book? Do you think this novel is a fair representation of Chanel? Why or why not?

9. "I forced myself to think not of what was happening, but instead of Angeline" (page 231). What did Angeline represent to Isabelle?

10. Discuss the themes of *The Collection*—female strength and independence, simplicity creating sophistication, ugliness draped in beauty.

11. "I had taken a bold step tonight and more bold steps would be needed if I was to move away from darkness" (page 256). What bold steps did Isabelle take in this novel? What other bold steps did you want her to take? Were you satisfied with the outcomes in her personal and professional lives?

Reader Tips

So, sew!

Join a sewing circle or take a sewing class.

Surf couture

View the Metropolitan Museum of Art's 2005 Chanel exhibit online at www.metmuseum.org/special.

Locate Angeline

Find the missing picture from the 1919 *Vogue* article on page 267: "Great success has attended the absolutely simple model of burgundy crepe de chine sketched at the left on page 56."

Quote Quiz: Which character in the book said,

"Elegance means something is as perfect on the wrong side as on the right." (Answer on page 31.)

"It is not healthy to be only with women, to have no life outside of work . . ." (Answer on page 70.)

"Everyone's a survivor of something." (Answer on page 94.)

"Style is French, just like painting is French." (Answer on page 161.)

"When the fashion history books are written, Mademoiselle will be a footnote. She doesn't even know how to sew." (Answer on page 168.)

"It's the Americans who are desperate for French couture." (Answer on page 216.)

"It might cost a guy three hundred francs to feed himself and his lady, but she's gotta put out a fortune just to get dressed." (Answer on page 221.)

"It's only a dress; it's not your life." (Answer on page 247.)

To learn more about the book, visit the author at
www.gioiadiliberto.com